STATIC

AFFAIR

By

Damian Bardell

I just wish to say thank you to all my friends,

family and work colleagues that have had to put up with me

chattering on about this book for the last several years.

I love you all.

CONTENTS

CHAPTER 1 Beer in a Glass..1

CHAPTER 2 Brown Crab Shells 18

CHAPTER 3 Boyfriend Material..29

CHAPTER 4 Smallest Bikini Top in the World..........................38

CHAPTER 5 The Other Park 52

CHAPTER 6 What Kid Only Eats Bran Flakes? 63

CHAPTER 7 Three Sea Kayaks..75

CHAPTER 8 Two Little Ducks 89

CHAPTER 9 Do You All Sleep in the Same Bed? 103

CHAPTER 10 Red High Heel Emoji 116

CHAPTER 11 Mum Alone Time 128

CHAPTER 12 A Suitable Supply of Batteries 144

CHAPTER 13 There's a Café at the Top 159

CHAPTER 14 The Telephone Call 174

CHAPTER 15 Cash on the Side 188

CHAPTER 16 Lady Right Leader Left...205

CHAPTER 17 Pebbles Caravan Park – THIS WAY 225

CHAPTER 18 Pink Inflatable Flamingo 247

CHAPTER 19 First Class..272

CHAPTER 20 You Have To Go Right Now................................302

ABOUT THE AUTHOR 330

CAST OF PRINCIPAL CHARACTERS

David WESTWOOD
Fun-loving former cruise ship bartender, now a painter and decorator who is about to 'discover' himself. Married to the vivacious Debbie and has five children.

Debbie WESTWOOD
Lively, voluptuous housewife and mother. Married to David, who discovers a new world of fame with her sun-tanned curves.

Charles COOPER
Larger-than-life former chef, now a boxing coach, with an impressive beer belly and a secret past. Married to his third wife Sharon, with three children.

Sharon COOPER
A passion for life, especially in the bedroom. A troubled housewife, married to Charles.

Andrew MITCHELL
Self-employed plumber with a secret addiction, who married his childhood sweetheart.

Gabriella MITCHELL
Teaching Assistant with supermodel looks and plenty of dark secrets.

Clifford SMITH
Self-made millionaire, married to Alison. Always well-dressed and adores his trophy wife.

Alison JOHNSON
Outgoing, bikini-clad character with a passion for bald men and a reluctance to let go of her first marriage.

Adam JOHNSON
Alison's ex-military, loveable rogue, first husband with a shady character, always up to no good.

i

Melissa WEBSTER
Sporty, bingo-loving police officer, married to Patrick with two doting boys.

Patrick WEBSTER
'Spider' to his friends, loves his beer and seems to know everybody.

CAST OF YOUNGER CHARACTERS

Danielle WESTWOOD
Sixteen-year-old eldest daughter of David and Debbie with a love of makeup and boys.

Daisy WESTWOOD
Twin daughter of David and Debbie; aged eleven.

Dolly WESTWOOD
The other twin daughter of David and Debbie; aged eleven-years-old, who is very outgoing and sporty.

Demi WESTWOOD
Nine-year-old daughter of David and Debbie.

Paris WESTWOOD
The youngest daughter of Debbie; aged three.

Jackson COOPER
Charles' sixteen-year-old son who divides his time between his mother and father's house.

Emily COOPER
Twelve-year-old daughter to Charles and Sharon.

Sophie COOPER
Five-year-old youngest daughter to Charles and Sharon.

Fabian MITCHELL
Tall, dark, and handsome sixteen-year-old wannabe online gamer, son to Andrew and Gabriella.

Jacob FERGUSON
Oldest son of Alison; aged twelve. Distant biological father works in the USA.

Molly JOHNSON
Seven-year-old daughter to Alison and part time ex-military father Adam.

Connor WEBSTER
Oldest son of Patrick and Melissa; aged sixteen. Tall and skinny with a love of computers.

George WEBSTER
Twelve-year-old sporty adventurous son of Patrick and Melissa.

OTHER PRINCIPAL CHARACTERS

CRAWFORD
Tall, handsome and muscular. This suntanned gardener pops up everywhere and seems involved with everybody and everything.

OWEN
Brother of Brynn and owns the south caravan site, married to Pam.

BRYNN
Brother of Owen, manager of the north side of the caravan park.

MEGAN
Charles' second wife and mother to Jackson.

FRANCOISE
Real name Phil. Former world champion ballroom dancer.

CLAUDIA
Real name Jenny. Second member of the ballroom dancing team.

LUCY
Caravan cleaner and all-round businesswoman of the year.

TONY
Metal-detecting character and permanent caravan resident.

BEATRICE
Charles' first love and first wife.

CHAPTER 1

Beer in a Glass

Charles pulled onto his driveway; the same frosty atmosphere hanging in the air as when they had set off from their caravan holiday home only a few hours ago. The car was quickly vacated as its occupants raced inside the house. Charles was left alone in the driver's seat to savour the 'coming home feeling' for himself. He casually opened the boot and gazed down at his three loyal and perfect dogs. They stared back at him.

"At least you still love me," Charles said aloud and gave each one a pat and a stroke for being so good on the journey home.

"You all right, mate?" came a loud voice from over the garden fence. "Did you have a good holiday?"

"Some are better than others," Charles muttered back to his neighbour as he ushered his dogs out of the car and into the safety of his gated rear garden.

"Come on round, I've got something to show you," added the neighbour, not really giving Charles any choice in the matter. Charles hesitated; he had just driven for nearly two hours (which had seemed more like six) and desperately needed the toilet, as well as a cold beer, but his neighbour had already disappeared back inside his house.

Well, at least it delays the verbal assault I am almost certainly about to receive from my wife, he thought. He turned around and with heavy shoulders and a big sigh, proceeded to go and find out what his neighbour wanted.

Charles walked around the end of his driveway to the main road and then up his neighbour Simon's drive. As he approached his neighbour's house, his attention was drawn to how tired and unkempt things had become next door. Since his neighbour's divorce, things had gone downhill a little compared to how his neighbour used to keep his house looking. It always had clean windows and a permanently pristine front lawn. The front door had been left open a fraction. Charles peeked inside the dark house first then, hearing a shout from inside, stepped in.

"Come in. Come in, man." It was the smell Charles noticed first; not a really bad smell, just an untidy odour from a house that wasn't getting cleaned or aired as often as it should. All reminiscent of a depressed divorced man living alone. Charles pushed open the door a little further and ambled into the lounge. The fixture and fittings were just how he remembered they were from only a few years ago when he was last inside. Nothing had changed. His neighbour Simon was tall and lean and an amiable man. With an out-of-date attire he looked a little older than his years. Charles was already thinking of any single women that he knew, it was time for Simon to move on and meet someone else. A new distraction and someone who could pull him out of the rut he was in. Simon had several attractive points, Charles was thinking as he entered the lounge. He has a full head of hair, his own teeth, and this house, surely there is a woman for him. A couple of years ago, Simon's wife had gone away for a long weekend with her girlfriends to Spain. Her travelling companions came through the arrivals gate and handed him a letter. The letter said that she had met someone else, a man some 10 years her junior, and she had moved in with him and wasn't coming home. Simon was optimistic that his wife would come to her senses and only be gone a few weeks but alas here we are two years later and no sign of her. Before Charles could speak, Simon said;

"Watch this," at the same time he pointed a remote control at an exceptionally large flat-screen television. In the corner of the room a screen came to life and up came a view of Charles' driveway and the main road. Charles was aware his neighbour had CCTV cameras, he could see them positioned on the side of the house, but he never imagined for one minute that the cameras recorded his house and his comings and goings.

Charles remained standing and he opened his mouth to object to this invasion of his privacy, when on the screen appeared a large, expensive-looking blue car. It had pulled up at the end of Charles' driveway, blocking his entrance. Charles remained silent and watched the screen with interest. He didn't know why but his heart was racing.

"Sit down, sit down," Simon repeated, at the same time pointing at the sofa and then gesturing back towards the television with his oversized remote control.

"This afternoon, this blue car arrived – wait for it." Charles didn't get a chance to say what he was thinking as his neighbour continued.

"One woman first, the pretty young one in the tight jeans first." Charles watched the CCTV recording and he saw a young woman get out of the blue car and walk up Charles' driveway towards his house. She disappeared out of view for a few seconds, presumably knocking the front door. The CCTV view remained focussed on the stationary blue car.

"I told her over the fence you were out," Simon added his commentary without looking away from the television. "Cheeky cow only then comes and knocks on my front door." Simon pressed a button on his remote control and a different CCTV camera view came up on the screen. Charles was now looking at the camera view that covered his neighbour's front door. The face on the screen was now clear and bright as the young woman walked up Simon's driveway and knocked on his front door.

"What did she want?" Charles asked with some hesitation and

looking anxiously at his neighbour.

"I didn't answer the bloody door. God knows what she wanted but that car looked expensive. The other one was just as fit," Simon replied and at the same time clicked back to the first camera view. This displayed the young lady walk back to the blue car and showed her standing next to the passenger side. It was then the driver's door opened, and another woman got out.

"Beatrice," Charles blurted out loud instantly.

"Ah Hah. You know her then," Simon shouted and began searching for more information from Charles. He was interested now and clearly proud of his CCTV equipment and technical skills. In silence Charles looked back at the TV screen and continued watching.

"Can you get me a copy of this?" Charles inquired, not really knowing what or how he could get a copy of it.

Simon grinned smugly. "I'll WhatsApp you the clip, but only if you tell me who it is." Then, after a pause, he repeated, "…. if you tell me who it is, come on, mate … what you been up to? Spill the beans." Simon was enjoying the excitement and the fact his CCTV investment had been worth it after all.

Charles' mind was racing. His emotions were mixed, and he was unsure of how to handle the situation. He glanced over at his neighbour.

"Beatrice was my first wife," Charles divulged.

Simon grinned and sarcastically offered, "I knew you had been married before, but I thought she was called Megan? Didn't know there was another one, *you dirty dog.* And that's your kid, isn't it? She looks just like you." Simon was excited now. Charles stood and walked out of the house. He didn't speak until he reached the front door.

One year previous …

"This beer is very quaffable," Patrick said as he smiled over the top of his cold glass of beer, which had an overflowing white frothy sudsy head. The beer glass was a European-style flute glass that had been previously chilled in the fridge. Sat on a very clean and modern UPVC decking, Patrick slowly sipped his beer, surrounded by expensive-looking frosted tinted glass handrails. Today Patrick was visiting his very good friends David and Debbie. Their newly acquired static caravan was located on a caravan park in Wales and in earshot of the crashing waves of the Irish Sea. You could definitely hear the sea, but you couldn't actually see it from their decking. Patrick made a mental note and something he thought he would remind Debbie about, when the moment was right.

Drinking beer out of a can wasn't allowed on the decking of Debbie's caravan, or *holiday home* as she referred to it. It wasn't a caravan; Debbie would often reaffirm that to anybody who called it such. She would strengthen her argument by adding that you *tow* a caravan, and that a caravan had wheels. Debbie often called her caravan *The HH* which was short for holiday home.

"If you want to drink beer from a can, you can go to the caravan park down the road," Debbie would often say. That was another one of her stock phrases if anyone ever tried to take a can out onto her decking. Approximately half a mile along the beach was a static caravan park that was considerably cheaper to purchase a caravan from. These low prices, however, attracted people who *drank beer from cans* and had *tattoos spelt wrong*, according to Debbie.

David and Debbie Westwood had bought their caravan and moved onto the Pebble Bay caravan park several months ago now, towards the end of last season. Everybody just referred to it as Pebbles. Their friends Patrick and Melissa were their first real visitors. It was spring and the start of the new caravan season and as their hostess, Debbie, was on top form. She was proudly showing off her *golden glow* fake tan, the maintenance of which was becoming part of her daily beauty routine. She was wearing her favourite push-up bra under an open neck shirt which offered up ample suntanned cleavage. All the children had been given strict instructions to disappear and go and play with their friends on the site and not to return for at least two hours. In reality, this was likely to be twenty minutes, but she hoped, for once, that she would be able to have some adult catch-up time with her two good friends.

With the oldest child Danielle in charge, the children had excitedly headed out in the direction of the onsite amusement arcade called Buccaneers. They would not return until all their money was spent and had been exchanged for a small handful of cheap plastic *tat* as Debbie called it. This season the site had installed in Buccaneers several new arcade machines. These, instead of money, spewed out endless vouchers or tickets as the kids called them. These tickets could be saved up and redeemed at the change kiosk for different prizes; the more tickets, the better the prize. The children had taken up this new challenge with gusto and all of them had decided to club together for one of the star prizes which was over 500 tickets. This could possibly take those in the consortium several years to amass that number of tickets. Friction was already building in the ranks as one child, Dolly, had decided to pull out of this mutual ticket sharing arrangement as she wanted to choose her own prize and go on alone.

Patrick and Melissa hailed from Shrewsbury, the same town as David and Debbie, and they had been threatening to visit them for weeks. Melissa and Patrick had initially owned a touring caravan, which they had for several years towed behind their car all around the country. This was really the reason why Debbie bought a static caravan, or so Patrick thought, anyhow. Patrick had a theory that Debbie had loved the whole caravan touring thing that Melissa and Patrick had been enjoying for years. They had visited them on several of their touring holidays and had been impressed with the caravan set up Patrick and Melissa displayed. In less than a two-hour drive, you could be totally relaxed by the sea, leave your troubles behind you, and enjoy a glass of *sparkling pink* in your hand. But Debbie regarded herself as middle-class – she wasn't from Shrewsbury, but Shro'ohs'bury. She had to buy a vastly more expensive static caravan instead of a touring one.

"What's great is, we don't know anybody here," David said and smiled. "It's lovely and quiet, no family or neighbourly dramas. We just jump in the car, and we are here in a few hours with everything all set up ready to go. Just unlock the front door of the caravan and – bliss." Another dig at touring caravan owners, Patrick thought again, but he just smiled over his cold beer and slipped his sunglasses down from the top of his head as he leaned back on his sun lounger. This is rather peaceful, Patrick thought as he took a cheeky glance down Debbie's top as she leaned forward in front of Patrick. Patrick regarded it as deliberate as there was no real reason for her actions. *Gosh, she is looking rather sexy*, Patrick thought to himself, *I wonder if she sunbathes topless on this very decking?* Patrick's mind wandered as he noticed Debbie's curvaceous curves. After five children, you would have thought that her boobs would have drooped, but clearly they had not. Patrick was mindful he had been staring at Debbie and he checked himself and glanced across at his wife. His wandering eyes had gone unnoticed. Patrick finished his beer with a compliment and suggested that he was, indeed, ready for another can. He smirked over towards Debbie at the mention of the word *can* and as he did so he lifted his t-shirt over his head.

Now suntanned and topless, Patrick maintained eye contact with Debbie and said, "Gosh it's a hot day," and he smiled, looking her up and down whilst he replaced his sunglasses back on the top of his head. Patrick knew he was in good shape and was repeatedly told his six-pack flat stomach was a very attractive feature to women. He winked at Debbie whose eyes had also dropped to check out his naked torso.

Patrick agreed that a touring caravan could sometimes be a lot of hard work. First, you pulled the thing along the road, at quite a slow speed. Then, once you actually found the caravan site, you were expected to reverse onto your assigned plot. This was often harder than you'd expect. If you were the last to arrive on site, you had the added problem of parked cars and other caravans all around your pitch. This was one of the reasons Patrick had paid for a remote-controlled motorized kit, so he could stand back and watch as his caravan manoeuvred itself around the site, much to the amusement of passersby. You first have to level the caravan and lower down the four corner stabilizing legs, next, you connect the fresh water, then waste pipe, TV aerial, special blue liquid into the loo cassette and finally plug in the electric. That's before you even think about erecting an awning, which Patrick wasn't a big fan of. An awning Patrick always regarded was a lot of work and it ended up just being a place to store coats and shoes.

George, the younger of Patrick and Melissa's two sons, had gone off to try and find the other children. His brother Connor, his senior by four years, asked again where Danielle had gone, forgetting that he had asked once already, only a few minutes ago. Danielle was sixteen and was David and Debbie's oldest daughter. Danielle, who preferred to be called Dani, was a very pretty girl and dressed much older than her years. Often seen wearing designer clothing and clearly was not the least bit interested in Connor. As far as she was concerned, at fifteen, he was far too immature for her. Debbie often protested that Danielle only appeared interested in older boys but in the same breath she would take her daughter shopping to buy her makeup and very short designer dresses.

Connor was your typical teenage boy; tall, skinny, but with very good muscle definition and a six pack like his dad. He was, however, pale and spotty – mostly due to lack of daylight, as he never went

8

outside much as his computer keyboard was inside the house. He didn't see any point in playing sports, but more recently, girls were constantly on his mind and Dani was top of his girlfriend *wish list*.

"I want to set off for the holiday home as soon as you come home from work," Debbie had said to her husband that very morning as he was loading the back of his van. David was preparing for a full day's work and stacking his painters van with numerous pots of paint and brushes. He ran an established company and employed several other painters and decorators. He worked very hard, sometimes seven days a week, but it gave him a good income and he could just about afford to pay for the six women in his life and now newly purchased holiday home.

"The Websters are coming to visit tomorrow, and I need to clean the holiday home. You have to wash the windows, cut the grass …" Debbie may have said a lot more, but David's attention had drifted back to preparing for work. He wasn't listening to his wife and the exhaustive list of household chores being dictated to him. *Even more DIY jobs to do at another house,* he thought, and he was starting to think that this whole holiday home thing wasn't such a good idea. *That's two lawns I have to cut now, two sets of windows to clean and that's without the list of new decorating jobs which I'm sure will start to be compiled.*

David went back inside the house and in ear shot of his wife's voice, "… and I want the place looking nice to show that it is better than a touring caravan," Debbie was using her assertive, firm *I'm in charge* tone and had started to walk upstairs, still dictating more orders as she went. David stared at his wife's bottom which was tightly confined within a pair of light blue jeans. *Gosh that's got bigger!* he thought to himself. *What happened to the slim young woman I met on that cruise ship all those years ago?* he pondered silently. David had wondered for some time now why he was no longer sexually attracted to his wife. He had very mixed emotions when he saw her naked, but he put it down to the fact she had changed. She had given birth to five children, and she didn't do any exercise. His wife was getting curvier by the day, and he simply wasn't seeing her in the same way he had done when they had first met.

The Westwoods lived in a lovely big semi-detached house just on the outskirts of town. They had been married for sixteen years and, aside from the children, also owned one very small dog which David wasn't keen on but whom the twins loved. His children were growing up quickly, his wife's bum was getting fuller, and he missed excitement and friendship in his life. More recently it was true to say he often thought about his wild bachelor youth and his past relationships.

When he had met Debbie, David had been a bartender on a cruise ship. He had grown up in a small mining village in the north of England and had left school with little in the way of education, in fact with no education whatsoever. Back then it was a given that he would go to work down the coal mine. His school career advice consisted of *when* he would be going down the mine, not *if.* He soon realised his skills lay in talking to people. He was often told he was very likeable and funny; that he was good looking and always the life and soul of any party.

After leaving school in the early 1980s, and with no credible career prospects, David had bluffed his way into a bartender's position at Camelot's, a trendy pub in the city. Camelot's was an old, converted church right in the centre of the town's night life and became the hottest place to be seen in. It was a different time back in the 80s, David would often tell his children the story of when he first started work at the pub. All the church pews and the church organ had been left behind and incorporated into the pub's fixture and fittings. You could come in, buy a pint of beer at the bar, and then take a seat in a pew. It was all very surreal and different and years ahead of its time. When Camelot's first opened for business, there were always large groups of protesters outside, some with strong religious beliefs displaying placards and banners. They were protesting against the church being used as a public house.

Often told to his children, David's stories from his youth would always include the trick he had pulled to secure his bartending position and then subsequently how he had ended up on a cruise ship and met their mother. David had not been as truthful as he should have been when completing his paper job application to work at Camelot's. He had said that he had previous bar and catering experience and that he was nearly nineteen years of age, putting a scribble on the form when it came to the year of birth. David had written born 197# and had a plan to say that his pen must have slipped if he was ever challenged about his age. David was in fact only sixteen years old when he started working at the pub and had never drunk a beer before, let alone served one. He was a long way off being legally permitted to pull pints behind a bar, but he was confident, tall, and had broad shoulders. The landlord's wife had interviewed him for the position and David had smiled and complimented her hair, the job was his.

David would often laugh to himself when he remembered the good old days. He would never miss out that when he was a lad, British pubs were only open from 12 noon to 3 p.m. every day and then open again in the evening from 7 p.m. till 11 p.m. This memory from the past always surprised David. The fact that you could be working in a really busy bar full of customers and one minute you would serve them a pint of beer and take their money then, in the next breath, you would ring a loud brass bell, turn the music off, turn all the pub lights on and ask them to drink up quickly and kick them out onto the streets. "Time please, gentlemen," David would holler, and his children would jump with a giggle every time. David's stories of working on a Cruise Ship and sailing around the world would often alter slightly but Debbie, who had heard the story so often, would smile to herself when the story was dramatised for their children's benefit.

David would sometimes ask his children if they were sitting comfortably. "You are? Then I will begin," he would say, smiling at each child in turn.

"It was a normal mid-week at the pub, and I was working a slow lunchtime shift," David began. "But it was a day that would change my life forever." He would often pause at this point in his story telling, in an attempt to build the excitement.

"I was bottling-up, as it was called in the trade," David continued. "You basically filled the fridges up with bottles of beer. Holsten Pilsner beer was very popular back then but being Camelot's, it was all very trendy and modern for its day. The beer fridges had see-through glass doors and the beer and other bottles all had to be placed in the fridges in nice, neat rows with their labels all facing forwards, like soldiers on parade. Back then it was a new concept, a fridge you could see inside without opening the door, groundbreaking." David smiled, trying to hold their attention.

"One day," David continued, "my best friend from school, Gary, had wandered into the pub and sat on a bar stool. Gary was still unemployed, and I served him a pint of his favourite beer." Gary fancied himself as a lookalike Simon Le-Bon and he even tried dressing like him. He had the looks and never struggled to attract persons from the opposite sex but with no job prospects his confidence had dwindled.

David continued telling his story to his beloved children. He told them all about how he wouldn't charge Gary for his drinks. How Gary would hold out his hand for the imaginary money that Gary would drop into his hand as payment, all in case anyone had been watching. David justified his actions to his children by saying that his friend was broke and that he believed that, as a good friend, he deserved a free beer now and again. David would add that he thought Camelot's could afford it and he would ask Gary to go around the tables and collect empty glasses as payment for his free glasses of beer.

David was accustomed to losing the attention of at least one of his daughters during his story telling, but he persevered. David continued to set the scene, describing one particular day when he was again filling up the beer fridges, and Gary as usual was nattering to him from his bar stool. That lunch time there were only ever a few customers in the pub, it was more popular in the evening for sure and David would adjust the music level to very low. There was just the one person sat reading a newspaper and a couple of smart businesspeople from the local office block, sitting very close to each other in one of the pews. This pair were clearly having an office romance as they appeared every lunchtime and would often get very generous with their hands. David concluded that they had decided to meet in a young person's pub so as not to be recognised or caught out by their work colleagues.

"You really like this pub job, don't you?" Gary said one day, and David told his daughters that he just stopped in mid beer fridge stocking. That he stood up and leaned on the bar counter, looking back into the eyes of his best friend, "I really do, you know," David replied with a smile to his buddy.

David continued. "Gary then said, 'So why not be a bartender on one of those big Cruise Ships and sail the world at the same time as serving drinks?'." Well, that got minds thinking and David looked around at his daughters and he knew he had regained their full attention at the mention of the words Cruise Ship. He told them how, that very afternoon, he had gone with his buddy and they had walked into a travel agent around the corner from the pub. David, describing the lady working there as wearing a bright purple jacket with matching skirt and scarf, and how she had pounced on them as they had entered.

He described in great detail how he had informed the lady, that his mum and dad, "Your grandma and grandad, girls," were thinking about taking a cruise, and how the kind lady had handed him several travel brochures to take home. David always looked forward to this part of the story, and he relished in describing that "There was no such thing as the internet in those days", and you communicated by writing letters. These memories always brought a smile to David's face, and he proudly informed his daughters that he had that very evening written to the address on the back cover of the cruise brochure, the one in small print at the bottom of the page. His letter simply stated that he was a first-class bartender and he was requesting to be considered for any future job vacancies.

David emphasised to his daughters that he had written a handwritten letter with a stamp on the envelope and everything. Two whirlwind weeks later, he informed them all that he was stood on a shipyard dockside in Old San Juan in Puerto Ricco, in the Caribbean, looking up at an enormous cruise ship called the Sun Princess. A ship which was part of the P&O Princess Cruises fleet, or "27,000 tons of oceanic splendour". David would say this aloud in his best American accent, explaining how the Cruise Director onboard would often say this repeatedly over the ship's loudspeaker system to all the passengers during one of his daily ship activities announcements.

David sometimes would throw in a quick test to assess his children's knowledge during this part of the story, asking if anyone knew the definition of P&O, and it was always Dolly that would shout out first "Peninsular and Oriental Steam Navigation Company" with a grin and a proud raised hand.

Several years later, Debbie captured bartender David's attention as she cruised with her parents. Debbie, tall, firm, young and single, had spent many an hour sat at David's bar counter. She would stare at him as he worked away and making her endless fancy cocktails. She liked what she saw and watched with an open mouth every time he deliberately bent down in his tight trousers to retrieve something from a fridge. She juggled her time with her parents and worked herself into a frenzy whilst she waited for David's shift to finish, knowing that she would soon be playing with his firm, naked, suntanned body. Debbie had her own cabin onboard away from her parents and with the balcony doors open and the fresh sea air pouring, the atmosphere of the sea roaring past would excite her. She would spend hours touching, kissing, and exploring David's entire body as he lay completely naked on her bed. This was her first-time having sex more than once in one evening and all the time with the lights on so she could see every curve of his body. Now, here he was, five children, a mortgage, possibly a dog (but more like a big hamster), a static caravan in Wales and a wife with a big bottom who constantly talked about home improvements.

Debbie didn't work, not as David recognised real work. In his eyes, she didn't have a job. Debbie would often remind her husband that she did, indeed, have a full-time job with a large family to organise. Danielle, their eldest daughter who was sixteen (going on twenty-six), twins Daisy and Dolly aged eleven, Demi who was nine, and little Paris who was three in a few weeks. Debbie would often say she was *so busy* with running the house and taking care of the girls, and yet would always find the time for her numerous social activities which ranged from regular visits to the hair salon, tanning salon, the nail bar, and more often than not a real bar which sold *Prosecco* on draft.

Early that day, the family bus had been loaded, mostly with clothes due to the majority of occupants being female. David had his small man bag tucked into a corner of the boot and now hidden out of sight under piles of other items which were mostly pink in colour. David had never heard of the music coming out of the radio, but there was little in the way of other traffic on the roads and he was making good time. David looked forward to making that left turn off the A748 at The Queen and Hammer pub towards the Welsh coast and his beloved holiday home. That, to David, was the signal for his shoulders to drop and for him to relax. He was on route to his slice of heaven, a place where he knew no-one, and he could unwind. He didn't have to talk to anyone if he didn't want to; he could just sit on his decking, drink cold beer, and relax whilst his daughters all grew up around him.

Debbie was a good social hostess and was fussing around their mutual friend Patrick. Things were made easier for her now as he had taken off his shirt and he was rather a tall hunk. They had glasses of cold beer, snacks were on the table, the sun was shining, they had healthy children and life was good.

"I tell you what I really like," David repeated and something Patrick noted that David had previously said many times before. David remarked how he didn't know anybody on the caravan park. He had made reference to getting to know his neighbours one day, but currently he only had plans to greet them when he passed and not to get too friendly with any fellow holiday homeowners. David was determined to keep hold of the quiet life. He didn't want to gather any drinking partners and he certainly didn't want anybody just popping round for coffee uninvited. He wanted zero stress, no dramas, and he definitely didn't want to talk to anybody. Well, that's what David thought he wanted. He was a bit mixed up in reality, and he wasn't sure how he felt, he had been feeling this way for several years now but didn't have anyone to really talk to about it. He had tried to talk to Debbie and had even considered discussing it with Patrick but, in the end, what was going on in his head he had kept bottled up.

"SPIDER ... SPIDER," came a deep bellow from across the site. Everyone turned in unison to stare over at a sizeable man with an even larger beer belly walking towards them. He wore a white vest, blue shorts, and flip flops and he was walking on the path that ran down through the caravan site. The chap was being jostled by three large dogs who were all barking and pulling in different directions on their leads.

"Hello buddy," Patrick responded with a wide-open mouth smile. Standing up he gestured for everyone to greet his close friend called

16

Charles from back home. Patrick's last name was Webster and he had grown up under the nickname of Spider. As a young man he had secretly relished the name as he thought it made him sound rather cool. Patrick leaned on the railings and as he did so, his biceps tensed, and his back muscles became more prominent. Debbie glanced over at Patrick and her eyes dropped to two perfectly round, hard mounds that were now stretched across his shorts as he leaned forwards. Leaving his beer glass on the table and picking up just the can, Patrick replied, "It's a small world. How you doing, mate? You on your holidays?" David stood and stared, and he enjoyed smiling at Charles as he looked him up and down. Charles was a big hunk of a man. David was unsure why he was so fascinated with Charles or why he currently had butterflies in his stomach. There was something about Charles that he took an instant liking to. Stepping back, David waited to be introduced. Debbie was aware that the men were talking to someone, and she was really having to concentrate on not staring at her friend's husband's body. Debbie had never regarded a man's back to be sexy before, but Patrick's was very muscular and exciting, all smooth and suntanned. He clearly lifted weights and Debbie tingled as she stared at his incredible muscle definition. Debbie nodded in reply to her friend who was talking but she was lost in her thoughts and not really listening, and she pictured her red fingernails as they scratched down Patrick's back whilst they made love.

CHAPTER 2

Brown Crab Shells

"Forty-two years I have been a visitor to this caravan site," Charles interrupted his wife Sharon and then unnecessarily added further, "I think that makes me qualified to know about the local area." Charles instantly regretted his strong tone. His confidence and firmness with his wife had come from the consumption of three pints of beer, however he knew instantly that he was already in for a hard time later for talking down to her.

Charles and Sharon were sat in the Pebble Bay club house bar. It had just undergone an expensive refit and everything still had that new smell. The bar had been modernised extensively to include moving the outdoor pool to inside. There was now a pool veranda viewing area in the style of a coffee lounge which was adjacent to the main bar. Large frosted rectangular windows overlooked the pool area and the restaurant with its new tables and tall brown leather-backed chairs had its own separate entrance. It boasted an environmentally friendly construction with patio seating area made from recycled plastic bottles and a hard-wearing beige plastic decking. In the evening it would all be lit up with modern, subtle, blue outdoor lighting.

Charles was not so keen on this refit. In his opinion the club house had become too upmarket and posh for his taste. Charles' beloved real ale beer pumps had mostly disappeared, leaving only a fancy range of expensive European lagers. There was now only one draft beer pump remaining, offering a real ale choice from a shiny chrome pump with flashing green lights. The bar was now also stocking a vast variety of gins and wines, and Charles felt that the average beer-drinking man was being pushed out. Sat at the next table were two young women who were new on site that season. They had started up a conversation with Charles about the bar refit and had asked about other activities and things to do in the local area and Charles regarded himself as a knowledgeable local guide.

Charles and Sharon had a static caravan pitched on the north side of the caravan park. The management situation on site had become a little complicated after the caravan park had been inherited by two brothers. The brothers' parents had successfully run and built up the business for many years, developing the park into the success it was today. Inheriting an equal share of the caravan park, the two brothers didn't see eye to eye on how to take the business forward and to the decrement of the business they couldn't even agree on simple daily matters.

Owen wanted to take the caravan park upmarket and attract the wealthy city holiday home customer and offer a quality, high-priced caravan experience. The club house would offer a wide range of wines and exotic cocktails, and the restaurant would use the best locally sourced ingredients and build an excellent reputation for its high-priced cuisine. This brother had a vision of all the caravans being of the same matching colour and design and to only have smart aesthetically pleasing artificial grass around the park. He even championed very enthusiastically a desire to enforce a strict clientele dress code around the site and in the club house.

Brynn, the older brother, had desires to cater for the average working man and continue in the business model as his parents had done before. Holiday homes for people who worked hard for a living; where they could come and relax for a few days near the sea and leave their troubles and ordinary lives behind them. He didn't care if the caravans didn't exactly match or whether his clientele walked around in shorts and took their shirts off in the sunshine. This led to constant arguments and disputes between the two brothers and, after a costly legal battle, the caravan park was split equally between them both. This technically created two different caravan parks and the two halves of the park became known as *The North* and *The South*. They did, however, continue to work around the one reception centre and offices and the one clubhouse bar which happened to be located dead centre between the now two parks.

The south side called themselves the *posh side* of the caravan park as this received heavy investment from Owen. One park rule which was immediately enforced stated that your holiday home would need to be replaced when it reached a maximum of ten years old. This ensured the park had a luxury, modern feel and was visually smarter, which in turn attracted the affluent paying client. The north side of the park continued to be run as it always had been done, catering for everyday people living everyday lives and with a relaxed sort of laissez-faire attitude.

Charles and Sharon had been married for just over twelve years. Sharon was his third wife. Charles' first marriage had been to Beatrice whom he had met at university. Beatrice was very pretty, petite, and slim with a few little freckles over her nose and cheeks. She had fallen pregnant after one of their many drunken university all-day parties and, as a result of the pregnancy, they had married three weeks after graduation. Beatrice was feeling vulnerable, but Charles had smiled and reassured her everything was going to be okay. The following week, at the university graduation party, on bended knee he had asked her to marry him. Two months later, a confused Beatrice had lied to Charles and informed him that she wanted a divorce as she had lost the baby. Things moved very quickly, and Charles was unsure of what was really happening and agreed to a divorce. Beatrice moved immediately out of Charles' mum's house where they had ended up living after Uni. Beatrice headed home and went back to live with her wealthy parents in London. After repeatedly attempting to contact his wife, Charles soon realised his marriage was over and he gave up trying to reconnect with her. He only managed to speak with the butler or other staff member that answered the telephone. It was all over as soon as it had begun. The fairy-tale university romance had all ended very suddenly with little or no warning, but they were both very young and had married far too early, so it had probably turned out the best for everyone.

For months, Charles had moped around at home, feeling sorry for himself and unsure of what to do with his life. He lost his confidence and his appearance suffered. He drank far too much and made poor choices in his diet. He quickly went from a young, tall, handsome, dark-haired hunk to someone who displayed poor skin and became overweight very quickly. His diet consisted of pizza most nights and he didn't wash as often as he should. Sadly, he had already started to lose contact with the new friends he had made at university. Not knowing what to do with himself, he managed to borrow money from his mother and decided to go travelling around Europe in an attempt to try and forget about Beatrice, sort out his head, and find himself. He smartened himself up with haircut and new clothes. With a better diet his skin quickly improved, and his round beer belly soon disappeared; the power of youth. His university culinary skills had given him the ability to obtain work wherever he went, and he felt the only way he was going to get through this heartbroken period of his life was to take himself out of it and start a new one. He questioned himself constantly – had he *ever* really loved her? Did they *only* get married for the baby? Did *she* really love him? What if …? Lots of 'what ifs'.

Charles had ended up in Southern France working as a chef in a busy, famous restaurant, and he had no plans to come home anytime soon. He was simply in the right place at the right time. Having found himself in the town of Montpellier, he visited every restaurant and café he came across in search of work. He was just about to give up and find somewhere to put his head down for the night when he stumbled on 'Bistro Jermain'. They had had a short notice 80th birthday party arrive and, with two chefs failing to turn up for their evening shift, Charles found himself putting on clean whites and being shown to a workstation within five minutes of walking through the front door.

A few weeks later, Charles was well acquainted with the menu and the kitchen routine. He had also started to become conversant with a much older, curvy, dark-haired French lady called Lisette, who waited on tables in the restaurant. She looked like a mature Sophia Lauren to Charles with her permanent olive skin and long flowing locks, all so very attractive to him. The language barrier prevented them from deep lengthy conversations, but this was of little importance. Most of their time away from the restaurant was spent in her small bedsit where the wrought-iron bed dominated the room. During these months, he grew from a fumbling teenager to a skilful lover and would be forever grateful to Lisette for the education he received during those long, dark evenings. Lissette taught Charles to take his time. She showed him how to excite a woman not with touch but first with what she could see and smell. Charles became a master of undressing very seductively and casually walking around the apartment completely naked. His semi erection dominating the moment as he turned and casually pretended he had a few things to do first before he joined a naked Lissette on the bed. His smooth, hard, muscular body excited Lisette and she would watch and reach out to hold his enlarged manhood as he neared the bed, but he would turn at the last moment, teasing her. His young muscular chest was smooth and hair free and he had a firm, round, shapely behind. Watching a naked and stimulated Lissette pleasure herself on the bed was always too much for Charles and with a fully erect penis he would approach the bed and enter Lisette easily whilst maintaining eye contact. She coached him to build her orgasm for both their pleasures. Exciting and fulfilling a woman during lovemaking was something Charles relished and more often also accomplished.

One particular day, having finished a busy restaurant shift in a hot kitchen, Charles was feeling down and, wanting to hear a familiar English voice, he telephoned his mother. Something he didn't do as often as he should. It was a bright spring day, and the streets were almost empty as Charles arrived at clear glass public call box, situated in the next street from the restaurant. A telephone call that stopped him in his tracks.

After pleasantries, Charles' mother explained that a few weeks ago a large, padded envelope had arrived in the post. Inside was a brief letter of introduction addressed to her, along with a sealed envelope marked *Charles only*. There was also a third envelope with the words printed in red, Divorce Papers, and a solicitor's name and address from London stamped on it. His mother told him all about the nice things Beatrice had said to her in her letter and Charles then asked that she open his letter and read it out, word for word. There was a brief pause whilst the handset was placed down, and Charles could hear his mother shuffling and tearing as she opened his letter. Charles glanced down at the green phone card that has sticking out and he hoped that he had bought enough credit. His mother began to read:

Dearest Charles

I am so sorry things didn't work out between us.

I'm not sure you ever really loved me, I think you only stayed with me at university because I had a car and a bigger flat and the fact my mum and dad gave me lots of money which we seemed to always buy beer with.

I have decided to keep the baby. I am so sorry I told you I had lost the baby, I was confused. Things happened so very quickly, please forgive me for that.

I don't want anything from you, and in time, if you wish, you can spend time with your son or daughter. I have a scan next week, so I'll write again and let you know the outcome. Please don't try and contact me, I will get in touch when I am ready and keep you updated on events.

I have given this letter to the family solicitor to send to you as I am staying with mummy and daddy before I move into my own flat which they have bought for me. The nursery is still being decorated.

I hope this letter finds you well. You are often in my thoughts. I really did so love you, my darling Charlie, with all my heart.

Forever yours

Beatrice xxx

Charles' mother asked after her son's health and whilst waiting for a reply made a negative reference to the fact that she was going to be a grandmother. Charles ended the call with a promise to call again soon. Although exhausted, Charles didn't sleep that night.

Charles had been working at the restaurant now for several months. The day following the phone call, he had been at work only an hour and he was in the middle of preparing two portions of authentic French bouillabaisse. Tired from lack of sleep and his mind had not really focussing on his work, he ended up putting some of his kitchen waste (only two brown crab shells) into the wrong waste bin; the waste bin belonging to a round ginger sous chef called Phillipe. In the restaurant, each chef had their own waste bin, and it was a strict kitchen rule that you didn't use anybody else's bin. On finding this unwelcome rubbish in his bin, Phillipe launched a verbal attack at Charles in French, his arms flailing wildly. The chef was going crazy at what Charles felt was a simple mistake on his part. Phillipe continued to shout obscenities in French at Charles and the whole kitchen stopped work to observe the commotion. Charles, still not really understanding what he was saying, decided to turn away from the troubled chef and continued his own work. In response, Phillippe picked up the said rubbish bin and emptied its contents all over Charles' clean workstation, ruining the meals Charles had very nearly finished preparing. Taking that as a signal that it was time to move on and, in one swift movement, Charles, with an experienced left jab, lunged forwards and punched said Chef squarely on the nose. Turning immediately, he headed for the door, collecting his coat on the way he casually walked out of the restaurant. Charles didn't look back at the chef who by now had all the other kitchen staff crowded around him, still moaning and rolling around on the floor clutching his bloodied nose. He did, however, glance briefly over his shoulder as he was mindful that his bouillabaisse sauce was about to boil over. He contemplated going back inside the kitchen to turn the hob down but made the right decision and he walked straight back to his flat to pack his bags.

"You said *hello* to our new neighbours yet?" Sharon bellowed at Charles from the kitchen of their caravan. His wife was cooking dinner tonight for a change as Charles usually did all of the cooking. Sharon had everyone on a strict diet, including herself, and she had banned the usual three nights a week takeaway. These takeaway meals were often referred to as *chuck outs* from the on-site caravan fast food restaurant. Charles had not said hello to his new neighbours yet, but he *had* noticed a rather busty blonde lady earlier and he liked what he saw. He used Sharon's question as an invitation to wander out to the very front edges of his decking to see if his neighbour was still walking around in the bikini, something she had been wearing when he first noticed her. To escape more shouting from his wife, who was now busy ordering the kids around to help prepare the super low-calorie dinner everyone was so looking forward to. Charles wandered down off his decking into his small, grassed garden area next to his caravan. He decided to show the second love of his life, his dogs, some much needed attention. Whilst fussing with his pets and looking over at his new neighbour's caravan, Charles was disappointed not to see the bikini neighbour wiggling about on her decking. However, he did see a short chap, with a very large forehead who was stood just staring back at Charles. He had a can of beer in his hand, so Charles thought he couldn't be all that bad.

"Good afternoon, mate, you all settled in?" Charles shouted across to him, lifting his chin and offering a smile. Charles could already hear Sharon chomping and moaning at him from the kitchen; she hated anybody shouting. Charles would soon find out his new neighbour with the big forehead was called Clifford and that he and the bikini lady were married. Clifford was the jealous type. He nodded across at Charles in response to his greeting. Charles, however, missed the acknowledgment as bikini lady had returned onto the decking and was waving frantically at him.

Gosh, I'm not sure how they stay in there, Charles thought with a smile. He struggled not to stare as Alison's boobs bounced and wobbled as she waved, her right hand high in the air, excitedly gesturing a welcome to Charles.

Sharon didn't miss a thing. She had clocked *bikini* lady and was now bending down in the kitchen to get a better view of next door's caravan along the side of their parked car. Sharon's view was partially blocked, but Sharon was now eye level with her waving neighbours. "Charles, walk the dogs before dinner please. Go NOW!" Sharon bellowed.

Who's shouting now? thought Charles, as he leaned briefly back inside the caravan and grabbed hold of the dog leads from the top of the small shelf as it was referred to. On seeing the leads, the dogs got excited, and Charles turned away from the looking at his neighbours but not before noticing Clifford giving Charles the downward glare. Charles used the excuse of sorting his dogs' leads to turn around and take another hopeful glance in Alison's direction, but she had gone and all he could see was the big forehead of the man staring straight back at him. Sharon was also staring at Charles through the open patio door. *For goodness' sake, I haven't done anything,* thought Charles as he took the leads and headed south, being pulled in all directions by his beloved dogs.

Charles had been on the site for so long he was sort of allowed to access and walk down across the southern side of the caravan park to reach the beach. North site clients were supposed to use the public footpath that ran alongside but Charles had built up such a good relationship with both site brothers he had special permission. He had practically grown up with the two brothers and he could tell a few juicy stories about them both from things that had taken place over the years. Charles' mind was still focused on the red bikini as he walked along past endless rows of caravans in the direction of the beach. He passed the visible dividing line of the north side of the caravan park and entered the forbidden zone of the posher south side. He zapped his *acquired* gate pass on the very swanky looking keypad and sauntered through the electronic barrier.

Gosh! thought Charles. *It's a much smarter looking park down here this year.* All the caravans looked exactly the same, shiny and new and they even had matching little green sheds, tucked away neatly at the back of their caravans to hide away their owners' junk. Even the red gas bottles were all glossy and shiny compared with the north side where any colour of gas bottle will do, as long as it contained gas. Over the years he had taken this route many times and soon he could hear the waves crashing on the beach. He had the glare of the sun in his eyes, but he was convinced he recognised someone. His dogs were pulling heavily on their leads, so his attention was elsewhere, but he stared hard at someone sat on the decking of a caravan. Looking through the expensive, designer-style smoked glass panels, something that Charles wish he had bought for his caravan. He didn't have the best view, but then the chap he was staring at stood up … *It couldn't be,* he thought.

Excited and now shouting, "SPIDER, SPIDER!" A bare-chested Patrick turned and leaned over the side of Debbie's decking, at the same time picking up a can of beer. Charles's dogs were now frantically barking, spinning on their leads longing to run free on the beach which they could smell was close.

"It's a small world, how you doing, mate. You on your jollies?" Patrick cried to his friend with a big cheesy smile.

"This is my site," Charles replied, "I've been coming to Pebbles since I was a kid. Just walking the dogs before dinner. You bought a caravan on here, buddy?"

"No. This is David and Debbie's van," Patrick replied, turning with an open palm gesturing towards David, who, on the mention of his name, jumped up from his chair and stretched his hand out over the railing to offer a welcome handshake. All Debbie could manage was a slight grin in Charles' direction as she glanced at Patrick and replied sternly, "It's a *holiday home*," but not before she looked a partially naked Patrick up and down again, her eyes stopping briefly at his groin as he turned, and her imagination turned briefly to what he would look like completely naked. Debbie didn't like the big dogs; they were noisy, and she also didn't like the fact that Charles was wearing a vest top with his beer belly hanging out the front. She immediately made the assumption that Charles must be from the north side. With a firm grip, David shook Charles' hand and gave him a courtesy look up and down. For an unknown reason David held onto Charles' hand for a split second longer than he should have.

CHAPTER 3

Boyfriend Material

Andrew and Gabriella Mitchell had been childhood sweethearts, both born in the same small sleepy village on the edge of Worcestershire in England. They both attended the same schools and went up through the education system together, even sitting next to each other in classes. Their parents were friends, and everyone knew it was inevitable that they would stay together forever. They married shortly after leaving school.

They lived at Gabriella's parents, in her old bedroom, until they had both secured jobs. With lots of parental financial support, they eventually moved into their own rented flat. Inevitably they soon fell pregnant. Gabriella was very much in charge and Andrew did what he was told but that worked for him; his clothes smelt of apple blossom and jasmine; they were always neatly ironed and hanging colour-co-ordinated in his wardrobe. He came home to deliciously prepared dinners which were anything but bland and, in comparison to most of his mates, he thought he had a pretty wild sex life. This was, of course, so long as Andrew did as he was told in the bedroom.

Gabriella had worked her way up through the education department and was now a qualified Spanish Teacher, working part time at the local school they had both previously attended as young children. Andrew had finished his plumbing apprenticeship and, with pressure from Gabriella to earn more money, had made the decision to step away from the security of the company he had worked for and was now self-employed. Gabriella liked the school hours and enjoyed lots of time off work, without the pressures of being a full-time teacher. It also meant that during the long school holidays, she was able to spend the maximum time possible at their seaside caravan. Unfortunately, this did mean she found herself mostly going without Andrew as he had to work, but to be honest, she didn't mind this at all – it gave her freedom, self-confidence, and the feeling of a double-life. She had an open mind when it came to their marriage vows and stood by the words; 'When the cat's away, the mice will play.' She had not been averse to the odd affair over the years. It seemed everyone knew about Gabriella's infidelity apart from Andrew. He was so besotted with her. Gabriella walked on water as far as he was concerned.

"I don't really want to go to this caravan," Fabian had repeated this phrase several times over the last few days and at least three times that particular morning.

"Honestly, son, you will love it, there is loads to do and we have bought that special fast Wi-Fi direct into the caravan so you can play your games." Gabriella smiled at her beloved son and placed a gentle reassuring hand on his arm. Gabriella was tall and slim with long dark hair, characteristics of her European heritage. She had small firm round breasts and she often preferred the look of not wearing a bra. Most days her nipples always appeared erect through her clothing. Something noted by her headmaster. She had a curvy behind which she emphasised as often as she could with tight jeans. Always immaculate in her appearance, anytime of day or night and she ran a tight ship with a very clean house. A bit too sparkly clean for Andrew and Fabian's liking, bordering on obsessive cleaning they would say. Always cleaning, spraying, polishing, dusting; ensuring every surface was 100% bacteria-free. They genuinely felt Gabriella had a cleaning phobia but had gotten used to it over the years, it was just how she was and what made her 'Gabriella'. The house was immaculate. Nothing was left out and Gabriella followed Fabian round, constantly tiding up after him. You would think you were entering a show home on a brand-new build estate, everything had a place, and everything was in its place. As a young child, if Fabian played with a toy, he was taught he must put it away back in the toy box before bringing out a new one. That's how Fabian was brought up and he became used to this style of living. He believed it was the norm and that everyone lived like that.

Andrew worked long hours to pay for this style of modern living and holiday homes by the coast. He didn't get much time off from work and there were never enough hours in the day. Always one more job to price up, one more customer to call back, one more boiler emergency call before going home to his family at the end of the day. The housing market was on the up, new homes were being built all over the county and, with business booming, Andrew's work mobile never stopped ringing with people asking for quotes and offers of more work. Andrew was a *Star Wars* fan and the movie theme tune which he had set as his ring tone blasted out constantly at all times of day and night. This arrangement of Andrew working long hours suited them both. Gabriella liked to keep the house tidy and if no one was home then it couldn't get messed up or dirty.

Andrew and Gabriella, well Gabriella mainly, had decided on buying a static caravan in Wales after Gabriella had not seen much of Andrew during the recent six weeks' school holidays. Her last affair had ended, and her remarkable lover had returned to Poland after finishing work on a school's roof, the same school where Gabriella worked. The school had been closed to pupils for the holidays and Gabriella was in desperate need of more male attention in addition to what Andrew was able to provide. Don't misunderstand Gabriella. She loved Andrew with all her heart, but she had an enthusiasm in the bedroom which Andrew was unable to satisfy. Gabriella sometimes got frustrated with Andrew as he was occasionally a little reluctant and hesitated when she asked him to get more physically adventurous during their love making. On a few occasions, Gabriella had wondered over the years if Andrew might be seeing someone else or was it simply that he had other things on his mind all the time. Andrew sometimes wanted to be affectionate with kisses and cuddles, or perhaps just talk, rather than engage in the sweaty thrill-seeking sex, almost bordering on hysterical passion sometimes which Gabriella constantly craved. This often left Gabriella frustrated and unsatisfied in her marriage.

Fabian was already sat in the back seat of Gabriella's car, seat belt fastened he had settled in behind the driver seat. He was wearing his red gaming headphones and was focusing on the bright lights of his fully charged gaming tablet held in front of him.

"I've checked the back door, it's locked. Let's just go." Andrew smiled at Gabriella, proudly looking her up and down. *He* was married to this striking woman who walked towards him in a crisp white shirt which was open almost to her waist and tight blue jeans. When she moved, the light would shine through her shirt and revealed glimpses of her stunning body shape underneath, her nipples erect and seductively on display. Andrew thought back to last night and the passionate love making that had taken them into the early hours of the morning. It still made him smile and nervous at the same time. He had been a little shocked as he hadn't seen that insistent side to Gabriella for some time, but he didn't complain as she had given him direction around her body, with specific instructions of what she wanted him to do. Those images would remain in his memory for a while.

The caravan purchase had been expensive but, with a loan and help from both their parents, they had managed to buy their second choice of caravan model and site it on a good pitch on the south side of the park. Gabriella had plans to fit out the caravan to a very high standard. She would have it looking like a show home in no time at all.

Several weeks previous it had been the closed season, when they had first visited the caravan park to decide on their pitch. After several hours of looking around, Andrew had not been sure they had made the right decision in choosing Pebble Bay Caravan Park over the other sites they had visited. The lady on reception had given them a map of both the north and the south caravan parks which displayed every available caravan pitch they could choose from. She had circled with a fluorescent pink highlighter the pitches that were available, and they could choose to rent, and ultimately site their beloved new caravan on. They had walked around for hours inspecting all the pitches and it was Gabriella who clearly preferred the south side over the north. It was evidently clear why most of the plots were available, too close to the recycling bins, too noisy next to the club house, no private parking, too overlooked. They eventually chose a pitch they liked, returned to reception only to be informed that it had unfortunately been reserved by another couple only in the last hour.

The receptionist was sympathetic. With a sideward nod of her head, she moved round to the far end of the reception desk. They swiftly moved with her. Lowering her voice, she asked them to return their map and, this time, using a lime green pen she circled another pitch. In hushed whispers, they were informed that although there was a caravan still on this pitch, it was possibly going to become available and that they could have first refusal. They were instructed not to walk directly onto the pitch but to nonchalantly amble by and, if they liked it, to come back straight away. The current occupiers were hoping to move sites and were still negotiating the cost of caravan relocation with the management. The couple moving had until Friday to make their final decision. Andrew and Gabriella loved the pitch location, an outside eating area was important to them both. The following Saturday they had a call to say the pitch was theirs, they just needed to pay a deposit to secure it.

Today, as Andrew turned their car onto the single-track lane and then onto the site entrance, the sun was shining, the seagulls were singing, children were playing, and Andrew liked what he saw. He pulled up competently into the only remaining parking space directly in front of reception. It was as though it had been reserved especially for them.

"You going to go in, darling. Collect the keys?" Andrew turned off the engine. Fabian remained looking down at his screen, in the same position he had been in for most of the journey. Gabriella opened the car door and was already halfway out of the car, her sunglasses on top of her head, her shoulders back, she pushed out her pert breasts as she walked towards the reception desk, knowingly catching the eye of every man around. Gabriella walked like a model; she had a confident elegant stride with her chin held high. She was always on the prowl for a new man's attention, and she had come to realise that you never knew who might be watching at any given moment.

"Crawford said that second right is the best way to go around as it's all a one-way system," Gabriella said with a smile as she got back into the car. She looked out of the car window, not towards her new second home, but back towards the reception desk she had just left. She smiled as she remembered the big muscular arms belonging to the suntanned Crawford who had been manning the desk. She was content with the knowledge that her new conquest had been found. He was a big man and had an air of confidence about him. He clearly worked outdoors and was used to manual labour. All things that excited Gabriella.

"What kind of name is Crawford?" Andrew asked sarcastically, trying to remember the way so he could find his caravan again the next time he drove in.

"That's it. That's it. FABIAN, FABIAN, we're here." Gabriella was very excited and bounced in her seat, but their son didn't even look up from his screen. Andrew always preferred to reverse into a parking spot but Gabriella, who hadn't replaced her seatbelt after getting back in the car, was in such a rush, had opened her door and already had one leg out. Andrew stopped the car and attempted to feign the same excitement as his wife. He reminded himself of the things he had resolved to do; one – forget about gambling and two – enjoy his caravan and the time with his beautiful family. The caravan still had that lovely new car smell and parts of the kitchen cupboards were still covered in thin protective plastic. The central heating had been left on its lowest setting, leaving the caravan all warm and toasty. There was a welcome food hamper on the kitchen counter containing a bottle of champagne and a card. It was from Pam & Owen, the south site managers welcoming them to Wales and to their new holiday home. Fabian was still sat in the car. He had decided to wait until his mother had stopped giggling with excitement before he undid his seatbelt. He was just going to finish this last level of his current game before seeing what his new bedroom looked like and, more importantly, how fast this promised Wi-Fi speed was. He was so hoping the signal strength reached into his bedroom.

"Shoes off, shoes off, please." Gabriella was standing guard by the caravan door. Her outstretched arm holding the door handle in an attempt to block access. She smiled lovingly at the new carpets inside that had never been walked on. She would love it to remain that way and would do her utmost to keep that look and smell of newly laid carpet. Andrew was already in the process of slipping off his shoes out on the decking. He didn't need to be told; years of being married to Gabriella had rammed this house rule into him. Gabriella led the way for the grand tour. Andrew followed on behind, she was pointing out all the features of the new caravan as if Andrew was seeing it for the first time, even though they had spent weeks deciding on what fittings to get together. Obediently, he joined in and followed his wife, smiling and nodding when she pointed out items such as the digital central heating thermostat that they had chosen together. But really, Andrew was watching his wife's behind as she moved from room to room and how the light shone through her translucent blouse and outlined her slim body.

Fabian had inherited his looks from his mother. He was a very good-looking young man, tall, dark haired, blue eyed, and with olive skin. He never had any problems attracting the opposite sex. Girls at school were always battling for his attention. As a result, he seemed to have a different girlfriend every other week but showed little respect to any of them. He would be 16 in a few months and Fabian was already starting to think about concluding his education. He wasn't really that academic and he was planning on taking a year off. He wanted to become a professional video gamer rather than the catwalk model his mother wanted him to become. Being a gamer meant he had to first dedicate himself to his sport and try to get in at least ten hours of gaming a day. Studying chemistry or other useless subjects would not be conducive to his future career aspirations.

Fabian thought he'd better go inside the caravan and show some enthusiasm. He put away his console and tablet and he stretched his legs as he looked around. He could hear the sea, but he couldn't see it. He decided to first go and find the beach. A short walk to the right, he saw a ramp up a slight incline and from there he had a view of a large sandy beach which spread out in front of him. The sea was calm, and the sun was hot. *It's okay, I suppose,* thought Fabian with a grin as he looked around at what could only be described as a stunning view.

Danielle jumped as she quickly turned her head. *OMG* thought Danielle, the same words had already been tapped into her phone without even looking at the screen, followed by *"sxy newbie"* and with a quick *click* uploaded a photo onto her friends' live social media chat group. Numerous replies pinged back one after the other, mostly with the request *"ptmm"* and a barrage of orders for a close-up photograph of this new fitty who had moved in next door to Danielle's caravan. Danielle, still grasping her phone, managed to raise the curtains off the floor as she jostled to get a better view of Fabian through the caravan lounge window. She watched, fixated on what was inside his tight jeans as he strode off in the direction of the beach, at the same time she attempted to obtain more photographic evidence to satisfy her online doubters.

"tlk2ul8r" Danielle tapped for the last time, she checked her hair and lip gloss in the mirror, at the same time as stepping into her heels, she had decided to go and bump into this new boy before he was bagged by one of her friends. He was, as she had decided after just a brief glimpse, definitely boyfriend material.

"I'm going out, Mum," Danielle hollered, and she was already out of the door with her phone on silent but still vibrating away with the constant barrage of messages of interest and excitement from her friends at home.

CHAPTER 4

Smallest Bikini Top in the World

"That's a wonderful idea, darling," Clifford had said, the same phrase he had repeated many times throughout most of their relationship to date. In fact, Clifford was very easy going; he thought he had to be as he was a short man in stature, with a pronounced forehead and he hadn't been blessed in the good looks department. He was, however, very rich. Several years ago, he had inherited a vast estate from his parents when they had both died. His family had suspected that Alison was only really with him for his money, and they had told him this on numerous occasions. Nevertheless, their relationship had stood the test of time and they had stayed happily married for over a year now.

Alison, he thought, was amazing and Clifford reminded himself how lucky he was every night when he climbed into bed and lay beside her. She looked like a 'classy porn star', as one of his friends had once described her over a drink. Alison was tall for a woman with broad shoulders and strong hips, always sun tanned with an ample cleavage and a voice that matched her stature. Wherever and whenever she went, no matter the climate or season, Alison always wore a bikini top. Even if she was wearing a dress, the style she chose would always resemble a strappy bikini top. The various Lycra bikinis and other stretchy materials were tested daily by her generous bosoms that constantly looked like they were about to pop out and say 'hello' to the world. This cleavage display, however, was a constant delight for Clifford, but also a constant headache to him, as this spectacle attracted the attention of other men. He felt it was his duty to defend his wife's honour from the barrage of both male (and sometimes female) attention and their wandering eyes.

After Clifford and Alison had married, he had adopted the two children Alison had brought with her from her previous marriages. Not formally adopted them yet but he had taken them into his heart and treated them as if they were his own children. Alison had been married twice before and her two children, Jacob who was twelve and Molly who was six (seven in only a few weeks), had different fathers. Jacob had retained his biological father's last name, Ferguson. Molly had also retained her father's last name, Johnson, along with his wife which was the elephant in the room of their marriage. Jacob's father had moved back to the United States of America, leaving Jacob behind, and had never kept in touch with his son. There was the odd phone call over the years from his dad and sometimes a birthday card, but the contact was poor and intermittent. Clifford remembered Alison once saying that Jacob's biological father was working as a bodyguard or stunt man in the USA, possibly San Diego, or at least somewhere in California. Clifford tried not to pay too much attention when Alison recalled her past conquests. It hurt him to think about this stunt man, a man who he had never met, but who was most likely tall, tanned, and extremely handsome with a chiselled six pack. All the same, Clifford loved Jacob and treated him as his own son. There was a special bond between them, and they did lots of exciting father/son activities together. It helped that Clifford was wealthy – everything Jacob liked to do seemed to always be very expensive, the likes of motor cross, jet skiing, flying and skiing to name just a few.

Molly, however, had a unique father and Clifford's relationship with her was very different. Adam was very much still on the scene, constantly in Molly's life which meant also he was also in Clifford's life and annoyingly often in his house. Adam was one of those ex-military, big muscular chaps that had left the Army because he hated it and couldn't wait to get discharged. After leaving service, his story changed, and he would say he had been forced out of the career he had loved and how he was honoured to serve his country. In civvy street, all Adam ever talked about was his military career and, over the years, he had developed a talent for being able to conjure up a story on every world topic imaginable. He always dressed in military clothing, even casual Sunday jeans and T-Shirt for Adam would not be complete without his regiment logo. Clifford had never served his country and he wondered if Adam's choice of attire was purposefully selected as a reminder to him of this fact.

Alison ruminated that her ex-husband could have PTSD as a result of his military experience, and she would always remind Clifford to try and make allowances. She would say that Adam was Molly's father, and she would ask him to tolerate Adam for Molly's sake, if only until she was a little older. Clifford was conscious that his wife seemed to sometimes spend more time on the telephone talking with Adam than she did with him. Whenever Alison's phone rang, it always seemed to be Adam on the other end, mentally draining his wife by relaying the challenges of his day and asking for advice on his personal issues and constant financial problems. Clifford struggled having Adam in his life but accepted that having Alison by his side meant having Adam in the wings. With the purchase of the caravan in Wales, Clifford hoped he would perhaps see a little less of Adam. His wish was that it would allow him and Molly to spend more time together and hopefully bond so that he could build up a similar relationship to the one he enjoyed with Jacob.

My god! I don't like big dogs, thought Clifford as he was carrying up bag after bag of Alison's belongings from the car. *This bag weighs a tonne,* thought Clifford. *If she only ever wears a bikini! What the hell is in these bags?* Charles' dogs from the caravan next door were barking due to the arrival of Alison and Clifford but they soon fell silent. Clifford made a mental note – *I guess I'd better say hello at some point* – and he looked around at all the other caravans surrounding him. It wasn't long before Clifford realised that his brand-new top-of-the-range caravan seemed to stand out a little from the others that were sited around him. With its newly erected gleaming white UPVC decking, carefully manicured landscape garden and ample driveway area, it looked considerably grander than any caravan within view. Clifford had hoped that Alison had chosen the correct caravan park for them and that he wouldn't be spending his evenings having to listen to his noisy drunken neighbours into the early hours.

Inside the caravan Alison seemed to be moving around as if she was on roller-skates, in the lounge one minute, on the decking the next. Clifford stood and smiled, forgetting the weight of Alison's luggage. He watched her excitedly bound around her new project, pointing out various aspects of their new living space to him and their children. The caravan was indeed 'top spec' with three bedrooms, large shower-room bathroom, and the master bedroom possessing an en-suite bathroom. Clifford had specifically requested an en-suite bathroom with a large walk-in shower where they could be alone and adventurous each day. It was the one place where Alison didn't take charge in their love making. Clifford enjoyed regular sex in the shower and this was the one place Alison was very submissive in their love making. It was probably due to the fact that Alison wasn't a water person and she preferred to let Clifford just do what he wanted, knowing that shower sex was one of her new husband's pleasures.

Well, that's going to be an issue, thought Clifford, as he stared across at the man in the caravan next door, someone he would later be introduced to as Charles. *I know what he is looking at,* he thought as Alison gallivanted around on the decking in her flimsy bikini top. Alison wearing denim shorts and the standard accompanying bikini top, which as usual was far too small for her bust size, waved excitedly across at Charles. Charles was now staring at Alison, so

Clifford decided to return the stare. At the same time, Clifford wondered why every bloke was so much bigger and taller than he was, but he gave Charles a brief 'hello' and a friendly nod of acknowledgement. Suddenly there was a screech. It startled Clifford, and he looked away from Charles. Clifford would come to realise that the noise came from the mouth of Charles' wife, Sharon. Clifford couldn't see her but noticed that, directly after the high-pitched screech, Charles moved very quickly and disappeared out of view, the sound of barking dogs becoming fainter.

Clifford found a cupboard for Alison's unnaturally heavy bags and settled himself down next to Molly on the large L-shaped sofa. *It's very peaceful here,* he thought and immediately decided he liked living by the sea. Down the hill, you could see the ocean in the distance. As you got closer the view disappeared behind a sea wall defence, consisting of very large, carefully placed boulders which protected the site. Alison opened the patio doors which led out onto the decking area and let in the fresh sea air. Jacob was nowhere to be seen but Clifford wasn't worried and thought he must perhaps be in his room or out exploring. He paused for a moment before sitting down, deciding that now was probably a good time to lay down some holiday ground rules. This would allow him to truly relax, knowing that the children could roam the site safely on their own. After a moment's parenting deliberation, it would be better to set out his ground rules only once, with both children present, and he stood up to go and search for Jacob. Molly was engrossed in her phone, and he had noticed earlier when he approached her with the intention of settling down next to her, she had immediately leaned slightly and angled her screen away from him. Clifford gave a whimsical sigh.

"Where's Jacob?" asked Clifford whilst looking in Alison's direction, just as her phone rang on the kitchen counter. Alison had it set with a specific ringtone for whenever Adam rang – the soundtrack from the military movie 'Where Eagles Dare'. Clifford seemed to be hearing this tune more often. He had come to hate that soundtrack.

"It will be about Molly, it's OK," Alison said, looking across at Clifford and smiling as she snatched up her phone and shot off in the direction of the bedrooms for some privacy to speak with Adam. "Hello darling ..." Clifford heard her softly say as she closed the door behind her, with the phone to her left ear.

I will find Jacob, Clifford thought to himself and off he went through the door and out onto the decking. He remembered the sea was just past the reception so, to take his mind off army Adam ringing *his* wife, he set off down the hill in the direction of the beach. Clifford was not truly concerned about Jacob, and he was promptly informed that Jacob had, in fact, gone inside Charles' caravan next door and was playing video games with the other children. He decided to go for a walk anyhow.

Clifford didn't meet anybody else on the site until he could see the reception building up ahead. As he neared reception, he passed a series of signs, written in both Welsh and English. The first green rectangular sign was made out of wood and had red painted letters on it which were starting to flake with age. This sign advised him he was leaving the north caravan park. A little further on, an expensive looking second sign, written in gold letters on a piece of large slate looked brand new. This sign advised Clifford he was entering a separate caravan park on the south side, and it highlighted the different site rules. Clifford hadn't been aware that there were two caravan parks. They certainly both looked the same in the brochures. He ambled past reception and entered the south side of the park. Heading down hill his destination was the beach. *Blimey! It's very different down here,* Clifford thought to himself as he looked at all the rows upon rows of elegant matching caravans, all very neatly maintained and grand looking. The grass looked like it had been cut with scissors, the flower beds were bright with fresh flowers, and it all had that modern special feel. Every car seemed to be expensive and brand-new, all proudly parked next to their caravans on their matching stone driveways. Clifford wondered why they hadn't looked at this side of the park, he had certainly paid enough for his caravan.

Charles was walking back from the direction of the sea. He was being pulled along by three immense dogs and as they approached Clifford, began to bark very loudly.

"You all settled in?" Charles asked over the noise of his dogs. Clifford smiled at Charles, he couldn't actually hear a word this bloke was saying, did he not realise how loud those bloody dogs were? Did he really expect him to stop and chat?

Charles stopped and Clifford could still see his mouth moving. Not really being a dog person, Clifford decided to wave and walk on, pointing at the dogs and smiling back – he hoped that would be enough. Clifford picked up his pace and, with Charles disappearing behind him, headed for the beach. For the next five minutes, Clifford could still hear the incessant barking and wondered whether it was only him who was clearly irritated by the noise. Standing at the top of a boat launching ramp he looked down over an almost deserted beach. A tall, good-looking young lad was walking across the shingles. He was looking down at his phone whilst a young girl, or at least a girl much shorter than him, almost ran alongside him trying to keep up, but she was struggling in the sand due to her ridiculous choice of heels.

This is wonderful, thought Clifford. *Sun, sea, sand and more importantly NO Adam.* He thought he would really push the boat out and go and discover the bar and enjoy a lunchtime drink. He left the beach for the exclusive use of the young couple. The bar, or clubhouse as was the term in the caravan world, was next door to the reception block. From the outside it resembled little more than a large wooden shack, but the sun was shining and there were a few people sitting drinking and chatting outside on the benches. Unfortunately, one of the seats was occupied by Charles but Clifford didn't register it was him until he was almost alongside him. The dogs had stopped barking and were busy lapping up water from shiny chrome bowls, water spilling out onto the stone floor. Charles acknowledged him and without hesitation invited him to sit down at his table.

"They'll soon be asleep," Charles said through a smile as he nodded towards the three bundles of fur under the table. "Sit down man," with a wave of his colossus arm. "Watch the dogs! I'll get you a beer seeing as you're the newbie." With that, Charles jumped up and, almost running, headed off inside and the direction of the bar, not really offering Clifford any choice in the matter. Tentatively Clifford sat down, not wanting to bump the table and disturb the now placid dogs. Clifford sat with his legs out to the side. There was no way he was going to put his bare skin under the table near to the mouths of these beasts. Looking down he couldn't believe how they looked even bigger laying down side by side. He was surprised he had allowed himself to get this close.

Charles hurriedly returned and with outstretched arms he was holding out two pints of frothy beer. He plonked them down on the bench with a thud. From one glass, the top inch of foam slopped out over the top of the glass and dripped down the side of the bench. One dog who must have been its recipient raised its head and looked up; Clifford knew this as he could feel its fur brush against his leg. The dog looked up from its sleep, but it just as quickly settled itself back down under the table with its two other napping accomplices. Clifford edged his backside even further out onto the edge of the bench seat and as far away from the dogs as he could possibly get.

"Cheers," Charles said, as he encircled his beer glass with his massive had and raised his pint, Clifford slowly reached across and hesitantly took hold of the glass.

"I was only going to have a small glass of wine, I'm not really a beer drinker," he said quietly. As soon as he had said it, he realised it wasn't the right thing to be saying in the presence of this very large man mountain.

"Cheers," repeated Charles, lowering his glass back down onto the bench, Clifford noticed that almost a third of Charles' pint had been drained already. Clifford took a sip of his beer and he looked over at Charles. "I'm Charles and my wife is Sharon. I think you saw her in the van."

Clifford offered an outstretched hand.

"Pleased to meet you. You have a van? I didn't see one," he added with a look of surprise.

"No." Charles laughed. "The caravan, we call it a van, in fact almost everyone on the north side calls their caravan a van," Charles scoffed as he picked up his beer again and drank even more of it.

"They have all sorts of posh names for their caravans on the south side. *Holiday Home, HH, Seaside Lodge,*" Charles smirked. "They think they are *rather posh* on the south side." He took several gulps of beer, his pint glass now almost empty.

"What do you do then, Clifford?" Charles asked, looking down with amusement at Clifford's glass. Clifford registered the look and, out of politeness, took a good large mouthful of beer as he replied.

"Real-estate, I'm in real-estate. I have a portfolio of houses and business lets etc."

"Very nice indeed," Charles said and, before Clifford could even return the questioning, Charles told him that he was a boxing coach and that he ran a series of classes throughout the week at local leisure centres which afforded him weekends off. Clifford heard that he had been married before, that Sharon was his second wife, and he had three children.

"It's my round," Clifford said. "Let me buy you one." He lifted his pint again as if to show Charles he would drink it even though he was only a third of the way down the glass. Charles had long finished his beer and was already light on his toes and heading inside in the direction of the bar. One beer turned into several and with every mouthful Charles' manly banter became more acceptable. Clifford was actually enjoying the evening.

With the sun setting and the spring evening turning cold, they moved inside the club house. The two new acquaintances stood at a raised table near the bar. The dogs fell into their customary routine under the table when their master was entertaining and they fell almost on top of each other, just a mass of twitching tails from dreaming dogs.

Beer after beer kept arriving and Clifford struggled to keep up, sometimes only drinking half of his pint before another one magically appeared on the table and, before he even realised it was dark, he was staggering drunkenly back to his caravan. Thankfully, he could amble behind Charles as he didn't really know the way home.

If Charles had been affected by the copious amounts of beer they had consumed, he didn't show it. Clifford, however, was struggling and had to really focus to even keep walking in a straight line. The dogs walked ahead of Charles, off the lead. They barked occasionally if Clifford walked into them as he staggered and concentrated on keeping pace with his neighbour. Clifford was surprised how different the place looked at night and, to be honest, he couldn't really recall which caravan was his, only realising he had reached his destination when he spotted his own car.

"Come in, Charles! Go-onnn! Come in and meet the wife. Have a night cap. One for the road old chum!" Clifford looked at Charles through a drunken grin, he was keen to show off his sexy wife. He was so very proud of Alison. Charles didn't hesitate and he tied his three dogs onto the handrail of Clifford's decking then walked up the steps, turning in through the open patio doors. The dogs were very well behaved and again lay down, looking attentively up towards the patio door after their master. Clifford slowly followed Charles up the steps, he was not as light on his feet as Charles. Inside the caravan Clifford didn't really notice how Alison squeezed past Charles at the side of the kitchen cabinet, pressing herself against him as she welcomed him into their new home. Neither did he see how she kept her right hand on Charles's bare bicep for slightly longer than she should have when she was asking him a question. Alison turned to Clifford, muttered something, then turned her attention back to Charles.

"Take a seat, Charlie! What can I get you?" she asked again suggestively with a lingering half smile, all whilst licking her top lip.

Clifford hadn't really registered what Alison had said but she hadn't told him off which he took as positive. It seemed Jacob and Molly had gone to bed, and Alison was now smiling and saying something about how great it was he had gone out with the boys. Inside the warmth of the caravan, Clifford very quickly realised that he had overdone it and, without saying a word, stood up and smiled at Charles. In his head, he had said that it had been great to meet him and that they should do it again soon, but the words which actually came out of his mouth didn't make any sense at all. He turned and wobbled down the corridor, still fully clothed he collapsed face down on the master bed. Two minutes later he was snoring deeply – the best dressed man in bed.

Charles and Alison were alone in the lounge, the lighting was low, and even though her husband had departed, Alison had convinced Charles to stay for one more drink. She offered that Clifford had only gone to use the bathroom. Alison knew her husband well. She knew he wasn't a drinker, and she knew he would be out for the count. The children were asleep in bed, and it was Alison's turn for some excitement with this bald hunk of a chap she had entrapped all to herself.

The opportunity had presented itself and, in the blink of an eye, the ambiance changed. Alison, who was well practised in the art of seduction, had already lit several scented candles. There was faint music now playing in the background, and Alison was ripping the foil off the top of a bottle of chilled French Champagne. Before Charles even realised what was happening, he was sitting on the sofa with Alison close beside him. She was facing him with one leg tucked underneath her and her other smooth bare leg draped across his lap.

"Cheers!" Alison smiled and they clinked flutes, Charles innocently looked down to ensure the very full champagne glass he had just been handed didn't spill as he clinked Alison's glass in return. She was face on now and all he could see was her ample bronzed bosom fighting to stay inside what had to be the smallest bikini top in the world. Her breasts stared straight back at him, and he liked what he saw. Almost immediately Charles was fighting an erection in his shorts.

Alison relished this new male attention and laughed at anything and everything Charles said, leaning back her head, pushing her breasts into the side of Charles's bare arm, her long hair falling down her back. She knew that the skin-on-skin contact with Charles's arm would make her nipples erect and that they would be easily visible through her bikini top.

Charles couldn't stop smiling. He had a belly full of beer and now he could feel Alison's almost naked breasts pressing into his upper arm. She giggled and moved closer. Charles had by now completely forgotten about Clifford and was so aroused by the attention from Alison that he found himself in that situation that him and many other married men before him had been in so many times. Just this one time, he thought. He had drunk too much. He had a very sexy and attractive woman making it clear she wanted more than just a chat. His inhibitions diminished through alcohol, and he found himself justifying his actions. He wouldn't get caught, not if it was just the once. He wouldn't do it again. What harm could it do? He played these thoughts over and over in his head.

Charles lifted his champagne flute to take another drink. "Cheers," he repeated, an excuse he could use to look down again at his glass, and once more stare at Alison's large, perfect breasts. They tapped glasses. Charles stared at Alison and this time he wasn't going to look away. Alison tossed her head back impulsively as she laughed, allowing her long hair to fall down her back, almost touching the sofa. She pulled her shoulders even further back and pushed her chest forward and upwards, pressing them even further in Charles's direction. She moved her hand gently onto the front of Charles shorts. Swiftly she had the zip down on his shorts and with skilful fingers she had her hand inside and was encompassing Charles full girth. Alison raised her eyebrows with a smile, wanting to show Charles how impressed she was with the size of his manhood. She moved her hand as best she could to please him, but she was restricted to only very small movements due to his clothing.

Charles leaned forwards and placed his face between her breasts. He had a burning desire to pour some of the champagne from his glass over them. Grinning, he raised his head and stared directly into Alison's eyes. Alison pouted in response, and she placed her other hand firmly and confidently at Charles' waist, searching for a button to remove his shorts. She mouthed the words that she wanted him now inside her. Charles raised his glass in preparation to trickle champagne teasingly over Alison's chest, when, without any warning, the caravan lights came on full. The mood was extinguished and there, silhouetted like a crazed bear in the middle of the open patio doors, was his wife ... Sharon.

She didn't speak at first, she just stood there with her hands on her hips and then growled, "Are you ever coming home to your wife and children?"

"Yes, sorry darling," Charles said as he jumped to his feet. The angle they were sat, he was almost certain that she hadn't seen the hand fully encompassing his hard penis which had been struggling to still occupy his open shorts. In one swift movement he was up and with a reverse shuffle type movement, all whilst he did his best to hide his arousal, he was out the door. The champagne flute still occupied his clammy hand, the other struggling to adjust himself and pull up his zip as he moved.

CHAPTER 5

The Other Park

"I do love visiting this site," Patrick remarked to his wife Melissa as they turned right out of the site and along the single-track lane up to the main road. They didn't speak again until the next right turn which led out onto the main road and then south. They chatted the remaining couple of miles, their destination was their own caravan park.

"We do seem to spend an awful amount of time here," Patrick again offered. "I bet when people see us walking around, they probably think we are permanent residents." Patrick laughed as he said it, clearly thinking it qualified as nearly a joke and was expecting a witty retort from Melissa so was surprised to hear her response.

"I like coming here too. I love seeing Debbie and David but it's great to leave." Patrick and Melissa had discussed their choice of caravan site many times over and had settled on Lobster Pot Park and *not* Pebbles for quite a few reasons. The main reason being that they could choose when to visit, pop over and see friends when they wanted. It could be on their own terms but more importantly they could leave at the end of the day and return to their own little slice of peaceful heaven.

"Yes, yes, yes I know, I'm just saying …" Patrick knew it was time to shut up as he didn't want to upset the apple cart. Tonight, Grandma was looking after the boys and bringing them to the caravan in a few days' time, which meant he had Melissa all to himself. This was likely to be his only chance for some intimacy with his wife; it had been over a week since he had seen any bedroom action and it was all that occupied Patrick's mind right now. He had been keeping the *wolves* from the door on his own, but it was becoming a tedious chore in the shower every morning.

Lobster Pot Caravan Park was only a few miles further down the coast, but it was a world apart from the Pebbles Bay site. Pebbles was loud and busy with big 4x4 vehicles, loud amusement arcades, numerous takeaway restaurants, and noisy jet skis, all centred around an immense sandy beach.

Lobster Pot Park on the other hand was a quiet caravan park situated on the edge of a small coastal Welsh village with just a pub and a single village shop stocking most of the essentials. Their caravan site had a club house, shop, and laundry and was set on a stony beach, with a few patches of sand here and there, depending on the movement of the tide. The main benefit of this shingle beach was that it kept the smoking noisy jet skis away, so ultimately it was a very peaceful park.

"Shall we stop for a drink at the pub?" Patrick asked with a smile as the village came into view. He was really hoping to mellow the atmosphere with a few drinks in the hope of getting Melissa *in the mood*.

"No, let's just get back. I've got a headache," Melissa replied unenthusiastically. Patrick's shoulders drooped and it seemed that the sky had turned grey. His hopes and dreams shattered, no sex again tonight he was thinking. The remaining part of the journey was completed in silence. It was all rather dull, Patrick even contemplated dropping Melissa off and going back to Pebbles and having another drink with his mates but, being the dutiful husband, he didn't for fear of another sexless barren week ahead.

*

"What did you think of Charles? Seemed a nice bloke to me," David asked his wife, without looking at her. He knew she was listening; she didn't miss a thing. Debbie didn't reply, which meant Charles hadn't made it onto Debbie's Christmas card list just yet.

David replied for her. "You can't just dislike him because he is from the north side. He is apparently a good mate of Spider's." David said, being a little more positive and assertive in his tone, hoping to generate a reaction from Debbie.

"If I don't like him, I don't like him. *You asked.*" David could feel her eyes upon him.

"Well, he is on our site, so we are probably going to be seeing—"

"He is *not* on our site. He is on the *north*, a *different* site last time I checked, and they pay a *lot* less in ground fees than we do on the south so no he is *not* on our site." Realising she was starting to raise her voice, Debbie got up from her spot on the sofa and pretended to busy herself in the kitchen. The mention of Patrick had again filled her head with the reoccurring fantasies of a hard naked body making love to her. The kitchen was her domain and David kept well away so he would have no idea she wasn't actually doing anything, apart from moving things that didn't need moving as she tried to get the naked body of Patrick from her mind.

David for some reason hoped he would see more of Charles. He wasn't sure why but again used the justification that he had used so many times before to himself, that he was surrounded by women. David realised he wasn't going to bump into Charles whilst he was sat on the sofa in his caravan so with a cheery tone said, "Well I'm going to the clubhouse for a quick pint. You coming girls?" Both twins jumped up off the sofa. They had had their headphones on but always had one ear open for any family activities that were on offer. They were now up and getting ready, arguing over who was getting which coat and whose turn it was for the portable power bank charger for their mobile phones.

"I'll stay here," Debbie muttered in her lowered 'woe-is-me' tone.

"Demi and Paris are both asleep."

"Ah-come on, we are on our holidays. It's OK if we wake them up," David stood up enthusiastically and picked up his wallet and keys, secretly hoping Debbie stayed home this time so he could talk to men instead.

"No, you go! Paris has a cold coming, I think. I gave her some medicine, so she needs to sleep it off." Debbie sat back down on the sofa and lifted a very large glass of pink wine to her lips. She was clearly happy not to have to walk anywhere or make any effort in her appearance and was quite content to stay in her spotted onesie, her hair tied up in a sparkly pink scrunchy she had found on the coffee table.

"I'm coming, WAIT," Dani said firmly as she came flying out of her bedroom, a full face of makeup, including her new brows. She was wearing a very short dress. David looked across at Debbie and creased his forehead in disapproval at the length of his daughter's dress. He opened his mouth in preparation to speak, but Debbie raised her eyebrows and shook her head nonchalantly.

David closed his mouth and slipped on his sliders. He was out of the door and down the steps in a flash. In his opinion, the dress would give off all the wrong signals but perhaps that was just him being an overly protective father. David walked slowly in the direction of the club house, within seconds his twin daughters, Daisy and Dolly, appeared either side of him, and slipped their hands into his. He was a proud dad, he smiled to himself on hearing his teenage daughter 'clip clopping' close behind him in her high heels. He could see the bright screen of her mobile phone reflecting in the windows of the dark empty caravans they passed. It always amazed David at how his daughter used the keypad on her mobile phone which never left her hand. She didn't ever have to look at it *and* she could even text whilst walking and talking. Earlier that evening Debbie had given David the heads up that Danielle had been seen on the beach with a tall good-looking young man who apparently was new on site. How Debbie found out all this gossip was beyond David. In reality, he thought Debbie was not that much different from Danielle, although Debbie could occasionally be seen without her mobile phone firmly glued to her hand.

David didn't get the mobile phone attraction yet. He still used an old Nokia 3310; it was often the butt of many a joke by his mates. "Text me, if you must, but I'd prefer you to ring me and speak to me. It's the best way," he would often say. He also liked to see who was ringing him before he answered and sometimes chose to ignore his ringing brick of a handset.

Debbie was finally alone; her two youngest children were asleep in bed, and she knew her husband would be gone for some time. She was very experienced in applying her make-up and, within just under two minutes, her hair was tidied up and make-up applied. She pulled down the zip on her onesie, making sure her boobs were elevated and in their best positions for the video call she was about to make. Debbie was going to call a friend, a new male friend called Martin. Martin was a good-looking single dad from back home who attended Daisy and Dolly's after school dance classes. It wouldn't be the first playful video call they had shared together. Debbie had caught Martin looking at her on several occasions during the dance classes and had thought perhaps he was, just like her, not sexually satisfied. He was clearly a single guy, no wedding ring and seemingly no partner. He was dark and mysterious with muscular legs and arms, and she found him very attractive. She started speaking and flirting with him and this had been going on for a few weeks now. It had started with the eye contact, then flirts and brief chats at the dance classes. This had turned into text messaging, and they had an understanding that, when she could, she would video call him. Debbie had sent several texts to Martin that morning and his excitement had been growing throughout the day. He was very much looking forward to his flirtatious call from this desperate housewife.

Debbie wasn't planning on being unfaithful to her husband, for her it was just a bit of fun but there was no doubt she craved sex. It made her feel good knowing that another man still found her attractive. For some time now, she had been feeling invisible and desperately unsatisfied by David. He didn't even notice when she had her nails done or her hair highlighted. He used to tell her how sexy and beautiful she looked but she couldn't remember the last time he passed her a compliment. She didn't know where this liaison with Martin would lead but, for now, it made her feel special and alive again, her own little secret.

Debbie took a large gulp of her rose wine and searched her mobile directory until she found 'Dance Teacher'. She'd read about using a code name for a phone contact in a woman's magazine and it seemed like a good idea. She tapped the video camera call button on her screen, glancing down at her two secret weapons again to make sure they were on point and hadn't dropped out of sight. She pushed her shoulders back slightly and lifted her chin, smiling, waiting for hunky Martin to appear on the screen. He appeared, his big white teeth filling the screen from his sexy smile. He wore an open shirt, and she could see whispers of dark chest hair. Debbie squeezed her thighs tight and she wished she could open his shirt and touch his chest right there and then.

The club was busier than normal tonight, David thought to himself. There was a live band playing in the far corner and a packed bar counter. David smiled and said hello to a few people he recognised, as he slipped past the crowds and found a gap at the end of the bar and waited to be served. "I will have a Bacardi and Coke, Dad," Dani shouted over his right shoulder, applying another layer of red lip-gloss as she scanned around the bar.

"You will have a diet Coke and that's it. Packet of crisps, girls?" David asked, looking down adoringly at his twin daughters by his side.

They both looked up at him and, with a smile that melted his heart, they nodded in unison as he knew they would. David had already ordered the crisps in anticipation of the positive response. The girls took one sip through the straws in their coke bottles, dumped them down on the table and with an open crisp packet shot out of the club house door. They ran straight round to the amusement arcade next door, eating and spilling crisps as they walked, their pocket money from Grandma and Grandad burning a hole in their pockets.

Family caravan rules allowed visits to the onsite amusements arcade if Mum or Dad were in the clubhouse next door, but children were not permitted anywhere else and had to report back every fifteen minutes or so to show they were OK. David glanced at the two bottles of practically untouched Cola. He was thinking about the two pounds that each one had set him back and the single sip the girls had taken before abandoning them for the bright lights of the amusements next door. The caravan had several very large bottles of cola from the supermarket in the cupboards, but the girls didn't touch them! They only wanted bottles of Coke if it cost the earth in the clubhouse bar.

"So, it's great you came out with your old man," David said, smiling, and turned to give his eldest daughter his full attention.

Before he could even say anything further, Danielle spoke, "Charlotte's here. Yes, I know. Back by ten and don't leave the site!" and with that, she was gone, off out the door in a flash, closely followed by her best friend Charlotte who David observed was dressed just as scantily as Danielle, in full make-up and heels. David knew Charlotte's parents. They had a caravan on the south side of the park. He couldn't see them, but he knew they would be sat drinking someplace in the clubhouse. It's what they did most nights.

Recently David had given up arguing over what his daughter wore or the lack of what she wore, and Debbie reassured him that she was having regular chats with her. That she hadn't had sex yet but was all ready and aware of precautions when the time was right. As a father, that didn't reassure David but with another four daughters in the wings and all of them growing up quickly he acknowledged that the next few years would bring with them a fair amount of door-slamming teenage tantrums.

David now stood alone. He lifted his pint to his lips and looked around the bar. He was secretly hoping to see Charles, but he didn't see any single men, just couples, men and women, mostly with several children loitering around them. David's attention was drawn to a tall man who he could only see from the back. He was wearing a formal type of jacket, a pair of smart skinny jeans and brown lace up boots. David liked his smart but casual look and it all matched and went together very well. The stranger had a full head of slightly greying hair and David was desperately hoping that he would turn so he could see his face. The man looked educated and smart, and David found himself staring at him. He thought perhaps *he* should wear a formal jacket more often and maybe make some new clothing purchases. He looked down at his misshapen faded shorts and tatty worn-out flip flops. He looked properly, for the first time, at his pale skinny legs. David had never shown any interest in his appearance before, he had never had to, but he decided at that moment he should definitely raise his game in the wardrobe department. He knew that he would need Debbie's help; she was the one with the dress sense, fashion magazines, and let's face it, she watches a lot of daytime TV so knew all the latest on-trend styles.

David turned his attention back to his immediate surroundings and moved the numerous empty beer glasses to one side, some pint glasses completely empty but several still almost full. David drank his beer with pleasurable contentment and, to be honest, he quite liked a little 'David time'. He always relished the first beer of the day, it always tasted better he thought.

With six women in his life, it was OK, he justified to himself, to have the odd 'man time' beer now and again. However, he would have preferred it if there was some male company with whom to share the moment. David again gazed around the clubhouse bar, he thought he could smell a dog but couldn't see one. He acknowledged the odd smile and nod from the few site members he recognised. There were quite a few new faces in the bar tonight he noticed. The clubhouse was open to both north and south residents. It was the only amenity that was open equally to both parks. After the big site divide between the two brothers, everything else, the pool, sauna, and laundry room, touring pitches, and the outdoor family barbeque areas had all remained with the south side and had received copious amounts of modernisation investment. This had seemed to work well in the most part but, much to their annoyance, south residents would occasionally sometimes see the north residents using the pool and laundry room which was strictly against the rules.

*

Patrick popped the cap on a bottle of chilled Belgian beer and half poured it into a specially selected clean glass. Before he drank it, he began the ritual of moving the glass, twisting the bottle label, and repositioning it for a better photograph, always being mindful of the background. Patrick had been challenged in the police station by a colleague to complete a book called *'101 different beers'* and Patrick had taken up the challenge with gusto and heaps of enthusiasm. This was much to the annoyance of Melissa, who also worked at the police station. Patrick was aware that Melissa wasn't assisting him in his beer quest. She showed very little interest in his *man challenge* and deemed it a complete waste of both time and money. Patrick had drawn the conclusion that, since he wasn't going to be getting any sex tonight, he may as well immerse himself in his love of beer. The beer photograph was being prepared and taken ready to log his #101beer drinking progress on social media. Beer number 24 was ready to be posted, only 77 beers to go and Patrick smiled to himself; tasty golden malty flavour with a frothy white head, he was already planning as his description for this particular beer post.

*

"He's there! There! The tall one! My future husband!" Dani pointed confidently to indicate the location of Fabian through the groups of people stood drinking outside the club house. Fabian was stood with a tall elegant blonde woman; Danielle could only see her from the back and immediately had that flash of jealousy in her eyes. It made her cheeks blush slightly. Fabian was holding a bottle of cider and talking with another boy of similar age. They all stood at the edge of the club house patio area, at the side of the entrance to the amusement arcade; the same amusements that Danielle had just seen her two younger sisters enter, she had ignored them as they had run past her chattering loudly, another bag of crisps in their hands.

"That's his mum, duurrrr," Charlotte said, knowing that look in her best friend's eyes and saying it all whilst pretending not to look up from her phone. "I saw the woman on Fabian's decking when I went to the shops earlier."

"You don't go to the shops past Fabian's caravan, *I* saw him *first*," Danielle protested, reinforcing her observations by clicking her phone off and placing it in her pocket. With the straw from her Bacardi and diet Coke tucked into the side of her mouth, she looked adoringly over in Fabian's direction. Eyes like a puppy dog. Charlotte's parents had bought Danielle the alcoholic drink on the understanding it had been OK'd with her mum and dad.

*

Patrick was in full flow with his social media post featuring his latest beer challenge conquest when his phone pinged. It was a message from his buddy, David. Melissa looked across at Patrick, taking her eyes briefly away from her latest TV programme that she had selected for that evening. She really wanted to know but didn't really want to ask who had messaged her husband, so she swivelled into her chair and fixed her attention back to the TV screen. *That's it,* she thought, *he's definitely not getting sex tonight.*

Patrick disappeared outside the caravan onto the decking, his mobile phone in his pocket, beer in one hand and glass in the other. He knew this would bother Melissa. She would be wondering who was messaging him, but he knew the damage had already been done that night and there was no going back. He attempted to take another picture of his beer with the moon and stars in the background. The message could wait a little longer.

It was David who had messaged Patrick, saying he was alone in the bar and that even Charles wasn't in there. Patrick had said Charles would probably be in the club house every night, he liked a drink. David continued with his messages and wished Patrick had chosen to site his caravan on the same site so they could have been drinking buddies. Patrick messaged back and replied that he wished the same, but it was Melissa who had wanted her space and privacy which had led to them choosing the caravan park a few miles away. Patrick returned inside. Melissa didn't even look up from the television screen as he entered. He had failed in his moonlight attempt at a cool beer photograph and began chatting to Melissa about how he might need a proper DSLR camera in the near future if he was going to take this social media beer blogging seriously. Melissa wasn't really listening and had decided she would wait at least ten minutes before asking who had messaged.

"David texted. He's saying he's in the bar alone if I fancied a pint." Patrick put his phone down and popped the cap off two bottles of beer, placing one down in front of his wife. "What we watching?" Patrick asked at the same time, taking a sip and looking up at the TV. He settled down on the sofa and tried to take an interest in his wife – it's not over, he thought, until the fat lady sings.

CHAPTER 6

What Kid Only Eats Bran Flakes?

After a busy day, Molly had fallen asleep earlier than usual, and she was now sleeping soundly. Alison could see a faint light coming from underneath Jacob's bedroom door, but she knew her son well and he would be wearing one of the many sets of sound deadening headphones that she seemed to be constantly buying for him. Sexually frustrated and feeling annoyed that her evening hadn't gone to plan, Alison had attempted to wake her husband. She had crashed about the bedroom, making as much noise as possible in an attempt to wake up Clifford. She wanted sex and she wanted it right now. As she prepared herself for bed she deliberately pulled at his duvet and knocked the bedroom door several times, accidentally but rather loudly. She knew that after a few pints of beer he could always be persuaded to fulfil his marital obligations and alcohol actually seemed to enhance Clifford's bedroom performance. To Alison's frustration it seemed that tonight would be different. Things hadn't gone the way she had hoped with Charles, and she lay awake thinking of him. Unsatisfied she had to ignore the tingling glow of her feet and reside herself to listening to her husband's drunken snoring instead. In her head she was visualising the incredible sex she would have with Charles one day; bald men really did turn her on. There was not a doubt in her mind it was going to happen. Still excited from Charles's company, Alison turned away from her unresponsive husband and closed her eyes. She let her imagination take her to another place, a place of desire, passion, and new male sexual conquests. As she drifted off to sleep, she thought about Charles and because he was tall and bald, she had no reservations that his large muscular stature was relative to all the other parts of his body. Alison adored big bald men, in fact baldness was very near to the top of her all-time turn-on list. As a fitness instructor, he would definitely have stamina as well, she thought. Alison was certain that he would be more than a willing participant in her number one fantasy, a fantasy she hadn't dare share with her new husband yet. She believed she was a strong judge of character and quickly formed the impression from watching Charles earlier that he was a man who was turned on by large breasts. Being well equipped in this department, she was determined to make sure Charles saw hers as often as he could, and she drifted soundly off to sleep.

*

Charles was awake and up and about early; he had an unimportant hangover but nothing he hadn't coped with many times before. In command of the kitchen, he was making copious piles of pancakes. The bacon was crisping nicely under the grill and a large bowl of scrambled eggs were nearly ready. The Welsh sunshine beamed in through the caravan windows, fresh sea air drifted in through the open patio doors and the 1980s radio channel played on low in the background. Yazoo screeched out *Don't Go* as Sharon surfaced.

"Good morning, pumpkin," Charles beamed with a wink and a smile whilst attempting to give his wife a good morning cuddle. Sharon was having none of it and she side stepped him quickly and marched past the kitchen and on into the lounge. Still in her pyjamas, Sharon's fluffy leopard-print dressing gown was firmly fastened over the top. She had been married to Charles long enough to know he loved to see as much of her body in the morning as he could. He liked her skin on show as she moved around the caravan, but today he wouldn't be getting any glimpses of flesh. After last night e*verything* was closed for him in that department Sharon had decided.

"Aah, come on, Pumpkin, nothing happened. Clifford was in the bathroom, she just jumped on me as soon as Clifford left the room," Charles attempted to lighten the mood with humour and added, "She's not made of wood. Her eyes aren't painted on you know, there's only one woman for me." Charles half laughed as he chased his wife around the lounge repeating the word 'Pumpkin' several times, something he knew she loved to be called. Sharon managed half a smile on her face, as she ran and giggled around the coffee table. She loved it when Charles used her pet name, however, she was adamant Charles was not having his hands on any part of her body this morning. He was very firmly in the *doghouse*.

Their eldest son appeared from the bedrooms and headed for the lounge. Only hearing parts of the conversation between his dad and step-mum, Jackson enquired:

"What happened then, Dad? Come on, do tell us." Jackson looked up from the sofa and smiled as he lowered his tablet. He was interested to find out what had gone on with the sexy bikini-wearing *bombshell* from next door. This description had been used to describe their new neighbour to his mates on Snapchat the previous evening. Jackson had even joked with his digital audience that he was considering his chances and telling his mates that he was going to ask if Alison might consider teaching him a few things after his 16th birthday of course. Sharon wanted to get in first.

"I caught your father about to have sex with our new neighbour last night," Sharon announced sharply in her forceful *hands-on-hips* voice. She was the victim here and she would make sure everyone knew. Even her own children.

"Erm, massive exaggeration, methinks," came Charles's quick retort. "I had a few drinks with Clifford last night at the club, that's his name, the new chap next door. He invited me back to his van for a night cap and when he went to the loo, his wife, whatever her name is, jumped on me on the sofa. Then your Mum walked in, being all grumpy and un-neighbourly like," Charles stood tall and seemed pleased that he had explained things the way he had wanted to without getting interrupted. He reinforced his innocence by signalling to the kids that breakfast was indeed ready. In his eyes, being the great Dad that he was he invited them to the table to sample the bountiful buffet of eggs, bacon, and heaps of pancakes, all lovingly prepared for his family to feast upon. Charles was a doting father. His children loved him and over breakfast he thought he saw a slight smile on Sharon's face. He began to believe he had got away with last night's shenanigans. At least he thought he had. He smiled to himself as he even considered, for only a split second, attempting a cuddle with his wife. Charles knew his children would all want to go to the beach, the café, or the amusement arcade as soon as breakfast was over, leaving Charles alone with Sharon in the caravan. His mind was thinking about sex, as only a man does. He could try and convince her that it was a new season, a new start. Things were currently great between them, and it would be a special way to start the holiday and, of course, more importantly if she had sex with him, he would wash up all the breakfast dishes.

Charles saw Alison walk past his caravan wearing a pair of skimpy blue denim shorts and, this time, a matching blue bikini top. In her defence she had to walk past Charles' caravan to get anywhere, to the beach or to the shop. He knew he would get plenty of chances to watch her saunter past, so he made a concerted effort to not look in Alison's direction. He busied himself with tidying the kitchen table and fussing over his children and their every whim. He also knew Sharon was watching him and he knew she would be keeping a very close eye on him from now on.

*

Nursing a thumping hangover, Clifford had stayed in bed that morning. He told Alison he wasn't well and put the pillow back over his head when she drew open the curtains. Alison, therefore, informed Clifford she was taking Jacob and Molly to the shops to see what she could buy for breakfast. It was a good excuse to wander around in a bikini again without Clifford at her side and to see what fresh male attention she could muster. Alison was thinking that she would be here at the caravan on her own most of the time, so it was important not to be seen in public with her husband in these early stages. At least until she got some regular male attention organised and booked in. Alison also made a concerted effort not to look in the direction of Charles' caravan as she passed. With her shoulders back, shopping bag in hand, she headed purposefully for the on-site shop. She was hoping and secretly relishing in the fact that Charles was probably looking at her right at that very moment.

Thinking forward to her next caravan visit, Alison had decided she needed to be more organised. It was essential to plan ahead and be a little more prepared for future caravan trips. They had driven past numerous supermarkets on the journey down to Wales but, in their excitement to get there, they hadn't stopped to buy any food or provisions. Alison made a mental note to stock up with food for the kids every time they come and, more importantly, she must also keep a plentiful supply of chilled champagne at the ready. She had wasted her only bottle last night on Charles. Not wasted as in not drank the wine but wasted as she hadn't got any attention.

The bubbles were Alison's secret man-catching weapon. She found men were not used to holding a delicate flute glass and drinking champagne. They could drink beer all night but when she hit them with a full glass of sparkling champagne whilst wearing a bikini, they soon caved into her sexual demands. She would deploy her favourite tactic. Whilst offering to clink glasses with a cheers, she would simply at the same time lean forwards. The man, having no choice other than to look down at their brimming glass, so as to check they don't spill any, would gaze directly into her cleavage. Over the years and the many times this trap had been set, Alison found that it wasn't very often a man could refuse. If there was any hesitation on the first *clink*, she would seductively tell her victim the story that it was customary, a French tradition even, to always drink the first glass of champagne down in one go, out of respect for the vines. Following up with her well-rehearsed dirty laugh, she would then top up their glass to the very brim for a second 'cheers' which never failed to get the desired result. The sparkling bubbles having the desired effect in greasing the married-men moral wheels.

The onsite caravan site shop didn't sell champagne, so she turned her attention to breakfast, letting the children choose what they wanted. After all, this was their special place. On her return journey and walking slowly past Charles' van, her bag was weighed down with two tins of spaghetti hoops, a ridiculously small pack of bacon containing only four rashers, a loaf of bread, three bars of white chocolate and a big bottle of orange fizzy pop. The bag was heavy, but, on the plus side, the weight of it made Alison's bicep muscles stand proud. Alison adored muscles on both men and women. She worked hard in the gym, almost daily to maintain her figure. She believed now was the right time in her life to be rewarded for all the time spent dieting and in the gym.

*

"Let's go, let's go," David jokingly cried out loud. His children filed out of the caravan onto the decking in what appeared coincidently age seniority order. Breakfast was over, most of the washing up was done and it was beach time. The Westwoods had plans to mess around on the beach until around lunchtime and then later they were all hoping to go to the club house for a meal and a few drinks. David seemed to be carrying everything down to the beach, every shoulder, hand and forearm laden down with *stuff*. He always thought he should be carrying surfboards, snorkels, and other cool sporty paraphernalia, but instead he found himself carrying several bags of different shades of pink, numerous fold down chairs and at least three multi-coloured beach umbrellas. He beamed to himself. He loved his family and had grown a fondness for the long-established colour pink.

Debbie had selected their spot on the beach. Down the ramp and over to the left, he could hear Debbie's bellowing orders. David was aware of the tide times and had to convince Debbie again that low tide meant that the sea was going out so they could pitch up as close to the water's edge as they wanted.

"Are you sure?" Debbie said with half a smile. "Surely low tide means the sea is low," and immediately realised that what she had said didn't make any sense.

"Trust me," David said with confidence as he began to lower all the gear onto the sand and only a few feet from the water's edge. He began to erect one of the many folding chairs for his daughters to sit on. They didn't like getting sand on themselves and all of them demanded a chair, apart from his youngest daughter Paris who loved nothing more than getting covered in sand, whilst at the same time eating it. Dolly was a twin, but she was so very different from her sister Daisy. Dolly was far more adventurous and outgoing, she loved nothing more than to splash in the sea. Dolly had requested a wet suit as one of her birthday presents and seemed to live in it since. Once at the beach, she never came out of the sea, jumping and splashing whilst her sisters stood at the water's edge working up the courage to get their toes wet. Dolly would shout at them to come deeper to join her, but they would just run and scream every time a wave splashed up onto their ankles.

The warmth of the sun made everything better and David sat and smiled at his family at play. No one noticed the smile as Debbie and Danielle were engrossed in their mobile phones and the younger daughters were playing and laughing in the surf. Things were good and David's thoughts turned to male company again. He wondered if his mate Spider was popping over to their site today or maybe he would bump into Charles later at the club. Either way, he hoped he would interact with another male today after being constantly surrounded by women. He wondered why he was craving the company of another man when he was surrounded by his beautiful family. David had had these thoughts for a while now, but he quickly dismissed them and felt sure it was nothing. He had five children and he had a very active sex life with Debbie, well not so much in recent years, or being brutally honest not since Paris had been born really. After the arrival of Paris, Debbie had informed him she didn't want any more children and that her boobs were drooping from breast feeding five children and she was thinking of having some *work* done.

Much to his relief, it hadn't cost David anything for the Botox, hair extensions, teeth veneers, breast enhancement and butt lift operations, apart from time off work when he was needed to look after his daughters. Debbie had gone away with her mum, leaving a house of crying children in her wake for just under four weeks. Very generously, her father had paid for the plastic surgery, and when Debbie eventually returned home, David had been genuinely shocked at her transformation. Debbie had been a tall slim attractive woman when he first met her, and they had fallen in love when she had cruised with her parents all those years ago.

She now presented a suntanned smooth clean complexion with a voluptuous pout, a big bold brave cleavage and round the back a Kardashian ass that looked like two eggs in a hankie that your eyes were drawn to. Was it all attractive? David had deliberated this when he first saw her naked for the first time. Debbie had clearly been spending. She presented a whole new wardrobe of designer clothes, all made to fit around her new shape and the first signs of a few extra pounds that she was putting on. She had new nails, fake tan, new hair extensions, the works. With presents and gifts for everyone on her dramatic and tearful return home, she genuinely had missed her children after being away for what at the time seemed like an eternity.

Later that night alone, David was given the full guided tour of her scars and he gasped when he was told how much that new bra had cost. Debbie explained the whole surgery procedure in full as David lay on the bed, looking up as her enormous static breasts. They didn't move. She sat on the edge of the bed turning and pointing out each scar in turn. At one point, David reached up with his left hand to take hold of her right breast but was promptly informed with a slap that she was still sore and there would be no touching for some weeks yet. David was more curious than turned on and felt a little concerned that he did not find these new additions to the family attractive at all.

After telling Debbie that she looked amazing, he turned to look at himself in the mirror and at that very moment he knew that something had changed, and he was no longer sexually attracted to women. Paris would be three in a few weeks and David can't recall if he had had sex with his wife since she was born. Debbie knew for certain they hadn't and, after completing her educational and thorough tour of her new 'toys', she soon covered herself up and prepared herself with painkillers for a much-needed night's sleep.

Was she having sex with someone else? Was she having an affair? David often pondered, recently she was always glamorous and made up with a full face of makeup. Even though the size of her bum, in his opinion, was now out of proportion, David loved her. He secretly hoped she would find love and sexual gratification in the arms of another man. She had a right to be happy. She was his best friend. He decided he wanted to be honest with her (the thought of touching those massive, silicone-filled lumps on her chest didn't excite or arouse him in anyway shape or form).

Over the years David recalled that Debbie had instigated sex more than he had, or had she? He wasn't sure. He wasn't sure about anything anymore, but he justified that his longing for male company probably stemmed from the fact that he was surrounded by females all day. His thinking was that his wanting to talk to the odd bloke now and again was perfectly normal. He was very mixed up.

*

"I'm up. I'm awake." Clifford climbed out of bed and, using the wall for assistance, made his way to the lounge and sat himself down at the breakfast table. He smiled and looked at his two children, well they weren't his biological children, but he liked to think of Jacob as his son and Molly his daughter. Alison loved to have everything set out for breakfast every morning, even though Molly would only eat enough to keep a hamster alive, and Jacob would only eat Bran Flakes. What kid only eats Bran Flakes? The breakfast table was quite a picture: a rack of warm toast, a plate of cooked crispy bacon, a bowl of spaghetti hoops full to the brim, a jug of fizzy orange juice, tiny jars of marmalade and strawberry jam, a pot of tea and a cafetiere of coffee. The table looked wonderfully presented and that morning, so did his wife. A small blue bikini this morning. Clifford loved the blue one. He smiled at his wife across the table, his eyes dropping briefly onto her ample bosom.

"So, kids," Clifford said with an air of authority, "I'm thinking we just go exploring today. Let's finish breakfast, we'll leave the dishes until later. Let's go and see what we can find on the site."

Alison didn't follow with any other suggestions, which of course would have superseded Clifford's suggestion, so caravan site exploring was on the family's agenda that morning.

"They have an amusement arcade," Molly said through a very big smile.

"Do they?" Clifford said, tickling Molly. "Well let's go and find it then."

With that they jumped down from the table and were racing to grapple with the laces of their shoes at the door. Alison tried her best to enforce more eating, but soon realised her children were paying no attention to her. Clifford was severely hungover and couldn't face eating anything. He was putting on a brave face, but his head was pounding and several times that morning he had fought back nausea.

With only one shoe on, Molly was busy texting on her phone. Clifford's immediate thought was she was probably texting her estranged father who Clifford really didn't like. He longed for the day when this man was no longer in his life. Clifford departed the kitchen and went back into the bathroom in a second attempt to put a toothbrush into his mouth without throwing up. From the master bathroom, Clifford heard Alison talking to someone.

"No no, not today. It's our first day, OK. Tomorrow." Alison fell silent. Clifford dressed and went outside to join everybody on the decking. The kids had got their shoes on, Alison was dressed in her usual bikini and shorts, but it fitted into their surroundings this time. They were all together on holiday and the sun was shining.

There had been times during the winter months when Clifford had felt a little uncomfortable about the amount of flesh his wife would have on show. When other women were dressed in jumpers and jeans, Alison would still be showing her midriff in a bikini top. That morning his wife looked radiant and sexy, and Clifford felt proud to be walking by her side.

They turned right and down the slight incline towards reception. In the distance the sea twinkled and shimmered, the warm sun on their faces. Walking slightly ahead Jacob laughed and joked with his half-sister and Clifford managed to hold onto Alison's hand for more than a few minutes this time. If she let go of his hand (as she always did whenever Clifford attempted to hold it), Clifford decided he would ask Alison who she was just speaking to on the phone, but she gripped his hand firmly and she walked by his side with two healthy, good-looking children skipping along out in front.

As they walked past the clubhouse bar, Clifford hoped that

Charles was not in the bar as he might ask them to join him for drink. Alison however hoped that Charles was in the bar, and she would certainly accept if she was asked. The amusement arcade was next door to the bar and Molly was at the entrance and looking back and forth at her mum for approval. It was clear, even on this beautiful sunny day, they would be going inside this dark and dingy amusement arcade.

CHAPTER 7

Three Sea Kayaks

"There's a supermarket in the town and I've made a list of what we need," Gabriella said as she handed her husband the shopping list. She had used the envelope from the welcome card, and she added, "Fabian will go with you and help you carry everything. I'm going to stay and clean the caravan."

"It's a *brand-new* caravan," Andy said with raised eyebrows in surprise, immediately regretting the tone of his response.

"I know. It's OK," Gabriella lowered her voice and smiled at Andy. "I'm not going to clean. Just tidy up and put things away in their correct place." Gabriella was still smiling at Andy as she reached forwards to hold his hand and settle him. She also realised that she needed him out of the way for a few hours, so she could go back down to reception and hopefully get chatting to muscle-man Crawford again.

Gabriella was yearning to find out Crawford's situation. Was he married or single? It didn't really matter either way; all she wanted to know was whether he was up for paying her some attention. In a few days' time her husband would leave and go back to work. Gabriella wondered about what the rest of Crawford's body was like, she couldn't wait to flirt with him again.

Andy's mind was racing, and he was thinking fast on his feet. His palms had started sweating a little and his heart rate was rising. He had prepared himself for the fact that he wasn't going to go to the betting shop or be able to gamble for a few days. He had come to terms with it in his head, but now there was potentially an opportunity to gamble, and the dopamine dump was building in his head. This trip to the supermarket could offer him an opening to pop into the local bookies and feed his gambling addiction. He would only need a few horse racing bets to get his fix and maybe a quick game of arcade machine roulette. Taking Fabian with him, however, would be a game changer.

For several years now Andy had been struggling with his gambling addiction. He had thought he had it under control and just before the kids broke up from school for the summer holidays last year, he'd decided that he was going to be honest and tell his wife everything. Andy totally believed that Gabriella was the only one that could help him and that everything was all going to be okay. Gabriella would sort him out and fix everything like she always did. He was going to choose a date to tell her.

It was the second week of the school summer holidays. Andy had left work early, something he never did and had headed straight home. Knowing that his wife Gabriella was off work that day and she'd probably be occupying her time by cleaning the fridge, sorting out the cupboard under the stairs, or finding something else to clean. He had arrived home to see a pair of large, big, tired work boots on his doorstep and assumed that Gabriella had another tradesman in the house to quote or fix something that was probably going to cost the earth as always.

As it turned out, there was another man in his house, and he could hear them upstairs. More importantly, he could hear Gabriella grunting and moaning with pleasure. The boots belonged to Kaminski, a Polish builder who had been working on the roof of Gabriella's school for the last several weeks.

Andy was aware that Gabriella liked things slightly irregular in the bedroom department and over the years he had tried and tried to up his game and satisfy his wife. He thought he had been doing a good job. He followed her every instruction, no matter how unnerving he had felt at the time. Despite his efforts he often wondered whether he was good enough for her. Deep down, he knew it was their son Fabian that kept their marriage together. Of course, he was sure Gabriella loved him but with his confidence diminished by his addiction, Andy had long given up trying to quench his wife's cravings.

Very slowly and quietly, Andy closed the front door behind him and retreated onto the driveway. With watery eyes Andy started his van and drove straight for the nearest betting shop. Right up until he entered the premises, Andy's mind was picturing the scene in his bedroom, in his bed, but as soon as he stepped over the threshold and he heard the announcement for the 2.45 p.m. race at Kempton going under starters orders, Gabriella became the last thing on his mind.

At the end of the school holidays, Gabriella had mentioned the idea of buying a holiday home by the sea. At first Andy had thought it was a bad idea. He couldn't get that much time off from work and Gabriella and Fabian would probably have to have to go on their own most of the time. Andy would only be able to join them at weekends. His initial reluctance to the static caravan idea had soon faltered after it dawned on him that it could be perfect mutual arrangement after all. It would suit them both; Gabriella could find someone to satisfy her insatiable sexual appetite without being disturbed, and whilst at home alone, Andy could spend as much time in the bookmakers as he chose. So, the caravan site had been selected, finances, caravan model, fixtures and fittings all chosen. The email had been received to say their caravan had been sited and connected and was ready for occupancy, so all three of them had set off for a few days away together.

"You don't have to come to the supermarket, Fabian, if you are busy," Andy had said quietly to his son.

"Cheers Dad, I'm going down the beach to meet someone. See you later," Fabian called back over his shoulder. He was already walking away at a pace; this was all going very well Andy was thinking. He smiled to himself and was busy preparing for his trip into town and frequenting a new bookmakers. "I might have a look around town while I'm there, darling," Andy said half-heartedly to Gabriella, he was unsure of the reply that would come back.

"Take your time, my darling," Gabriella said, placing a hand either side of his head and planting a lingering kiss on his lips. Gabriella pretended to busy herself with housework as she watched her husband walk out of the caravan, heading towards his parked car.

"Oh, come on," she muttered under her breath as Andy sat in the driver's seat with the engine running for several minutes before he slowly drove away. She shot into the bathroom, at the same time undoing another button on her new crisp white shirt. She slipped on her short black leather mini skirt which accentuated her figure whilst she applied another layer of red lipstick. Smiling at her own reflection in the mirror, her heart was racing slightly in anticipation of what might be about to happen. She knew she was a stunner with her curls of thick dark hair. She had been asked many times in her life if she was a catwalk model. Gabriella felt sexy and alive. She couldn't stop thinking about Crawford and loved this exciting new holiday destination. Steadying herself on the bathroom sink, she leaned to one side and slipped off her underwear. What little there was of it she left on the bathroom floor where they fell and was out the door. Slipping on her sunglasses she pushed her shoulders back and headed in the direction of the site reception and hopefully a sight of Crawford's muscular arms. It was a new thing for Gabriella to not wear underwear in public, but she had found it exciting and exhilarating and it had proved a lot easier in the past when seizing the opportunity to have quick sex with Kaminski in one of the empty school offices. At first Gabriella had been very careful and had only taken a few risks whilst on the school grounds to enjoy the young hard body of her new lover. Often it had meant that they had to wait late into the evening until the last teacher had left and even the cleaners had finished and left for the evening. They would find an empty office or unlocked cleaning cupboard. The first time Kaminski had discovered Gabriella's lack of underwear, it had made these passionate brief occasions even more memorable.

She had started to take more risks as the date got closer for Kaminski to return home to Poland. Gabriella was smug that she had not been caught, but that was in the past. Now, as she walked towards reception, she started to get that exciting sexy risk-taking feeling back. Only she knew she was not wearing any underwear, but she was hoping to put a big smile on Crawford's face when she gently whispered this fact in his ear.

*

David had mentioned to his wife that he wanted to modernise his wardrobe and had asked her if she would help him to create a new style for him. He had informed Debbie of the gentleman he had seen in the bar recently who had been wearing brown boots, slim fitting jeans, and a brown checked jacket. He had liked that look. David had been pleasantly surprised at how enthusiastic Debbie had taken to this fashion assignment. She had already started her online research and had already several screenshots of suggested outfits on her phone's camera roll.

"Of course, we will have to wait until we get back home to go shopping properly," Debbie had informed her husband, but she had continued researching and cataloguing style suggestions that she liked. Debbie had also informed her husband that she had decided to make some changes and she was going to raise her online profile. She advised David that he should do the same, but he was just keen to look smarter. Excitedly Debbie had suggested that she was going to take a few photographs of David before and after. In his tired usual shorts and T-shirts and then afterwards with his new fashion style. Also planned was a trip to an expensive barber's shop in the city, and

Debbie even suggested that beards would be very fashionable but left him with that thought.

Debbie gave David a hug, the first show of physical affection they had shown each other in the last few years and David reciprocated. He hugged his wife back and leaned on her shoulder. That act of tenderness marked the first step to them both realising they were best friends now, and no longer lovers.

Debbie knew in her heart that her husband was gay. She knew it and had known it for several years. The fact they conceived Paris was a miracle, but David had been drunk one night and Debbie had taken full advantage of the situation. There was potentially one glitch to this whole saga. A few days before David's mysterious drunken erection, Debbie had been on a long weekend trip away enjoying her sister's hen party. After a full evening of drinking under the Blackpool lights, Debbie had scant memories of chatting in the Hotel bar to a group of men who were also on a stag do. Before she knew it, a very willing Debbie had gone back to the hotel room of a charismatic dark-haired man from the group and had enjoyed a passionate drunken night of sex. The following morning after a fulfilling night but now wracked with guilt, Debbie had woken at 5 a.m. feeling exhausted and ashamed, she had sneaked out of the stranger's room. She had left him completely naked on the bed face down. Before she left, she had taken a moment to look him up and down, she liked what she saw. He had a good firm body and she believed he was at least half her age from how smooth and muscular he looked. Looking down at his naked bum she had even reached out to touch it again, but hesitated as she knew she looked nothing like she had the previous evening. She had no memory of what he looked like, and she was unable to see his face without waking him. Debbie collected her underwear that had been scattered around the room and left. She remembered thanking the person who had invented the idea to emboss room numbers on Hotel key fobs.

Still tingling and glowing from the physical contact she had longed for so much, Debbie crept into her own hotel room. She was sharing with her sister and immediately darted into the bathroom and dropped all her clothes onto the floor. Debbie flushed the loo and then ran from the bathroom to her bed naked. Her sister woke briefly and asked the time. Debbie replied that it was only 5 a.m. and apologised for waking her but she had needed the toilet. She turned away from her sister, lay her head on the pillow, closed her eyes, and smiled with satisfaction.

The Hotel had specially laid on an early morning breakfast just for the hen party. At the table everyone was laughing, and nobody mentioned that Debbie had disappeared at the end of the night. She had clearly got away with her explosive unprotected one-night stand. The hen party was up early as they were all going for a surfing lesson, and they had to be up early to catch the tide. There were a few people in the group who had clearly drunk far too much, including Debbie, and were probably still a little drunk. They had already decided that they were not going into the cold sea. This rebellious offshoot had agreed to spectate whilst sipping their warm cappuccinos from a nearby café, of course whilst offering lots of encouragement to the remaining brave hen party surfers.

Over the years Debbie had a gut feeling that Paris might be the result of the Blackpool trip. Debbie didn't even know his name; she couldn't remember his face and had never heard or seen him since. She had closed this uncertain chapter in her head, David had had a sort of erection and they had had sex – end of.

"Spider and Melissa are coming over this morning, girls. He's bringing his three sea kayaks." David looked around the room for any signs of excitement. Dolly jumped up and ran into the bedroom to retrieve her wetsuit but the others, including Debbie, had not even looked up from their phone screens.

"You getting into a wetsuit today, darling?" David said cheekily, looking in the direction of his wife. They had a special, different kind of relationship now. It was as if a weight had been lifted. There was time for fun.

"I might, you know, be great for my Instagram page being all sporty and sexy in a tight wetsuit." Debbie stood up and placed a hand over her bloated stomach, but she looked serious. David wasn't sure what to say so decided to keep his mouth closed.

"I'm going to message Melissa to see if I can borrow one of her wetsuits," Debbie said, tapping her thoughts into her phone and walking away towards the bathroom without looking at David. David had a grin on his face. He compiled a sarcastic retort in his head to the suggestion that Debbie, a size 14 and 38EE breasts, might get into one of Melissa's size 10 wetsuits. But he decided not to say anything and started to think about what he was going to wear that day. Giving any thought to his choice of outfit and appearance was a new concept for David.

There was a very audible alert on David's phone – a text message. It was a rare moment. Everyone looked at David's old brick of a phone vibrating and pinging as it danced vigorously on top of the dinner table. He read his message.

"I'm going to the site barrier to buzz Spider through." No one offered any acknowledgement. Patrick had sent David a text asking to be buzzed through the park's south side barrier on the understanding that Patrick could park in David's caravan parking bay. He would have three sea kayaks on his roof, which were expensive and highly desirable to thieves.

Dolly was already in her wetsuit when Patrick and Melissa pulled up alongside the caravan and shot down the steps to ask lots of questions. Patrick picked her up into his arms with a smile and told her all about what kind of life jacket he had brought for her to wear. Patrick explained how she would use her paddle to go forwards and how he was going to teach her all the safety things to do if her kayak overturned.

"Morning, everyone," Patrick said as he stood in the open patio door entrance to David and Debbie's caravan. He gently placed Dolly back down on the ground. Patrick already had his wetsuit on, but he was wearing it pulled down around his waist. This revealed his broad suntanned chest and with his sunglasses on the top of his head it was Patrick's surfer dude, come and get me girls, look.

"Morning, hun!" Debbie gave him a peck on his cheek, as she did so she placed her hand firmly on Patrick's muscular arm and she knew her breasts had pressed into his side. She said hello to Melissa with a smile and a nod and they both disappeared into Debbie's bedroom with a choice of several wetsuits for Debbie to attempt to squeeze herself into. Patrick had been surprisingly aroused at Debbie's touch and had never really looked at her sexually before. She was a friend and his mate's wife BUT if he didn't want her Patrick liked what he saw. He imagined her naked as she left for the bedroom with his wife to try on wetsuits. Patrick's wife was tall, slim, and firm. She was sporty and carried no excess weight. Patrick liked that Debbie was very curvy and his mind was racing. Stopping himself from staring he also contemplated a sarcastic 'tight squeeze' joke but, like David, he refrained from commenting. Debbie can be a tad fiery sometimes about her weight.

"No Connor and George?" David enquired after Patrick's children.

"No, Grandma's bringing them down tomorrow," Patrick replied and with a smile he returned to his car. He was closely followed by Dolly who continued to ask many more questions about the proposed kayaking day ahead. Most questions Dolly asked were then followed by another question before Patrick even had time to answer.

Patrick lifted down the three kayaks from his car roof. They filled the road and parking area around the caravan. He only had two sets of road wheels, so he fitted them to the end of two of the kayaks and then rested the third kayak on top. Dolly was wearing her selected blue lifejacket open at the waist, straps dangling down on the floor. Patrick lifted the front of the kayak trolley and led the way with a shout of "Follow me, Captain!" Dolly laughed and toddled on behind with an oar in each hand.

It was just a short walk to the beach and with David pulling along the third single wheeled kayak, they proceeded down the ramp onto the sandy beach and towards the water's edge.

"No one else coming down?" Patrick remarked. It was a lovely summer's day and the sea was flat calm with little or no wind.

"Debbie's is coming down when she has crowbarred herself into that wetsuit!" David smirked.

"That's going to be a sight for sore eyes," said Dolly immediately.

"DOLLY," David said, alarmed, and then everyone started laughing. Although he thought it a bit cheeky, he was secretly proud of his daughter. It was clearly a demonstration that Dolly was growing up fast and she didn't miss a thing that went on or was said in the family.

Patrick seemed to enjoy the importance of his role. He emphasised how they must respect the sea, even on flat, calm days. He continued with requests for life jackets to be worn at all times and to stay together when out at sea. Patrick then showed Dolly what to do if she got into difficulty. He told her to always hold onto her oar and he reassured her that her sit-on top kayak could never sink.

With a puzzled look on Dolly's face, Patrick instructed her to pay attention and watch whilst he demonstrated. He selected the orange kayak and walked out into the sea towing the kayak behind him. He walked out until the sea came just above his knees. He jumped up and popped over, landing on the kayak seat in a showing off display of competence. He was emphasising that he had years of kayaking experience. Paddling around only a few metres he then abruptly turned the kayak with skill and faced the shore. Dolly was very impressed, and she stood on the beach staring. He shouted across to her, "Oh no! I'm going to fall in!" Laughing, Patrick rocked from side to side in an attempt to topple over the kayak which was harder than you could imagine, which was one of the reasons he preferred sit-on top kayaks over canoes. Patrick then half threw himself over the side of the kayak and managed to end up in the sea. It wasn't that deep, but he was soon splashing and floating because of his lifejacket. He bobbed along with his arms and toes sticking out of the water and Dolly just laughed.

"You see, it's actually very hard to tip the kayak over, but if you do, hold on to the oar." And at that, Patrick lifted the oar out of the water to show Dolly the strap which connected the oar permanently to the kayak. The kayak couldn't drift away from Patrick and the strap could easily be seen.

"Then, with a kick and a splash, you just flop back over the side onto your belly then wriggle around back into your seat." Patrick finished ungracefully by climbing back into his seat and rowing the four metres back to shore to an excited Dolly who had been paying respectful attention.

Dolly was (seated correctly) in the fast red kayak and with one slight oar adjustment, Patrick gave her a gentle push followed by the command to wait around for him and David before paddling away. David was in the yellow kayak. Patrick called it the newbie kayak. It was a very stable wide kayak and specifically designed for the apprentice. A discussion around seat comfort started between them just as Debbie and Melissa appeared at the top of the ramp which led down to the beach. Debbie caught Patrick's attention in her tight, flattering wetsuits. He watched them both as they lumbered over the sand, both chatting and laughing together. Debbie looked at the group, her attention mostly taken with Patrick's broad muscular shoulders and the hint of dark fine chest hair. For a brief moment, a hint of jealousy flashed through her thoughts as she recalled previous drunken stories from her friend as she had described her husband's large manhood. Melissa had joked that Patrick's penis was so large he took its time becoming fully erect and the fun she had playing with it whilst it flopped around. As Debbie walked towards the group, she could stare at Patrick without it becoming obvious she was singling him out. She looked him up and down and just as she neared the group, he looked at her briefly and she knew. There and then she knew it was going to happen. Patrick made a concerted effort to only have eyes for his wife and he thought she looked a million dollars as she walked barefoot over the sand towards them all. All that watching what she ate and going to the gym three times a week really showed when she wore something skin-tight around her body. Patrick thought back to the previous night when they had made love, chatting for hours afterwards whilst sharing a bottle of wine. Patrick could feel the sea salt stinging the scratches on his back. Melissa had made a real effort last night and had surprised Patrick by wearing new lingerie, along with his favourite bedroom item of all, high heeled shoes. Patrick would always say that his favourite high heel shoe colour was whatever the colour Melissa was wearing at that particular moment, this would always make Melissa laugh as she wore a different shoe colour every time in the bedroom.

Debbie was certainly a different shape to Melissa. Patrick still thought she looked curvaceous and sexy and leaned his shoulders back ever so slightly to accentuate his broad shoulders and ever so gently he clenched his stomach muscles to reinforce his flat firm stomach. He was amazed that Debbie had made it into a wetsuit. You could see every bump and curve and she certainly filled out the wetsuit at the rear and most definitely at the front. He tried not to look but he found it difficult to avert his eyes. Debbie loved her new sporty look and she thought she looked amazing. She laughed and noticing Patrick's eyes upon her she flirtatiously started to run the last few metres towards the men. As she got within earshot she shouted, "I'm Pamela Anderson on Baywatch!" with a big smile and flash of her straight, whitened teeth. It was certainly a sight as Debbie's large breasts were bouncing around. If only Patrick had a beer right this very minute that would have been an awesome Instagram beer post. Debbie on a beach wearing a bikini and running towards a beer would surely go viral and get a million likes. Patrick was going to get her alone and ask her if she would help him promote his page.

Dolly had been quick to pick up kayaking and she was paddling around in the surf only a few metres from the shore. She was easily turning and controlling her kayak and waving proudly at her mum. She was in a kayak on her own and over the moon that her mum was joining in with a sporting activity. Her mum historically didn't really join in with any sports.

"Do you want to try the yellow beginner's kayak first?" Patrick asked, also still amazed Debbie was getting involved.

"I will try but I'm not going out very far, I only want some photographs," Debbie replied, and she plonked herself ungracefully down with a thud into the seat of the kayak. The kayak was still on the sand and several metres from the water's edge. In a seated position Debbie was now at eye level now with Patrick's groin. It's all she could think about, and she couldn't help herself but look. She surprised how well the wetsuit emphasised Patrick's large mound. Debbie was going to get Patrick alone and ask him if he would help her with some modelling pictures for her social media page. Patrick in just a pair of skimpy shorts laughing and walking hand in hand with Debbie along the beach had to go viral she was thinking.

"Take lots of pictures," Debbie directed Melissa who was clicking away with her iPhone. Debbie leaned back in the kayak seat and let her hair fall down her back. She pushed her shoulders back and reached for the zip on the front of her wetsuit. She pulled it down a few centimetres more to reveal the start of even more cleavage.

"Gosh, don't pull that down too far!" Melissa shouted. "It was an effort to get that zip up." Patrick, who had been staring in silence the whole time, made himself look away laughing, he was very conscious that he was starting to get aroused from these large breasts, something he was unused to seeing. It would be difficult to hide an erection in his tight thin wetsuit and he could feel the burning sensation in his groin. He was intrigued by this curvy woman. Debbie pulled the zip down even further and Melissa clicked away on the camera. Debbie was the perfect model, and she threw her head back and tossed her hair.

"That's loads of pictures," Melissa said to Debbie, "but you can really see you are not actually on the sea." Melissa passed back the phone to her friend Debbie who immediately started to browse the camera roll and already she was deleting some of the more unflattering photos.

"Why all the pictures?" David asked his wife.

"For my Instagram page," Debbie said. "I'm going to make these very expensive additions pay for themselves," looking down at her chest.

"I'm going to need your help with the camera, Mr Westwood, if you can up your photography skills, please, unless anyone else wants to help," Debbie said aloud as she looked Patrick up and down. She had noticed that he was again staring at her body. The mood was relaxed, everyone was busy and Patrick found himself fussing over Debbie as he pulled her to her feet, again having to concentrate so as not to stare.

CHAPTER 8

Two Little Ducks

"No, not tonight, Dani. I can't take you tonight, I'm afraid," David said as he stared back at his daughter. Danielle was becoming more irritated by the second, partly because she was trying to plug her phone into the charging cable, which was proving difficult as she was also waiting for her nails to dry. Danielle had big plans tonight with only one thing on her mind, Fabian. Her father's social commitments were insignificant. Finding out via Snapchat, Fabian had said that he was going into town 'on the pull' with his new mate Dafydd. His new buddy was an older local lad whom he had somehow recently met.

On hearing this startling news Danielle had arranged with her best friend, Charlotte, to dress up and accidentally 'bump' into Fabian in a bar in the local town. They were simply going to stalk Fabian via social media to find out which bar he was in.

With her new hair style, very high heels, and the shortest dress Danielle owned, she was hoping Fabian would pay her some attention and see her for the sexy young, sophisticated woman she thought she was. She had told her mum she wasn't ready to have sex yet, but she secretly was ready and had been ready for some time. Everyone in her year group seemed to be having regular grown-up sex in hotels and in the parents' double beds. Danielle had decided that tonight it was her turn. She was hoping that Fabian was going to be her future husband.

Danielle couldn't give Fabian her virginity. This had been given to a fumbling boy from school some months ago, in his bedroom whilst his mum ironed on the landing directly outside. She had confidently taken the condom from him and applied it rather expertly. Her banana condom training with her bestie had reaped rewards and she had positioned the condom in seconds, much to the astonishment of her boyfriend. Two brief physical movements later he had rolled off Danielle with a huge grin on his fresh spotty young face. Danielle hadn't been impressed.

In her handbag Charlotte had two condoms that she had acquired from her older brother's secret stash. They had both been practising putting condoms onto bananas for weeks and had used up the other eight from the box. Only two left, but they both agreed that was all they needed. Danielle smiled, remembering the laughs she had had with her mate, Charlotte, practising with the bananas.

"I only want a lift into town, I can get a taxi back. God I never ask for anything," Danielle screeched in a typical teenage strop. She had added the taxi home part as she was hoping that she would be coming back to the site with Fabian.

"Not tonight," David repeated. He couldn't keep it to himself any longer, "I can't give you a lift, Dani, as I'm the bingo caller up at the club tonight."

"WHAT?" Debbie bellowed as she darted out of the bedroom and into the lounge. Danielle had looked away and probably didn't really hear what her father's reason was for not driving her where she wanted to go. All she could think about was how she was going to get into town tonight. She was already messaging her accomplice regarding the parental taxi dilemma.

David turned from his disgruntled teenage daughter and smiled at his wife. Debbie, with her hands on her hips, just stared.

"I was in the shop earlier," David offered as a start. "Brynn was in there and he just asked me. He said that Jackson who normally does the calling is out of town. He's doing something on his cousins' farm, and they had no one to do it. So, he asked me. And I just said yes, why not!" The new confident David stood proud.

It had seemed a good idea at the time, but he was regretting it a little now.

"I told him I hadn't done it before, but he was so enthusiastic about me doing it I just thought I'd go for it!" David was after his wife's support with this little venture into the entertainment world, but Debbie just rolled her eyes, just slightly, but enough for David to see and she disappeared back into the bedroom.

Debbie was making their bed and, whilst changing the pillowcases, she suddenly smiled to herself, with both David and Danielle going out, she could video call Martin. She felt annoyed with herself. She should have encouraged him a bit more in his little bingo task. She had missed an opportunity. She smiled to herself for being such an amateur and her thoughts turned to Martin's smile and his big hands she so desperately wanted on her body again. She needed to switch onto this affair game if it was going to work out for her. She quickly reminded herself that it wasn't an affair, it was just a bit of fun. Justifying it in her head, she had womanly needs and with David not interested, what option did she have? Martin had always caught the eye of the other women when he entered a room. He was tall and dressed casually but always smart. What had caught Debbie's eye were his legs. He had been a Rugby player for years and he had thick muscular legs which made whatever he wore tight around his thighs. Debbie had often glanced towards this area of Martin as he had walked towards her, and she just knew that what was between those thick legs would be very pleasurable.

With that, Debbie plumped the last pillow and looking down at the bed she pictured Martin chest down on the crumpled duvet, exhausted and fast asleep after the hours of lovemaking they had shared. She imagined the faint visible scratches down his back that

Debbie had inflicted as she orgasmed. She turned swiftly and left the bedroom, but not without catching a glance of her curvaceous figure in the full-length mirror. She smiled to herself, and she felt alive for the first time in years.

"Two little ducks twenty-two," Debbie sang aloud, beaming as she walked back into the kitchen. She placed the duvet cover and pillowcase into the washing machine. Danielle, with her mobile telephone held to her right ear, had disappeared out of the caravan onto the decking.

"I think Brynn had said that it was all in aid of a local charity," a puzzled David continued. "He was dropping between English and Welsh to Pam in the shop, so I didn't catch it all." David looked at his wife for support. "You are going to come up to the club and have a go at the bingo?"

"Don't be ridiculous!" Debbie swiftly replied in a tone of utter disgust. "I wouldn't be seen dead playing bingo with the north crowd." Seeing the disappointed look on her husband's face, she softened her voice.

"No, you go. It's not really my thing. It is great you're joining in on the site, I'm proud of you and it's for charity. I'll go for a walk along the beach with the girls. We might come up to the club for a drink with you when it's over."

*

"David's just messaged, he's calling the bingo tonight," Patrick said, laughing, as he popped his head around the caravan door, looking his wife up and down as she sunbathed on the decking.

"Oh really? What time does it start?" a startled Melissa said, who couldn't see anything as she was staring at the beaming sun. Melissa was a secret bingo lover, but she kept that a secret from her friends and especially her work colleagues. If they found out at the police station, she would be the butt of numerous jokes. Melissa imagined the bingo numbers that would appear on her locker door and the bingo cards that she would constantly find in her desk drawers. At work she tried to project a youthful, sporty image to her colleagues, but as a child her mum had loved playing bingo, and it had rubbed off on her.

"David says it starts at 7 p.m.," Patrick continued as he looked down at his wife. He hadn't noticed before that she was wearing a very skimpy green bikini. For a better look Patrick wandered slowly out onto the deck. He was wearing just a pair of small tight shorts and he went and stood near Melissa, trying to attract her attention with his attire. Patrick liked what he saw, and he wanted his wife right there and then. He was hoping the sun had got her in the mood, and he imagined her naked. "Charlie and Sharon are going too."

Melissa attempted to get a few more minutes of sunshine to top up her suntan, but now she had bingo on her mind, so she got up and wrapped her towel around her waist. She hadn't realised her husband was stood that close and she gently ran her hand across his large, firm chest. She tugged on his chest hair with a smile.

"We could go on the train if you fancy a drink," Melissa said with a wink, and she ran her hand down over Patrick's groin. She was surprised at how large he was through the thin shorts.

"Later darling, promise," she said, with a full hand she squeezed hard. Patrick laughed but was disappointed, he had to work to keep the mood cheery. It was always later, why is it never now? Patrick was becoming restless in his marriage.

From the bathroom, Melissa shouted, "Or I don't mind not drinking, I can drive." She was not a big drinker anyway and she knew if Patrick had his two mates together in the same club house, he would end up having too many beers tonight.

The trains weren't as frequent as they were used to at home, so in the end Patrick decided to drive to Pebbles caravan site. As he parked, he handed the keys to Melissa.

"Thanks, darling. You look lovely tonight. New jeans?" he asked with an adoring look up and down.

"No, I've had these ages," Melissa said, grinning. She walked a little quicker to get ahead and out in front, knowing that Patrick would be watching her. They were brand new jeans. It was the sales lady in the shop who had explained that they were specifically designed to accentuate the shape of your bum. Melissa was confident her ass was on fire tonight and would attract a lot of male or female attention, she didn't mind which. She walked on and her thoughts turned to when she had reached for Patrick's penis earlier. She had expected to be the one who aroused him and made it grow and she was surprised how erect it already was. She wondered if he had been thinking of other women. Her husband looked after himself and was constantly in the gym. He was also a well-endowed man, something which Melissa had enjoyed exhaustively when they had first started dating. Tonight she was in an excitable mood, and she was also excited to see if she still had the magic touch to arouse him in an instant, like a light switch being flicked on.

Patrick had parked in front of the site takeaway. It was the weekend, and with the season well underway, the site would be very busy. It was a warm summer's evening so they knew the club would be packed.

"Good evening, Brynn," Patrick said as he entered the club house. Brynn was stood near the door doing some last minute promoting for the bingo.

"What's it like down in the cheap seats?" Brynn replied with a smirk. He took the opportunity to have a dig at Patrick and Melissa, knowing they had come from the Lobster Pot caravan site a few miles down the road. "I've got a few spaces left on the elite north side if you change your mind," Brynn laughed and immediately turned his attention to a woman who was stood in respectful silence, as if she had a question to ask of Brynn.

Patrick was going to ask Brynn if he wanted a drink, but he knew he would have ordered a double whiskey as he always did. As Patrick had never known Brynn to ever get a round of drinks in, he moved on inside the bar. The club house was indeed starting to get fill up. Some people were persistent seat preservers, putting coats on the back of most of the chairs for their friends and family who were yet to arrive. One scraggy long-haired man went flying past Patrick, making him step to one side in fear of being knocked over. The man's arms were full of coats and like a military operation he proceeded to put them all on the back of at least seven chairs, centred around a single square table. He then sat down on the eighth chair looking all innocent, but inwardly proud of himself and his seat-reserving accomplishments.

"I'll get the drinks, darling," Patrick said as he placed his hand gently on his wife's bum. He was startled slightly as he thought she wasn't wearing any underwear, something very unlike his wife. "You grab a table, anywhere you want, I can't see Charlie yet."

Looking around the club Patrick could see David on the left of the dance floor. David hadn't seen them arrive, as he was trying, unsuccessfully, to assemble a folding table. On the floor next to David was a large metal cage containing numerous different coloured bingo balls. Lying next to that and propped up against the wall was a wooden board with lots of rows of holes drilled into it. This was presumably where the bingo balls were placed after they had been called out. With several feeble waves, Patrick tried to attract David's attention to get him a drink, but he'd sort of joined a queue at the bar and didn't want to lose his spot, so thought he would get him his usual pint of Guinness. He might need the Dutch courage, he thought to himself.

Melissa sat down at a table against the far wall opposite the bar. It was a table for four with two chairs and then a bench style seat that ran along the whole length of the back wall – ideal if seats became short. Melissa looked into her handbag. She always kept several different coloured bingo pens in her handbag. They were the special felt-tipped pens used to mark-off bingo cards. She knew they would be in there, but she didn't want to get them out of her handbag yet. She didn't want to give the appearance that she was a regular bingo player. She was a young, slim, sexy, sophisticated woman, at least that's how she had been described on a recent night out with her mate Rossi from work.

Melissa and Rossi had both had spray tans in preparation for a forthcoming work colleagues' wedding. The night before, whilst out with some of the hen party in the city, they had both been walking drunkenly slowly behind the group as they changed bars. They both agreed that they had far too much skin on show for their age, but with spray-tan confidence they strutted along in their heels. Ahead were a group of very smartly dressed, very good-looking young men, all wearing designer suits. As they approached the young men parted along the path, allowing the two girls to walk through the middle of them. As they did, they cheered and had asked the girls for their respective phone numbers, one calling them both 'Sexy MILFS'. Melissa and Rossi had giggled, secretly relishing the compliments. They had laughed with the group of lads, saying they were old enough to be their mothers. One lad had got down on one knee and even asked Rossi to marry him there and then. Rossi admitted afterwards that she thought he was gorgeous and had wanted to say yes.

After Patrick had been served, the club had got busier and the queue to purchase drinks behind him had become even wider and longer. Patrick was doing that careful 'I'm going to drop them' walk as he turned with the three glasses in his hands. Melissa hadn't said what drink she had preferred so Patrick had ordered her a glass of wine, David had a Guinness, and he had bought himself a pint of

Welsh beer. It was from a brewery he had never heard of before and he certainly couldn't pronounce its name. It was a beer Patrick had never tried before and he had annoyed everybody in the bar queue slightly, using his phone to take several photographs of his new beer with the bar and pump in the background, all for his social media beer page.

"Hello mate, Mr Bingo Caller," Patrick shouted as he made his way through the crowds and out into the clearing on the dance floor. David was sitting at his little table with his spinning ball machine.

"I've got you a Guinness, son," Patrick said, proudly offering the beer but not really sure how David was going to get the glass out of his hands without dropping the other two drinks.

"Ah cheers, mate but I'm off the Guinness, I'm on a diet. Trying to get a flat stomach," David smiled back at him, tapping his paunch with his right hand and Patrick laughed back at him. David was pleased to have Patrick here. He now had a male companion to talk to later. David said he would sort himself out for a drink and told Patrick to tell Melissa that the bingo cards were about to go on sale.

Patrick was laughing a little as he walked away to the table Melissa had found. He over exaggerated the shaking of his head in laughter at his mate's diet so David could see as he walked away. Patrick very skilfully lowered the three drinks onto the table and took a seat on the bench, so he had his back to the wall. He wanted to be able to see what was going on in the club. He wondered what Debbie would be wearing.

"Who's having the Guinness?" Melissa said, looking down at the table. "You thirsty?" She reached over and pulled the wine glass nearest to her. She had wanted a gin and slim line tonic – it was less calorific than the wine, but she realised she should have replied to Patrick when he had asked what she wanted to drink. She quickly stopped her bottom lip from grimacing and lifted her wine glass to her mouth with a cheerful cheers and took a little sip. The wine was cheap and bitter, but she had decided that it was going to be her one and only drink this evening so would hopefully last her all night. Melissa had promised herself; she was adamant she wasn't going to get drawn into drinking the same amount as Sharon and Debbie. She had heard recently that Sharon's drinking was becoming more frequent and not only confined to her social nights out. Under the table, Melissa reached across and grabbed her husband's groin again and squeezed, hard this time as she had to search for its contents through folded clothing.

Patrick didn't jump, he just smiled, whispering, "Are you wearing any underwear?" Melissa smiled, leaving her hand where it was. Melissa had decided she was on a diet. She was very mindful she was turning forty in a few weeks which had started to scare her to death. She was going to make some changes in her life. Exactly what changes in her life she was going to make, she wasn't sure of yet, but there were definitely going to be some changes. Sat there in the club she decided she was going to get away more with her girlfriends and she was going to dress more sexy all the time.

"The Guinness was for David, but he says he's on a diet and only drinking wine and soda now as it's non-fattening," Patrick replied without looking at Melissa and instead he took a sip of his new beer. It had a very lemon taste and wasn't all that nice. Over the top of his beer, which he was determined to finish, he looked around the now 'bustling' club house. Quickly raising his other hand, Patrick gave a wave to a man on the other side of the bar who was vaguely familiar. At that particular moment he couldn't remember his name but this man clearly recognised Patrick.

Blurting out over the club house loudspeaker came *"Good evening, Ladies and Gentlemen, Boys and Girls,"* in a surprisingly friendly and professional tone. Everyone in the club replied with a cheer and immediately started clapping, including Patrick who was probably the loudest supporter of his friend. David was going to be a natural on the microphone Patrick remarked to his wife.

Perched behind his now solid folding table that Brynn had supplied, David rotated his Bingo ball machine. Balanced on the edge was a tall glass thing of pink wine and soda and next to David's left hand was a small bright red petty cash tin. A box of pens sat on top of the tin and David held a wireless microphone which had one of those big black round foam heads over the end. When he lifted it towards his mouth, it covered most of his lower face. David continued his barrage of 'ice-breaking comedy', as David had referred to it later to his friends.

"If you are driving home tonight, watch the police on the road, they drive like maniacs. Thank you for coming tonight, and if you haven't come tonight, I hope you do so later." Most people instinctively laughed, including Patrick, who was in hysterics, but some of the parents had resorted to putting on their serious 'I'm a responsible parent' faces, and had put down their drinks and reached out to place their hands over the nearest child's ears.

"No. No. No, it's family night, no rude jokes," Brynn blurted out as he ran from the bar at nearly full speed across the dance floor towards David. Brynn had only just managed to come to a halt without knocking over the bingo table and immediately placed his hand over the microphone. He pushed it down with force and away from David's mouth. The microphone, disapproving of this blunt action, made an awful piercing feedback and a crashing noise around the room as it hit the bingo board.

"OK, sorry. Yes of course," David replied in a soft calm voice apologetically. A brief lecture from Brynn included the fact that his brother Owen, who ran the south side, didn't want Bingo on his site, but Brynn had reminded his brother that the agreement from his parent's estate gave him as much right to put on entertainment in the club as he had, and the north residents wanted Bingo.

Brynn so wanted the bingo night to be a success. He wished he could rub it in his brother's face on how successful the charity bingo event had been. He was now just wishing it wasn't all going to be ruined with numerous complaints about the choice of inappropriate jokes from the bingo caller. All would become evident at the reception desk in the morning.

"OK I've got it, I've got it, I understand," David said repeatedly, reassuring Brynn with smiles and several nods of his head. Gently removing Brynn's hand from the top of the microphone, David lifted the microphone slowly back into place. David dropped back into his loudspeaker announcements, this time with none of his cruise ship jokes. After a few minutes David nodded towards Brynn who had backed away towards the bar again. Brynn turned to face the bar to pick up his drink and David saw him relax and smile once more. David proceeded to explain the rules of the game and that Bingo cards were now on sale. He offered a gentle reminder to all participants that all the profits from tonight's Bingo were going towards the local lifeboat charity. Almost immediately a long queue formed in front of him. David scanned the club looking for Brynn to assist him in the selling of bingo cards, but he had miraculously disappeared. David hadn't realised that selling bingo cards was going to be such hard work. The first customer in the queue was a very large woman wearing a hand-knitted orange jumper. She had both hands in a fist shape on her hips. She wanted only one bingo card priced at £2 each and she stood there with a stern face and an outstretched arm. She had no change and thrust a £20 note in David's direction. David had not been given a float or any change and had to think on his feet now – he wanted to keep everyone happy!

Charles and Sharon walked down to the club bar, just the two of them, no children. They arrived in the middle of the second game of bingo. Charles had tried to be quiet but had proceeded to say hello to everyone who wanted to acknowledge him as he entered, much to the annoyance of several guests. Those who regarded themselves as professional Bingo players had loudly *shushed* Charles several times. Even Melissa, without taking her eyes from her bingo card, instinctively *shushed* out loud so as not to miss the next number being called.

Melissa had purchased the maximum ten bingo cards that were allowed per person. She was having to concentrate as she would have a least one number to mark off on her cards every time. She loved bingo. Fond memories were flooding back of her mother and her childhood as she played. Patrick had bought one bingo card. This had been to the annoyance of his wife who had tried several times to persuade him to get the maximum number allowed per player. She had even offered reassurances that she would keep her eye on his bingo cards and help him, thus massively improving their chances of winning. Melissa wanted to win. She wanted the thrill of calling a winning card. Patrick was content with his one bingo card and was only really there to support and see his friend David. He had plenty of time to check his one bingo card between the numbers being called. He also had time to drink, and he even had time to briefly chat with Charles who had plonked himself next to Patrick. Charles had squeezed in on the bench, Sharon taking the empty seat next to Melissa. Deciding she wanted more room, Sharon had, on purpose, knocked several people as she sat down, which was her way of telling them their chairs were too close. Sharon had that 'don't mess with me' air about her, and sure enough people sat nearby, quickly seemed to move away to give her more room.

"Two little ducks, twenty-two."

"On its own, the number nine."

"Five and nine, the Brighton line." David raised his right hand with a *"Whoop Whoop"*, hoping everyone would join in with the imaginary train whistle. None of his audience had heard this cruise ship style of bingo calling before. David carried on with the task in hand and after a

while began to thoroughly enjoy himself. He even considering whether he might throw in one or two more of his jokes, clean family-friendly ones of course. This centre-of-attention volunteering was completely new to David. At first, he had felt a little out of his comfort zone, but it was all part of the *new* David, he thought to himself. He had decided the new David was an outgoing, fun kind of chap.

Charles dropped a pink wine and soda on the table next to David without asking if he wanted another drink. David paused in calling out his next bingo number and took the opportunity to look in Charles' eyes and he gave him his biggest smile. Over the microphone came a loud "Thank you," adding, "Big round of applause please, ladies and gentlemen. This good-looking chap is called Charles and he has just bought your bingo caller a beverage and isn't he cute?"

The entire room started clapping and cheering. Charles was laughing as he carried four drinks at the same time easily in his big hands back to his table. Melissa had said she didn't want another drink, but Charles bought her another glass of wine anyway.

CHAPTER 9

Do You All Sleep in the Same Bed?

Even though they had only arrived that morning, Alison and Clifford had taken the children out sightseeing the local area for the day. Returning to the site, they had eaten their evening meal in the club house. The children were playing outside the caravan and Clifford and Alison were settling in for a quiet evening together in front of the television. Everything was peaceful and Clifford was sat thinking how he was getting used to the leisurely drive into Wales. The drive past the lake and the turn north to the site was enjoyable and he was pleased with the route he had chosen. It was not the direct route to the caravan site, in fact it was a few miles longer than some of the other routes, but there were a lot less single-track roads which Clifford disliked. The television was murmuring in the background as Clifford contemplated giving his wife a cuddle. Suddenly, from outside, came the dreaded words …

"Daddy! Daddy!"

It was Molly screaming. Clifford's head turned and he looked across at Alison with a stare that could have stopped traffic. He stood up from the sofa to get himself a drink, he was going to need one.

"Don't look at me! I didn't know he was coming," Alison immediately threw back at Clifford. "Looks like he's here now though, so just think about Molly – she's still very vulnerable from the divorce." Alison was firm in her tone but not quite brave enough to look in Clifford's direction as she said it. She shot off into her bedroom and leaning her head back she shook her hair and adjusted her cleavage, lastly she applied a fresh coat of lipstick, turned, and slowly and very calmly she walked back into the lounge with her shoulders back. Hearing her daughter laughing and giggling, Alison went outside onto the decking to see her ex-husband, Adam, standing in the road holding his beautiful daughter high above his head.

"Hello Adam, what are you doing here?" she said with a smile as Adam carefully placed his devoted daughter down on the floor. Maintaining eye contact, he walked directly towards her and without any words he leaned forward and kissed her firmly on the cheek.

With hands still holding his ex-wife, he leaned around her and shouted, "Hello, Clifford," in the direction of the open patio doors. Clifford had yet to show his face as demonstration of his disapproval of his wife's ex, having shown up at his holiday home *uninvited*.

Maintaining physical contact, Adam, with his face only inches from Alison's, said, "I was in the area, and I thought I'd surprise my wonderful daughter." Alison was surprised how she fell under his spell so easily. She could feel the power in his arms as he held her, and she was unable to speak. Adam knew he could still influence his ex and he pulled her ever so slightly just a little closer, his lips only inches from Alison's before he let her go and turned to find his daughter. Seconds later he was laughing and tickling Molly as he swung her into the air again with his large muscular arms. Adam knew he needed to justify his actions and he continued.

"I knew Molly was here, so thought I would just stop by, only for a few minutes. I'm not staying."

On hearing the words, "I'm not staying," Clifford's mood was lifted and knowing he couldn't hide forever, he unhurriedly walked towards the patio door. Leaning out he greeted Adam briefly before disappearing back inside and into his bedroom.

Why does he have to wear camouflage clothing all the time? he thought to himself. *Is there a war on? He has left the bloody army, he hated it!*

Whilst Adam was being fussed over by Alison, Molly never left his side. Adam was now inside the caravan and sitting in Clifford's spot on the sofa. To add insult to injury he was drinking one of Clifford's cold beers from his fridge.

This is taking the piss! thought Clifford.

"Cheers!" said Adam, looking in Clifford's direction as he surfaced from his hiding place. Goading him further, he added, "You joining me in having one?" Adam raised his glass a little in an imaginary clink.

"They *are* my beers," Clifford muttered to himself. He opened the fridge door and selected a beer for himself. He didn't really want a beer now, but he felt obliged to join his adversary.

The conversation was constant between Adam, Alison, and Molly. Even Jacob was now sat staring at Adam, interrupting to ask questions about the army and guns in general. Adam seized this opportunity to change the subject and talk about his past military career and answer Jacob's many questions. Clifford rolled his eyes. He felt like a stranger in his own caravan.

*

David and Debbie had plans to visit the HH just for the weekend and had both been waiting patiently for their daughters to get home from school. David had received numerous text messages that morning from Patrick to let him know that over the weekend a friend of his from work would be arriving on his site. Patrick asked that David look out for him and his wife and help them out if they needed anything. Frank and Sylvia would be passing through on their grand tour of Wales and staying for a few days in their motorhome on David's caravan site. They had reserved a rental plot on the touring caravan pitches. Patrick had informed David that he couldn't miss Frank and Sylvia as their motorhome was enormous. He could imagine it struggling to get down the narrow lane onto the site. David had attempted to pass this information onto Debbie, but she had taken little interest and was busy showing disgust at several comments that had been left on her Instagram page regarding her recent bikini beach post. She'd also received some unpleasant direct messages, or DMs as she liked to call them.

"What is *wrong* with these people? *Block!*" Debbie applied the same procedure to another follower who had left a similar rude comment on her latest photo. Debbie had considered her latest photograph to be very tasteful. What was not to like about her ample cleavage in her favourite red bikini?

"That's the third rude comment today and the second picture I've been sent of a penis this morning! What is *wrong* with these people?" she asked again to whoever was listening. Debbie's online profile was growing well, and she had now gathered several thousand online followers. She had mastered the art of hash tagging and was clear of the direction she wanted to take her Instagram page. She wanted to be regarded as a tasteful, glamorous fashion influencer, or something similar. Although she was in her mid-forties with five children, Debbie's 'bio' claimed she was just arriving at forty, she was slim and sporty and wanted to discover love again. She was confident that David would never see her online page and was also confident she could explain it if he ever did. Everyone removed a few years online and she had to say single for the allure and fantasy of her online followers. She often reminded David that she didn't make the influencer rules and that 'exposed flesh' created more followers. The more followers the more royalties she would receive. David wasn't ready yet for the revelation that Debbie had also considered *only fans* but even she wasn't ready for that yet.

David was aware of Debbie's recent obsession with her Instagram page, and he was mindful of the time she was spending online. Debbie had started asking David to take pictures of her wearing just her underwear as she lay on the bed, telling David, "It's all about the lighting and the camera angle." He had also noticed that Debbie was now incapable of going to any restaurant without at least ten photographs of the food being taken, before David was allowed to even take a single bite. She would thrust her phone into his hand and instruct him to make sure her cleavage was included in the food shot. David didn't find it at all interesting that Debbie's chest and backside were posted all over the internet until, one day, Debbie sat down next to him on the sofa and started to flick through page after page of men on Instagram. Most of them being part naked and nearly all suggesting they had a large item under their tight shorts. All were of a similar age to David and Debbie used the guise that she was showing him new outfit suggestions, but David suddenly became very interested in the stream of very good-looking men he could follow and converse with. Shortly afterwards there had been a thunderous round of applause from his children when he revealed to his family he had been into a phone shop and had spoken to a lovely sales lady about an iPhone he was considering purchasing.

On hearing from Patrick again, the Westwoods had gone for a walk to see if Patrick's friends had arrived onsite in their gigantic motorhome. Danielle had declined the invitation; she was always too busy for family walks these days.

"Talk about road rage," Debbie commented as they rounded the corner near reception. The loud, long, disapproving drone of several car horns pierced the usual ambient atmosphere of the caravan site.

"Go on, Mum! Honk your horn," Fabian encouraged his mother with laughs. He sat in the front seat because his dad, Andy, had stayed at home to work. Gabriella and Fabian had arrived at their caravan for the week only to be prevented from accessing their site because of a monstrosity of a motorhome blocking the final left turn onto the park. The motorhome was stationary and blocking the entire site entrance. Gabriella was now leading the queue of impatient holiday makers.

Frank and Sylvia, who were very experienced motorhome travellers, had found the site easy enough from Spider's directions but as they turned to take the last bend onto the site, they had been met with an illegally parked car. Frank had considered reversing and pulling over to the left-hand side until the owner of the car moved it out of the way but now some woman had driven up so close behind him that Frank was unable to move and, before a plan of action could be implemented, it was gridlock. There was only one possible outcome to this mess, Frank would need to find out who owned the small white van parked inconsiderately on the corner on double yellow lines and get it moved. Sylvia had ventured down to reception and Frank remained unflustered by the cacophony of aggressive car horns and stayed monitoring the situation.

"Oh God! He's coming over!" Gabriella said, rolling her eyes. She was not attracted to Frank in any shape or form, which was unusual as Gabriella could often find something to fancy about most men. Frank wore cheap worn-out beige shorts over skinny, hairy pale legs which were not high on Gabriella's tick list although she did take note of the cravat around his neck.

"I'm terribly sorry, young lady. It's not my fault, you see! There's a bloody little van illegally parked at the entrance." Frank spoke to Gabriella through her open car window. The sun behind him illuminated the interior of Gabriella's vehicle. Frank moved closer to the car and stuttered slightly as he looked down to see a pair of very long suntanned legs. Below the steering wheel, Gabriella's mini skirt had ridden up almost to her waist due to the long drive. Frank had been unprepared for the glimpse of her brief red underwear and was now distracted at how wonderfully sexy her legs looked; they were so perfect and so very long.

"Oh! Crisis averted; I think," Frank acknowledged his wife Sylvia who was now beckoning him back to the motorhome.

"Tootle Pip," Frank reluctantly left the view from inside

Gabriella's car and with a little jog headed back towards his motorhome. He lifted himself into the driver's seat in anticipation of moving onto the site.

Those breath-taking legs, thought Frank, *will have a place in my memory for some time.*

The van had been moved and Sylvia was standing on the pavement next to a lady who was wearing a name badge. Another woman with a small blue tub containing numerous cleaning bottles and cloths climbed into the driver's seat of the parked van. Lucy, the on-site cleaner, claimed she only parked illegally for a few seconds every day when she dropped off any rubbish from the rental caravans. Frank didn't believe this for one minute and drove the last few hundred metres and pulled over in front of reception. A continuous stream of cars filed past and dispersed onto the site. Frank stood and waved at the steady flow of drivers; an oblivious smile planted on his face.

"Are you Frank?" David said, offering his hand inquisitively. Frank turned in surprise to face the chap who had just spoken to him. He greeted David with an enthusiastic grin and a firm handshake. David explained that he was friends with Patrick and Melissa and that they were coming over to the site later and had told them of their imminent arrival in the motorhome. Frank faced everyone and held court, being a retired senior police officer, this was an arena he was used to. Offering David and Debbie an equal amount of attentive eye contact, Frank proceeded to tell them the dilemma of the illegally parked van and how the site would be charging him for two rental pitches due to his motorhome being so large. Everyone, including the children, hung onto Frank's every word.

Frank was an accomplished storyteller and no doubt later that evening, as he always did, he would be holding court and securing everyone's attention as he told of his adventures around Europe in the infamous motorhome. It was a given that Frank would probably also explain that he would, in writing, be challenging the company policy regarding charging him for a double pitch. He owned one motorhome and it certainly only had one engine. Where was the justice?

Frank and Sylvia's motorhome eventually got parked and, once in situ, it did indeed spread across two pitches, mainly due to the overhang. Everyone had stopped to watch as Frank skilfully completed what appeared to be a 75-point turn whilst Sylvia communicated via walkie-talkie with Frank, high off the ground in the colossal cab. They made it all look effortless, no shouting or stress. It was clearly the largest motorhome that had ever been shoe-horned onto the site. At first glance, the onlookers had thought that it would never fit on, but now in position it looked like it had always been there.

Frank connected the water and electricity whilst David and his family wandered off in the direction of the club house. They had made arrangements for a fire on the beach later. Frank had brought with him a supply of suitably dried firewood, a perk of having many compartments in his motorhome. He suggested that everyone should bring a folding chair, marshmallows, and something to drink and they'd make a night of it. It was the children's first campfire party, and they were suitably excited at the invitation. Debbie, however, wasn't impressed at all with this suggestion. All she could think of was the smell of smoke on everyone's clothing and how she would need an extra trip to the laundrette.

Once settled, Frank took to the task of penning his letter of complaint. From years of complaining about the same issue, Frank's letter had the usual paragraph that had been well used. He noted that just because his particular motorhome had a slight overhang onto the adjoining pitch, he strongly believed he should be charged only one pitch fee. Frank again, as he always did, would include in his defence with the site manager the tale of the 'ten items or less' at supermarket checkouts. Frank using his silver tongue and years of police negotiation skills would attempt to come to some arrangement with every site manager that wanted to charge him for two touring pitches. Skilfully jousting back with the question that his motorhome had one engine and was a single box containing twelve eggs, actually twelve items or one.

*

"Was it me or did I hear that you were unfortunately unable to stay long, Adam?" Clifford attempted to sound sincere before taking a sip of beer.

"I'll be off now, I don't want to get in the way," Adam said, standing up. Clifford could almost see his reflection in his polished military boots.

"Please stay, Dad! Please! Please!" Molly was almost in tears. Clifford's heart sank when he saw his daughter, well *almost* his daughter, was about to cry.

"It's up to Clifford," Adam retorted in a stern tone. Everyone had turned to look at him. Clifford was now in an awkward position. Things had backfired. Molly smiled at Clifford, and he knew he would have to put his issues with this man to one side despite it being obvious that his wife still had feelings for him.

"Of course, Adam can stay," Clifford said, quickly adding, "for dinner." Clifford thought he had been quite articulate in adding *for dinner*, but that clearly had fallen on deaf ears.

"It's only the sofa, Adam, but it's very comfortable." Alison passed Adam another of Clifford's beers from the fridge. Clifford looked down at his own glass, it was still full, but he would have liked to have been asked if he had wanted another.

I hate this bloody bloke! Clifford thought but he had backed himself into a corner now and if he asked him to leave, he would look like the bad guy.

"Who fancies a walk to the amusements?" Clifford tried to sound enthusiastic. No one responded – not even an acknowledgement. Alison appeared to ignore him as she fussed in the kitchen making their new guest his favourite sandwich. Jacob had his headphones on. Molly was sitting close to her dad, enveloped by his huge arms whilst he read a story from a book she had brought over for him. Clifford resigned himself to the fact that, even here at his special place, his wife's ex-husband would be part of their life.

"I'm going for a walk," he said, without waiting for approval or response from Alison and he was out the door and away, walking in the direction of the beach. As he passed his neighbour Charlie's van, Clifford offered a wave and Charles took a break from whatever he was doing in his shed and shouted over.

"Having a beach campfire tonight around seven. Bring the kids. I'm just looking for the folding chairs."

"Thanks," said Clifford. "Sounds great. See you then." He smiled and walked on, thankful for a break from Adam and his military woes. *Goodness!* thought Clifford as he walked into the shadow of the largest motorhome he had ever seen. Sat comfortably under a canopy on the side of motorhome were two pasty-looking Brits in shorts sipping what seemed to be large gin & tonics with no ice!

"Lovely evening for a stroll," Frank gestured, raising his glass slightly and offering a smile. Clifford managed only a shallow leer, but no words came out. He regretted this instantly, they seemed nice people, he knew he was being rude, but the moment had passed and he continued on in the direction of the beach.

*

Patrick had been helping Frank with armfuls of firewood by making several trips from the motorhome to the beach. It was dark now with only a half moon and Frank was wearing a head torch on his forehead. Melissa and Sylvia laughed every time they returned with a load of wood as they could initially only see the head torch, bobbing up and down and appearing out of the darkness like a steam train in a long tunnel. "You just relax, ladies," Patrick said sarcastically to the girls who by now had blankets over their legs as they sat on their camping chairs, both proudly holding aloft full wine glasses. In between drinks, they both placed their drinks down onto a large blue cool box that Sylvia had made Frank carry to the beach. It worked well as a beach coffee table.

"Hi everyone," David said as Debbie and the children appeared out of the darkness with only Frank's head torch guiding the way.

"Where's Danielle?" Melissa asked.

"Oh, you know – she had already made plans," Debbie said as she watched Frank and David exchange a handshake.

"Good to see you again, David. Glad you could make it, old chum."

"Of course, you all met when you arrived," Patrick realised. "I heard all about your poor parking, Frank."

Frank didn't rise to the bait and asked, "Have you brought chairs?" He could already see that they had but asked anyway to move on from his buddy's attempt at a joke.

"If you make one big circle around the fire, ladies, everyone can then take turn telling stories," Frank instructed the group. There was more wood to bring down to the beach first so Frank also recruited David to help out by carrying the final load from the motorhome. Debbie busied herself with sorting the girls, she erected the folding chairs to form a circle. David set off following Frank and Patrick back to the motorhome. As the three men reached the ramp up from the beach, they bumped into Charles and Clifford, both with their families. They were with another chap who no-one knew.

Alison did the honours and introduced Adam as Molly's biological father and explained that he would be joining them, if that was OK with everybody.

"More the merrier," Frank said loudly and set off, leading the charge back to the motorhome with a raised arm. David directed Charles to the area where they were seated on the beach and once again shared the advice on forming a large circle. This was, apparently, the order of things. Clifford followed the men back to the motorhome to help carry the wood. It was a good excuse to get away from Adam – he didn't wait to be asked.

"So, that's your wife's ex-husband. The father of the little girl?" Frank inquired. Clifford, who had already apologised for not saying hello when he had walked past earlier in the day, blamed Adam for the distraction and added, "Molly. Her name is Molly. And yes, he's her biological father."

"Well, don't we all live in very modern times," Frank chuckled and gave an approving grin whilst he divided up the remaining firewood between the three waiting helpers. "Do you all sleep in the same bed?" Frank snorted, immediately regretting the crude comment. Everyone laughed except Clifford.

"I'm sorry. That was out of order. Sorry! I've had a couple of gins," Frank offered sheepishly, looking in the direction of Clifford, his head torch shining straight into his eyes. Patrick and David, still giggling, picked up their pace and walked on ahead towards the beach, chatting.

"No. It's okay. It's complicated, but it's all about Molly and, *no* we don't all sleep in the same bed," Clifford felt the need to emphasise the fact he was the one who got to sleep next to Alison every night, not Adam. In the darkness, the laughs and chatter became more apparent as the wood-laden men approached to join the others around the beach campfire. Everyone seemed in an excitable mood. Adam had brazenly taken a seat in Clifford's chair and was sat next to Alison. He was in the middle of telling yet another military tale to Charles and anyone else who would listen. He showed no sign of moving to make way for Clifford.

"Let's get this fire lit, Mr Chumble," Sylvia bellowed. She was clearly already drunk, holding aloft her glass in the air for no apparent reason other than having consumed too much wine.

"Is that your nickname for Frankie?" Melissa asked, laughing and digging her feet into the sand, her chair nearly toppling backwards. Melissa was also well on her way to getting drunk. She already had the excuse in her head that she hadn't seen her good friend Sylvia for a while, and they were having a girlie catch up.

"Bugger! I've forgotten the matches." Frank looked around the large group in search of a smoker but with no luck.

"Do not fear!" Adam said in a deep, firm, manly voice which caused Clifford to roll his eyes north.

"A military man is always prepared for every situation." Molly looked up at her dad with admiration. The remaining women stared a little too long at Adam's muscles and his chiselled flat stomach. They secretly appreciated Frank's head torch helping to illuminate his body. The group fell silent as Adam unfastened the end of the handle of a very large combat knife which had been strapped to his inner calf. Frank was about to mention the legalities of brandishing such a large weapon in public, but the moment was lost as an arc of bright sparks filled the night sky like a firework. Two strokes of the flint and steel was all that it took and in what appeared to be only a few minutes, the campfire was well alight. Clifford found it hard to hide his annoyance. Adam was, yet again, the bloody hero of the hour. Was there nothing this bloke couldn't do? He forced a smile as he took the opportunity to occupy the vacant seat next to *his* wife as the hero saved the day with his combat knife.

CHAPTER 10

Red High Heel Emoji

Frank and Sylvia booked to stay on at the caravan park for an extra night. Frank had again tried to negotiate paying for only one touring pitch fee but to no avail. Debbie, who regarded herself as the sexy popular hostess within her circle of friends, had organised a trip into town to the local nail salon, and had made plans for a few girls only drinks afterwards. Sylvia was very interested in attending the salon, something she never got the chance to do at home, neither did she usually have the inclination. Would Frank notice if she had the odd treatment? A new hair colour? Nice nails? Probably not. Melissa managed to get completely wasted the previous evening at the beach campfire but she was still up for the trip. although adamant that she never wanted to drink again for the rest of her life. She had ended up, much to her embarrassment, crashing out on Frank and Sylvia's plush motorhome sofa. It wasn't the first time that had happened, and it wouldn't be the last. Sylvia took pleasure in reminding the group chat of Melissa's antics. She even surprised everyone by using an appropriate emoji.

Alison also had no hesitation in accepting the invitation, although she believed there was little room for improvement, salon visits were high on her agenda. She loved nothing more than being pampered. That just left Sharon to commit. Melissa took it upon herself to convince Sharon to come and set off to find her. Melissa didn't share on the chat-group that she was going to find Sharon and personally ask her; she didn't want her to see it. She was acutely aware that

Sharon was still very wary of Alison and that she had convinced herself that Alison was after stealing her husband.

"Hi girls! How are you both today?" Melissa genuinely liked Emily and Sophie. With two boys herself she had missed not having a daughter in her life; someone to shop with and visit the hair salon with. She yearned for that mother-daughter bond. Sharon was lucky to have two strikingly pretty daughters but, like Melissa's two boys, they were growing up fast.

"Good morning," Sharon called out to Melissa. Melissa had decided to message ahead that she was popping in. Sharon greeted her friend, walking out onto the decking with two cups of tea, placing one down directly in front of Melissa.

"Is everything OK?" Sharon asked just as she sat down.

"Yeah, it's all good thanks!" Melissa replied as she leaned forward to take a sip of her tea. Melissa continued, "We're planning a girls' night out, that's all, and I really want you to come. It wouldn't be the same without you." Melissa looked over at Sharon for any flickers of a reaction.

"Is, err, you know," Sharon nodded her head in the direction of Alison's caravan, "is *she* coming?"

"Yes," Melissa replied. There were a few seconds of silence before Melissa began the persuasive speech she had pre-prepared in her head. Sharon was a little reassured at the suggestion that Alison would be unable to get her claws into her man if she was sitting next to Sharon getting her nails done.

"Anyway," Melissa added, "since when has Charles got time to be sleeping with anybody else?" Melissa leaned closer into Sharon and lowered her voice. "Aren't you still bonking him every day?" They both laughed at the remark.

"Sometimes even twice a day, if I have my way," Sharon replied with a raspy laugh, and she squeezed Melissa's arm. They both fell about laughing and Alison was forgotten for a moment.

"Well, I can implement code *Red Shoe Emoji* right now if you want me to look after the girls for an hour," Melissa said, unsure if it was the right time, but then it was always the right time for Sharon. 'Red shoe emoji' was Charles and Sharon's secret password to each other to suggest that sex was imminent. Sharon smiled with a nod as Melissa stood up and finished the dregs of her tea.

"You want to go for a walk with your Aunty Melissa, girls? Where do you fancy going? We could go to the coffee bar for cake and milkshakes?" Melissa was already moving towards the edge of the decking as the girls stepped into their flip flops. Sophie slipped her hand into Melissa's.

"Where's Jackson?" Melissa asked of the girls.

"On the sofa, with his headphones on," Emily said, looking at Melissa. Melissa could already hear Sharon in the bathroom. *Poor Charles,* she thought, with a grin.

Popping back inside; "You coming for a walk, Jack?" Melissa lifted the left side of his headphones up. He seemed startled. He had been engrossed in his YouTube clip. Melissa only caught the briefest glimpse of it before Jackson lowered the screen but caught sight of some muscly body builders working out in a gym.

"Oh! Hi Melissa," Jackson smiled up at Melissa. Melissa was one of his parents' better friends. She was cool. Jackson described her to his mates as the sexy cop.

"Come for a walk with me and your sisters." Melissa nodded towards the bedrooms. Jackson looked up at her, shrugged his shoulders with a brief shake of his head, and replaced his headphones.

"Look, Jackson. You're old enough now. You're a man," Melissa leant in to get Jackson's attention. "Let's just give your mum and dad an hour to themselves, some quality alone time." Melissa beckoned Jackson to follow her as she grinned and raised eyebrows. The penny dropped. Jackson shot up from the sofa and darted past Melissa and through the door.

"Don't tell me things like that. I will be scarred for life. Here in the caravan? Ewww." Jackson was half laughing, and half disgusted as he stumbled to slide his flip flops on. One flip flop on, he scrambled down the decking steps and caught up with his sisters as they headed towards the south site amenities. Melissa ran to catch up with the three siblings. After a few seconds, Jackson looked across at Melissa with a horrified face – still traumatised from their recent chat. The two of them burst out laughing. The girls however were oblivious to the joke as they all walked through the caravan site.

Sharon seized the alone time opportunity with her usual enthusiastic gusto. She was determined to make full use of every minute that Melissa had instigated. She dropped everything she was wearing onto the bedroom floor and stood completely naked. There was no time for lingerie or foreplay this morning. She had already ensured the patio doors were locked. She didn't want to be interrupted. She slipped under the duvet and placed her mouth next to Charles' ear. He was lying face down, his head fully ensconced in the pillow.

"Melissa's taken the kids. You have exactly one-hour, Big Boy!" Charles began to unfurl in a state of dozed confusion. Sharon moved her mouth from his ear and ventured under the covers. Charles smiled as he realised what was happening. He turned fully onto his back to assist in his wife's chosen activity, closed his eyes, and smiled. On all fours she climbed slowly down his laying body. She allowed her sizeable heavy breasts to drag across his muscular chest, knowing her nipples were erect with excitement. When she arrived, he was almost ready to receive her and without using her hands she only just managed to encompass him into her open mouth. With enthusiasm she worked, her goal was to turn this mountain of firm dough into something as hard as iron which she craved to be inside her.

Melissa sent Debbie a message to say that Sharon was up for the girls' night out. Sharon was initiated into the girls' only group chat, to be greeted by a picture of a bare chested, six pack yielding and very good looking man. Debbie added the words "I would". This was closely followed from Melissa with the words "So would I" and a series of laughing emojis. The evening soon arrived, and the ladies made full use of the group chat with constant questions about what everyone was wearing and was a coat required.

The men had also set about making their evening arrangements, and, as men do, it was all very last minute of course. Charles had offered to babysit, but Jackson had volunteered to watch his sisters. This allowed Charles to go to the club bar, alone for a change, to enjoy a few beers. His son's only condition was that his father returned swinging the coveted white carrier bag containing a takeaway meal for him. He knew Frank would have similar thoughts with Sylvia being out. Clifford had decided to stay in. His ex-wife's husband had finally left, and he had ordered pizza and had plans to watch a Disney movie with Molly and Jacob. Patrick had driven Melissa over for the night out but had headed back to his own site. David was still unsure what his oldest daughter's plans were. He had asked her if she would babysit but Danielle had pointed out, under no uncertain terms, that she couldn't fully commit until later. She had more important things on her agenda. A lot would depend on whether Fabian was around tonight. Danielle was still waiting to hear from her network of informants around the site. Snapchat had been quiet so far this evening, but she expected things to heat up. If they did and Fabian was spotted out on the town, then babysitting would be called off.

The minibus arrived outside the clubhouse and the girls hauled themselves inside. Alison, who was wearing the skimpiest of outfits, had to climb over the back seat. She couldn't help but exaggerate lifting her skirt to get her leg onto the first step. Frank got more than he bargained for as he stepped outside to wave them off. The girls laughed hysterically when they realised he'd caught an eyeful of Alison's almost naked bottom.

"Good luck," Frank whispered to the driver. "They haven't even started drinking yet!"

Debbie sat in the front, half turning in her seat to chat with the girls behind her. Her stance also helped to show off her figure. She was wearing a revealing dress that was open to the waist. The driver couldn't take his eyes off Debbie's breasts, Debbie knew this and took great pleasure in twisting around in her seat, chatting to the girls behind, whilst managing to fix a sultry smile on the driver.

*

Frank was nearing sixty years of age and had been a seasoned drinker most of his life. Being a retired police officer, he took drink-driving seriously but as it would be days before he drove his enormous motorhome again – and considering he had a night off from Sylvia, he decided he was going to partake in several alcoholic beverages that evening. He was disappointed that Patrick wasn't going to be at the club later, but he understood his parenting obligations. Frank's children were both grown up and living on different continents. It was a warm summer's evening; the site was busy, and Frank enjoyed the buzz and feel of the Pebbles caravan park. He had been pottering around his motorhome and chatting with almost everybody who had walked past. The abundant comments about the size of his motorhome, however, were becoming a bit tedious. Frank remained polite and never tired of talking with people, especially when the conversation was regarding his motorhome.

"Hello Lucy," Frank was gifted when it came to remembering names. Lucy, the site cleaner, shot past, with her trolley piled high with loo rolls and bed linen.

"Got many vans to clean today?" Lucy liked a natter and any excuse to stop and talk. In less than ten minutes Frank had heard her life story. She had worked at the site for twenty-two years, how she had watched the two sons grow up and how they had changed when their parents had died. He was updated that she hated the park split into two halves and that she herself had four grown-up children, all with different fathers. Frank made enquiries regarding one of the see-through containers on Lucy's cleaning trolley. The container on the middle shelf had what appeared to be over twenty bottles of shower gel of various brands and sizes, some were almost empty. Before he knew it, Frank had bought eight bottles of half-used shower gel, three half jars of coffee, and six tins of unopened baked beans, all for only £3 cash. Frank regarded it as a complete bargain. Lucy always had a full trolley load of offerings which she sold on for a bit of extra pocket money. These were all items left behind by holiday makers from the rental caravans. She then felt the need to justify her side business with references to waste, the environment, and landfill. It was her duty to completely remove any trace from the caravans before the new tenants arrived. As she was preparing to leave, Lucy had made a sexual reference to Frank which seemed to go straight over his head. Only later that evening, when chatting to Charles in the clubhouse, did it all become clear.

Charles and Frank were getting on rather well in the club bar and so far they had consumed several pints of various brands of beer. Frank wore the same clothes he had been wearing all day and had not even contemplated changing his clothes for the evening. He was slightly out of practice and was unaccustomed to socialising with a seasoned beer drinker such as Charles and was already thinking about moving onto whisky as he was rather full and getting rather drunk.

Earlier Charles had kissed his wife goodbye and he had reinforced his promise to his son to return with takeaway food. Showered, shaved, and with his favourite cologne, he strode down to the clubhouse with his belt around his waist firmly fastened. He was starting to get conscious of his girth and had made an effort recently, but it was too late tonight, he thought, he was doing the best could. He wore expensive shoes and fashionably tight jeans. It was worn but he felt special in his brown checked formal jacket and with his best smile, he was looking forward to having a few drinks with Frank. Charles was also hoping to verbally engage with any female company that might be attending the club tonight, he enjoyed chatting with other women as it made a stimulating change from his wife.

Charles had been coming to this site for years and explained that if Frank needed any *relief* during his stay, then he was to call Lucy, who had a diverse and varied supply of contacts who would be able to offer discrete massages at very reasonable rates. The conversation turned to the time Frank spent as a police officer. Over the years, Frank had discovered that people often had a fascination with police work and so a few exaggerated tales regarding traffic stops and the antics on nights at the station with randy policewomen had Charles in stitches. As the men relaxed in each other's company, they chose to send out a few messages to Patrick, Clifford, and David, telling them to get down to the club bar immediately. Charles felt compelled to buy another round and he desperately thought of a tale to add to the story telling.

"So, I've got this boat. It's a Rib with a fifteen horsepower engine on the back," Frank enthused first before Charles could offer his tale of sex in a car wash story. "I don't often get the boat out of the motorhome."

"It's inside the motorhome?" Charles asked with surprise but then remembered that Frank could probably fit ten boats inside his enormous moving house.

"Yes, it's deflated in one of the driver's side compartments in its own special protective bag," Frank proudly informed Charles. "The engine has a special stand and it all fits under the master bed." Frank then proceeded to tell his boat story, leaning in so Charles didn't miss a word. The club was filling up and it was becoming increasingly difficult to hear over the noise. Frank continued.

"The last site we stayed at, we got this flat calm sea weather window, so out came the boat. I had been motoring around all day, Sylvia had been water skiing, in a bikini I might add, and all in all, a rather super day was had by everyone." Charles had water-skiing on his to-do list. He wanted to ask more about the boat, but he didn't want to interrupt.

"So, the boat is pulled up on the beach with a short anchor rope and I was going to have a shower and a bite to eat with the intention of fastening the boat down securely for the night later on. Sylvia is all salty and wet and she also wants a shower and, before you know it, I'm proceeding with my manly obligation with a sock on the motorhome door handle, if you know what I mean," Frank nudged Charles on the arm and winked.

"I know what you mean," Charles said coldly. He now had the image of a naked Frank in his head which he feared would never leave him.

"Alright lads. What you both having? I'll get them in." David had been given the clearance by his oldest daughter to go out. Dani had not been given any updates on what Fabian was up to, so she had agreed to babysit but on condition that he brought home a chicken kebab with mayo and no onion. David had agreed to these demands as he would also be eating later himself after only cooking a meal tonight for his younger daughters before he left. Charles and Frank welcomed David into the group with drunken gusto and he was soon catching up with the drinking. David nestled in next to Charles at the table and enjoyed being squashed up next to the big bear of a man. After explaining as to why Clifford and Patrick were missing and the whole saga around David's babysitting drama, Frank skilfully brought the conversation back to himself and after a brief recap he continued with his tale.

"So, I've left the boat on the beach, not fastened down properly and I've been distracted by Sylvia in the shower." He winked at

Charles with the shower reference again. Charles cringed inside. He wished Frank would shut up about his sex life.

"And before I know it, we have both fallen fast asleep. The next thing, it's 3 a.m. and I shot bolt upright in bed realising I had forgotten to tie the boat down properly." Frank was an avid storyteller and both Charles and David were hanging on every word. Their expectations of an interesting punchline were building.

"I am awake and running up and down the beach, Sylvia's awake and so is the bloke in the caravan next to me. Someone gets one of those powerful torches and is panning the sea and we spot my boat in the distance, just floating free." Frank made eye contact with both David and Charles whilst his boat story unravelled. Charles became lost as a tall, slim woman around forty years old entered the club and offered a full, opened-mouthed smile at Charles as he passed. He maintained the eye contact and then watched how she placed her hand gently onto another woman's bare back to attract her attention. The friend opened the circle further to greet her friend and the woman, before she engaged with her new group, turned fully to stare in Charles' direction and return a smile. Charles got that instant burning sensation in his groin as men often do when they see a woman they are so sexually attracted too. Charles was distracted but turned to give his attention to his friends as Frank continued to paint the scene.

"So, I've got my wetsuit on and I'm wading into the sea with one of those children's blue rectangular floats that you hold out in front of you to teach kids to swim. The chap in the next caravan had offered it to me and I thought it was better than nothing.

"Then another site member comes running over with one of those tiny little rowing boats for kids. I mean tiny, like it was designed for a three-year-old in a paddling pool. It seemed better than my float, so I just manged to squeeze myself into it. It was a squeeze but with my legs tucked under me I start out rowing to rescue my boat. Every time I look up it seems to have drifted out even further," Frank paused, building the tension.

"So, what happened next?" David asked. He loved stories that didn't involve shopping or things that were pink. Charles was struggling to stay with the boat story and with a firm distraction in his tight jeans he was searching the room for the tall lady. He had decided when he found her, he was just going to go over and tell her how beautiful she looked. His drunken game plan was to keep it simple. Maintain eye contact and just start with low level compliments about her hair and try his hardest not to look down. Frank continued his story even though he suspected he had lost Charles.

"So, I start to settle into a rowing routine, and I think I'm going to make it. Then I could feel cold sea water around my legs. It's only gone and burst and I'm bloody sinking. Then the torch that's been shining from the beach disappears and I'm cold and wet. My little rowing boat is sinking, and I can't see a thing. It was pitch black."

Charles spotted her but she was the centre of attention in her group of friends and was about to turn back and show a little more interest in Frank and David when she turned around. Alerted by her friend, she knew she had Charles' eye as she stared at him over her drink. She lowered her glass, seductively released the sipping straw from between her plump red lips and smiled. She raised her other hand slightly and mouthed the words 'Hi' at Charles. Charles smiled in return and began to imagine slowly unfastening her dress and under its own weight watching it drop to the floor. He knew this would reveal some expensive lingerie and expose what must be a perfect, firm, olive-coloured body. Charles was bored of drunken bloke's stories, and he wanted to flirt with the slim lady in the red dress.

"So, I'm nervous now and I'm considering, albeit ashamedly, I'm actually considering phoning the coast guard to ask for assistance, when a small wave turns me round and I find myself only a few meters from my drifting boat." Frank had expected a little bit of laughter during his tale and made a mental note to add a bit more humour into his next tale.

"So, then what?" David enthusiastically asked.

"I clambered over the side of my boat and brought it back to shore, anchored it properly, and got back to bed, not to sleep, mind, with all that adrenalin pumping." Frank gave Charles another wink and, lifting his pint in a congratulatory manner, gave him a gentle prod with his elbow. Without speaking, Charles stood up and walked directly across the room. David watched him as he walked away.

CHAPTER 11

Mum Alone Time

"I did ask Gabriella from next door to come out with us tonight, but she declined, saying she was meeting a *friend* later for coffee." Debbie refrained from turning in her seat this time as she spoke to the group instead, she faced forwards to look out of the front of the taxi. Debbie had over exaggerated the word friend and waited for the retort from her fellow passengers.

She was actually becoming rather concerned about their taxi driver, Aeron. His driving ability was questionable to say the least. Debbie had just hurt her neck on the seatbelt when they went round the last bend in the road, and she decided that it may be best if she stared straight ahead from now on and stop distracting the driver with her exposed boobs. She reached down and adjusted her skirt, trying to cover as much of her thigh as she could. She also pulled up her dress again to cover her breasts and to try to make sure that Aeron was watching the road ahead rather than the curves of her body. She braced herself for the next hairpin bend that she could see was coming.

"Oooh, a friend," Alison sneered from the backseat.

"Have we met Gabriella? What does she look like?" added Melissa inquisitively.

"She looks like a bloody supermodel with legs to die for. She's got the holiday home next to mine. I would!" Debbie added and she laughed at her own smutty comment and threw a wink in Aeron's direction. The minibus swerved theatrically as Aeron, speechless after overhearing Debbie's comment, once again fixed his eyes down to Debbie's cleavage instead of the road ahead.

Aeron was a tall, broad-shouldered man in his late 50s. Even though he showed signs of greying, he still had a full head of hair. He was accustomed to the on-board banter of his fare-paying customers, but it had been a while since he had enjoyed blatant-flirtatious female company in his taxi. He was taking everything in, and he turned a blind eye to the bottles of open *Prosecco* that were being passed and spilled around his taxi. Driving towards the sleepy Welsh coastal town, his thoughts turned to the locals. They were in for a shock tonight. The local lads wouldn't know what had hit them! Aeron chuckled to himself.

"I bet you've caught David eyeing up Gabriella then, if she's that sexy." This was Alison's mild attempt at provoking Debbie. Alison gave Sharon a little nudge, in a bid to gain support as she goaded Debbie. Debbie didn't reply and noticeably fell silent in the front of the minibus. Melissa, noticing this unusual silence from her best friend, made a mental note to ask Debbie about it later. Debbie flushed, her cheeks bright pink, but no one noticed, except for Aeron. She took a deep breath and looked out of the window towards the sea beyond the beautiful dry-stone walls as they sped past.

The ladies had decided that they were all going to drink tonight. Each participant had deposited £50 into a kitty and sensible Melissa had been elected to oversee the fund, whether she wanted the responsibility or not. Several bottles of *Prosecco* and numerous rounds of double pink gins had given the kitty a respectable bashing. The pub had been quiet; the barman was euphoric to see his night's takings double on their arrival. He had given them a cheery wave as they left to descend on the next booked establishment, the restaurant.

Earlier that day, the restaurant owner had insisted they made a reservation for the evening. Looking around now at the practically deserted restaurant, the women couldn't fathom as to why this had been necessary. However, they were pleased with the efficient service and the waitress did not delay in supplying the insatiable women with copious amounts of alcohol. The lone waitress delivered every round of shots with unreserved efficiency and professionalism. She even managed a smile once or twice. When the majority of food had been devoured, Debbie's attention turned to her social media profile, and she primed the gang to get ready for a series of photographs.

"I want lots of skin in this shot," Debbie's high pitch startled the waitress who was on her way with more drinks. "Alison, get up front! This is for my Instagram page! Let's give them massive tits of yours some glory, Hun!"

"Yours are bigger than mine," Alison replied, giggling as she slipped her right hand through the front of Debbie's open dress. She gave a quick squeeze, perhaps keeping her hand there a little longer than was necessary. Debbie didn't seem to show any sign of disapproval, nor was she in any rush for Alison to remove her hand from her slightly sweaty breast.

"Ready? Smile! Say 'sex'!" The waitress had been commandeered into becoming principal photographer. Using Debbie's phone, she snapped away, the poses between each photo becoming more provocative with each shot. Alison's hand had found its way back inside Debbie's dress. Debbie appeared to prolong the photo shoot, requesting more and more photos.

"*Enough*, woman!" Sharon rolled her eyes and sat back down in her allocated place at the dining table. Others agreed with her, muttering that the photos were distracting them from their drinks. Debbie thanked her friends for their commitment to her online cause and proceeded to explain how it had been too good an opportunity to miss. She attempted to explain how Instagram worked; her long-term advertising goals and the requirement to boost her followers whenever she could. She also, rather unsuccessfully, tried to explain that she wasn't selling sex by insisting on them revealing more flesh.

It was just the way it was and that she didn't make the social media rules. More skin meant more followers, she repeated.

After a while, Sharon wandered off to the toilet and had still not returned, despite several minutes having passed. Melissa had noted her absence and had abandoned the raucous table to head towards the bar to settle the very large bill. The kitty was virtually depleted. Melissa glanced across the bar to the dining area. Her friends were oblivious to the fact that the kitty was short. Suddenly, Alison appeared at Melissa's side. She placed her left hand on Melissa's backside and gave a firm squeeze and giggled.

"Clifford's loaded," she winked as she laid down two crisp fifty-pound notes onto the bar counter. Crippled by her heels, she hobbled off towards the loo.

Melissa welcomed the extra cash and was surprisingly unoffended by the grope she had just received from her new friend. She placed the remaining money from the kitty on top of the two newly placed notes and deposited it onto the shiny steel tray that had carried the bill. Waving at their waitress, she was relieved that she hadn't had to ask the group to top up the kitty again for one last time. By now, the party were too drunk to make sense of financial matters. On top of that, they had lost one. Sharon was still missing.

The combination of skimpy dresses and the lack of jackets meant that the group certainly stood out in this sleepy little fishing village. Melissa couldn't remember the last time she had seen her friend Sylvia so intoxicated, but it was good to see her laughing and letting her hair down. What had surprised her was that throughout the entire evening, Sylvia had managed to flirt with every man they encountered. They hadn't actually met *that* many men but, as the evening had progressed, the cruder and more laddish (not to mention desperate) her advances had become.

Through her drunken slur, Sylvia proceeded to inform the ladies that her husband wasn't interested in sex anymore. Frank's idea of something hot in the bedroom was a cup of tea. In simple terms, Sylvia wasn't getting any, and she had decided that tonight was the night to rectify matters. It didn't matter who with, but she had decided it was going to happen. Sylvia had accepted that she wasn't as firm as she used to be around her midriff. She was a woman in her mid-fifties; these things happen. But she was still a woman with needs and if her husband wasn't interested, then the taxi driver would need to step-up to the challenge. The girls roared with laughter at this suggestion, not really sure if she was joking or not.

'Hey! There she is!" Debbie spotted Sharon just across from the restaurant.

"What the hell are you doing out here by yourself, you crazy assed fool?" Debbie blurted out as she wobbled over to join her. Sharon was no more than a silhouette in the pale light from the harbour. She was just sitting on a bench, alone looking out to sea. It was nearly midnight and Aeron wouldn't be picking them up for another hour yet.

'For God's sake! Why the hell did we change the friggin' taxi? I'm freezing my tits off!" Alison blurted out. They had all consumed far too much alcohol, the cold sea air hitting their senses as they settled in next to Sharon along the cold damp benches. The warm sea air that rolled in off the beach onto their exposed skin and faces seemed to instantly calm everyone and the group fell into a huddled silence. After several minutes of just listening to the sound of the rolling waves, Debbie spoke first.

"I haven't had sex with David for nearly three years."

A small, silent tear rolled down her left cheek. It had been a lot longer than that. It hurt to think about how long it had truly been. No one spoke, Melissa put an arm around Debbie, and they leaned into each other on the bench looking out into the darkness. Minute after minute passed without anybody saying another word.

"I think I'm addicted to sex," Sharon said quietly, finally breaking the silence. One of the girls involuntary sniggered.

"I'm being serious," Sharon bit her lip. "I pester Charles to have sex with me every day, even if he's not in the mood. I even carry my vibrator in my handbag, just in case!" As if in unison, everyone along the bench leaned forward to look at Sharon. Debbie was grateful for Sharon's confession; she was starting to regret baring her soul. Again silence, only the sound of distant seagulls and crashing waves on rocks. They all leaned back on the bench and gazed out to sea, each lost in their own drunken haze. The mood began to feel special. A bond had been formed and, although no one spoke, they all knew that things between them were different.

It was Debbie, again, who broke the silence. "I don't think my husband finds me attractive anymore."

"David is as camp as they come! God, it can't just be me that's noticed? Surely it's not just me?" Alison jumped up from the bench, looking for support from her allies. The girls stared back at her in disbelief!

"Melissa, you must have noticed? Come on!" Alison singled out Melissa, her arms outstretched, beseeching her to agree. Everyone again leaned forward on the bench to look along at Melissa. They waited with bated breath for her reaction to Alison's bold statement. Melissa felt like there was a spotlight on her. She thought carefully about her response, careful not to allow the alcohol to speak on her behalf. She stayed silent for a few more seconds, preparing her answer when Debbie broke the silence and fired the question at her friend, forcing a response.

"Do you think David is gay? *My* David?" Debbie spoke softly and turned to look at her dearest friend. There was a pause. Alison was still standing, holding centre stage, not seeming to want to lower her accusatory arms until Melissa replied.

"He is, Debbie," Melissa whispered with a gentle shake of her head. "But it's not anything bad. It's not like he's ill or anything. And it's not anything you've done. He's going to be okay; you know. So are you."

A few seconds passed before Melissa leaned into her friend for a hug. "He's just gay! It's no big deal. He'll probably feel loads better when he comes out. But it *is* a bit obvious." Melissa hugged her friend and Debbie leaned in and rested her head on her shoulder.

For a few moments, Debbie felt totally alone in the world as she stared out into the darkness of the ocean. Melissa broke the silence.

"He is so lovely and kind. I really, really love David. But not in *that* way! I don't *fancy* him, and he doesn't fancy me!" Debbie's eyes welled with tears and Melissa pulled her in for another hug. She also tactfully pulled at her friend's dress to help to re-cover her exposed chest.

"God! Your tits are huge, Debbie!" Melissa laughed and the mood of the women was lightened as they all leaned back into the sanctuary of their benches and once more gazed out towards the sea.

"Sharon! You have sex *every* day! *Every* day?" Sylvia's anxious exclamation interrupted the silence.

"Yep! I've decided – he's getting it! I'm going to shag that taxi bloke, Arran." Everyone laughed as the tide appeared to wash away the night's revelations.

"*Aeron!*" Melissa said. "His name is Aeron, and he is about 100 years old!" The mood was lifted. Alison was thinking about her ex-husband and how he was still in her life and if he was here right now, he would also be getting it. Melissa's mind wandered, not to her committed, loyal husband but to a certain new recruit, a tall, olive-skinned police officer at work on D Squad. Sylvia, excited and rejuvenated from the prospect of propositioning Aeron again, broke the silence.

"So, what's going on with you, Alison? Do you and Clifford sleep in the same bed as Adam when he visits? One, big happy family?" The group burst out into roars of laughter as Alison protested that Sylvia had crossed a line. Her objections went unheard. The reflection of headlamps on the water announced the arrival of their taxi. Debbie linked Alison's arm as they precariously walked towards the stationary vehicle.

"I've just told you my husband is gay!" Debbie said.

"Being gay is no big deal. Just see him as a new best friend and, more importantly, you now have permission to start shagging anyone who takes your fancy!" Alison replied, smiling and squeezing Debbie's bum as if offering a subtle suggestion.

Leaving her hand in place, Alison leaned into Debbie and whispered, "You're lucky if that's all you got going on! I'm married, I have a crazy jealous ex-husband who rings me every day and I can't stop fantasising about bald men." Alison giggled and ran ahead towards the waiting taxi, still very drunk and unsteady in her heels. She smacked Sharon's bottom as she ran past her and threw her a wink.

Alison climbed into the back of the minibus. It was easier this time as she had lost all her inhibitions through drink and didn't care what parts of her anatomy were on show as she tumbled and fell onto the back bench seat. Sharon looked out of the window. She was wondering whether Charles would be interested in experimenting with a threesome. Alison had mentioned earlier that she had been interested in trying one for some time. Alison was thinking about Charles, and she glanced in Sharon's direction from the back seat wondering if Sharon would be up for it.

*

"No! I'm *not* going swimming and, no! I am *not* going for a walk along the beach," Debbie put on a brave face and concentrated on not being sick in front of her children. Last night's drinking was catching up with her. She was functioning but she was still hungover and very fragile.

"I'm going for a jog, girls. You going to follow me on your bikes, like Rocky in the movie?" David smiled at his daughters and threw a few practice punches, like a boxer. Running and boxing where things David had never done in his life before, but he was enjoying this freedom that he seemed to have discovered and this desire to better himself.

"Jogging?" Debbie shook her head in disgruntled disapproval and looked down at her phone.

"I've been chatting to Charles. It's a massive calorie burner. Come with me. I'm not going far. I'm just starting out," David replied with some seriousness as he warmed up, not really sure what he was doing. He was secretly hoping it was something they could do in the future together. David knew he would need a running partner to keep him motivated and get him up to the long distances. She wasn't his first choice, but Debbie would have to do to start with, until he found a new running partner. Maybe an experienced male running partner would be better, someone he could learn from. David didn't get any acknowledgement from Debbie. She didn't even look up from her phone. Unbeknownst to David, Debbie had already just searched online gyms and sports bras. She was shocked at the price of them, but she liked the muscular tall young men that seemed to work in all the gyms. She liked the idea of jogging, it meant she might lose a bit of weight, but she also liked the idea of a six-foot tall, late twenties, dark-haired personal trainer teaching her how to work out in the gym. She also smiled at the thought of working up a sweat in public in what was essentially her underwear!

"I've also been thinking about joining a gym." The words seemed to blurt out from Debbie's mouth. "Yes! Let's get a joint membership, me and you, when we get home. That could be our thing that we do together, and it will be great exposure for my fan base." Debbie gave David a smile, secretly knowing that she needed

David to sign the membership forms and for him to take care of the monthly direct debit payment. She had started earning, but she didn't earn enough yet to join an expensive gym and hire a personal trainer. She was pleased with her idea. *There must be loads of fit men at the gym,* she thought to herself. *Some of them may even be single.* She knew her secret weapons were going to pay for themselves in finding her another man. She had been thinking about what Sharon had said last night. In fact, all the girls had been thinking the same thing, but no one had been brave enough to say anything on the group chat. Instead, Debbie had been receiving individual messages from the girls and she was having to concentrate when she replied to ensure that the right message got sent back to the right person.

Sharon was getting sex *every day* and she wasn't getting anything. Nothing. Zero. She hadn't had so much as a quickie in years. Where was the fairness in that? Debbie had also been thinking about the adult toy comment that Sharon had dropped on everyone's toes. She decided that she would discuss this in more detail with her. She was behind the times in this department and knew she needed advice on what to buy. Sharon, it appeared, was the expert on the matter.

*

"Morning, sleepy head! Had a good night?" Patrick stood up to make his wife a cup of tea as she finally entered the lounge.

"Are you still drunk, Mum?" George asked as Melissa surfaced after lunch and walked awkwardly into the lounge. She was very hungover; her head was sore; her mouth was dry, and she smelt of stale wine.

"I wasn't sure what you were doing today so, me and George are going gold panning," Patrick informed his wife.

"Gold panning!" Melissa replied, looking up, she wasn't sure whether she had heard him correctly.

"Yes!" Patrick replied with a large grin. "Gold panning. Are you coming with us?"

Melissa shook her head delicately as she cradled her hot cup of tea and ambled to her spot on the end of the sofa. She was still dressed in her furry leopard-print onesie, and she pulled up a blanket over her knees. Their youngest son was busying himself, preparing for today's adventure with a map, a yellow shovel, and a compass whilst Patrick was proudly holding aloft a green gold-panning dish which he had bought from eBay several weeks earlier.

"Bye, Mum! Hope you feel better soon," George said as he smartly exited the caravan and headed out into the sunshine. He had put on his walking boots and was ready for whatever adventure his dad had in store for him that day. Patrick was quick to follow his son's lead and so both father and son set off to seize the day, leaving a hungover wife and mother drinking tea on the sofa and staring at her phone and a teenage son still snoring in bed.

"It's just at the end of this lane I think, son. Here we go! And here's a parking space. Boom!" Patrick grinned as he manoeuvred into the empty space. He often worried unnecessarily about being able to park down these single-track lanes, deep in the Welsh countryside. Patrick had carried out plentiful online research. Several years ago, gold had been found in the Ysgethin River. He and George had also watched several YouTube videos on gold panning and today they would chance their luck and give it a go. Patrick had invested the £12.99 on the special green pan and the excitement and expectation of actually finding gold was high. Both prospectors grabbed their rucksacks from the boot and set off.

"Which way, Dad?" George enquired, walking off in the same direction as the car was facing, which seemed logical to him.

"It's just down there, son," and, with a nod of his head, Patrick indicated the way George was walking. "Hang on! Hang on! I just need to sort out my wellies!" Patrick called. "One minute, son."

The river here was very shallow, which pleased Patrick, his biggest concern in all this gold hunting was putting his son at risk. They both dropped down their rucksacks on the grassy riverbank and Patrick produced the shiny new pan, holding it aloft like a trophy. George held out both hands, ready to receive it. It was decided he was going to be the first to try it out. Patrick plonked himself down on the riverbank and with an overwhelming pride and a love so deep it scared him, he watched his son at work. How could a child so young have such a bottomless amount of confidence and ability to perform any task requested of him?

George waded out a few metres into the river and dipped the green pan below the water. Up came a big pile of water and soil from the sandy bottom. The weight and current flow surprised George, who immediately lost his grip on the gold pan as it was now so heavy. It floated away downstream at an alarming speed.

"DAD, DAD," George was screaming and pointing, and Patrick was startled that something else must also be wrong and not just a dropped bit of plastic. Patrick jumped into the shallow river and waded after the gold pan. The current was fast flowing, but it was only a few inches deep, and the pan kept getting stuck on the river bottom and it ended up only floating a few metres away. Patrick recovered the pan and tilted out the remaining soil. He lifted up the pan and with a big grin he held it aloft, laughing, and shouted back in his son's direction, "Got it."

Still stood in the river, his shoulders dropping and whilst looking down, George started softly crying. Patrick walked back towards his son and still smiling said, "Aah son it's OK, it was an accident, we got it back." With an almighty hug, Patrick lifted his son into the air with a show of affection he wanted the whole world to see. Patrick was heartbroken that his son was upset. George let his cheek fall onto his dad's shoulder but after only a few seconds George wriggled slightly, an indication he was OK now and wanted to be put back down.

"Sorry, Dad, I thought I'd lost the pan," George blurted out, still with a low bottom lip. The last few tears had dried up. More shock than anything Patrick thought, he will be OK. "I love you, son, with all my heart. It's OK, it was heavy, that's all. Come on then," Patrick said enthusiastically, handing the gold pan back to George with a big smile. "This is the one, a big gold nugget in this one." Patrick waded back to the bank to take up his spectator's seat on the grass. He anticipated that they could be here for some time.

George's smile and contagious enthusiasm quickly returned, and he grabbed the pan with gusto. He positioned himself about a metre from the riverbank, in about four inches of water, and he leaned over to dip the pan into the river bottom for a second time.

"Just a bit of soil, that's all you need, son," Dad added unnecessarily as a reminder at the same time as his son lifted up the pan with a small amount of dark soil in it from the riverbed. As the youth so often do, George picked up the technique of swilling the pan around very quickly and within seconds he had swilled the majority of the excess soil and stones away and out of the pan. With his view from the bank, Patrick thought that the pan was empty. George stood frozen, just staring down at the green pan, and his dad saw that he was trembling slightly. George walked slowly back towards his dad, not lifting his eyes from the prize, he offered up the pan to his dad. There was the remnants of the last few grains of stones and sand. With the biggest grin on his face anybody had ever seen, George's trembling had turned into almost visible shaking.

"Noo," Patrick half screamed whilst looking down into the pan and then immediately looking up. He looked directly into his son's eyes and then back down into the pan, over and over again. "GOLD, that's gold, son," Patrick said, staring at this small oval shape gold flake in the bottom of the pan. A shape that resembled a squashed grain of rice. It was only a few millimetres around, but it was so shiny and unmistakably gold looking, compared to the soil and stones that surrounded it. The world seemed to stop spinning for a moment, and they both just stared into the pan for a few more moments. George was speechless and after a few seconds he asked,

"How much is it worth, Dad?" Repeating the same request several times before Patrick could reply.

"I'm not sure, I'm guessing about £50 pounds with the current gold price," Patrick stated, over pricing this little speck of gold in the pan to compliment his son's enthusiasm, something he would come to regret.

Patrick carefully lifted out the speck of gold with the end of his car key, which is all he could find for the task, and they used a small clean sandwich bag to put it in. The sandwich lunch getting instantly discarded onto the grass. The gold pan now empty and the precious cargo secured away, George was immediately back into the river. Pan after pan of riverbed soil was lifted and swilled around, checked for gold and then what remained in the pan discarded. George was relentless and moved further downstream as he continued his search for more gold. Patrick shouted to his son twice to not go too far.

After a while George walked up and handed his dad the pan. "You want to have a go now, Dad? My hands are cold," George said, at the same offering up his blue-coloured shaking hands to his father. Patrick became immediately alarmed and his fatherly protection head switched on. His son's hands were shaking almost violently with the cold. Frostbite crisis averted, they both sat on the riverbank edge, feet dangling over the side. George was warming his hands inside Dad's coat which he had taken off and put over his son's legs with instructions to keep one hand under the coat at all times.

"So, lunch is served," said Patrick, "you've a choice of cheese and ham or just cheese sandwich." George smiled at his dad and grabbed the packet of custard cream biscuits instead that were also on offer. Melissa had been in no fit state to supply her men with packed lunches for their expedition so Dad had grabbed what he could find in the fridge and cupboards. He had, however, given consideration to a beer photograph opportunity for his up-and-coming Instagram page that he was working on. With the last of his sandwich still hanging out the corner of his mouth, Patrick re-positioned the European beer bottle and glass. He had the Welsh sunshine behind him and the river trickling away into the distance. Patrick took the first photograph with the beer unopened, just next to the glass. He checked the image on his phone. *Awesome!* Patrick thought. He was certain this beer post was going to be a guaranteed minimum of fifty likes, something that he so hankered to achieve. George had become distracted, his hands now warm, and he was climbing the nearby trees. The gold pan discarded on the riverbank.

With numerous beer pictures taken for posting later, it was time to taste the beer.

Oh, my goodness! That's terrible! thought Patrick. *I can't drink that!* He secretly tipped the remaining beer out of the bottle into the grass. He glanced around, checking the location of his son, so he wasn't aware of the beer waste that was going on. Melissa was already disapproving of this beer challenge that Patrick had been set, if she knew he was tipping away some of the beers, she would only moan even more. Anyway, Patrick was content that it was a good use of his time and that he knew he couldn't like every beer listed in the challenge.

*

"Mum! Mum," George shouted, his seat belt off the minute Patrick even touched the handbrake on the car. He flung open the car door and ran for the caravan steps. Family rules meant that no seatbelts were to be removed until the handbrake had been applied. George was already inside the caravan as Patrick lifted the boot and retrieved their rucksacks. It took him a few minutes to remove his wet boots and as he entered the caravan, he could hear his son explaining to his mother how he was going to-buy a drone with the fifty pounds that his dad was going to give him for the gold.

Melissa held up a small, clear sandwich bag and was trying hard to find the gold speck contained within it. Melissa loved her son beyond words, and he loved her back just as much. As he watched them hugging each other, Patrick was beginning to regret the overpriced quote that he had excitedly given for the miniscule speck of gold. Patrick turned his attention to unpacking the rucksacks, taking the wet coat and gold pan out and leaving them to dry on the decking in the sunshine. He then took the two rucksacks to the spare bedroom, which was the junk room in reality. He couldn't stop smiling as he mentally ticked off another father and son adventure and a day he hoped his son would never forget. He also secretly hoped that one day, he could do the same thing again with his grandchildren, maybe even here, in this very same caravan.

CHAPTER 12

A Suitable Supply of Batteries

At the beginning of the week, Debbie had suggested a weekend visit to the family holiday home. However, with his favourite football team playing at home this weekend, David was adamant he wasn't going anywhere. He had apologised to his wife profusely, saying he would make it up to her. For a few seconds, she had hesitated on whether to accept this apology but, still made the decision to take the children away for a couple of days without him. As was normal for a weekend visit, she planned to set off on Friday evening as soon as the kids got in from school.

Debbie was looking adoringly at her two daughters as they moved around the stage. It was a well-attended after-school club and tonight was a full-dress rehearsal. Debbie, struggling with the discomfort of the hard, plastic school chair, glanced periodically around the room. She had hoped that Martin would be here tonight. She *wanted* Martin tonight. On arrival, Debbie had casually checked for him in his usual spot but, alas! No sign of his thick muscular legs or chiselled jaw just yet. However, this was not a surprise. Martin was often late. He also didn't bring his daughter to every class and, very often, didn't stay to watch. Debbie, on the other hand, loved watching her daughters on stage. This evening, however, she was distracted by her thoughts of Martin and what she needed to take with her for the weekend.

Debbie closed her legs tight, squeezing her thighs together in a meagre attempt to distract herself from her cravings. She began to make a mental list of all the clothes she was going to need this weekend in an attempt to take her mind of Martin and everything she was planning to do to him. Her thoughts soon turned to her recent purchases. Her new toys had been discreetly delivered in plain brown boxes. The wonders of anonymous online orders!

Debbie's social media presence was beginning to take over her life. She had plans for her weekend by the sea and was hoping to capture some great photos of herself in her new outfits. She hoped for numerous shots of herself on the beach with the sun and sea in the background. She had even planned her status update. The weather forecast for the weekend looked good. She had learned quite early on those sunny days made for better pictures which attracted more *likes*.

Debbie smelt his aftershave before she saw him. His thick muscular leg pressed very firmly and deliberately up to hers as he sat. Unable to stop herself, Debbie let out a soft groan of pleasure at his touch and her cheeks flushed with anticipation. It took all her willpower to not throw her arms around him and press her lips on his. Martin sat down on the chair to her left and leaned in closely to Debbie. "Alright, Gorgeous?"

His lips almost brushed her ear as he spoke and, as Debbie turned to look at him, he flashed her a sexy welcoming smile. Martin restrained himself from looking directly at her. He had glanced at her as he had taken his seat and still had a mental image of her large, tanned breasts through the top of her open-neck white shirt. He stared towards the stage for a few moments, aware of the other surrounding parents, but he couldn't resist it. He had to sneak another look. The tiny plastic chairs had caused Debbie's skirt to ride up, exposing her tanned thighs. He tried to act as if they were just two normal parents watching their children, and not two adults who were about to embark on a wild, steaming hot affair. They hadn't *actually* done anything yet, but Martin so wanted to take Debbie there and then. He started to fidget uncomfortably in his chair. He crossed his legs to hide his arousal.

Debbie smiled back, taking him all in. She pressed her thigh firmly against Martin in response. Glancing down, she could see Martin's muscles through his suit trousers. What she would give to move her hand across and touch his inner thigh right there and then. Her thoughts spun around her head; desire mixed with a lack of sexual confidence. She doubted that she was capable of still arousing and satisfying a man. She dismissed any negative thoughts. Things had changed. This was the *new* Debbie. The more confident, adventurous, and daring Debbie. Wasn't that how Sharon had described her? Her friend's words rang in her ears and yet her inner thoughts and desires continued to play tricks with her. She stared straight ahead but couldn't focus. She pictured herself kneeling down in front of Martin and unbuttoning his trousers. She had visualised many times how it would be with Martin. Although she had never seen him naked, she knew he would have a lot to offer. She knew that he would have a muscular, hard body and she wanted him right there and then.

"I need to speak to you! It's really important," Debbie whispered, hardly moving her lips. "Wait two minutes then follow me to the disabled toilet." Without giving Martin the chance to reply, she rose gracefully and ambled casually in the direction of the toilets.

The dance classes were well attended, and the music was always way too loud. The hall was packed full of parents on uncomfortable chairs; younger siblings ran around at the back in an attempt to ease their boredom. Fortunately for Debbie, the toilets were tucked well away from the main hall area. She headed straight for the disabled toilet, spotting the 'vacant' sign she relaxed as she approached. She opened the door and offered a casual nonchalant look back over her shoulder. Debbie was confident that no one had followed her and that no one had seen her go inside. Initially, she found herself relieved it was clean and modern but within a couple of moments, she froze, already having second thoughts. Whilst she waited, she looked herself up and down in the mirrors that covered the walls around her. Several times she double checked that she had locked the door. Then she just stood there trembling. She felt as nervous as she had when she had lost her virginity, all those years ago, in the back of a rusty looking Ford Escort!

Once again, Debbie looked towards the mirror to check her appearance and she unfastened another button of her blouse. What the hell! She unbuttoned another. She actually contemplated removing her knickers, something she had seen in a film once; it had turned her on at the time. Her thoughts flashed to her underwear; she couldn't even remember which knickers she had put on this morning.

A knock on the toilet door startled Debbie, too late to check. She slid the chrome latch to the left, and, through the crack of the door, she saw Martin. His eyes immediately fell to her exposed cleavage and Debbie forcibly grabbed his hand, pulling him lustfully into the generous cubicle. Debbie was about to have wanton sex with a stranger, something she had never done in her life.

"Oh my God!" she whispered, pressing her lips onto his. It was the first time Debbie had kissed a man since her breast enhancement. She leaned in hard, her ample breasts almost preventing her from getting close enough to Martin.

Martin responded and kissed her back just as passionately. Within seconds, he had untucked the back of Debbie's blouse. He placed his large, open palm onto Debbie's naked back. She tingled at his touch and her back arched. She groaned, unable to hold back. Debbie's knees dropped a little as Martin unfastened her bra with one experienced twist. Martin guided Debbie and her back was now up against the toilet door. His left hand found the front of Debbie's partially open blouse and he caressed her right breast, searching for her nipple. He moved his lips from Debbie's as he let his mouth trace the outline of her neck, kissing it softly. Through explosive gasps of pleasure, Debbie managed to speak.

"I'm free! David has come out and I want you, Martin! I want you right now!"

Martin's lips found Debbie's mouth again. His hands still exploring her body. Debbie ached to see Martin's body. She had dreamt of this moment so many times. She reached down with her hand and was shocked and pleased at how hard Martin had become in this short space of time. She was also impressed with his size. She pressed firmly with exploring fingers. She fumbled and searched for his zip. Martin dropped his left hand and pulled Debbie's skirt up to her waist. He spun her around, Debbie instinctively leaning forwards. Martin slid his fingers inside the waistband of her knickers, pulling them to one side.

*

Lucy only had five caravans to clean that day, compared to the fourteen units she had had last week during the school half-term holiday. She was pleased the caravan season had peaked for another year and things would now start to get easier for her. Autumn had arrived, it was starting to get cold outside, and the nights were drawing in. The large metal loop of keys jingled as she searched for the key to B22. Key located, she unlocked the door and entered. "Hello, housekeeping," she called out instinctively, just in case. The previous tenants had left all the lights on, and the central heating had been turned up to max. Lucy was pissed off. What was wrong with some people? There was so little regard for the carbon footprint from some of these tourists. Lucy regarded herself as a bit of an environmentalist. She was constantly infuriated at anybody who didn't do their part in protecting the planet. The planet we had been invited to share. She turned off the unnecessary lights and heating and glanced around at the mess. Her first job, the thing she did on every caravan rental clean, was to search the caravan for anything that had been left behind by the previous tenant. Lucy regarded these items as unwanted and, she was, therefore, completely within her rights to claim them as her own. She regarded it as a perk of the job and considered it to be a sort of gratuity.

Years of experience had taught Lucy the hot spots. The bedside table was always a high contender. She checked the master bedroom first. She frequently found items in here, sometimes of great value like a watch or jewellery which she moved on very quickly for cash. Always for cash. Both bedside drawers were empty, but she spotted a phone charger in the socket next to the bed. Crawford would easily give her a couple of quid for that. Next, the bathroom. An almost full shower gel, half a tube of toothpaste, and a toothbrush. Lucy used the toothbrushes to clean the hard-to-reach places of the caravan taps before recycling them. She would resell the shower gel from her cleaning trolley and use the remaining toothpaste for herself at home. Save her the expense of buying any. The lounge was a let-down, just a discarded biro down the back of the sofa. She moved into the kitchen. She would be surprised if there wasn't something in here. On opening the cupboards, Lucy found a half-used box of Oxo cubes, nearly a full litre of virgin olive oil, and one tin of beans. Not bad. Lucy picked up the oil and Oxo and hid them discreetly inside the pillowcase full of dirty laundry. She reached for the can of beans. It was light. Who puts an empty can of beans back in the cupboard? But as she lifted the can, she knew it wasn't a real can of baked beans. She had seen one like this before. It was a can safe, the type you hide things in. Lucy's heart quickened slightly. A warmth of excitement ran through her body. She pulled at the lid of the can and peered inside. In shock, she released her grip and the plastic lid dropped almost silently to the floor. Inside the can were two large, compressed rolls of bank notes, they were reddish in colour. The notes filled the can completely, one roll on top of the other. Lucy knew instantly that they were fifty-pound notes and that there was an awful lot of them.

With her heart racing with anticipation, she grappled to pick up the lid and she quickly deposited the can safe into her pillowcase. She was on edge now and looked nervously out of the caravan window. Her cheeks glowed and she sat down on the sofa for a few seconds to catch her breath. Sitting down, she composed herself and she switched into business mode. That money was now hers. Finders keepers, right? They'll be back for this though, she thought. She moved hesitantly to the door, taking her pillowcases with her. Looking around she switched the lights back on as she left. On hearing an approaching car, she fumbled to lock the door. She ran to the rear of the adjoining caravan and crouched down between the two red gas bottles. Her heart was pounding, and she struggled to control her breathing. From her hiding place, she could see the site manager's grey van come to a stop on the parking space next to the caravan. A blacked-out Range Rover also came to a sudden stop directly behind the van. An enormous bald man climbed out of the Range Rover. He was wearing shorts and she watched as Owen, the manager, lifted a site radio to his lips, as if to speak. Lucy leaned to her left and, without looking down, minimised the volume on her site walkie-talkie with a well-practised click. If she was going to keep the money for herself, it was time to leave. Lucy ran as fast and as quietly as she could.

Knowing the area well, she managed to disappear between the caravans and sheds, making her way to a wooded area that surrounded the site and that would discreetly lead her back home. On her way, she had time to think. She formed a plan in her head. She would tell her boss that she had been unwell today and had gone home early. She would say that she hadn't been inside any of the rentals yet, but that she would make up her cleaning time first thing in the morning. Lucy felt no guilt; she had convinced herself the man she had seen was a drug dealer with more money than sense. If he had nothing to hide, why didn't he just use a bank like everybody else?

*

Gabriella enjoyed the drive through the Welsh countryside en-route to her static caravan. Maybe it was because there was never any traffic on the way into Wales or maybe it was the anticipation of some male attention. She was starting to love this time away from her husband and, unbeknownst to her, Andy enjoyed it just as much when Gabriella was away. Things were working out for both of them, and Gabriella had decided that she was happy with this new arrangement, and she was really enjoying her new life. Little did she know that Andy was just as enamoured with his bachelor weekends of drinking and gambling.

Gabriella had re-arranged the caravan furniture to her liking. Fabian had settled in with a group of likeminded friends of a similar age. Whenever she saw Fabian around the site, he was always with girls; Fabian was just as happy as she was. Having visited barely a week ago, Gabriella had not switched anything off when she had last left. Now the caravan heating was on low which gave the place a warm welcome and the fridge was ready at the perfect temperature. She unpacked the food she had bought on the way and put away into the wardrobe some extra clothing that she had packed for herself. Opening the patio doors wide, she let the warm air and salty sea breeze drift into the caravan.

"I'm going to the slots, Mum," Fabian didn't wait for a reply and disappeared out through the door. Gabriella was alone for the first time since her arrival, and she had a list of things to do. She watched as Fabian turned the corner and headed for the beach. Glancing at the clock, she gave it another fifteen minutes, just in case he had forgotten something. She closed the patio doors and locked the front door. Making sure all the windows were also closed, she made her way into the master bedroom. She locked that door as well and sat nervously on the end of her bed. The conversation Gabriella had had with Debbie on her last visit had played on her mind for days. Debbie had told her, in confidence of course, about a friend of hers on the north caravan site who had made a series of confessions on a recent girl's night out. Apparently, once you had used an adult toy, there was no going back!

Astonishingly, this sex toy idea was an arena which Gabriella had not explored before. Gabriella had also been secretly surprised that Debbie herself hadn't invested in this area until recently. After some serious online research, Gabriella had made various purchases which she was now in receipt of. She was alone, she had a good supply of batteries, and more importantly, she was in the mood.

A few minutes later, Gabriella knew that she had made a good investment. Through heavy breathing and burning cheeks, she had imagined it was Crawford's body next to her in that bed. She placed the vibrator to one side. There were still three more curios to try out, still in their boxes, hidden under clothing in her wardrobe. Gabriella experimented with a couple of her less expensive purchases. She discarded them as a lost cause and, in her frustration, threw one across the room, narrowly missing the mirrored wardrobe. An hour later, with no sign of her son, she took out the final item. This was meant to be the *pièce de resistance* and at £190 she hoped it was worth the hype. Undoubtedly money well spent, she thought as she smiled to herself. She lay still for several minutes. Her feet burning and a flush of pink on her cheeks. She could still picture Crawford's tanned muscular body lying next to her on the bed.

*

Lucy had checked over her shoulder several times on her way home. She had switched off her mobile phone knowing that Owen didn't know where she currently lived. She had moved three times in as many years, a side effect of her hectic lifestyle but she was very happy in her current rented flat. It was on the new estate on the far side of town. Lucy's neighbours were mostly businesspeople who were out all day and kept themselves to themselves. This suited Lucy down to the ground. She closed all her curtains and double locked the front door. She went into the spare bedroom which she used as her office and for storage. An array of mobile phones, mostly iPhones, lay across a desk. She turned each one off, one after the other which Lucy thought wouldn't do them any harm. She rummaged around inside the pillowcase she had brought with her. Her stomach fluttered for a split second when she struggled to locate the can of money, but she soon felt the tin at the bottom of the pillowcase and tipped it upside down to dislodge it. The tin rolled away from the dirty washing as though aware of its own importance. Lucy smiled and stared at the two rolls of notes for a moment before she reached down and picked one of them up. It was weighty and thick in her sweaty palm. Each roll was held together with two wide yellow elastic bands. She ripped them off and let the notes drop loose to the floor. For a few seconds, the money kept its shape before the roll sprung open to reveal a thick band of crisp fifty-pound notes. The gasp she let out caused her to cough slightly. This was a lot of money. Lucy had never seen this amount of cash before in one place. She began to count it. Putting two fifties together she decided to count in piles of one hundred. Lucy soon realised that she would soon cover the entire floor, so she regathered them and began to count out piles of five hundred pounds. Straightening the money as best she could, Lucy smiled as she contemplated just how much was here.

Rather than feeling elated, Lucy actually felt a bit sick as she stared down at just over twenty-seven thousand pounds. She checked it again, at least three times. The fat bloke was going to want his money back and she could be killed in the process. Lucy had seen enough gangster films to realise that she needed to keep her wits about her and launder the money slowly, a little at a time. It was important that she was not seen as someone who had suddenly come into money overnight. She couldn't be flash. She hid the money in various locations around her flat. Some went under the kitchen sink, under the mattress, and some in her knicker drawer. She quickly changed her clothes, threw a hat on her head, and headed to the local off licence to celebrate with just one fifty-pound note in her pocket. She needed to carry out the ultimate test. Was the money real? Lucy knew the shop staff well and had a story prepared for the cashier if she was asked about the bank note. She would say that Owen had included it in her wages. She was only intending to spend a few pounds just to get rid of the big note. Fifty-pound notes were rare around here. She wandered slowly around the store, waiting for the other customer to leave. She approached the till and placed her item on the counter. The shop keeper checked the note on his machine and without so much as a glance, handed Lucy her change. With her tote bag swinging, she glanced over her shoulder a few times before almost running back to her flat with her four cans of beer.

*

The site was quiet tonight, only a handful of regulars in the club bar. With autumn approaching, the wind had been blowing hard for several days. All the *sporty* people, as Debbie called them, were moaning on the site's social media page that they had not been able to go out onto the water for days on their jet skis.

Debbie had been surprised that her eldest daughter, Dani, had actually seemed keen to come to the caravan this weekend. It was nice to spend quality time with all her daughters. Shortly after arriving, Debbie had received a text message from one of the other residents to say that they had seen Dani kissing a rather tall boy in the corner of the arcade. From the description, Debbie had realised that this must be Fabian, Gabriella's son, from the caravan next door. A *Southsider*, thank goodness!

Debbie was still building her online social media pages. It was a lot harder than it looked to build a big online audience. However, little by little, she was increasing her influencer status and pushing the on-line nudity rules to their uppermost limits. Her Instagram page was mostly filled with pictures of her breasts and numerous short video reels of her beginning to get undressed. She had taken on board some good advice to avoid her account from being blocked. She was doing well, and her followers were increasing steadily. Yes, there was a lot of flesh on show but not one nipple on view. Good advice!

Debbie now had five separate Instagram accounts and flicked between them on a regular basis. As well as this, she was also the admin for the underground social media site for the caravan park; a site set up for the south residents only. Debbie had also volunteered to help both Owen and Brynn with their respective social media business presence. At first, Debbie had enjoyed this new responsibility and was very proficient at the task but, after only a few weeks, she had realised she had taken on too much and had told them she would have to charge them £250 a month each if they wanted her to continue. Brynn, on the north side, had said he wasn't bothered and didn't have a budget for advertisement, something Debbie was secretly pleased about. Owen, however, was more than happy for her to help promote the events on the south side. Debbie therefore regularly received messages from Owen with news and site event updates. Debbie would then promptly post this information across the main social media platforms.

Over the last few months, David had made numerous sarcastic comments to Debbie about her excessive mobile phone use. He didn't believe she was setting a good example to their children. Debbie couldn't hold back a grin when she placed £250 in crisp red notes down on the table in front of David, explaining it was one month's wages from just one social media client. David soon changed his opinion on the power of Debbie's mobile phone. He suddenly became very supportive of his wife's new business ventures, even offering to help with some of the photography. Debbie had managed to convince her husband that she was on the verge of earning some real money; she was close now to 100K followers on her main account. Debbie had asked David's thought on her being paid in cash and, as a self-employed painter and decorator, he didn't see this as a problem whatsoever. He was very accustomed to not paying as much tax as he possibly should, and he openly encouraged Debbie to accept cash as often as she could.

Although Debbie was meeting Martin at least once a week, she was already starting to get a little bored with the quick, sometimes unremarkable sex. She wanted more. Sometimes their meetings would only last twenty minutes, and she hadn't been impressed with the choice of his last meeting venue. It wasn't really that good anymore, once the initial excitement had gone. Debbie wanted bigger and better things. She knew she looked good and suggested to Martin that they book a few days away in a five-star hotel. She was prepared to tell her husband the truth. They no longer had any secrets from each other. Debbie planned on telling her daughters that she was having a few girlie days away with her mate. There was no need to confuse matters.

Martin was very excited about these proposed days away with Debbie but hadn't actually got around to booking anything just yet. One day would turn into two until a month had passed and Martin was still no closer to making any enquiries. She was starting to get tired of Martin's lack of organisation. She had decided that, unless Martin upped his end game on tonight's video sex call, her bra wouldn't be coming off and her blouse would remain securely buttoned all the way up to the top.

David had chosen to stay at home for the weekend. He had tickets to watch his favourite football team. He also had a date planned, something to which Debbie was completely oblivious. It was his first date with anybody since he had dated Debbie all those years ago. He was very nervous and had even started to panic now. It wasn't really a date, he kept telling himself. He was just going for a drink with another man. Another man who also happened to be gay. A man who David fancied like crazy – oh, and he was something of a celebrity! David had certainly made himself more appealing over the last few months. In doing so, he had almost completely changed his appearance. He had finally realised the importance of healthy eating and had lost a little weight around his waist just from cutting out the junk food whilst at work. His skin had improved from his new diet, and he had taken to going to the gym with his best friend. David had firmed himself up around his shoulders and had the beginnings of a six-pack. Maybe not a six pack but he was certainly a lot trimmer. His new wardrobe was his finest achievement. Debbie had spent many hours traipsing around the shops and waiting for David whilst he tried on piles of new clothes. Debbie fortuitously used this time to grab a few minutes here and there to work on her numerous social media accounts.

Very recently, Debbie had taken on a new client. A friend of hers ran an estate agent and she had asked Debbie to handle the company's online presence. It was easy money. She literally just had to wait for a notification of a new property being listed for sale. The rest was easy. The only pressure being that she needed to duplicate the new house listing without delay onto the various social media platforms. Sometimes this meant that Debbie had to pull over and spend a few minutes listing a house, whilst sitting on the hard shoulder. All worth it though, when that £250 dropped into her bank account at the end of each month. This was the first time in a long time that she had had her own income and she didn't have to ask David for money.

Conrad was a wealthy, famous actor. He had purchased a brand-new caravan on the south side, near to Debbie and David's caravan. He had selected all the extras, decking, landscaping, outdoor lighting, and seating. News around the site was that it must have set him back at least £150,000. However, Conrad's lifestyle meant he was rarely able to take time out. His acting career took him all over the world and he paid the cleaner to visit his caravan every week just to air the place and have it ready, if ever he was going to visit unexpectedly. Conrad would send Lucy a text message requesting that milk, tea bags, and several bottles of champagne be placed in the caravan for his imminent arrival. One of the reasons for Conrad choosing the site was the proximity of a small airfield on the outskirts of town, ideal for his piloted helicopter. On hearing about Conrad's helicopter, Owen had immediately applied for planning permission for a helicopter landing pad to be built on a disused field on the south site of the park. The planning application was promptly rejected by the local Welsh planning authority, but Owen had a family member on the planning appeals board. He knew he would get permission for his helipad soon enough and it would be exclusively for use by the south residents. Owen had instructed Debbie to keep his social media followers updated on his planning application. He needed to attract the right kind of wealthy park resident. Owen had placed a few traffic cones in the shape of a cross in the middle of the proposed field so people would get the idea of the helipad location.

David and Conrad had become instant friends and had taken several long walks together along the shingle beach. Conrad walking with his hands behind his back, a straw hat pulled down over his forehead. He told David that he loved his visits to the caravan and the secluded nature of the area was a welcome distraction from the emotional drain of being famous. There had definitely been an immediate spark when they met. It had now been several weeks since Conrad's last visit. However, one Saturday morning, Lucy knocked on David's caravan window, post-it notes in her hand. David had been washing the dishes and leaned his hand out of the kitchen window. Lucy thrust the yellow slip of paper through the gap and into his open palm and left without a word. The note just said, 'Phone Conrad!' David stared down at the new mobile telephone phone number scribbled in purple biro. David had, of course, told Debbie. She had suggested that David should send a text message first before a phone call, just to check they were 'on the same page'. After painstakingly observing David write and delete at least seven text messages, Debbie snatched his phone and composed a message herself. She read it out loud and with a nod of approval from David, she clicked the button – *sent*. The date was arranged.

CHAPTER 13

There's a Café at the Top

Charles' second wife had been called Megan. He believed her to be the only real true love of his life. She was a curvy girl, with an ample bust and someone who enjoyed boxing, horse riding, and almost any kind of sport. She had a penchant for tight skimpy clothing and had once spent a lot of money on a permanent all-over laser hair removal; a procedure which had fascinated Charles at the time. Charles thought about Megan often, even now after so many years. After all, they had a son together. Jackson who was now sixteen and shared his time between his parents' houses. The arrangement suited them all. "One family, two homes." Megan would often repeat this mantra to her son. This arrangement meant that Charles needed to speak with Megan fairly frequently and, on occasion, it meant he would also get to see her. This always pleased him. The sexual attraction between them was still very evident.

When they were married, Megan had had a brief drunken affair which had broken Charles' heart. After several unpleasant arguments about it, Megan had eventually moved out. She had ended the affair as promptly as it had started and had begged Charles for forgiveness. At first, he had struggled to come to terms with the possible end of his second marriage but, at the same time, he found it incredibly difficult to forgive her infidelity. It also broke his heart to imagine losing the woman he loved. What made it worse for him was that he had known the man who had ended up in Megan's bed. *His* bed. Charles was not a man who found it easy to forgive and forget. He also had a nasty temper which sometimes got the better of him. The house seemed empty without Megan at home, days turned into weeks, which turned into months. Before Charles really knew what was happening, Megan had left him a voicemail telling him she was moving on with her life. In fact, she had already found a new partner and was now, apparently, very happy. Charles had been floored by this message and had been left completely bewildered. To him, it had all happened in the blink of an eye.

Three years later, Charles married Sharon, who was evidently aware of the flame that still flickered between her husband and *the lovely* Megan. Sharon was always on her guard whenever Megan needed to make contact with Charles. She made sure that Charles was never alone with Megan and Jackson was under strict instructions to also be aware of this and to keep his eye on them both, for his father's sake of course.

Charles often wondered how things could have been so different. It had all ended so quickly between him and Megan; he had never really wanted a divorce. Megan had admitted to making a big mistake. She still genuinely loved Charles. But it was all out of his hands now. Megan had re-married. Life had moved on. Charles became a boxing coach, one of his passions, along with cooking. He was a big man, but he was very fit and flexible and a good instructor, someone who had a natural flair for teaching. He enjoyed his job; he enjoyed his food but all not as much as he enjoyed his beer. Since meeting Sharon, he had constantly carried a little more weight around his mid-rift than he should for a boxing coach. It was in the gym that he had met Sharon, a young, pretty, blue-eyed boxing student. Their first date had been at a local working men's club in the city. They had hit it off and Charles began to feel that life was on the up. Sharon was gregarious and exciting. Charles thought he had hit the jackpot; she constantly instigated sex and seemed completely wild and uninhibited in that department. There was a physical similarity between Megan and Sharon that was certain, the ample bust, suntanned skin, and a boisterous air of spontaneity. He was conscious of these similarities and wondered whether anyone else was aware of them? If they were, they hadn't mentioned it. Not to his face anyway.

Charles was well travelled. This was something that Sharon had found attractive when they first met. The fact that he could cook was a bonus for Sharon. Charles was creative in the kitchen and Sharon was creative in the bedroom. It was a good combination.

Most weekends consisted of time spent as a family at their holiday home. This weekend, however, Charles had made a few alterations to their usual routine, alternative arrangements had been made for the children and it would just be Charles and Sharon. It was unusual for the couple to be alone at their caravan and he had plans for something that, as a couple, they had never participated in before. Instead of the usual weekend caravan schedule – a short walk along the beach, a drunken night in the club house, and bowing down to Sharon's sexual demands – Charles actually had plans to explore the surrounding countryside.

Charles wanted to bring something new to their relationship. Their caravan was sited on the coast of North Wales, a stone's throw from the beautiful Snowdonia National Park. Charles had plans to explore the great outdoors. He had a trek up Mount Snowdon planned for them both. Snowdon was the highest mountain in Wales, with the carpark at the base of the mountain and after all, the car park was only a thirty-minute drive away from their caravan. Unbeknownst to Sharon, Charles had booked a couple of seats on the train to bring them both back down the mountain. He knew this amount of physical exercise would be a challenge for his wife in one go. Sharon certainly seemed to have boundless energy for sex but, when it came to outdoor physical exercise, she never seemed to muster up the same amount of energy or passion. As part of the weekend surprise, Charles had bought Sharon a new rucksack, water bottle, and walking boots, all which he had hidden in the boot of their car.

On the journey to the car park, Charles had to keep reminding Sharon to relax and enjoy the surprise. After all, this was their special time together. Sharon, however, was relentless. "Where the hell are you taking me? This seems like the bloody road to nowhere!"

Charles smiled and reiterated that they were going to have a good time.

"You know what? Apparently loads of people come to this area for the remoteness," Charles glanced over towards Sharon.

"Dirty buggers!" Sharon laughed, her thoughts then drifting to the plentiful opportunities for outdoor sex.

"Is this it?" she asked as they eventually pulled into a very busy carpark.

"It'll be great! I've even bought you some new gear!" Charles was desperately hoping that she would enjoy the day he had planned.

New kit tried on, they set off for the summit. Sharon lagging behind her husband along the footpath and displaying a distinct lack of interest towards the immediate task in hand.

"Seriously, do we actually need to get to the top? I'm bloody knackered."

"Come on! You can do it! We're past halfway!" Charles replied. On hearing Charles' determination to push on to the summit, Sharon started to well up and tears began rolling down her cheeks. Her feet were hurting, and it turned out she had a fear of heights.

"Charles. I'm scared. I can't do it. Oh my God, these boots are killing me!" She perched her bottom on a smooth wet rock and began to undo the shoelace of her right boot.

"Don't take your boot off! Don't ask me why – they say it in all the films! Come on, darling. We're nearly there and I've got a surprise for you at the top." Charles gave his wife a reassuring smile.

"I'm not moving. What surprise? I'm not moving unless you tell me the surprise. Surprise? What surprise? Seriously, I'm not bloody moving unless you tell me!" The look on Sharon's face could have stopped traffic. Charles realised the seriousness of the situation and sat down next to Sharon, his backside half hanging off the edge of the rock seat. He placed a firm hand onto her thigh, lowered his voice, and met her glance.

"It's only a walk, all on paths, we are not climbing a rock face with rope or anything like that. Yes, I should have said but I didn't want to scare you," Charles paused briefly then continued. "We are well past halfway and only just under an hour from the summit." Charles offered a reassuring smile. "We're on a footpath that thousands of people walk every year. People like you and me."

Sharon was looking down at the floor, rubbing her bare red calf. She was clearly not happy!

"It gets a little steeper for a short while but, at the top, there's a café with a proper toilet and everything! *And* I've booked us two tickets on the train that takes us directly back down the hill to our car. So, you don't even have to walk down," Charles smiled. He was so pleased he had actually remembered to book the train.

"*And,* tonight, we're on our own in the caravan. No kids. I've got a couple of bottles of champagne and some beer in the boot. If you're tired later, you can just rest up. I'll do all the work." Charles winked and squeezed her thigh hard. Sharon's mood was clearly lifted. Her thoughts turned to getting to the top, getting down as soon as possible, and then getting her husband into bed. As Sharon got older, her need for sexual gratification had gone through the roof. Fortunately for Sharon, Charles had always managed to satisfy her needs. He was also well-endowed which Sharon believed was the reason he was usually able to pleasure her. Charles needed to brace himself for when they got back to their caravan, she thought. She turned and smiled at her husband and, for the first time that day, she skipped ahead of Charles and continued to make her way along the muddy path.

*

Owen's wife had been nagging him for several months now to do more regarding organised events for their onsite caravan guests. Pam wanted to show the north side that they could organise more cultural and classier events in the clubhouse other than the bingo that they constantly arranged.

"I've booked someone for the last six weeks of the season," Pam informed Owen whilst they were all gathered in the reception back office. Pam had chosen her location and allies well to drop this spending bombshell on her husband.

"How much is it going to cost me?" Owen didn't even look up at his wife. He continued to stare at the spreadsheet for the forthcoming rental caravan bookings.

"Bloody hell, Owen! You haven't even asked who I've booked. You only ever think about the bloody cost!" Pam rolled her eyes. "Anyway, it will add glamour to the site, bring an air of class to the south side *and* improve our professional standing in the local community." Pam spoke with an air of confidence and began spinning around the office, her arms uplifted like she was dancing on a stage.

"How much?" Owen spoke sternly this time.

"And I think we should open up the classes to non-residents," Pam ignored her husband's negativity and turned her attention to the two receptionists who seemed very keen to hear about Pam's plans.

"Introducing Francoise and Claudia!" Pam bowed to her audience. "They are very highly regarded within the ballroom dancing scene. In fact, they've even been world champions. Or maybe it was national champions? Something like that anyway. They're good!" Pam emphasised the word *ballroom dancing* for her husband's benefit. She was very excited about the project, and she had pre-arranged for

Crawford, who was on lawn mowing duty that day, to enter the site office under the pretence he was just looking for something to fix the tractor. As Crawford entered, Pam shouted across to him.

"I've booked ballroom dancing classes to take place in the club house, Crawford. They are going to teach lessons to the residents. What do you think?" Pam said, who was now standing with her arms in a dancing pose with a big grin on her face. Pam secretly knew in advance that Crawford was a skilled and experienced ballroom dancer.

Crawford, dressed in grass-stained overalls, walked directly towards Pam and with slight bow he raised his hands, taking her hands in his and said, "That's a fantastic idea, boss. May I have this dance?"

"I would be honoured, young man," Pam replied, smiling back at Crawford, and she placed her left hand into Crawford's in the correct Waltz position. Exactly in the way he had secretly shown her that very morning. Laying her open palm into Crawford's, she then reached up and held firmly onto his muscular upper right arm. Crawford reached around and placed his right hand onto Pam's shoulder blade, and he guided Pam around the office. Pre-arranged music was now being played from one of the office girls' phones, and they both floated effortlessly around the desks, guided by Crawford's dancing skill set. Crawford made it look easy, but it was actually no easy feat with the office layout, but Crawford managed it with style. The remaining reception staff members cheered and clapped. Pam was shocked at how much she enjoyed the dancing but shocked even more at how sexually stirred inside she had become at the touch of Crawford's firm body. Owen did not look up from his spreadsheet, even when the dancers glided past his chair. He was now looking and researching who had block booked one of his most expensive caravan rentals for a solid six weeks. He became even more alarmed as he was struggling to find any payment details – the payment field just repeatedly said 'See Pam'.

"Where are they staying, these ballroom dancers?" Owen asked.

He was beginning to get a sinking feeling in his stomach. He turned in his chair and was now looking directly at his wife, still in the clutches of one of his better-looking muscular employees. A twinge of jealousy and a little rage started to creep across Owen's cheeks.

"Well, thank you, sir!" Pam gestured a bow to Crawford and, with rosy cheeks and butterflies in her stomach, she turned and skipped across the office floor towards her husband who was sat staring at her from his desk. Pam was shocked at how tingly and alive she felt from dancing with another man. Owen remained seated in his *I'm the boss* black leather chair, still waiting for an answer to his question. As his adoring wife neared, he already felt his resolve weaken. Pam stood directly in front of her husband. He stared at her firm body, emphasised by her tight clothing. He knew he was beaten. Placing both hands on her hips, she switched from business partner into wife mode. She spoke firmly and deliberately to allow everyone in the office to hear what she had to say.

"Look! You never organise anything. *Ever!*"

Opened mouthed, Owen lifted his chin in protest, but Pam thrust a finger in his direction to silence him as she continued.

"I've booked two professional ballroom dancers for six weeks. They're going to live rent-free in one of our premium rental vans. It won't cost us anything apart from that lost rent revenue. They keep the dancing fees they charge. I was lucky to get them. They had a cancellation from their regular booking on a site down in Pembrokeshire – the owners found asbestos in the club house roof."

Owen knew he was beaten, and he found it impossible to argue with the woman who had stolen his heart all those years ago. He dropped his shoulders and looked away, turning his attention to the calculator on his desk. He began to work out how much six weeks of lost rent was going to add up to.

*

Francoise and Claudia, *aka* Phil and Jenny, had been professional ballroom dancers almost all their life. They had won numerous titles in Scotland before travelling the ballroom competition circuit all over the world. They had won copious amounts of trophies and medals and had built a formidable reputation. Things had changed unexpectedly after Jenny had taken a bad fall in the semi-finals of the 2008 Detroit Ballroom Dancing World Championship. Whilst attempting an under-turned spin in the Cha-Cha-Cha segment of their new dance routine, Claudia, feeling the pressure, had mistimed the pivot. She had completely failed to catch her partner's outstretched hand and had fallen badly. Being rushed to hospital, Claudia had undergone emergency surgery. She had been bed bound for several months with a complicated broken hip and had never really recovered from it. She had also never regained her confidence to compete professionally again. Phil, devastated from not winning the competition, spent a few days alone in his hotel room before eventually visiting the hospital. As a couple and best friends, they drifted apart and Phil's contact with Jenny became less and less as each week passed.

Arrogantly Phil continued to blame Jenny for the missed dancing opportunities. Almost effortlessly he found a new dancing partner and he picked up his pursuit of ballroom dancing notoriety. Weeks turned into months without any contact whatsoever with Jenny, as Phil threw himself into his dancing with a talented young partner who was half Jenny's age. He racked up numerous competition wins, medals and trophies were abundant. Phil became financially stable after winning gold and a big money prize pot in Australia, a competition sponsored by a blossoming social media company. Things were good for Phil, and Jenny was far from his mind.

No sooner had Phil's new young dance partner appeared than she disappeared. She had been photographed all over the world and was now regarded as a better dancer than Phil himself and unbeknown to

Phil she was a YouTube sensation. With little warning she thanked him for the dancing experience and all he had taught her but said their time together had concluded and she was moving on to greater things with a younger dance partner and her own TV show. Overnight, Phil's world-famous standing seemed to disappear, he was now a lonely old man and a washed-up former ballroom dancing champion.

Without a dance partner, Phil rattled around in his big *paid for* empty house in London. Months had passed and he was aware that he was drinking far too much. One morning's cough and a spit into the sink Phil saw the colour of blood and he knew he needed to take back control of his life. Three weeks dry and on a bright spring morning, he finally found the courage to drive down to Plymouth and knocked on Jenny's front door.

The last few years had been hard for Jenny, and they had taken their toll on her appearance. First the injury and then being dumped for a younger partner, Jenny's self-esteem had hit rock bottom. To escape her loneliness and self-resentment, she also had sought solace from the bottle. She covered her tracks well, often sipping Vodka from an *Evian* bottle. Jenny was a functioning alcoholic with just the odd, silly vocal outburst making its way to the surface. Phil had missed Jenny more than he had realised and after several weeks of living in each other's pockets they had become best friends again, Jenny confessing all regarding her additional drinking. Phil decided he could tolerate Jenny's drinking, he felt partly responsible for her addiction after leaving her when she was injured and when she needed him most. The old magic was reignited and what followed was years of dancing and celebrity performances all over the world. They easily took the sideward step into teaching ballroom dancing after accepting a contract on all-expenses-paid cruise around the world. All they had to do was host a few one-hour ball room classes for the on-board passengers twice a week, the rest of the time was their own. And so was born the Francoise & Claudia Ballroom Dancing Company.

Years of teaching and working on cruise ships and hospitality venues around the world had given Francoise and Claudia invaluable experience in teaching ballroom. Weeks in advance, with military precision, a bundle of glossy posters were delivered to the caravan site. A buzz was generated around the caravan park. Building anticipation led to numerous questions being asked on reception; people wanted to know the dates, the times, even the type of dancing clothing required.

Crawford had systematically hung the posters all over the park and in several key locations in the local town. Phil and Jenny had previously charged £5 per person for an hour's ballroom instruction but more recently they had discovered a secret weapon to fill the dance floor. They decided not to charge men to attend their dance classes. For years, they had struggled to fill the dance floor with any men. The women were always very keen to learn to dance, but they struggled to get their partners interested. The price had been raised from £5 per person to £10 per woman. Men could dance for free, and no money had been lost. Phil believed that this new advertising would make it easier for the women to persuade the men in their life to come along. At first Jenny feared that it was sexist, printing this on their posters, but after the system worked, and no one complained, they carried on. Over the years one or two people had made reference but after explaining their way of thinking and the fact that nearly all of the men actually loved the dancing, they thanked them for getting them to try it in the first place. Most said they wouldn't have tried it if it hadn't been free to attend.

"Do I really have to, darling? I can't dance for toffee," Clifford pleaded with his wife. Alison didn't even bother replying. She wanted to learn to ballroom dance and Clifford was joining in whether he liked it or not. If he didn't, then he wasn't getting any sex ever again. It was a simple as that and she made that very clear to him. Alison had spent a lot of time recently wondering what other men would be at the dance classes, she hoped she would get the chance to dance with different partners. She'd already chosen her outfit; high heels, denim shorts, and a blue bikini top – after all, that's what she wore day in day out, why change to go dancing?

*

Crawford and Gabriella had been texting each other constantly about this afternoon's ballroom class. Crawford had already had the backing from Pam that he could attend classes during work time. Gabriella, who was very interested in dancing, had insisted that they should each arrive at the club separately. She wanted it to appear as if she was on her own and would have to end up dancing with Crawford as he would also be without a partner. That had been the plan, but it had all fallen apart when Gabriella had forgotten to close her caravan bedroom window a couple of days ago. Crawford had popped round to *fix a leaking tap* after receiving a text from her letting him know that she was alone. Her husband was not with her, and Fabian had gone out with his friends. Over the months of their affair, Crawford had eagerly obliged in Gabriella's many fantasies, and she had responded positively to his touch, on this occasion, rather vocally. It was during this one occasion that Gabriella had expressed a desire to try something new and she wanted to have her hair pulled during their love making. Crawford, with a firm handful of Gabriella's hair, at the same time positioning her over the kitchen table, Gabriella was in the throes of her orgasm when she had repeatedly screamed Crawford's name out loud. As a result, it appeared the entire caravan site was now aware that Crawford had been paying regular visits to Gabriella's caravan when her husband, Andy, wasn't there. It was also perfectly clear that he was there for a completely different type of maintenance check!

Charles had made it crystal clear to Sharon that he wouldn't be learning to dance, under any circumstances whatsoever, and there was nothing she could do to persuade him. He knew Sharon wasn't going to go without sex. What else could she do to him? He had made it categorically clear, albeit politely, that ballroom dancing wasn't for him. Sharon had been relentless, but she knew she was onto a losing battle and, in desperation, had even asked Jackson to go dancing with her.

"I think it would be very cool dancing with your step-mum," Sharon said to Jackson one evening but without looking him in the eye. She stared at the floor and made a feint attempt at trying to get the sympathy vote.

"I am sixteen years old. That question is not even worthy of a reply," Jackson said and walked away to lock himself into his room and away from his crazy step-mother.

The day of the first dance class arrived and Sharon asked Charles once more as she was exiting their caravan.

"Oh, darling PLEASE come with me. I don't want to go on my own, I will be the only one there on my own."

"I love you with all my heart and I will do anything for you BUT not ballroom dance," Charles replied and looked directly at his wife.

"Just walk me to the club then," Sharon requested.

"No because A, I'm not drinking today and B, you will ask me again as soon as we are there. I'm not dancing." Charles was getting agitated at the repeated requests, but he wasn't angry with his wife, he secretly had a twinge of regret, but he had set out his stall and he was sticking with it. In complete desperation, as Sharon walked out of the caravan, she made reference to their wedding vows, but it didn't receive a reaction. Sharon fled the caravan with a raised bottom lip and over exaggerating the door closing, not slamming it but enough for her husband to realise she wasn't a happy bunny. She walked alone down the hill towards the club house. En route, she saw several men lagging behind their partners as they walked, everyone was heading in the same direction.

"Hello. Welcome, welcome!" Claudia greeted each guest as they entered the club house in a respectful single file. Her petty cash tin was set up on a nearby folding table and her open palm held out firmly to everyone who entered.

"That's ten pounds please, thank you and you, young man, are free, get in there you." Claudia was offering each guest a few seconds of her time with a smile before looking beyond them to the next person in the line.

"Ten pounds is what we charge for the hour's dancing instruction, but your husband is free, go on give it a go, see how you get on. I promise you will have a great time." She sometimes had to persuade the odd couple who had wandered in to see what was happening, after seeing the long queue of people entering the club house.

Francoise was working the floor of new dancing recruits. After many years of experience, he had learnt to spend a maximum of thirty seconds with each couple before moving onto the next. He seemed unflustered at the repetitive questions thrown at him, answering each one in turn and adding a skilful personal touch to each of his answers.

"Hi, Sharon!" Debbie beamed as she walked towards her friend. Sharon's eyes immediately dropped towards Debbie's excessive cleavage that seemed superfluous at a ballroom class. Sharon was now glad her husband had stayed away.

"Hi!" Sharon smiled over her shoulder at David. David wasn't looking. He was busy shaking Francoise's hand and discussing the future class and his willingness to participate and learn.

"I couldn't keep him away!" Debbie nodded towards her husband. She was proud that she was here doing something with her best friend. "No Charles?" Debbie enquired, looking around the room. Sharon didn't reply but shook her head with raised eyebrows and offering her sad face.

"Hello everybody! Good evening!" Claudia's voice boomed loudly over the loudspeaker, followed by a little unwelcome microphone feedback. She was wearing a red glitzy evening gown with matching heels. Everyone smiled as she unashamedly twirled into the centre of the dance floor. Her left hand reaching out to her side, her right holding a silver wireless microphone to her lips. Her enthusiastic smile lit up the room.

CHAPTER 14

The Telephone Call

For the umpteenth time that day, Charles checked his phone. He was uneasy but, on seeing that there were no missed calls or messages, he relaxed a little. He assured Charles he would be checking his test results thoroughly and would telephone immediately if he had any concerns. He assured Charles this would be before six o'clock. It had gone six. It was ten past. Charles tried to turn his mind to other things, but he had a terrible gut-wrenching feeling that there was something wrong. He walked into the bathroom and locked the door behind him. Sharon was out at her ballroom dancing. The class finished at 4 p.m. so he assumed she must have gone for a drink. The children were down at the beach. There was no real reason to lock the bathroom door, but Charles felt that it was the right thing to do. He unfastened the first couple of buttons on his jeans and, with his left hand, reached down to his groin area. Charles knew exactly where it was; this hard lump to the left of his genitals had been there now for several weeks. He thought it was getting bigger, but he may have been imagining that. The mind does funny things when you are worried. Several days ago, he had attended a biopsy appointment at the hospital. Now he just needed the results of the test. The good news, which Charles tried to focus on, was that the doctor had thought it was 'just a cyst'; a 'harmless fluid-filled sack'. Charles' eyes had brimmed with tears on hearing this news from the doctor, a personable man with many years of experience in these matters. All Charles could think about was his family and the endless list of things he still wanted to do with his life. He had been on edge now for several days and now six p.m. had passed and the call had not come. *No news is good news, isn't that what they say?*

"Bloody hell!" The shrillness of the ringing phone startled Charles who jumped, banging his arm on the cupboard door. He couldn't reach his mobile. His trouser pockets were at an angle and folded over the top of his legs. Panicking, he attempted to untangle the phone from the inner lining of his pocket. "Don't hang-up! Don't hang-up!" Charles flipped the phone over and saw a red dragon on the screen. Sharon's calling card. Christ! What was wrong with him, he thought? His heart was racing. His palms were sweating. Charles slid the screen bar to answer his wife's call. He placed the phone to his ear and took a deep intake of breath.

"Hello darling," he said. There was a blanket of loud background music and general noise.

"I'm in the clubhouse! Everybody's here! You coming? Come on, my big precious lump of man love!" Shrieks of laughter could be heard from the people around her. Charles heard shouting. It sounded like his good mate, Spider.

"I'm on my way," he replied and ended the call. He sat silently on the edge of the toilet seat; his trousers still undone. All alone, he wasn't in any rush to do anything. He sat and stared at his phone. He definitely wasn't in any rush to go to the clubhouse. Standing up and dressing he decided he was going to make a few changes in his life. Rushing around and singing to Sharon's tune was going to be one of the first things to go. Charles loved his life and family and regarded himself as a very lucky man, but today, today he wanted to draw a line in the sand. He would take more care of his body. He would cut down on the beer and eat more fruit and vegetables. He also had a long mental list of adventures to tick off. Not a bucket list as such, but adventures to do sooner rather than later. Loose ends in his life.

Charles washed his face, ironed a fresh shirt, and, eventually ready, he set off walking. Calmly he headed in the direction of the club, taking in all his surroundings, noticing things he hadn't noticed before. As he made the turn to walk down the hill to the joint site bar, he stopped and gazed across to the sea. The sun was setting in the distance. It was a perfect straight line as it disappeared over the horizon of the still, silent ocean. Charles marvelled at this spectacular sight, his thoughts drifting to his eldest son. He had spent many evenings in Jackson's company watching this familiar scene. For countless years, he had led Jackson to believe that there was a green flash just as the sun set but you could only see it if you looked really carefully. Charles had seen this in a movie; however, he had convinced Jackson that it really was a thing, albeit a very rare thing. So, every night, they had watched the sunset together and, if they were lucky, they would see the green flash.

Charles carried on walking, but something was different, Charles knew it. He walked with a calm gait, smiling and acknowledging everyone he saw. Quietly, he made his way towards the club. On reaching the door, he checked his phone one more time. He still had a full signal and yet, he had not received a call from his doctor. Everything was going to be OK.

*

"Please, come over!" Gabriella spoke softly into her phone. "Crawford, I need you, right now." A pause followed.

"I'll try," Crawford said and then immediately ended the call. Gabriella sat on the end of her bed staring despondently at her phone's black screen. The door was closed, and the caravan suddenly felt cold and empty.

This was a new feeling for Gabriella. Never before had she had to practically beg a man for sex. She stood and looked in the mirror, turning slightly to look at the reflection of her bum. She still considered herself to be desirable. She definitely still had her looks. Why was she having to beg? She put in a call to her husband.

"Hello, darling, how are you? What's that noise?"

"It's just the radio, I'm in the car. I'll be with you in an hour or so." The line was silent for a few seconds. "Hello? I can't hear you. Are you still there?" No response. Seriously, what was it with the phone signal in Wales? Surely some phone company would have managed to find a solution for getting a decent signal strength in the Snowdonia Mountains, Gabriella thought to herself.

Crawford disappeared from her mind, and she busied herself with tidying her caravan, even though the place was spotlessly clean. She was getting sex that evening after all, not with her first choice but her husband would have to do. She had already decided that sex tonight would be on her terms. Thank God for the perks of married life! Gabriella was alone. Fabian hadn't joined her at the caravan this time. He was getting older now and had plans of his own. She had never experienced time on her own before. Maybe that was the weird feeling she had had experienced earlier. But she didn't think so.

A gentle flurry of taps sounded on the kitchen window. It was Crawford. That was his signal. He was outside! Gabriella had forgotten about her call to him. And now Andy was on his way. She should have felt panicked. She should have felt sick but as Crawford slid open the patio door, she felt nothing but excitement and lust. She had trained him well. Gabriella had often told Crawford exactly what she wanted and how she wanted it. It turns out that Crawford had listened attentively.

As he stepped into the small kitchen area, he smiled. Unbuttoning his shirt, he stared into Gabriella's eyes and walked towards her. His shirt still on his shoulders, she could make out the outline of his chest in the lights of the candles she had lit ready for her husband. He was close to her now as he unbuckled his belt. He grabbed

Gabriella firmly around her waist and pulled her towards him, pressing his lips against hers with some force. Leaning into her, he ran his hand over her bottom, and gave it a squeeze. He pushed her up against the kitchen cupboards. Gabriella resisted. This was all part of the game. Fighting to keep her mouth covered with his, he lowered her bra straps and exposed her breasts. She pulled to the right quickly in an attempt to refuse to be kissed and repeatedly saying "I'm a married woman" but with no real meaning. Crawford was trained to be firm and carry on regardless of what she said aloud, instructions she had given him over the recent weeks.

"He's on his way! He'll be here in less than an hour," Gabriella gasped as she began to unbutton her tight jeans and peel them off over her feet. Crawford lowered his eyes and watched her beautiful slim legs come into view.

"Then we need to be quick." His hand on her waist, he turned Gabriella around and passionately kissed the back of her neck. He took a handful of her long hair in his left hand, gently twisting it he steered her head forwards. He continued exploring her body with his free hand, his kisses continued to rain down on her exposed, long, sleek neck. Yanking her knickers to one side, almost tearing at them, the way he had been schooled, he entered her. Gabriella's entire body rippled with pleasure at his invasion. Crawford didn't wait for any further instructions, and Gabriella was unable to give any. The only sound to be heard was the sound of their bodies beating against each other. Slowly, Gabriella began to whimper and she pushed back to meet Crawford as she attempted to direct his work. But she knew it was too late. She had already come.

*

Charles had arrived at the club and had easily located his wife, sitting amidst the rest of the gang. Greeting everyone in turn, Charles squeezed through the circle of bodies and chairs and leant in to kiss his wife lovingly on her cheek.

"Hello, darling!" He squeezed her hand gently as he spoke and looked directly into her eyes. She stared back at him with a nervous smile. "I love you," he mouthed.

Even though there wasn't enough room along the bench seating, Charles was adamant he was going to sit next to his wife. Previously, he would have plonked himself wherever there was an empty seat but tonight, he needed to be near Sharon. He didn't quite know why.

"Ahh!" Melissa said, sitting next to Sharon, not missing a trick. She glanced over at her drunken husband, wondering when he had last made a public show of affection towards her. She turned to look away from him, a loud slurp of her straw indicating that her gin and tonic had come to an end.

"Drinks, anybody? It's my round," Charles announced with an air of authority as he smiled at the noise from Melissa's straw. He raised his right hand and headed for the bar. He tossed his head back as he walked. It was his way of a joke; his infamous imitation of a tour operator giving the signal for the men to follow him to the bar. David jumped up. Placing a hand on either side of Charles' hips, he started singing to the tune of the imaginary Conga.

"Dah, dah dah. Dadadadadadada!"

Charles joined in with an exaggerated swagger of his hips as he led the precession forwards. Patrick, still seated, raised his hands in the air, alternating each in a desperate attempt to keep with the rhythm of the familiar tune. He had consumed far too many drinks and knew his limitations. Now was not the time to stand, let alone attempt a dance.

"Anything else?" The dull drone of the bartender interrupted the men's banter.

"You alright, Owen?" Charles asked with a smile. "You don't seem your usual self?"

"Sorry, buddy! Just people letting me down last minute. Leaving me short staffed." Owen took the two twenty-pound notes from

Charles' hand and turned to face the till.

"One for yourself!" Charles shouted across to Owen. Owen raised his chin in acknowledgement as he concentrated on how to operate the till. As the south site manager, Owen felt that he had full responsibility for managing the club bar. Legally, it was a duty and responsibility he was supposed to share with this brother, but Brynn showed little interest in the club house management. His only contribution was organising the occasional bingo event, which he would spring on his brother at short notice. The lack of business acumen was another thing the brothers argued over. Since the death of their parents, they were at the point of hardly speaking due to the park split and last-minute social events. Owen had repeatedly requested to be given more notice so that he could organise extra bar staff and amend the barrel order for the draymen and complete the long list of other tasks that were required to be completed to run a busy bar. On many occasions, they had almost come to blows over this.

Apologetically, Charles again squeezed in between the tables and chairs on his return from the bar. People lurched forwards to grab their fresh drinks to prevent them from being knocked off the tables as he wobbled along the bench next to his wife. He raised his glass to his lips and looked around the group with a smile. A smile fixed many misdemeanours. Charles enjoyed this group of friends and today, he was a lucky man. Putting down his drink, Charles called over to his friend. Over the noise and bustle of the room, Charles had to attract his friend's attention, Charles shouted to Spider loudly.

"Hey, Spider! Have you heard from Frank and Sylvia lately, how are they getting on?" Before Spider had chance to reply, a loud screech ricocheted around the room.

"What the *hell* are you drinking?" Sharon lifted up the tall, delicate glass that her husband had placed down on the table, and she stared at the clear effervescent liquid. Two slices of lemon floated lifelessly either side of a striped red and white paper straw. Sharon looked quickly around the group for support at her mocking of her husband's beverage choice.

"Soda water," Charles exclaimed proudly. He was hoping his tone portrayed an air of normality.

"Are you alright, mate?" Patrick leaned in towards his friend, a serious expression on his face. The group fell silent. Something was clearly wrong.

"I'm okay. Honest, I'm alright! I had a few too many yesterday, that's all. I'm still feeling a bit hungover." Charles forced a smile as he looked around the group. "Seriously, I'm fine. Stop staring at me!" Sharon shook her head in exasperation and carried on her conversation with Melissa, almost irritated by the diversion. They were still discussing a plan to recruit more dancers to bolster the ballroom lessons. As they chatted, they both took it in turns to glance in Charles' direction and then down at his lifeless soda water.

"I just love my ballroom dancing so much. All I need is a decent partner!" Sharon said aloud and gave her husband a quick dig in the ribs. She had been trying to persuade Charles into becoming her dancing partner for months. She wasn't ready to give up just yet. Everyone in the bar heard Sharon, Charles understood the meaning of the dig in the ribs from his wife. With a smile he enquired anyway to its meaning so he could invite the question. He was also hoping it would distract everyone's concerns away from his drink choice.

"What was that for, my bundle of love?"

"You know *exactly* what that was for, Charlie boy!" Sharon was aware of her audience now. "Making me go all on my own. Me, the only woman there without her husband for moral support." Sharon tilted her head to one side, pouting her lips and widening her eyes in a sorrowful puppy dog manner.

"Okay! Point taken. I'll come with you next time. I'm a shit dancer though. You won't be asking me again!" Charles flashed a smile at his wife and, out of sight of everybody else, under the table he placed his hand on Sharon's bare inner thigh, probing and searching the opening of her shorts with his little finger.

"Will you? Seriously?" Sharon turned quizzically to her husband. Charles nodded repeatedly, smiling, and gave her thigh an extra squeeze. Ever so slightly, Sharon adjusted her posture in response to Charles' touch. She said nothing. Her gaze now fixed ahead of her.

Charles was surprised at how much gratification he received from this very discreet and yet so very public sexual act. He found himself becoming uncomfortably aroused. His ill-fitting jeans constraining the signs of his erection.

"They're in Chamonix at the moment," Patrick broke the silence around the table. "Frank and Sylvia. You asked where they were." Patrick began to relay the recent conversation he had with his friend, the numerous emails they had exchanged. Holding out his phone, Patrick proceeded to show Charles the few photographs that his friend had sent him. He went onto explain that Frank took hundreds of photographs on his travels but that he kept them all on his laptop and he wasn't into sharing any of them. With only a few photographs to share, Spider told the story of how Frank had been livid recently at being charged the same price as a coach on his trip through the channel tunnel over to France. Evidently, Frank had argued at length with the French authorities, saying that there were only two people in his motorhome; it wasn't the bloody *National Express*, which carried 50 people on a coach. Frank had attempted to back up his argument with facts regarding wear and tear of on-board facilities and presented toilets occupancy as one example.

"Well, it's his own fault for having such a big one!" Debbie said, in an attempt to lighten the mood. "Lucky Sylvia, I say!" and everyone laughed.

*

Following Frank's recent event, Melissa had made plans for her own campfire on the beach. Her sons, Connor and George, had taken to the task they had been set with gusto. Searching the entire beach, they had already gathered a considerable pile of driftwood in preparation of the campfire, and they had hidden it amongst the rocks on the beach. Melissa had also been busy organising drinks and buying sausages and marshmallows. There was no need for folding chairs on their site; it was a rocky beach and there was always a plentiful supply of large stones to sit on. With their children already on the beach waiting to light the campfire, Patrick and Melissa set off on the short walk from their caravan to find them.

"Patrick, there. Slow down! Slow down!" A startled Melissa said then casually tugged on her husband's arm as she gestured to a couple who were walking ahead of them also towards the beach.

"There! See that couple in the dodgy, matching outfits? I know them!" Melissa lowered her voice and leaned in close to her husband. "From *work*." This last comment immediately gained Patrick's attention. He loathed any crossover with his private life. This was his special place. A chance to escape from it all. It had happened only once before. That time, he had been lucky. They had all just left a restaurant in the nearby town. As they walked down the street, Patrick recognised a man walking towards them. Patrick had arrested him on several occasions for burglary. *Bloody hell*. The man would have recognised Patrick, without a doubt. Patrick wouldn't have minded so much if he'd been on his own, but he had Melissa and the kids with him. On that occasion, without saying a word, he allowed his family to carry on walking. Patrick just stood completely still at the side of the street, putting into practice his surveillance training. He didn't move a muscle. He didn't even blink. He just stood and pretended he was looking in a shop window. This guy walked straight past. Not even a glance. Fortunately, Patrick never saw him again.

This was another of those moments. Patrick was tense and he

switched to being very serious. He needed to know who these people were and why they were walking around his caravan site. He hoped that he hadn't arrested them on some occasion.

"Stop! Let them walk on," Patrick instructed Melissa in a calm manner. The couple were walking hand in hand towards the beach, directly ahead of them.

"It's the married couple. From the rooftop flat," Melissa whispered to her husband, and she smiled as she recalled watching the CCTV footage after they had both been arrested.

"Who?" Patrick asked, "Who do you mean?"

"The two doctors. Remember? They'd rented out that flat they owned, and he had put in that hidden camera," Melissa said. "Remember, when he was interviewed, he had said it was to protect his investment against damage from tenants? But there had only been one CCTV camera and it had been hidden in the smoke detector in the main bedroom." They were both now standing still, waiting for the couple to walk on.

"He'd been watching the new tenants having sex!" Melissa said, giggling. "He was a doctor for God's sake! What the hell was wrong with him?"

"Will they know you?" Patrick asked, his tone solemn.

"I imagine so. I arrested the wife; I can't remember her name. She hadn't actually been part of it, but she was the joint homeowner. She was mortified when she found out what her husband had been doing. Poor woman."

"Well, looks like she's forgiven him." Patrick watched them walking away, turning right along the beach, still hand in hand. "What did he get?"

"Two years, suspended," Melissa said, unremarkably. "But he was struck off."

"They've gone. Come on. Let's get this fire started." Melissa pulled ahead of Patrick and turned left along the beach. She could see her youngest son, George, waving in the distance. She could also see Connor dropping down a big bundle of firewood at their chosen spot on the beach.

*

Charles had asked Jackson to sort him out a laptop. It hadn't been a secret, but Charles had asked his son when Sharon hadn't been around. Jackson had done his research and had ordered his dad a suitable device. When it had arrived, he had set it all up for him. Charles was aiming to write a few songs, or his memoirs, or even a few poems; he wasn't sure. He just knew that he had an inner desire to write, and it had been on his mind for some time. This desire to complete new projects had come crashing to the surface following his recent health scare which he had still managed to keep from everyone. He hadn't wanted people to worry unnecessarily. More importantly, he didn't want people to treat him differently.

His first masterpiece was a song. He was aware that it needed more work, but the words had come easily to him. It had been odd. When he had first sat down to write, his thoughts had drifted to his first wife, Beatrice. Charles read back over the lyrics. It didn't really reflect his relationship with Beatrice and how it ended, but it helped him to identify his feelings about the child he had never known. The son or daughter who was living somewhere in this world. The son or daughter he had never spoken of. To anyone. Only his mother had known about Beatrice and the baby, but she had since passed and had taken his secret to the grave. Charles had never told anybody else, and, over the years, it just became too difficult to talk about. Charles watched his eldest son. Somewhere, there was another son or daughter out there. They would almost be an adult now. An adult who could potentially come knocking on his front door at any time. Charles actually hoped they would. Then the secret would be out.

He stared at the words he had typed on his screen.

When you ran you left us, and we don't want you back.

You left our home, your things, your clothes, and you haven't been back.

You left our son without a mother, and he will never bounce back.

You said goodbye, you left no note, no message and you never said why.

Our son has his dad, a dad that stays.

A dad that cares and a dad that will never say goodbye.

You found a new man; you found a new life, but you made no time for the son in your life.

I leave our son alone in his bedroom at night, I can hear him crying and I know he is there.

I stand outside his bedroom door, as a dad I am unsure what to do, he just wants his mum to be there.

I start each day being positive and strong, but my son wakes and asks for his mum and then all my strength is then gone.

He has started school with new uniform and shoes, but you still don't ring and still you don't show.

I hear things about you from family and friends. I hear about your travels and your lovers and the things that you send.

He was pleased with himself and his first attempt at being a writer. He hadn't written anything since leaving school, other than the occasional birthday card. He hoped this would be the first of many new projects. He pushed the laptop into the middle of the table and pulled the lid towards him. It was complete coincidence that his laptop closed at the exact moment that Sharon walked into the room.

"What you up to?" Sharon planted a kiss on the top of Charles' head. He was in her good books today. He was always in her good books after they'd had sex. Sharon had instigated it this morning, but Charles had been happy to lie there quietly, letting Sharon run her fingers up his inner thigh.

"I'm writing a book," Charles said, the idea of writing a book just coming to him at that very moment.

"Writing a book? You dickhead! Fancy a cuppa?" Sharon laughed as she clicked the button on the kettle.

CHAPTER 15

Cash on the Side

Tony was born in the local area and was a very proud Welshman. He was around forty-five years old, no one was sure of his correct age, not even him after being born on a rural farm in the Welsh valleys. He wasn't a chatterbox, and he would at all times do his best to keep himself to himself. On the odd occasion he actually ventured out of his caravan, he would, more recently, be wearing a large pair of over-ear headphones. This would allow him to walk straight past anyone who attempted to engage him in pointless conversation; he would just pretend he couldn't hear what they were saying and be on his way, sharpish.

Growing up in the local area, Tony's school attendance was not as good as it could have been. He would sometimes be missing from his classroom desk for days on end, but it was a computer-free era and where a poorly scribbled note of absence (written by your best mate) was all that was needed to satisfy any teacher. Tony had only loved one lass in his village, but sadly things hadn't worked out, and after a long, slow, drawn-out divorce, she had got the house and Tony had ended up living in the family caravan. Fifteen years later, he was still here in a static caravan on the north side of the caravan park.

There were rumours on site that Tony was not short of money, after several inheritance windfalls falling in his favour. Other residents had taken note that Tony seemed to be replacing his caravan for a newer, upgraded model more often than anyone else on site. As a permanent resident, Brynn would occasionally ask Tony to help him with odd jobs around the site. It was clear to onlookers that they were close; a friendship going back many years. Over the years, he had occupied numerous different caravan pitches, in different caravans. He wasn't too fussed. If Brynn offered him a good deal on an available caravan for sale, he was able to pack up and move his worldly belongings within a few hours. His old caravan, with the use of a crane, would then be lifted off and towed away from the site, never to be seen again. His old spot would then be freshened up and replaced with a brand-new caravan, ready for the site's newest residents.

Historically, Tony had worked for Brynn's parents when they were alive. As a young lad he turned his hand to all manner of odd jobs for some extra pocket money. He regularly helped pick up litter, collecting car parking fees, and even dog walking. During the summer months, one of the empty fields surrounding the site was used as an overflow car park for tourists visiting the beach for the day. From dusk to dawn Tony would sit on an empty beer crate at the entrance to the field, offering out his grubby palm to every vehicle that arrived. As the sun began to set at the end of the day, Tony would climb into the front seat of Brynn's father's old grey beaten-up Land Rover, unable to see over the dashboard.

"Have we made our fortunes today?" Brynn's father would always ask, with a big smile and a rub on the top of his head.

"Not many visitors today, uncle!" was always Tony's stock reply as he handed over a jingling carrier bag full of shiny ten pence coins. Some years later, one drunken evening, Tony let slip to Brynn (when they were both staggering home from a lock-in at their local pub) how he used to keep every fifth ten pence coin he collected to boost his wages. He had cleverly crafted a secret pocket inside the lining of his coat. He remembers years later he went to throw it out and finding a few coins still in there.

Tony was now an accomplished artist, and he made a living from selling his oil paintings. Before the big caravan site divide, he had been allowed to hang his paintings he had for sale on the club house walls. It suited both sides; Tony would get the odd sale, and the site had some decoration for their large bland walls. He would attach little brown tags to the corner of each piece using a piece of bailing twine with the price clearly displayed. This had worked well until after the split when Owen, seemingly now in charge of the club house, had asked him to remove all his artwork. Since then, Tony has rented wall space inside a local gift shop in town. At least once or twice a month Tony would get a telephone call to say another piece of art had been sold and there was now room to hang another, the shop owner taking a percentage of the sale.

Tony was a tall man and lean from the many years of living alone and only ever having to cook for himself. His everyday look would be deemed as 'scruffy' to some or perhaps looked like someone who lived on a surfboard, but when he did make an effort, he actually scrubbed up very well. Since his divorce, he had shown little interest in the dating scene. He would often emerge from his caravan in well washed, thread bear clothing. Even after he had washed his hair it would soon look wild and unkempt and as if it needed another wash. He was healthy, happy, and single and he enjoyed his own company. He loved his hobbies, mostly putting down on his canvas what he experienced and things he saw with his own eyes. He would paint what happened around the caravan park, families on the beach, buckets and spades displayed for sale in shop fronts and seagulls landing on fence posts. He had learned from experience to adapt his paintings to what sold the best. Paintings which featured views of the local area, the harbour, or the wonderful Welsh beaches all resulted in better sales. Another little feature Tony had learned to include was a small but discreet Welsh flag, fluttering in the wind. Tourists loved this and it almost certainly helped them sell faster. So, begrudgingly for someone who liked to express himself through his artwork, he added these money-making little extra touches to every painting. He was also mindful that Marion at the Gift Shop would only continue displaying his artwork if she was making some money out of it, so they had to sell, or he was out. In the last couple of years Tony had also discovered a new passion and he had thrown himself into this new hobby with all his ability and enthusiasm.

*

Today, Lucy arrived early for work and signed in at reception. Looking at the back-office whiteboard, Lucy discovered she only had three caravans to clean that day, and on finding out that they were not being re-let straight away, Lucy went straight to find Crawford.

"There is only three today, you got my new number, right?" Lucy said in a tone that didn't give Crawford much choice in the matter. Crawford just offered a smile and a quick nod in reply as Lucy disappeared. She left her site radio on the top of her cleaning trolley and sent a quick text to Crawford that she wouldn't be long – just in case. Lucy changed her mobile number often. The two-way radio that Owen had insisted she carry with her at all times wasn't something Lucy liked. Owen was her boss, so to keep him happy she carried it with her but only whilst cleaning his caravans. Whilst cleaning she would often change the channel and listen to radio transmissions from ships out at sea.

Lucy was still in the throes of laundering her recent cash windfall and had tasked herself in getting this cash discreetly into her bank account as soon as possible. She was uncomfortable with all that cash being hidden under the mattress in her flat. One such money laundering scheme Lucy had generated was a contract with the local chip shop owner in the town, and this is where she was headed. She would collect and deliver all their weekly business supplies from the wholesalers in the city. Lucy's payment for this fetching and carrying, which included items such as potatoes, plastic forks, and copious amounts of cooking oil, was very reasonable. In fact, Lucy only just broke even with her time, petrol costs, and wear and tear on her cleaning van. The benefit for Lucy however was that Mike, the chip shop owner, would electronically transfer £500 into Lucy's personal bank account for every trip she made. Lucy would then pay cash at the Wholesalers using the acquired fifties. This agreement enabled Lucy to steadily get the abundant amounts of £50 notes she had in her possession into her bank account, without alerting any suspicious bank clerks. She had big plans for her steadily growing bank balance, which included buying a flat of her own. She even had plans beyond this to sub-let the flat to one of her massage girls to bring in yet another income. Lucy had notions to get a property portfolio in the local area off the ground, but to do this she needed to turn her excessive cash into legitimate funds. She was paid in cash by Owen every week for cleaning his caravans. She sold her caravan finds which included the likes of shower gel, cooking oil, and phone chargers, for cash. Her share of the massage introduction money was always in cash and added together with the find from the drug dealer, she was constantly looking for ways to launder money. One long term goal was to contract out cleaners and employ staff to clean Owen's caravans. This would enable her to concentrate on her other varied business ventures. Lucy had a very keen business mind, but she liked to maintain an air of being just a dithering cleaner, getting along day by day; little did everyone know that behind the scenes was a sharp intelligent business mind who was building a substantial business empire!

Crawford was a trusted ally of Lucy's, and he would often assist with whatever opportunity arose, so long as he could make a little money on the side. Crawford was naturally good looking, a tall muscular man who was a keen gym attendee. He kept himself in good shape. Working outdoors he always sported a suntan and had recently successfully performed the role of a naked butler at a party organised by Lucy. This was another business venture that was taking off for Lucy, but again people insisted on paying cash for these special Hen parties that she organised. Cash, thought Lucy, was no good to her in this modern digital world.

*

Pam and Owen had been married for as long as anyone could remember. What only a handful of people knew was that Pam had visited the caravan park on holiday when the two brothers, Brynn and Owen, had been teenagers. An innocent young Pam had arrived on the caravan park, holidaying with her parents, and had come to stay for two weeks in the school summer holidays. Feeling very comfortable around the caravan site, Pam had immediately settled in with the local young crowd. Almost immediately she had chosen Brynn as her holiday romance conquest, and the man to whom she was going to offer her virginity. She had at that particular time shown no interest whatsoever in Brynn's younger brother, Owen. As a young man Owen was the skinny, spotty, younger, immature choice of the two brothers. Pam was smitten with Brynn, the strapping tall Welsh lad who appeared to be in charge and run the caravan site. He always appeared busy and could be seen driving around the park on tractors and forklift trucks. Brynn nearly always wore shorts and was bare chested, showing off his muscular torso and his strong, thick, suntanned legs.

During the summer season Brynn was accustomed to being the centre of every young girl's attention. He had grown up on a popular caravan park where new girls had arrived every few weeks. He would be the love of their life for this short period of time. It was a time long before mobile phones were invented and he would always tell them that he would write letters every day when it came time for them to go home. They would be in tears as they kissed and said their goodbyes and waved from the back seat of their parents' car. Within a few hours, Brynn would have forgotten their names as the new batch of holiday makers would arrive and the cycle would repeat itself all over again.

Pam had been another one of Brynn's fortnightly girlfriends and they had been inseparable for the entire two weeks. Pam had willingly given Brynn her virginity in the changing rooms of the onsite swimming pool after it had closed for the evening. The same activity repeating itself many times over during Pam's holiday. As it inevitably did, the holiday romance had come to an end and with the normal offer of keeping in touch, Pam had reluctantly gone back home.

On this rare occasion however, Brynn had felt a tinge of sorrow; he quite liked this one, she was a keeper, he thought.

"I promise, I will write you every week," this rolled off Brynn's tongue with ease.

"You promise?" Pam replied through watery eyes. Brynn hugged her again and gently kissed her on the lips.

"I promise, I mean it."

Brynn waved back to Pam as she stared at him from the back seat of her father's gold-coloured Vauxhall Viva. As it drove away and then turned right down the lane and out of sight, Brynn took a deep breath. He stood there for a minute, staring at the empty space in the road left by the car before he strode off back to his tractor. From his experience he knew that he never saw these girls ever again, so he decided he should just forget about Pam. Sure enough, it wasn't long before his attention was drawn to a twenty-one-year-old curvy red head called Susie from Swindon. She had just arrived with her elderly grandmother and was staying in one of the rental caravans for a week. Grandma fortunately went to bed early most nights, so Susie was then free to do as she wished. Susie had told him all this within the first ten minutes of chatting to him at Reception, so things were soon looking up for Brynn.

It was just under five years later before Pam returned to the site. There had been no letters, but she had never forgotten her first. It was towards the end of the summer holidays and this time she arrived on the train with an older friend called Marge. That wasn't her real name, but her friends called her this as she *spread easy*. They had rented a caravan for ten days that had two separate bedrooms. Pam had never forgotten about Brynn and her excitement built as over the train announcement came 'Next Stop, Pebbles Caravan Park' with the usual reminders to take all your possessions and belongings with you before you depart the train. Pam's heart missed a beat at the train announcement. She so longed to believe that Brynn had never forgotten about her, and it was all going to be like before.

It was only a short walk from the train station along the lane towards the site reception. It was made slightly more difficult than it should have been by the fact there was no footpath, so the girls, and surprisingly many other pedestrians, had to share the road between them and the numerous cars which went back and forth. It was busier with cars than Pam remembered. They arrived at the site boundary, and they turned left off the lane and headed for the site's reception. Pam immediately noticed a rather large and flamboyant new welcome sign which included a Pebbles company logo that she didn't recognise. Pam became worried and her stomach fluttered slightly as she thought that maybe the caravan park was now owned by a different company and Brynn may have moved on. The site layout hadn't changed and remembering her way to reception, all the fond memories of her previous visit came flooding back.

"Hello, yes checking in, we have rented a caravan for ten days," Pam said to the lady on reception. Pam had booked everything and talked Marge into coming with her. Marge was therefore very laid back and let Pam sort everything out. Marge was there for one reason only and she was busy smiling and flirting with a man who was also in the queue for the reception desk.

"Yes, here we are. I have your booking. You are staying in 14 Sea View. Oh, this is a lovely new caravan, you will be very happy here," the receptionist said through a warm smile and continued talking without taking a breath as she handed over two sets of caravan keys along with numerous coloured brochures full of information about the site amenities and facilities. Whilst everything was being explained in glorious detail, Pam incessantly looked around her as she half listened to what was being said. She was looking for anybody or any sign that might signify that Brynn was still around. She contemplated just blatantly asking the receptionist but secretly she was afraid she might not get the answer she was looking for. She also wanted to play things cool, and not alert Marge to the fact that she was still deeply in love. Marge wouldn't get that, she used men and discarded them easily.

*

Tony's metal detector batteries were fully charged, he had glanced over his checklist several times, giving a nod of approval to himself as he read aloud each item. He was organised and hadn't missed anything that was important to take with him on his next expedition. This checklist idea was something he had learned the hard way, after one day finding himself miles from his caravan with a forgotten piece of important metal-detecting equipment. Wearing his sizeable headphones, he strode boundlessly through the site at an enthusiastic pace, heading in the direction of the beach. His very expensive, military-looking metal detector balancing in his left hand, a rucksack on his back containing all manner of essential metal-detecting paraphernalia and, in his right hand, a yellow-handled shiny chrome spade.

Tony's preferred treasure-hunting ground was the beach. This particular beach and area of North Wales was heavily occupied by military personnel in the Second World War. With numerous finds now under his belt, Tony's caravan spare bedroom was beginning to look like a military war museum. He was, however, still looking for that one big find or *coin-cache* as was the term used in the metal-detecting underworld. A treasure discovery that would put him in the history books and up on the wall of 'metal detecting' fame.

He had plans to search in a virgin patch of beach today. Owen, the south site manager, had recently invested heavily in bolstering the caravan park's sea-wall defences. Massive boulders, each resembling the size of a car, had been shipped in one at a time on the back of a lorry. The delivery lorry had accessed the beach at low tide and with an agreement with the owner from the nearby caravan park further down the beach, a complete sand dune had been excavated away. This had allowed the building of an access road for the lorries to drive onto and off the beach. Tony was sure that a financial incentive had been made between the two parties but as yet, and luckily for him, the sand dune had not been repositioned. This access road offered a substantial open area of virgin sand and Tony wanted to search every square inch of it for possible treasure. He had learned his hunting skills from watching many hundreds of YouTube videos that are available on the subject of metal detecting. With his shirt off in the sunshine, his lean, toned, muscular torso was on show for all to see and it wasn't long before he started getting his first hits. In his headphones, he had learned to distinguish the many different tones that the metal detector gave off. These different beeps in each ear depicted what type of metal had been found and an approximately what depth it was buried at. So far today, Tony had found six 2p coins, numerous iron nails, and a good handful of complete and almost brand-new looking metal can ring pulls. Tony was always amazed at the ring pull finds as they had stopped making these beer and soda can ring pulls back in the 1980s, but here he was still finding them almost every time he went out detecting.

Tony projected an air of complete and utter metal-detecting professionalism, up until it came to back-filling in the hole he had just dug to retrieve his buried treasure. He regarded this back-filling task as a complete and utter waste of time and would just leave these gaping holes all over the beach in his wake. He believed it burnt precious daylight hours as the tide would soon wash them all full again. One thing he always said to people who complained was that there was one certainty in life and that was the tide was always going to come in again. On numerous occasions dog walkers and general beach goers had stopped and politely attempted to inform Tony that their dog or child had just nearly fallen into one of his recently dug and dangerous gaping holes, and that he should fill them back in. He often chose to just completely ignore them and pretend he couldn't hear them because of his headphones, or sometimes he would just shout at them, over exaggerating the volume inside his headphones and explain that high tide was only a few hours away.

On a few occasions these ongoing beach health and safety concerns had been highlighted to Pam and Owen. Tony had been spoken to by Owen who had politely requested that he fill in the holes. In fact, Owen had told Pam he had spoken to Tony about it many times but in fact Owen hadn't bothered. In truth Owen was a little nervy of his old family friend and didn't want to rock the boat. Something unknown to everyone had happened in the past between Owen and Tony and it was best forgotten. Back then, Owen's older brother Brynn had sorted it all out. As a young man, Owen will never forget that his older brother had to go away for a while. Everybody had been told that Brynn had gone to visit a family friend overseas. He was gone for over two years, and everyone secretly knew he had gone to prison for badly beating up Tony's uncle after an incident at a wedding.

Tony was getting low on battery power now; he had a spare battery in his backpack, but he was also getting hearing fatigue. He was starting to find it difficult to distinguish between the many different pitches and tones. He straightened and stretched his aching back, looking back over his shoulder he could see his searched route, clearly identifiable from the abundant holes in the sand. Tony lay his equipment down on the sand to rest. He stood there wearing only a pair of green shorts and boots. He had a dark hairy chest and legs but the hair on his arms and head had been bleached blonde from the many years of living a beach bum lifestyle.

Tony was aware of a person heading in his direction along the beach. He didn't look, he assumed it was another hole complainer. Out of the corner of his eye he saw a pretty, middle-aged woman walk past him. She was walking her small white dog. She was alone and unnecessarily came within a few metres of Tony. On her head was a large round straw hat and her thin flimsy yellow summer dress blew up and around her long shapely legs in the sea breeze. She lifted her left hand to hold down her hat from blowing away as she turned and looked at Tony.

"Hello," she said, her blue eyes scanned up and down his almost naked body. She smiled, her lips slightly apart, it was a smile that said she liked what she saw. Tony watched as she walked away. In the bright sunshine he could see her hour-glass figure, transparent and silhouetted through her dress. It revealed long slim legs and an alluring gap at the top of her thighs. Tony liked what he saw, and his muscles tensed, remembering and missing the touch of female skin. He stared as she appeared to flout away across the sand, and he regretted that he hadn't said hello back when he had the chance. He contemplated running after her, but the moment was gone. He reminded himself that not everyone was the enemy.

His attention was then drawn to a gold spectacle-wearing man in a brown cardigan hurriedly walking towards him. He was gesturing politely for Tony's attention with his raised left hand as he struggled to walk in white socks and sandals across the sand. Tony was in no doubt what this man wanted and saw this as the cue to finish for the day. He quickly gathered his equipment, turned, and began striding back to his caravan park. The words "I say, young man, hello there," were being bellowed at him constantly from behind. Clearly this was going to be another polite lecture on the dangers of not filling in the holes he had been digging and the potential health and safety infringements. As the shouting abated, his thoughts turned to the lady in the yellow dress. He smiled as something yellow in the distance caught his eye and he strode with a purpose in its direction.

*

Pam and her friend Marge loved their modern rented caravan on the posh side of the caravan park. It was theirs to do exactly what they wanted with. No parents' rules to follow this time. They each had their own bedrooms, each with a double bed.

"I'm loving this sea view out of the window but the only view I want to see is this caravan's ceiling," Marge said to Pam, giggling before she could even finish her sentence and throwing herself backwards onto her bed.

"I want to experiment on this very bed," Marge continued to inform her friend and added that she was on the search for a man to tie her to it and make love to her for hours on end. They had each saved well for this holiday and with nobody else to look out for apart from themselves, they had decided they were going to have a wild time. Their caravan was tucked away in the corner of the park behind many other caravans. They hadn't paid the extra for a sea view as Pam stood staring out the window, mesmerised by the distant rolling waves and lost in her own thoughts. Pam could still hear Marge talking about sex from her bedroom, "… there are so many different shapes, sizes, and colours, I'm starting to enjoy large …" Marge continued talking as Pam drifted again in her head and she blocked out Marge's words. Her thoughts turned to holding Brynn's hand as they walked along that very beach, just like they had done before. It seemed like only yesterday in her head. After deciding who was having the bedroom with the en-suite shower, they looked around, opening numerous empty cupboards before placing several bottles of pink sparkling wine into the fridge. They both opened their suitcases on their respective beds and after a quick application of more lip-gloss and mascara they were ready to leave. Within thirty minutes of arriving, they locked up their caravan and were heading up to the club bar, their heels clinking along the footpath.

Walking through the site, Pam was constantly looking around her for any sign of Brynn. She was trying to remember her way around the park, it had certainly changed quite a bit since she was last there. As they walked past the swimming pool, she smiled to herself. She recalled the times she had spent in Brynn's embrace, in the pool; out of the pool, on the changing room benches, in the showers, on the changing room floor and all the positions she could never have imagined were possible if Brynn hadn't had taught her. Pam could remember that when she had visited with her parents all those years previous, they had driven past reception and then turned left in the car and gone up a slight hill. The site layout looked different she thought, but the bar was still in the same place, a little more modern but the walls and front door were unchanged. Entering, she didn't recognise anybody, she had this wild idea and secretly wished that she would be welcomed and recognised by everybody. Being served quickly, they stood sipping large glasses of white wine. Within minutes Marge was already chatting to a tall muscular chap who was wearing a green polo top. Pam also thought that he was gorgeous looking, and he had a thick chiselled chin and deep suntan. He wore works clothes which had the new company logo printed on the chest and shirt sleeve. Pam recognised the logo from the entrance. *If Marge flicks her hair to the right, then God help that poor chap,* thought Pam. She watched her experienced friend at work, flirting was something Marge was very good at, but at the same time Pam constantly scanned the area for any signs of Brynn. Pam couldn't wait any longer and with her heart pounding she wanted to know, she needed to know right now, once and for all.

"Excuse me, sorry Marge," Pam said, forcibly leaning in, touching her friend's arm to silence her before she could object. "Do you work here?" Pam enquired.

"Yes, hi I'm Crawford," and he offered his hand to shake, all the time presenting his sexy smile. Crawford carried on talking, something about his name not being Welsh and about what he did onsite. He continued rambling and he began to turn his attention back to Marge. Pam interrupted him with a raised finger and a gentle squeeze of Marge's arm. Pam was not trying to steal her prey.

"Sorry, but does Brynn still work here?" Pam said with wide open eyes. She was on the verge of bursting into tears if he didn't say what she wanted to hear. Crawford maintained eye contact with Pam, but he paused in his reply. She didn't know why he was hesitating, but she was now on tender hooks anticipating the answer that she was so hoping for.

"Erm no," said Crawford. "Well yes and no. He still works here but he has gone away for a while. It will be another year yet before he is back." Crawford could see that Pam was upset at the news and he contemplated telling her that he was travelling around Europe or something similar to let her down gently. But she was soon forgotten as Pam strode off to the bar for more drinks and he turned his attention back to Marge who had regained physical contact and was now so close to him they were almost glued at the hip. Quickly and without being invited to do so, Marge reaffirmed her position that she had claimed, and she kissed Crawford full on the lips. Crawford kissed her back and then smiling he softly stroked the side of Marge's large left breast, the hidden side so no one could see as they both leaned up against the club wall. The touch was very slight but very intimate and they both knew what it meant. Only the two of them knew what he was doing with his hand and Marge, whilst maintaining eye contact with Crawford, used her tongue seductively to search for the red striped straw in her drink. Marge laughed at everything he said, all the while she caressed his naked arm, fascinated and complimentary at how hard his muscular body was. She found his firm erect nipple through his shirt and she squeezed it, all the time staring into his eyes. Marge was overpowered by how aroused she was that a man could be so hard to the touch, pure firm muscle, and she so longed to reach down and place her hands between his legs.

She wanted to see if he was getting an erection. They both knew what was going to happen later, Marge pleased she had found a man so soon to fulfil her endless sexual desires.

At the bar, Pam ordered two more drinks, she looked back over to ask Crawford what he wanted but he was too engrossed with Marge, so she didn't offer to buy him a drink. Pam felt alone and she knew that Marge had only one thing on her mind. Pam waited at the bar counter for a few minutes, she contemplated asking the young lady who had served her if she knew Brynn but decided against the idea. Crawford had been convincing, and her beloved Brynn had gone away. Had he gone away with another woman? Her mind was racing. Realising she couldn't stand at the bar forever, she re-joined the lovers. They didn't notice as she approached, and Pam coughed to attract their attention and remind them she was still alive. Crawford registered Pam's awkward cough and said aloud;

"Owen, Brynn's brother, is about, he won't be long, that's who I'm meeting here. He will know for sure when Brynn is coming home." Crawford had moved his body to one side and was now covering and partially screening Marge from anybody else in the bar. They were both still leaning up against the bar wall, where Marge had pulled her shoulders back and was pressing her exposed ample chest into Crawford's body. Expertly he used his index finger of his right hand as he slowly caressed Marge's bare arm, lingering at the shoulder blade before slowly and seductively trailing back down, neither of them talking, but both of them filling their heads with what they wanted to do with each other's bodies.

"Hello mate, you busy, or do you want another beer?" came the voice of a cheerful young man who had appeared in the bar and the group became four. Owen looked at his friend Crawford, then over at Marge, looking her up and down, and then smiling back at his friend. Owen knew that his friend was going to be busy for the next few days.

"This is Pam," Marge said aloud and gesturing towards Pam

without really looking. She only had eyes for Crawford. Owen, who was stood in green shorts and a black T-shirt, turned and stared at the prettiest girl he had ever seen in his life, and his heart missed a beat. For Owen it was love at first sight, he would never forget the first time he laid eyes on Pam. With her long blonde hair and curves in all the right places, he liked what he saw. Immediately, he assessed the familiar situation. Knowing his friend Crawford well, he could see that he was making plans for his night ahead, leaving Pam all alone. Owen introduced himself to Pam with a polite handshake and his best smile, hoping that he didn't have bad breath after being at work all day, and regretting that he had not taken time to freshen up and iron his shirt.

Twenty years later and here they are, Pam and Owen, still happily married and running the south side of the caravan park. They were inseparable during the holiday, so much so that Pam decided to stay on after being offered a job onsite and didn't return home for several months. She fell in love, they soon married after falling pregnant with their first child. When Brynn did eventually return from a short stay at her majesty's pleasure, he was different, and not how Pam had remembered him. Brynn kept his distance from the happy couple and Pam and Owen were so in love they took no notice. This arrangement suited them all just fine.

CHAPTER 16

Lady Right Leader Left

'Not everyone is coming to the future, because not everyone is learning from the past'. Charles had written this as a chapter title on his laptop. He was still very keen to write a book, or something similar, and release his inner creativity. He knew this was deep within him someplace. He was thrilled that at long last he had actually started to write his novel. He wasn't sure if he had read this sentence someplace else, because he was impressed and felt it sounded particularly good. He was shocked at the possibility that it may just have been conjured up from his very own imagination. He made a note to research; after all, he didn't want any copyright issues when his novel became a world-wide best-seller. This arena of creative writing was very new to him, and he was struggling to get ideas off the ground. To get started, by typing a few words onto the screen in front of him, was an enormous achievement in itself.

Charles sat there looking at his open computer screen in silence. His thoughts, for a reason he didn't realise, always seemed to turn to his first wife whenever he began to write. Perhaps it was because Beatrice brought back fond memories of his university days. Although he had studied to be a chef, the course involved a great deal of written assignments, spending long hours staring at a laptop screen. The more he wrote, the more he thought about her, and the more he realised that one day he must tell his family all about her.

That night, as Charles slept, he dreamed he was sat in the doctor's waiting room with Beatrice holding his hand. He was sat crossed-legged waiting to be called forwards by the doctor who would be able to explain the hard lump he had recently found in his groin. He had not received a telephone call from his doctor, so he was sure nothing was wrong, but something had changed and awakened inside him. Thoughts of his past, and the possibility that he might have another child someplace in this crazy world, who may look just like him, featured heavily in his thoughts. As each day passed this was becoming more and more important to him.

After consulting Sharon's family organiser, Charles noticed that a family trip was planned to the *holiday home* the following weekend. This could be the perfect opportunity, he thought to himself. His entire family would be together in their happy place by the sea. He would pick his moment, and when he had everyone's attention, he would get it all off his chest and out in the open once and for all. He imagined gaining their attention, perhaps whilst they were all sat down enjoying a meal together. He would tell them firstly about Beatrice, and then his recent doctor's check-up, sparing no detail and telling them everything. Perhaps by sharing his past secrets with the family he loved, he would be able to move on in his predicament. It was becoming increasingly difficult to get to sleep at night and by sharing his thoughts and feelings with his family, he was hoping to find inner peace. The biggest dilemma for Charles was whether to tell Sharon about him fathering another child, before he shared this bombshell with the rest of the family. In any normal relationship he thought he should. But with Sharon, a self-confessed sex-addict, he decided that if she got the hump, that might give him a few days respite from sex which wouldn't be a bad thing. He knew in his heart he should have told her about the check-up, but it was all too late now. He had made his decision; it was all going to come out in one unforgettable family speech.

"I have booked at table at The Lamb & Dragon pub for tomorrow night," Charles enthusiastically informed his family. He told each of his children in turn throughout the course of the evening, as they arrived back home after school.

"Hi, Emily. How was school?" Charles said as the front door opened and in swaggered his eldest daughter. Emily just nodded in acknowledgment, not even looking up from her mobile phone screen and showed no interest whatsoever. Her unimpressed attitude towards her father's meal planning was evident on her face. For Charles, this was a nerve-racking time, but with a slight nod she simply walked past him. She flicked off her school shoes in the hallway, leaving them precisely where they landed and with one precarious step at a time, she unhurriedly headed upstairs to her bedroom.

"Did you hear me? I have booked a table at The Lamb & Dragon pub for dinner tomorrow night." Charles was eager to at least glean some sort of reaction.

"Whateva," Emily replied in a sarcastic tone as she passed on by.

Charles smiled lovingly. He had been informed many times over by friends and other parents that his daughter would grow out of her teenage attitude and he wasn't to take anything personally. It never surprised him, and sometimes he found it remarkable how much her mannerisms mirrored her mother's, and indeed how much she looked just like her. His younger daughter Sophie still had that loving respect for her dad. When she arrived home from school, as soon as she saw him, she ran towards him, and Charles lifted her up in his arms and gave her the biggest cuddle.

"I have booked a table at The Lamb & Dragon pub for tomorrow night," he informed her. "What are you going to order?" Charles said. He then recited a list of her favourite foods, each with a gentle shake and laugh, unsure even if the restaurant even had these choices on the menu.

"I'm going to order a pizza I think, but I'm going to watch TV now," Sophie said, and she also wandered off, leaving Charles alone in the hall with his own thoughts. Perhaps he was doing the wrong thing, was Sophie too young? After all, he didn't want to upset her. But he decided he was going to stand by his plan and tell his entire family everything, all at the same time. He also thought that being in a public place, Sharon would be less likely to start screaming and shouting and punching him. Or so he hoped ...

*

In each other's company, when they were alone, they were always Phil and Jenny. Many years ago, when they started out dancing, they had chosen Francoise and Claudia as their ballroom dancing stage names. These names had stuck and remained unchanged for years. On numerous occasions, Phil had often remarked that he sometimes regretted his stage name choice. People struggled with the spelling and pronunciation. This often led to competition organisers getting his name wrong in programmes and missing his cue when they announced him incorrectly on stage.

Phil wasn't a drinker, in fact it was very rare for Phil to drink any type of alcohol, but the previous evening, alone in their rent-free plush new caravan, Phil had joined in with Jenny's daily habit. He had facilitated in polishing off a bottle of Vodka, mixed with diet coke. He generally disapproved of excessive alcohol consumption, and as such he scarcely found himself drunk. However, this evening he found himself laughing and joking whilst imitating a competition judge from a country he couldn't remember and laughing hysterically.

Staggering around the caravan lounge holding the empty vodka bottle as an imaginary microphone, "and the winner of the 2006 something or other Ballroom Championships ... FRANSOW and CLOWDIA," Phil said out loud, with his free arm raised to emphasise the point. They both laughed and fell onto the sofa, arm in arm, sharing a brief intimate physical encounter together.

That day they had four back-to-back ballroom classes scheduled.

They had introduced an extra lesson at the end of the evening, something they sometimes did for students that had done a little dancing before and wanted to progress quickly. Tonight's class was an introduction to the Quick Step and all the different dancing groups were progressing well. Most had attended regularly for several weeks now, and it showed in the high standard of dancing on display. Some classes were better represented than others with only a few couples having dropped out so far. Phil and Jenny both knew this wasn't a reflection on their teaching ability, and it was nothing personal. It was simply down to who was at their caravan on the day of their classes.

Jenny was delighted with the cash tin contents with over £150 in it so far. Turning her microphone upside down she flipped the switch on the bottom, and the red 'on' light flashed. She then dropped effortlessly into her well-rehearsed routine speech. With her microphone switched on, she instantly transformed into Claudia.

"Good evening Ladies and Gentlemen. Let's have a row of men and a row of ladies please," Claudia said aloud, indicating with her free arm where she would like people to stand. All eyes were on her now. "Come on, as quick as you can please, don't be shy. Let's get them hips moving and warmed up, let's get started." Claudia was very clear in her instructions and very firm and fair in her praise. All she wanted was the group to get their monies worth.

"If I say *bar* then everyone should be facing the bar and if I say *door* then everyone should be facing the door." Claudia pointed with her free hand to the main entrance door. "That door, the main door you came in, not any other door," she said to clarify.

"Just watch for now, please, I'm going to demonstrate," Claudia said and without being asked a silent and obedient Francoise offered his raised open hand and took up his dancing posture in front of Claudia. They looked elegant and perfectly in tune together. The only thing that appeared out of place was that Claudia held a microphone to her mouth as they danced, but with years of practice she described the moves as they were performed, and everyone followed the dancing steps, words booming out of the speakers. Every move was made with grace and expertise, gliding effortlessly around the room and the obedient students, who stood in awe of their teachers, smiling and clapping in admiration.

It wasn't only Sharon who watched every move as Francoise pivoted and spun around the dance floor, his tight white trousers smoothed over his two round buttocks and his perfectly formed large mound at the front. Sharon caught Debbie's eye and they both smiled and were on the same wavelength. They both stood admiring Francoise's thick muscular legs and his toned body as he moved. Francoise's dancing costume, as expected during competitions, was tight, it had however been getting a little tighter over the years as he had aged. As he moved, his muscles flexed and beads of sweat appeared on his forehead and down the centre of his back.

"Side close side to the bar. Side close side to the door," Claudia repeated over and over through the microphone. Francoise released his partner and stood attentively by his laptop computer, selecting and controlling the music that was now coming out over the club's loudspeakers.

"Everybody just keep repeating these moves on your own. OK, let's go, everyone. Side close side to the bar. Side close side to the door," Claudia continuingly repeated over and over as the group of individual dancers moved in a large circle around the dance floor.

"OK let's do it now with partners, please. Come on, quickly, let's go," Claudia instructed firmly as the music ended and the next track began.

Gabriella made a lunge towards Crawford before anybody else bagged him as a dance partner. "Can I dance with you please? What's your name?" Gabriella asked, smiling in case anyone was listening.

Crawford wore a tight, short-sleeved open-neck black shirt which exaggerated his muscular body and emphasised his large, suntanned biceps. Gabriella took pleasure in placing her hand on Crawford's bare upper tattooed arm as she squeezed in very close to him. Crawford was a big man and even when he wasn't erect, he had a firm mound, and he pressed his manhood into Gabriella as they danced, and she melted at his touch. It never stopped surprising Gabriella how solid Crawford's body was, all from his working outdoors lifestyle.

"Lady right, leader left. OK everybody, get ready please. Let's go. Let's go." Claudia's commands were booming through the speakers with a perfect pitch and pace to the group's dancing ability. Experience gained from many years of doing the same thing over and over.

"Side close side to the bar. Side close side to the door." The dancing pairs moved around in an anti-clockwise direction to the music, each couple spinning like a flywheel, some better than others but all with laughs and smiles and sometimes with intimate looks from their public physical contact, looks that partners had most probably not given each other in a long time.

"Will you look at them pair!" exclaimed Debbie as she leaned over and whispered to Sharon as they came unusually close together on the dance floor. Sharon leaned forwards to reply.

"Does she think that we don't know they are at it like teenagers?" Sharon replied as they danced passed each other on the next turn of the dance floor. David loved his newfound ballroom dancing and was oblivious to his wife's excessive cleavage display. All he could think about was concentrating on the dance steps and taking every opportunity to glance over in Francoise's direction for guidance. The hour's lesson ended with a brief display of dancing showmanship from Francoise and Claudia. The aspiring dancing students would stand in a circle around the dance floor and watch in awe at their magnificent, highly talented teachers. When the music stopped, the fabulous display ended with an enthusiastic round of applause, a bow to each other, and then a bow to their delighted audience.

Most would slowly vacate the bar still clapping and cheering with a warm feeling inside, certain they would return for another ballroom dancing extravaganza.

Before the microphone was turned off, Claudia would thank everyone for attending, before her attentiveness was drawn to the next class of excited students who had started to arrive, and who, more importantly, were offering up their £10 notes as they entered. David took this opportunity to leave his wife's side, she was gossiping with Sharon anyhow. Debbie didn't even notice as her husband slipped away and had gone to catch Francoise's attention.

"I'm very keen to purchase some dancing shoes," David enquired, and Francoise fell into his well-rehearsed response. This question had been asked of him *many* times during his dancing career.

"Have you seen Prince Charles and Camilla over there?" a bitching Debbie whispered into Sharon's ear.

"Doesn't he look gorgeous," Sharon replied, who was now sipping through a red straw on her second Gin & Tonic of the day. With a mouthful of gin, the straw still in her mouth, Sharon was looking in the direction that her friend had indicated. Gabriella was still physically holding onto Crawford's arm, even though the dancing had ended. Crawford had secretly enjoyed himself and the memories of his dancing past had all returned to him. He had found that the constant female contact had aroused in him a passion, and he hoped it wasn't too evident through his tight trousers. He was aware he had the beginnings of a burning erection and was eager to take Gabriella as soon as he could. A promise offered if he attended the dancing class. Gabriella, aware of her friend's eyes upon her, leaned into Crawford and whispered in his ear that she wanted him in her mouth right now. Crawford, instinctively reacting with pleasure, reached and took a firm hold of Gabriella's bottom, this had gone to plan, and she knew that her friends would have seen the sexual chemistry apparent between them. She especially wanted Sharon to see that she was getting big, firm, tattooed bad boy Crawford tonight, not her.

"Your tits look great, you know," Sharon said, looking down at Debbie's exposed bosom as they both stared over at the other side of the room.

"Ahh thanks Hun, you're so kind." Debbie smiled back, stroking Sharon's bare arm with her hand. "I know they cost enough," Debbie laughed and pulled back her shoulders to push them out even further. This was all for Sharon's benefit, or maybe Charles who was having to really concentrate on not looking down at Debbie's chest, or at least not get caught looking.

"Right then, dinner, young lady," Charles said, interrupting the gossiping damsels, and he offered out his raised elbow for his wife to link arms. Sharon, smiling, and with a slight curtsy in return, replied, "I'm all yours, young man," giving her friend Debbie a wink as they walked out of the club. *Poor Charles,* Debbie said in her head, *he is getting it tonight whether he likes it or not* and she giggled to herself, hoping that she hadn't said that out loud. Charles and Sharon left the clubhouse, and they could hear the music start for the next dance class and the booming voice of Claudia over the microphone.

Family all collected, seatbelts on, the restaurant was only a short drive away from the caravan site. On the journey all Charles could think about was his forthcoming prepared speech and what the future had in store for him. Charles had offered to drive even though Sharon was very insistent on them getting a taxi. She liked to utilise a taxi so her husband could drink. From experience, if her husband drank, when they were alone later, he would last longer. With no uncertain terms, Charles had decided he was staying sober tonight. He needed to if he was going to survive the dropping of his two prepared bombshells.

"Oh, and by the way, I fathered another child before I met your mum, yes you all have a half brother or sister. I recently had a cancer scare but I got an all clear," Charles repeated over and over to himself in his head as he drove. What could possibly go wrong, he thought? He reversed into a car parking space and applied the handbrake. He was worried sick now and his stomach churned.

*

"I know it's our caravan, but Adam is between jobs and at the minute he has no money coming in," Alison pleaded to her husband, lowering her voice, and leaning in closer to him and pressing her breasts up into his arm as she finished talking. She knew how to coerce and control her husband.

"For Pete's sake, does he have to?" Clifford replied, staring at his wife. Alison pressed her body in closer to Clifford, noticing he was getting aroused. "Well, it looks like it's already arranged now, I guess," he responded. "But just so you know, I'm not very keen on him staying here at all, to be honest," Clifford replied as he continued to stare at his wife who was wearing a red bikini top. She was now stood directly in front of him with her shoulders back, pushing herself into him. Pressing her breasts firmly into her husband's chest, she reached down and rubbed her hands in his whilst he shook his head in disapproval.

"I'll make it up to you later, I promise, darling," she whispered in Clifford's left ear as she reached down and squeezed his manhood through his shorts. She squeezed through his clothing as hard as she could, her tongue flicking his ear. She could feel his member instantly firming in her grip as she massaged the end skilfully. The fact that her current husband was extremely wealthy and had a very large penis had been a surviving factor in their relationship and a key reason for Alison to get married again.

Alison knew she was asking a lot. She added, "And it can be *the special* if you wish, my darling," whispering softly into his ear, her lips touching his ear lobe as she spoke. Alison only reserved *the special* for when she really needed Clifford to change his mind over something.

Earlier, Adam had begged Alison during one of their daily telephone heart-to-hearts if he could stay rent free in their caravan for a few days.

"I've been feeling a bit down lately and it's only for a few days, of course it's when you aren't using it of course, you wouldn't know I was there," Adam said softly.

"He won't go for it; he's only just paid for it," Alison had repeatedly replied. Adam had explained he was out of work again and had no money. He wanted a short holiday to clear his head, as recently he had been feeling down. He had continued pestering and successfully persuaded Alison that a good mate of his, who was currently working away on an oil rig, had offered to loan him his car. It all seemed plausible, and he had promised, on their daughter's life that it was just going to be him, and he would keep the place clean and tidy. With a slight hesitation in Alison's voice, he then resorted to using Molly as his final angle for the free holiday. He explained that if he were able to experience the area and get a better understanding of Molly's caravan holidays, he would be able to talk to her about it more, and it would be something they would have in common. Of course, he would sleep in Molly's bed, that was a given. Alison was no fool, but as always, she softened where Adam was involved and she had ended the call saying she was sure she would be able to convince Clifford to allow him to use their caravan, no promises of course, but she would try.

Later that day she messaged Adam to confirm that he could use the caravan, provided he looked after it, and left it as he had found it. Feeling incredibly pleased with himself, Adam immediately sent a text to his latest girlfriend. He had only met her a couple of days before in a bar, and he told her that he had rented for them both a plush new caravan by the sea. He told her to pack her best lingerie and prepare herself for a weekend of excitement. He added the 'ear' emoji to his message. Adam had to later explain to Kate that his fingers were too big, and he had meant to press the kiss emoji directly next to it. The only request was that she would need to drive, as his Range Rover was in the garage being fixed! Lying came easily to Adam, it was something he had mastered and had become part of him, it was how he survived.

*

After their ballroom dancing class, Debbie requested of her husband, "If you don't mind, I want you to take a few photographs of me this afternoon, darling." They were walking side by side back to their caravan through an unusually quiet caravan park.

"Yeh no worries. I do so love ballroom dancing, don't you?" David replied eagerly, still smiling from ear to ear and looking out into the distance.

"Hello girls, shall I make you lunch?" Debbie said, greeting her three daughters who were all sat slouched along the giant cream corner settee in their caravan. The TV was on, all the lights in the bedrooms were on, Paris was asleep on the end and the twins were both just looking at their mobile phones.

"Not hungry," replied Dolly without looking up.

"Dani cooked us Spag Bol," replied Daisy, again not even looking up from her screen.

"Erm ... Where is Dani?" asked Debbie, as she stared across at the mountain of dirty pots and plates that had all been piled in the kitchen sink. She shook her head in annoyance at the lack of interest from her oldest daughter to placing dirty items into the dishwasher. Debbie had to remind herself that she shouldn't complain. Her teenage daughter had taken care of her younger sisters and had cooked them a meal. Not washing up was the least of a mother's worries.

"I know we have just been out dancing, but me and Dad are just going for a quick walk on our own along the beach. We won't be long, is that OK, girls? When we get back, we will all do something together as a family." There was no verbal response offered, but Debbie could see her daughters nodding their heads in unison.

"Let Paris sleep for a little while longer please, OK?" Debbie added, giving the twins further instructions.

"OK, Mum," they replied promptly, after hearing a slight raise in their mum's voice on the word 'OK'.

Debbie needed some bikini pictures for today's social media pages. The sun was out, it was mid-week down at the caravan park and she knew the beach would be deserted. She had high hopes for some great material. Debbie had in her mind a few ideas of what poses she wanted to do, and she was even considering a running picture. She had seen it done by another online influencer and thought it was very sexy. She wasn't sure if her big boobs were up to the challenge of running in a bikini, but she was going to give it a go. She had seen one of her Instagram idols, who had over a million followers, do a short video recently of her posing whilst laying on the sand and then she jumped up and ran along the beach into the sea. Debbie thought this would be a very sexy clip indeed. Bikini on, with easily removable loose clothes over the top, she grabbed her husband's hand and pulled him out onto the decking; he had no choice in the matter, he was coming for a walk and was going to be the photographer whether he liked it or not!

"That's it, the big red button," Debbie was holding up her phone and instructing David how to take a 'Boomerang' video clip.

"I will nod, and you immediately hold the button down, that's it," Debbie said over her shoulder as she ran away towards the sea in her bikini of choice. She then turned and immediately ran back to David. Several attempts later, David felt he was really starting to capture the moment and was feeling confident with the phone camera.

"Press and hold as soon as I run away," screeched Debbie. "Yes, film me as I run away first," she continued, as David clicked away, hoping he was doing it right.

Debbie had dropped her clothes in a pile on the sand and was happily jumping and running around on the beach in her skimpy bikini. Even though she was a mother of five children, she still looked amazing, the expensive surgery she had, had certainly helped, but she looked after herself, and it showed. A few men had started to walk past. David was sure the same chap had walked past three times! After ten minutes Debbie felt she had enough material and she was bursting to see the results. As she dressed, a man walking his dog strolled past and he offered a sexy, sheepish smile. He was middle aged and well-groomed. She had started to look at men's clothes more and she instinctively looked down at his shoes. He wore expensive brown designer shoes, and Debbie, for a reason she wasn't quite yet sure, certainly liked what she saw. She looked up and smiled back at him, and to her surprise, and with her newfound confidence, she boldly said "Hi."

On seeing Debbie talking with someone, David soon lost interest and wandered off back home towards their caravan. Debbie started chatting with the stranger, who turned out to be a widowed dad, on site with his teenage sons. She quickly dressed but refrained from covering up her top half for just a few moments longer and continued to walk along the beach with her stranger. She explained about the photographs, and he sounded genuinely interested. A few minutes later she took a big breath and asked him out loud if he wanted to grab a coffee sometime. "Sure," he replied and reached into the back pocket of his jeans for his phone. They exchanged numbers and Debbie double-checked by calling his number and letting it ring just once.

"I'll message you," she winked, and slowly and sexily walked away from her blue-eyed, chiselled-jawed, expensive-shoe-wearing tattooed new friend. She walked with a skip in her step back to her caravan and her loving family. She thought of turning to see if he was watching her, but she didn't. Her concentration was on her camera roll. "Ooh that's a good one," she said aloud to herself every few seconds as she walked, before climbing the steps onto her decking.

*

"No pudding for me, thank you," Charles said, handing back the sticky laminated dessert menu to their waiter. The waiter departed, and Charles decided it was the right moment and turned to address his family.

"Right, phones away please, everybody!" His children lowered their respective mobile phones, just out of sight under the table, but at an angle so they could still see their screens.

"NO, I mean it, away properly please. Mobiles away please. I have something to say to everyone and it's important. I'm calling a family meeting." His children knew that tone. They stared in nervous anticipation. Sharon froze and lowered her fourth G&T slowly onto the table. Charles had suddenly gained everyone's attention. They all knew this was serious.

The calling of a family meeting was something that only happened occasionally in the Cooper household. Every family member was authorised to call a family meeting, at any time, day or night, and discuss any topic whenever they wished. The rules being that the rest of the family had to immediately stop what they were doing and listen in. Emily's right to call family meetings had recently been revoked after she called at least seven family meetings in one evening. This had coincidently been after a disagreement with her mother over what time she had to be back home from a party at her best friend's house.

Charles looked around the restaurant table. Jackson was getting tall now and turning into a man. His two daughters sat opposite him, and they were both looking at him with awe and respect. His wife now of many years, Sharon, sat to his left, and was looking puzzled and concerned about what he was possibly going to say. Her mind raced in anticipation of the next words out of her husband's mouth. *My god, what if Charles 'comes out', like David,* Sharon thought briefly, before shaking her head and trying to think of something else he might say. *Is he leaving me?*

Charles coughed lightly, he didn't need to, he just wanted to, and he looked everyone in the eye in turn. This was something he had seen Frank do when he addressed a group, and he liked it. Charles began his well-rehearsed speech.

"I am married to your mummy now and we are very happy, we love each other dearly and nothing is going to change that," he said, scanning the table, continuing to look everyone in the eye. He moved his hand across the restaurant table, and he squeezed his wife's hand gently, in a show of public affection. Sharon's stomach churned. *Oh my god, he has found someone else,* she thought.

"I am about to tell you all something important and I want you to let me finish. I want to tell you everything before you interrupt me or ask me any questions," Charles said. "I will tell you all when I am finished, and I will then invite you to ask any questions you wish. You can ask me anything at all, I will have no secrets after this." Charles paused, he looked everyone in the eye one more time to ensure he had their utmost attention. He dared not look in Sharon's direction, and he quickly continued.

"As you know, Jackson has a different mummy to you two. That is because I was married to Megan before your mummy. Well, before that, I was married to a lady called Beatrice." Charles could feel Sharon stiffen, and he felt her eyes burn into the side of his head as she violently pulled her hand away from his.

"YOU WERE MARRIED BEFORE?" Sharon screamed.

"Mum, don't interrupt. Wait till the end, like Dad said," exclaimed both Emily and Jackson in near unison, and both giving their mother and step-mother a firm glare. Charles was prepared for Sharon's reaction, and he didn't rise to her loud interruption. He continued.

"I met Beatrice at University, that's how long ago it was, and long before I met your mothers. We were both very young and Beatrice fell pregnant. It was just before graduation. Her parents were very influential over her, it was different times back then, and Beatrice left to go back and live with her parents in London." Charles paused briefly, he was aware of the enormity of what he was off loading on his family.

"We were only married a short time and Beatrice requested that I never contact her again. I am not sure if she had the baby. I don't know. I wish I knew. It could, however, mean you have a half-sister or half-brother someplace." He paused again, smiling at his daughters and giving his son's arm a fatherly stroke of reassurance. Charles continued in his tale, and he told them all about the pressures of university exams and all the studying he had to do. That there was always drinking parties on campus, and it was after one of these parties that Beatrice had got pregnant. He explained how they had married quickly in a register office around the corner from the campus, with friends from the University as witnesses. They had both travelled to London on the train to tell Beatrice's parents. He went on to explain how they arrived at her parents' house, and how nervous they both were, walking along the banks of the River Thames for hours to get their story straight, and how they had built up some Dutch courage with several bottles of cider. Charles explained in detail how Beatrice's parents had been upset and disappointed with them both and persuaded her into leaving Charles. He never saw her again. He continued explaining how upset he had been for a long time afterwards and after leaving university he went to find work in France. "That was close to 20 years ago and I don't know if I have another son or daughter out there somewhere."

Charles paused and smiled at his son and daughters with an overwhelming, all-consuming feeling of love that he couldn't describe. He took a deep breath, and not wanting to invite any further interruptions from his wife, he continued quickly, changing stories, and outlining his very recent hospital check-up. He explained to his children that he had found a lump on his private parts but had undergone a hospital check-up and had been given the all-clear and that nothing was wrong. He emphasised to his children that the doctors had given him the all-clear and he was all OK. He reassured them all with smiles. Again, he talked quickly, still not wanting to invite any questions just yet.

"It's not that I kept any secrets from anyone, it was just a long time ago. I was very young, and I never thought about it much until now. It wasn't really a real marriage, not like with your mummies. Then the hospital thing, and now I want to write a book about everything that's happened in my life. OK. That's it, I have finished." Charles took a deep breath and then said, "Does anyone have any questions?"

He didn't look at his wife who he knew would have a long list of questions. Jackson was first and quickly said, "Is that it? I thought you were going to announce that we were going to Las Vegas or skiing or something." He shook his head briefly and looked down at his phone.

Sophie said, "Can I look at my phone now?" And everyone at the table fell silent. They all knew their mother well and she had a temper and that she was high spirited, as it had been described to them all before. Charles gradually turned his head and looked at his wife. Her hand, which she had snatched back from Charles's grasp when he had mentioned another woman, was now clenched in a fist on the table.

"You OK, darling?" Charles said softly.

It was as if Sharon was in shock as she didn't move or speak for a moment. She then twitched and her head moved ever so slightly, and her cheeks went a rosy, pink colour.

"Does *she* know?" Sharon asked very calmly but she was now gently shaking.

"No, you are the first to hear about the doctors," Charles ducked the question. He knew exactly what his wife was asking. He wasn't prepared for that question, and he hadn't thought of a reply. He sat at the table, his mind racing, and he remembered that Megan knew all about Beatrice. When he had been married to his second wife, they had discussed starting a family. At that time, it had seemed only natural to tell her all about his previous brief marriage. As far as Charles was concerned, Megan was the love of his life and he was never ever going to get married again, so why not tell her everything about his past.

"DOES MEGAN KNOW?" Sharon asked again, almost shouting. Jackson raised his head slightly on hearing his mother's name said out loud. He was ready to defend his mother's honour from his step-mum, something he had done before and would gladly do again. Charles could think of no other words to say.

"Yes," he replied. Sharon knew this answer was coming and had subconsciously prepared her stance under the table in readiness so she could storm out of the restaurant. On hearing the word *yes* from Charles' lips, she jumped up aggressively from the table, and stomped away through the restaurant. She bounded for the exit, nearly knocking an elderly chap down in the process who was not looking where he was going.

"It's OK, kids. It's just a shock for your mum. She'll be OK," Charles said reassuringly.

Just then, the waiter came over carrying bowls of ice-cream piled high and smothered with sauces, chocolate buttons, and sprinkles. "Wow kids, don't they look great?" he exclaimed, and they all tucked into their desserts. Charles looked across at his wife's empty seat and the delicious desert at her place setting.

"Can I have Mum's?" asked Jackson.

CHAPTER 17

Pebbles Caravan Park – THIS WAY

"Good afternoon. Pebbles Bay Caravan Park Reception, how can I help you?" came the joyless tone of the young staff member, who was manning the phones that morning.

"Oh, hello there. Yes, good afternoon. My name is Beatrice," she said slowly, in her aristocratic, warm, southern accent. "I'm trying to speak with Charles, Charles Cooper, and I seem to have misplaced his mobile number. I remember his mummy telling me he has a caravan of some sorts on your site, and I wonder if you can help me with his telephone number." She hesitated for a moment and, clearing her throat, she said, "It's rather terribly urgent."

The receptionist responded by reciting the onsite company policy on the passing out of personal and private information regarding site guests. This policy had been printed on a small, laminated card, about the size of a credit card and stuck discreetly under the counter of the reception desk. It was one of many policy signs that could be seen by employees when answering the telephones. The receptionist refused to pass out Charles' mobile number, but Beatrice was persistent, and, after a little persuasion, the receptionist agreed to write down Beatrice's mobile number and pass it to Charles when she next saw him walk past. It confirmed to Beatrice, however, that Charles could still be located at the caravan park.

In London, that very morning, things had come to a head between Beatrice and her daughter Evangeline. Emotions had been building in the household for the past several weeks, and Beatrice knew her daughter had inherited her father's hot-blooded European temperament. Beatrice had been subjected to many months of deep discussions and debate with her daughter. Evangeline was now 19 years old and planned to marry next year. She wanted her biological father to walk her down the aisle. Rupert, the future husband, had no views either way on the subject, but he had added that it was rather unfair on her stepfather who had raised her from a baby. He also was now firmly in the doghouse for his unwelcomed and unsupportive opinion.

Beatrice had known in her heart that this day would eventually come; she had been honest with Evangeline about her father, for most of her life. But, over the years, she had on the odd occasion painted an incorrect picture of Charles. This had been done with the best intentions but she had made him out to be a bit of a rogue, and someone whom her daughter should try and forget about. She had sort of allowed her daughter to believe that Charles had deserted her, in her time of need, and as such should be forgotten and was not important to them anymore. In fact, it was Beatrice's parents' idea to tell Evangeline that her biological father had ran out on her, and she should regard Beatrice's successful new husband as her father now and to forget about Charles once and for all.

The previous year, at the end of Evangeline's 18th birthday party, in the early hours of the morning, all the party guests having finally left, mother and daughter had decided to go for a sobering walk along the side of the River Thames. It was high-summertime, and the warm bright sun was rising early. Added together with excessive alcohol consumption on her daughter's special day, Beatrice uncontrollably had blurted out the significance of the very path they were walking on, and she had taken Evangeline back those 18 years when she and Charles had walked along the same towpath. All alone in the world and in love.

Evangeline, who had been affectionately holding her mother's hand, startled at the revelation, suddenly let go. Realising her actions could silence her mother, Evangeline gently searched for her mother's embrace again and begged her to continue. Beatrice let everything pour out of her broken heart and, with skilful probing questions from a young sharp mind, Evangeline started to slowly unravel the truth of the past.

"Where were you going, Mummy?" Evangeline enquired.

"Oh, just walking, darling, we were so in love. In love and alone. He held my hand and then we would stop, and Charles would place his hands either side of my face and he would gently hold me as he kissed me." Beatrice smiled as her hidden affection for Charles warmed her inside, her inhibitions relaxed from the several flutes of champagne that had passed her lips that evening. Reminiscing, she lifted her free hand to her cheek, imagining her Charles was there with her.

"The sun was rising, just like this," Beatrice stopped and pointed over the Thames to the brilliant morning sun. "We both didn't want that morning to end. In my head I could feel you growing inside of me, and Charles would place his hand on my belly to be close to you." Beatrice looked at her daughter through blurry tearful eyes and said, "Your father would always smile and sometimes cry when he did this." And she touched her own stomach.

They walked for hours, and they both enjoyed the peaceful empty streets and warm glorious morning. Beatrice, once started, never stopped talking, and Evangeline didn't miss a detail of the tale. She told her daughter that her biological father was in fact a wonderful, kind man and that she had loved him dearly. One passionate account followed the other, as mother reminisced of her first, young love and Evangeline lapped everything up. Beatrice recollected an endless list of romantic gestures and outings they had been on together in such a short time. Her words just came tumbling out as they walked, as she repeatedly blamed Grandma and Grandad for the split. She explained how they had insisted she leave Charles immediately to have any hope of bringing her daughter up successfully. They demanded that she should of course also stay in London, where they could protect her and where she belonged. Grandma and Grandad believed that if they wanted Evangeline to have the best start in life, with all the trimmings of a first-class private education, then working-class Charles should not have any part to play in her upbringing. They wanted no life distractions for their only granddaughter.

Beatrice was relentless and continued to open her heart to her beautiful daughter who walked beside her. Both now had tears rolling down their flushed cheeks. Beatrice was relieved to tell her daughter the truth after all these years, and to explain the course of events that happened all those years ago.

"I left quickly, in the middle of the night." Beatrice stopped walking, as if to emphasise this point. "Charles was asleep, and I only grabbed a few things. Staff went back to collect my belongings; I wasn't allowed to return. I don't really know why I did that; it was cruel, and it didn't feel right, it wasn't the right thing to do!" Beatrice had regrets as she spoke, and tears again filled her eyes. She told her daughter she had given Charles no chance of ever contacting her, but again repeated it was what she was told to do. Beatrice got everything off her chest, all the heartache and years of pent-up emotions. Through a moment of soberness, Beatrice pondered on not revealing the love letters, but she was committed now. She told her daughter about how Charles, over several years after she had left him, had sent numerous handwritten love letters to her, and how he had posted them to Grandma and Grandad's house.

"Do you still have them?" Evangeline eagerly interrupted and spoke for the first time in over an hour. Beatrice hesitated in her reply.

"Yes," Beatrice sheepishly replied as she looked down at the ground and she briefly fell silent for the first time as they walked. Her thoughts turned to the bundle of handwritten letters, hidden for years

228

in the zipped, inside pocket of an unused black handbag in the bottom of her wardrobe. Fingered and dog-eared from being lovingly read many times, she had kept them all in their respective envelopes and bundled in date order together with what now was a frayed red ribbon. They contained endless words of love, backed-up with promises of fatherly support and devotion. After five minutes of silence, Evangeline searched out her mother's hand and squeezed it reassuringly. She knew what she was doing.

"Please continue, Mummy, please tell me everything tonight, everything, once and for all," Evangeline whispered firmly with a reassuring smile. As they continued, they realised how far they had walked as the iconic Tower Bridge came into view. The sun was rising beautifully behind it, and without communicating they both paused to admire the magnificent view.

Beatrice continued talking again, slowly at first but soon dropped back into where she left off, feeling surprisingly free and alive from clearing her conscience. She recited all the antics of university life, the all-night parties, falling asleep in lectures, and the amazing friendships she made. She told her daughter about how her biological father had ventured off to France shortly after she had left him. And when he found out about his daughter, how he returned to England and immediately travelled to London to find them both. Evangeline was now tearful again, overwhelmed with the things she was hearing, and feeling the effects of the earlier party.

For years she had laid awake at night, hating an unknown man for deserting her when she needed him the most, but in truth, everything she had been told was a lie. Evangeline was starting to drift; she had decided what she was going to do, and she had heard more than enough for one evening.

But Beatrice continued talking. She described how Charles had knocked on their front door and how she had heard his voice on the doorstep from the open guest bathroom window. She listened to

Charles pleading with the butler to allow him to speak with her. Beatrice unsuccessfully attempted several times to explain how in just these few eighteen years, how things back then had been so very different. A different world, a different way of thinking and a different era of parental dictatorship. Beatrice found it easy to recall, having thought about that day often over the years, describing how Charles had sat on the doorstep for hours on end before the staff eventually moved him on. Through tears again, Beatrice explained how after night had fallen, she saw a dark figure loitering around at the end of the street, and she knew it was her Charles. She chose not to tell her daughter how she had cried for weeks after the shadow had eventually gone, not eating or sleeping, lost in her own broken heartache night after night.

Evangeline continued to listen attentively to her mother talking and knew when to listen and when to speak, but her silent rage was boiling inside of her now as they strolled, linking arms, now in the shadow of Big Ben. She was Charles' daughter and, just like her father, she had a temper when she was goaded.

As they neared home, Beatrice concluded her historical tale. Evangeline believed that her mother added insult to injury by repeating to her daughter that she had sat on this very bench, all those many years ago with her Charlie. A bench in the street, very close to their house that Evangeline had grown up sitting on with her friends as they had chatted about boys and looked out over the Thames.

With a rotten hangover that lasted for several days, Beatrice kept a low profile from her daughter, which was easy in such a large house which had many rooms on many different floors. Beatrice was aware her daughter was processing emotions that she had not experienced before, and she was under no illusion that the kettle was probably going to blow. Sure enough, it did.

Weeks turned into months and Evangeline continued to stomp around the house at every opportunity. Slamming doors and shouting uncontrollably at the slightest occurrence or thing that was said to her. Around the house, Beatrice had to listen to her daughter's loud opinion on a vast range of topics. These included what a bad mother she was! How could she be so weak to let others dictate her life, and that she was going to find her biological father on her own and required no assistance from anybody. She was in charge of her life, and she was not going to be dictated to. The thing that hurt Beatrice the most, was the evening when Evangeline yelled that she hated her mother, wasn't speaking to her for the rest of her life, and wanted nothing more to do with her. After many uncomfortable days and sleepless nights for everybody in the household, Evangeline eventually calmed, and Beatrice agreed to help her locate Charles.

One part of their plan was to journey north and see if Charles still lived in the same house. Beatrice still carried a secret torch for her Charlie, and unbeknown to anybody else, she was looking forward to making the trip with her daughter. After their discussions, Beatrice had shown Evangeline the letters Charles had written to her all those years ago. In those days, when people sent handwritten letters, they would often write their return address on the rear of the envelope, in-case they did not reach their destination, they could be 'returned to sender'. Charles on his many letters had done just that, and this address was spotted by Evangeline almost immediately as she read, re-read, and examined every letter. What followed were many more days of verbal outbursts as Evangeline accused her mother of always knowing where her real father lived.

The car journey north, under the guise that it was a mother and daughter bonding weekend away, had been mostly made in silence. Whilst Beatrice had been driving, she had often glanced across at her daughter, who for most of the journey had just stared out of the window, lost in her own emotions and thoughts. They had driven directly to Charles' house and Beatrice had waited in the car. She had watched with a knotted stomach as her daughter had walked up her first husband's driveway. Evangeline walked with purpose and stood at the front door with a positive stance, turning briefly for a reassuring glance in her mother's direction. Evangeline knocked the door several times, but nothing happened. No reply.

Charles' next-door neighbour was a tall, pale, skinny man who always wore a thread bear grey cotton tracksuit. On hearing the repeated door knocking from next door, the neighbour opened his side door and looked over the adjoining garden fence. He shouted over to her.

"They're not in. At their caravan," he yelled this only once, and then disappeared back inside his house, almost immediately as he had said it. Evangeline stood frozen to the spot, unsure of her next move. She had numerous unanswered questions running through her head, trying to decipher the words just shouted at her. After a few short moments, she gathered herself, and turned to face the direction from where the voice had bellowed. Evangeline had questions to ask so she marched round to the neighbour's house, not even looking up to see her mother's reaction as she came close to their car and switched driveways. After numerous repeated door knocks, it was clear that the occupant was refusing to answer his front door. With drooping shoulders, Evangeline walked unhurriedly back in her mother's direction. She checked repeatedly over her shoulder, in case he appeared at the door, but he clearly must have heard her and was choosing to ignore her.

"What now?" Evangeline said. With no more ideas on what to do next, she looked to her mother for guidance and direction. At that moment, she became a young, nervous nineteen-year-old child, with little life experience. Beatrice had had many days to think over this plan to find her Charles and fortunately had already planned their next move.

"I heard him say this many times. Charlie's parents had one of those static caravans by the sea. It was in Wales." Beatrice was now conscious of the intimidating, track-suited neighbour, now scrutinising them both through his raised grubby net curtains. They swiftly reversed back off the driveway, trying to avoid his glare.

"The caravan site was called something like, 'Stones' or 'Pebbles' … something like that," Beatrice said enthusiastically to her daughter.

"As a child, Charles was always at his caravan. He was constantly telling me stories of the things he got up to there. All his adventures on the beach with his family. Come on, let's go and get a coffee first, and then see if we can't find this caravan. We will give the caravan site a ring, I'll ring them, darling." Beatrice offered a smile followed by a gentle reassuring squeeze of her daughter's hand. Evangeline, through wet eyes and a quivering bottom lip, could only manage a nod of her head.

*

Debbie and David had gone alone this time, just for a few days to their caravan. This was something they hadn't done for a long time, but it was just the two of them and they were looking forward to being child free. They were both now sleeping in separate beds, not because they had fallen out, but both agreed that a good night's sleep was priceless and very important. It also helped that if ever their mobile phones rang from their new partners, then they could speak in peace without any conflicts or embarrassment. They were getting on better now than they ever had before in all their married life, and they cherished this newfound friendship.

David was a very house-proud partner and didn't need telling. He always wanted to keep the place looking smart and tidy and today he had decided that the outside of the caravan could do with a scrub, and the windows a good clean. Whilst he was busying himself sorting out his brushes and sponges, he glanced across at a neighbouring caravan. It wasn't a new caravan; it had been sited there since they had arrived on site. In the past, David had walked past several times and said 'hello' to the new occupants. Today he could see a man up a ladder installing a new TV aerial on the side of his caravan. David didn't give it another thought and moved round to the front of his caravan, focussing on the cleaning task in hand. It took him a good hour to complete a full exterior clean and end up back where he had started. He was in the process of getting fresh water into his bucket when again he looked across at his neighbour, who was still up his ladder, in the exact same position as an hour ago, and still obviously trying to fix his TV Aerial.

Inside the caravan, Debbie had been messaging Hunter all morning. He was the hunky caravan site occupant that she had met down at the beach the other day when she was on her bikini photo shoot. Since then, over the last few weeks they had been corresponding on a regular basis. With Debbie's newfound confidence, she had not been pulling her texting punches. Sometimes the text content had got very explicit. It turned out Hunter was a widow, still bringing up his children, but as they were now teenagers, they didn't really need him anymore. He explained how after his wife passed, he had decided to keep the caravan as some normality for his children. He wasn't looking for a relationship, he just yearned for the touch of female skin again. He had told her all about himself, that he didn't get much free time to date but that he found time for the gym and he was covered in tattoos. He had made it clear to Debbie that he missed sex. For Debbie, this was music to her ears.

On her friend's group chat, Debbie had described Hunter as a Bradley Cooper lookalike, and this had caused a free-for-all of sexual innuendos of what Debbie should do to this man. Several comments also saying that if she wasn't going to shag him, then there was a long list of her friends who would do the honours. An excited but nervous Debbie was ready. It had been a while, but it was happening today.

"I'm popping out for an hour, darling," Debbie said, pulling her big coat tight around herself as she passed her husband. She clinked in her high heels along the path, but didn't hang about, and was out of sight before giving her husband any real opportunity to respond. She didn't want to explain that she wanted something else, and she wanted it right now.

Hunter had a caravan on the North side, which unusually on this occasion didn't bother Debbie. She was hoping she would be able to get in and out of Hunter's caravan completely unseen. They both had around an hour of free, uninterrupted time. His caravan was empty, so Debbie had told Hunter to brace himself as she was on her way round. Debbie wore heels, no bra, and a full face of make-up. With a very short skirt and her shirt unbuttoned almost to her waist, she had wrapped herself in her big coat. She had previously worked out the quickest way to get to his caravan, but it still meant the inevitable walk past the clubhouse. She walked with pace and determination, staring directly forwards, all the time hoping she would not bump into anybody she knew.

David again paid little interest to his neighbour who was still up his ladder, fiddling with his aerial. With a full bucket of fresh water, he finished cleaning the complete outside of his caravan. He was now in a position to do another loop of his caravan. This time to give the windows a last rub down with his chamois leather and make everything sparkle. He couldn't help, however, but look over in the direction of his neighbours, as this time he could hear raised voices. The man, still up his ladder, with a woman, presumably his wife, waving her arms around and shouting, as she disappeared back and forth inside their caravan. David could feel the tension but made a conscious effort to stay out of it. He wiped down his first window and, after more shouting, thought to himself, *I have to go over and help*. He dropped his chamois leather into his bucket under the window he had just cleaned and ambled over to his neighbours.

Wearing his best smile and from a short distance away, David shouted across to his neighbour so as not to startle him.

"Hi, how you getting on?" He was mindful that his help might not be welcomed.

"Not good, mate!" came the immediate reply from a broken man, who was shaking his head as he spoke, whilst he still stood on the top rung of his ladder. The man fell silent and continued to stare at David, hoping to be rescued.

"Can I offer a suggestion?" David enquired with the neighbour. "I don't want to stick my nose in!" David added. The distressed man immediately waved David to come closer and help. The neighbour was clearly at a loss on what to do next and welcomed any suggestions from anybody at this stage. This was a man on the edge.

David now walked on at a pace, with a skip in his step, knowing his presence was welcomed. He alighted the steps of his neighbour's decking.

"Hi, I'm David. Is that your wife inside?"

"Yes. PAULINE," screamed the stressed man up the ladder, and a lady came running outside. She was wearing a different outfit when he had seen her a few moments ago. He had started to notice things like this now.

"Hi, I'm David," he said, shaking the lady's hand and noticing how soft her skin was. "Can I tell you both a quick story which might be, well it will help, I can see now it will help. It's a quick story that might fix your problem." David was smiling at both parties in turn and at the same time he took a quick look around at the adjoining caravans. He was certain he knew how to fix the aerial issue. David had the full attention now of both of his neighbours.

"When I first arrived on-site, I paid for the TV aerial company in town to put up my aerial. I had young children back then and the TV was important." Pauline raised her hands in the air and gave her husband a filthy look. David assumed from her exaggerated arm waving that Pauline had also wanted to call a similar such company.

David continued, and with an attempt to calm the situation, raised a finger slightly to indicate he had more to tell.

"Well, whilst the guy was putting up the aerial, the engineer man told me a story about how he was on our caravan site a few months earlier fitting an aerial to another caravan. I think he pointed over there someplace. Anyhow, he said that there was a chap fitting his own aerial to his caravan, just like you next door. And just like you he couldn't get a picture on his TV.

"The neighbour asked for advice and the aerial company chap, I can't remember his name, but he had informed him that this is what he does for a living and explained that this is how he pays his mortgage and that he doesn't give out free advice. He had told him that it would cost £20 for the aerial installation advice. Reluctantly this neighbour had paid the money and the engineer had said, 'Take a look at all you neighbours' aerials, which way up are the rabbit's ears? Is the rabbit laying down asleep or is the rabbit stood up, and are his rabbit ears sticking up to the sky or laying down?' This reference was to the antenna prongs on the aerial." David then made pretend rabbit ears with his fingers and twisted his fingers from side to side as he looked around the other caravans.

The man up the ladder caught on very quickly indeed and turned his TV aerial through 90 degrees to match his neighbours' aerial's positioning. Almost immediately a child's voice shouted from inside the caravan "IT'S WORKING." Pauline ran inside and then almost immediately reappeared with a smile and the words "Thank Goodness, thank you," and she leaned forwards as if to hug David, overwhelmed with the once stressful situation.

David smiled and began to walk away, his good deed for the day was done. Pauline dashed back inside again and reappeared very quickly waving a £20 note and repeatedly saying the words "Thank you". David persistently declined the offer of the money. He appeased the woman by asking that they buy him a beer in the clubhouse the next time they see him in there. A content David walked on back to his window cleaning, he didn't really get a thankyou from the man up the ladder. David put that down to stress and manly embarrassment.

Debbie was relieved to have now passed the clubhouse, and her excitement returned to what was in store for her. Only one more turn and she would be moments away from Hunter's caravan. Her thoughts turned to sex. She yearned for sex, it had been so long, and she was surprised at how excited she was. She felt like a teenager again. She was partially naked and on her way to spend time with a man she hardly knew. She had missed this type of excitement. She felt alive and she liked this feeling.

Knocking the door and taking hold of the handle, she took a casual look over her shoulder. She didn't wait for a reply, and she entered the caravan without being asked. It was an expensive, modern caravan and she liked what she saw. She felt immediately comfortable, and she also liked that Hunter stood staring at her whilst holding two glasses of champagne.

"Hi," Hunter said and offered out a glass in Debbie's direction. He was wearing a light blue long-sleeved crisp shirt and had tastefully folded a couple of turns of each sleeve so that it tightened across his dark, tattooed forearms. His shirt was tucked into a pair of expensive slim fitting jeans, and he wore designer tanned brogues. Debbie turned and locked the front door behind her. Turning back around, they both stared at each other. After a few seconds of smiling, Debbie lifted her coat off her shoulders, and it dropped to the floor where she stood. She felt it was the right thing to do and she felt empowered and alive. With her shoulders back, Hunter's eyes were drawn immediately to her open blouse and Debbie's almost exposed large breasts. Hunter couldn't tear his eyes away from her body. Near to where he stood, and without looking, he placed his glass down on the counter. Whilst maintaining eye contact, he began to unbutton his own shirt. Debbie was very attracted to Hunter who was several years her junior. His opened shirt revealed a sleek muscular suntanned physique covered in a fine whisper of dark soft chest hair and endless tattoos covering his entire chest.

His resemblance to the famous actor Bradley Cooper was extraordinary, and Debbie was feeling very aroused in the presence of this man standing before her. Holding his stare, she slowly walked towards him. As she got closer, he instinctively reached out to caress her breasts which were now completely hanging out the front of her open blouse. Debbie pushed his hand to one side and raised a finger to his lips, silencing him. She looked into his eyes.

"Do not speak. Do not move," Debbie said softly and then slowly she lowered her gaze and her hand moved at first along his jaw line then it dropped to his muscular, solid, granite-like chest. She pressed firmly and wove her fingers through his chest hair as she sought out each nipple. She looked again into his eyes and one finger again silenced his lips.

"I have wanted to do this for a long time," Debbie whispered. She broke eye contact and left her hand caressing his chest hair, whilst reaching across with the other hand for her glass, she drank down the remaining champagne in one gulp. Placing the glass back down, Debbie slowly moved her fingers over his tattooed shoulders, down the centre of his chest and down to his groin. She was startled at his size, and she caressed her hand in a circular motion firmly through his jeans. Debbie lowered herself slowly to her knees and knelt directly in front of Hunter. She knelt staring at his belt buckle. Hunter had listened to Debbie's wishes and had remained silent throughout.

She unfastened his belt with ease and she opened the top button of his jeans. She pulled down hard on the zip, as it eventually made its way over his growing mound. As soon as the zip was down, Debbie pulled aside his crisp white Calvin Klein boxers and out dropped a substantial, partially erect penis. She was initially startled at its length, and she lurched backwards slightly as it moved towards her face. It was the biggest penis she had ever seen, and it was not yet fully erect. It was not pointing upwards but directly towards her. What she was also unprepared for, was that Hunter was fully shaved. Everything gone, all his pubic hair had been removed, even around his balls. Reaching up she took it in both hands and at first caressed it slowly, intrigued at its hair-free smoothness. She was captivated by his balls which were smooth and firm, something she had not been used to. Everything about Hunter she found exciting and sexy. As Debbie leaned forwards, she instinctively closed her eyes and opened her mouth as wide as she could.

David, satisfied with his aerial good deed, returned to his caravan cleaning chores. Only occasionally did he look over at his neighbour whilst he finished cleaning his windows. He saw that his neighbour had put away his ladder and was presumably inside his caravan watching television. Debbie had returned after just under two hours, informing David that she had been delayed as she got caught chatting to the girls. Still tingling all over, a red flushed-face Debbie disappeared quickly inside to the bathroom to tidy herself and shower. Later, Debbie smiled lovingly at David when he eventually came back inside and began to put away his cleaning things.

"I do so love you," Debbie whispered and planted a warm kiss on David's cheek as he recited the story about their neighbour's aerial shenanigans. What followed was several hours of calm silence as they both busied themselves around the caravan, enjoying each other's company.

"Do you agree we are being honest in our relationship now? I would hate anything to ever ruin this." Debbie asked, beckoning for her husband to come over and sit next to her on the sofa.

"I agree. I have never been so happy!" David replied with a smile and a gentle stroke of her bare arm as he sat down next to her on the sofa.

"Do you have anything you want to tell me? It's OK, I know, I forgave you years ago. It's all in the past," Debbie added. Debbie was fishing, she had nothing on David. He had been a wonderful faithful husband, as far as she knew. Wracked with guilt, she was trying to compensate for the life-changing sex that she had just experienced only a few hours previous. Feeling empowered, both from her financial independence and her blossoming celebrity status and of course the sex, Debbie had decided that she wanted more of Hunter, and many more men who looked exactly like him. She had several years of catching up to do, and she didn't want to waste another minute.

For the first time, as far as she could remember, she had enjoyed reaching orgasm through intercourse. She liked it, and she wanted it to happen again. David was puzzled and his mind was racing, *how does she know?* he thought. *Or is she on about that last stag-do to Cornwall I went on?* David couldn't think straight, and he had a worried look on his face. Debbie saw the look on David's face and smiled to herself, thinking *He has been a naughty boy then,* making a mental note to get that information out of him one day. Debbie's confidence grew.

"Look. The past is the past. Don't you agree?" Debbie said whilst reaching out to hold her husband's hand.

"Yes. Let's just go forward. Life is so short," David responded. "I have Conrad now and you are so successful with all your online show-biz stuff."

"It's important that you listen. I really don't want things to change. But I want us both to be honest from now on. No secrets whatsoever," Debbie said firmly and nodded at David, inviting a reply.

"Yes. If it's in the past it can stay in the past," David offered. Debbie smiled to herself, and she was pleased that she had got those words out of David's mouth without much effort. Finding the words easily, she continued to take charge of the situation.

"Well. I have something to say, being mindful of what you have just said," Debbie paused, pointing a finger at David. He knew when to be attentive and stay silent.

"You know when I went on my sister's hen night, to Blackpool?" Not wanting or waiting for a reply, Debbie continued. "Well. We all got very drunk, and I mean drunk. Drunk, drunk. All the girls were flirting and snogging this group of guys. How we met them I have no idea, it just sort of happened. Anyway." Debbie couldn't believe she was saying this out loud. "Anyway. I woke up in this bloke's hotel room!" Debbie didn't stop for breath, she wanted her confession out in the open, as quickly as possible.

"I don't know if anything happened exactly. I was that drunk, and I just tried to forget about it in my head. No one else knew. I just sneaked back to my own room." Debbie had used lots of body language whilst explaining her incident in an attempt to invite sympathy and understanding. She lowered her voice and tilted her head to one side. Nervously, she was anticipating an angry response from her husband.

"It's in the past. Let's move on, and let's not mention it again," David replied.

Debbie didn't say anything else for several moments. Her eyes watered at his loyal understanding, and her head lowered even further as she stared at the floor.

"Honestly. I don't know if anything happened. But it must have. I am so sorry. I have let you down! I have let our marriage down! I don't know his name; he doesn't know my name. I can't even remember what he looked like, and we never saw any of them ever again." Debbie was frantically rambling now, with tears rolling down her cheeks. Placing an arm on each shoulder, David looked loving at his wife.

"Why are you still going on about it? It is in the past," David said, and he started to stand in an attempt to defuse the uncomfortable situation his wife was in. He started looking for his next DIY cleaning task around the caravan. He was dealing with the situation the only way he knew.

Debbie continued talking as he walked away towards the kitchen. She knew David was listening. She hadn't reached the punch line yet and she continued calmly.

"It's my sister's wedding anniversary in December. We've been invited to a party to celebrate it. It's four years since they got married," Debbie paused; David was walking around the kitchen. "The Hen night was the week before the wedding." Debbie had a lot more to say to David, who hadn't grasped what Debbie was trying to tell him. David was unsure how to process the situation.

"I'm sorry, what you on about?" David said, who had now ducked down behind the kitchen sink looking for some cleaning cloths.

"Please come back and sit down. I want to tell you something else!" Debbie asked, almost sobbing now. David returned to his wife's side, sitting down next to her, he maintained eye contact. He gently lifted his hand to Debbie's mouth and spoke first.

"I know Paris is not mine, she looks nothing like me. I have always known but I will always love her as my own. That night you jumped on me when you came back home. I didn't know what was happening, I thought you had drugged me or something with Viagra, but I know I didn't ejaculate, that is for certain," David continued.

"I was so mixed up I just wanted you to be happy, so I kept my mouth shut and let you do your thing." Debbie started to cry as she held onto David's arm. She had kept that in all these years, and all this time he knew. Debbie didn't know what to say next and they both laid back onto the sofa and hugged and her tears slowed to a gentle roll down her cheeks. David's eyes watered and he also found comfort in talking about the past. They both calmed and realised that, at that exact moment, they were now more in love than they ever had been.

"Nothing must ever change between us. Never!" Debbie whispered after several minutes as they lay together. "I think she should never know," Debbie added, sitting bolt upright and staring at David, waiting for his reply.

"But that's just my opinion. I will be guided by you; we do this together."

"I agree. Why should we ever tell her? Let's take this secret to our graves, especially if you don't know his name." David questioned with raised eyebrows. "Was that true, did you not even know his name?"

"Oh My God. I can't even picture his face!" Debbie jumped to her feet, emphasising her regret for that evening. "We were so drunk, all of us. Me and you had not had sex in years, and he was showing me some affection and, and, and well that was that, it was quick I remember that much, god it was all a bit uneventful and strange and quick." Debbie, feeling comfortable talking about sex with another man to her husband, offered an awkward laugh. Debbie had dreaded this day for years, but it was all going OK with her loving companion.

"It's good to talk. We must always talk," Debbie said. "Promise me we will always talk and tell each other everything," Debbie asked lovingly.

"Promise," David replied with a hug and a smile, their new relationship now even stronger than ever.

"Loved your heels earlier," David said with a wink to his best friend. Debbie blushed and remained silent as she stared at her David with a newfound respect.

*

After cake and coffee, Evangeline had regained her composure. With a new-found purpose she had wrestled them from her mother's grasp and taken charge of the car keys.

"Right. You book the hotel, a nice one, and I will start driving west. That's right, isn't it, west towards Wales? That's how I remember it from school, they both begin with a W!" Evangeline commanded as she turned left at the next roundabout and began following the signs for the motorway.

After several minutes of silence, as Beatrice stared at her phone, which had no reception, she said aloud, "I can't believe we are going to Wales." Beatrice continued as best as possible to search online for a hotel. As the miles ticked away, Beatrice stared across at her daughter with pride and boundless love in her eyes. Beatrice felt her phone vibrate as messages and emails connected with her phone as they drove near to a town. Beatrice ignored them all and turning away from her daughter, she again typed '5-star hotel Wales' into the search engine.

As she drove, alone in her own head, Evangeline pondered on her predicament. She was driving to find her biological father, someone she had never met, at an unknown caravan site in Wales. A country she had never visited before and a man who didn't know she even existed. She had a range of emotions that one minute lifted her spirits to shear and utter excitement, and to the next making her almost cry as she drove.

Her entire life, her mother had led her to believe that her biological father was an immoral, awful man. She was still processing how she was going to move forwards with her mother over these years of being lied to, but now she was going to find the man she wanted to walk her down the aisle.

That night. The night when everything had come out into the open. Her biological father's description had been offered. His mannerisms, his features and character had been described to her, as well as all the antics from their university partying. Over the subsequent months her mother had occasionally repeated stories from their time together, forgetting how much had been revealed on the sunrise walk along the River Thames. Evangeline was now satisfied that she knew almost everything there was to know about her real father. When she saw him, she would know straight away that he was her dad. She believed she would recognise him immediately.

Beatrice had been productive. The in-car Sat Nav had been updated with the caravan site postcode. She had spoken with the receptionist at the only four-star hotel in town and she had reserved two rooms without even asking the price; the only request being that they were the best rooms available. A second call was required to finish the booking as the telephone connection had dropped out as they drove through the Welsh valleys. Her chores complete, Beatrice looked out of the car window and smiled at the beautiful mountain scenery. Her thoughts also turned to Charles. She was starting to get a little excited herself and was enjoying the quality time and adventure she was undertaking with her daughter. It had taken a long time, longer than would be acceptable in this modern age. But she recognised how much of her young adult life had been controlled by her parents. They were now old and frail and didn't hold the influence over her as they once had. Beatrice held no anger towards her parents for her strict upbringing.

After several hours of what appeared to be continuous green valleys and fields, they both knew they were getting close to the caravan site. Having to stop on red at a set of traffic lights, directly opposite was a road sign that read 'Pebbles Caravan Park This Way'. There was an arrow directing visitors to turn left down a country lane.

Evangeline burst into tears, heart-wrenching bouts of tears, and loudly blurted out, "I've changed my mind. Can we go home please?" Evangeline was inconsolable and had completely forgotten she was in the driving seat. The lights turned green, and they didn't move an inch before they turned back to red. Beatrice started to pull the steering wheel gently towards her, whilst calmly and reassuringly convincing her daughter to take back control of the car and pull over to the side of the road, in order to appease the now horn-beeping traffic behind and allow them to pass.

CHAPTER 18

Pink Inflatable Flamingo

That is definitely gold, thought Tony as he hastily laid down his metal detector onto the warm golden sand. He was still searching the area of the recently excavated sand dune. It was a big area, so he had lots of virgin ground left to explore. So far today he had found a few worthless items including an old rusted knife minus its handle, an old penny, and a rusty bolt fastened to a rotten lump of wood. This particular tone in his headphones, however, was strong, a new sound with a deep rich tone, which he didn't instinctively recognise. Each metal had its own unique sound. He hadn't heard this sound before, and he was secretly hoping it was gold. As he started to dig, his heart was racing in anticipation of a prize find. He started attacking the sand vigorously with his spade, he then used his bare hands to dig deeper and deeper into the ground, throwing handfuls of loose sand into the air.

*

"I'm going up to the club, darling, to read my paper and have a coffee," David informed his beloved wife, kissing her on the cheek. It was followed by a big smile and a friendly stroke of her bare shoulder.

"OK. I've got online work to do, about two hours' worth so I'll see you later," Debbie replied, pointing at her laptop, and settled in at the dining room table with her notepad and pen. She didn't watch as David left the caravan, and she also didn't see that he was wearing his new smart jeans and an open neck light blue shirt. Debbie's social-media management work was becoming serious now. She had secured several new business contracts, which all required daily posting and each account earned her around £250 a month. One of Debbie's accounts that she managed was an estate agent. Each morning, Debbie logged into the company's website, where she had 'Read-Only' access and this provided her with the new house listings for that day, as well as information on any new house sales. It was Debbie's job to make sure these new listings all went out on *The Big Three*, Twitter, Facebook, and Instagram. Debbie found this work thoroughly enjoyable. She had started to get systems in place, including example templates which allowed her to simply cut and paste the information across all platforms. She had also compiled a list of suitable hashtags that she could use to speed things up.

One account done, time for the second. But before she moved onto her next account, she checked herself in the mirror. She quickly unbuttoned a button on her blouse and, ensuring her new expensive black bra and its contents were partially visible, she began taking numerous selfies. Using the 'sexy secretary working hard in the office' theme, she then posted the shots immediately over her numerous different social media platforms. The final picture, with her blouse coming completely off and everything on show, she posted to her *Friends Only* account. She wanted to keep this last account a secret for as long as she could from David, but it was really starting to take off with over 450 subscribers now all paying a monthly fee to see her 'exclusive' adult pictures.

David had never been so content and happy in his life as he was right now. He had a spring in his step and a smile and wave for anybody and everybody he passed on his caravan site. He walked with the sun on his face and love in his heart. His first stop was into the little onsite shop to purchase a newspaper, before heading for the clubhouse bar. David now had a smartphone, and his daughters had recently been nagging him about how many trees were being chopped down every day, just so he could read a newspaper. His environmentally conscious children's ultimate goal was for their father to read his newspaper on his mobile phone. He had tried to defend his argument by stating that there are some things in life that shouldn't change, and how good it feels to hold a book or magazine, rather than looking at a bright screen. His young daughters said they didn't really understand this argument. Owen, the south site manager, was the only person behind the bar when David entered the quiet and deserted clubhouse.

"Good afternoon, Owen," David offered with a nod and a smile as he approached the bar. First double checking that the bar counter wasn't all wet with beer slops, he then leaned on it with both elbows, clasping his hands. "Nice and quiet for you today. Cappuccino please, young man, when you are ready." David added a cheers at the end of his sentence as he glanced around, looking for a suitable well-lit table to plonk himself down on and read his old-fashioned newspaper. David had noticed that his eyesight had not been great for some months now, but if he sat next to a window with the sun beaming in, he found he could read even the smallest of print. The coffee machine began doing its *whoosh* thing as David again attempted to instigate conversation.

"I don't often see you behind the bar much, Owen?" David enquired. Owen had his back to him, watching the coffee machine gurgling and making strange noises.

"I'm just covering Beryl's shift. It's only a couple of hours. She's gone to a funeral. Hopefully with this sunshine I will be lucky if I see anybody else. They'll be on the beach all day."

"Oh. I'm sorry about the funeral," David replied.

"Distant family member, I think. She's OK. Back tomorrow," Owen said, and as he turned and started to walk, the cup and saucer began to wobble. As he lowered the cup of coffee down on the bar, David noticed a small amount of coffee had escaped from the cup and spilt down the side.

"It's on the house. I'm out of biscuits," Owen stated, relieved that he had managed to work out how to use the coffee machine and continued replacing the pink gin optic with a new 1.5 litre bottle. The gin bottle was specifically designed for commercial optic use, with the label stuck on upside down, so it would be the right way round for the customer when he lifted it onto the optic stand.

"Thank you. I hope it remains quiet for you," David replied and glanced along the bar. "You have a new guest beer in today?" David's attempts at polite small talk continued and he pointed at a new shiny copper-coloured beer pump head.

"Arrived last Tuesday," Owen responded, "but we have nearly run out of branded glasses already." Owen bent down and lifted a jug-type beer glass that had the new beer's logo neatly printed on it with bright green and black lettering.

"Smart-looking glass," David replied, giving a nod of approval.

"That's the problem," Owen interjected. "They are being stolen as fast as I can order them in."

"No!" David spurted out, genuinely surprised. "People are stealing the beer glasses?" David's thoughts turned to the last time when he was in Charles' caravan. David couldn't help but comment on Charles vast collection of pub beer glasses that he had on display in his illuminated glass-fronted cupboard.

"They steal every glass you could imagine. Do you remember those big bowl gin glasses? *All gone.* Every single one," Owen said with raised arms, searching for an answer on what to do about it.

"I know, I saw it the other day. Right in front of my eyes," David said, pleased he had a story to tell and continue chatting with Owen.

"I was in early just for one pint and a young chap, tall with curly blonde hair and suntanned arms. He ordered one of your new beers, he was sat with a lady next to my table. She was older than him," David continued his story even though he was unsure if he had Owen's attention who was now opening and closing fridge doors.

Owen raised an eyebrow and looked over at David, "Did he rob one of my glasses?"

"Well, this chap finishes his beer and goes back up to the bar for another. As he stood up, he slid his empty glass to the edge of the table in front of the woman he was with. She immediately opened her handbag on the chair below. Bang, it disappeared. At the bar, Beryl refused to serve him another pint until he brought his glass back. He did the walk of shame back to his table, the woman with the coordination of a magician lifted the glass out of her handbag. I couldn't believe it. Shameless. He was good looking as well," David smiled at the memory of the curls. Owen just shook his head and continued to busy himself around the bar.

David made his way over to his selected perch, a table in the far corner by the bay window. The smell and feel of a newly printed newspaper excited David and he decided the feeling was priceless. He did, however, understand the environmental issues, and he was aware he had young daughters. Hopefully grandchildren one day, so he had made a mental decision to make more of an effort. Today, however, he was going to read his newspaper from front to cover and enjoy every minute of it, in complete peace and quiet. Along with his free coffee!

*

It had been a long and excruciating drive home from the caravan. As a family they had planned to stay a few days longer, but after Charles' aforementioned marriage revelations over dinner the previous evening, Sharon had told everyone to pack their bags now as they were going home immediately. Sharon was packed and ready to go in minutes and she had gone and sat in the back seat of the car. She hadn't spoken with anyone that morning and her arms were firmly folded, seat belt fastened. Charles was also packed within a few minutes, but he took care of his children first. He offered them reassurance that Mummy and Daddy were all OK and that Mum was just a little shocked after hearing about Beatrice. That's all it was. On the drive home, Charles asked several times if anybody wanted a toilet stop, but this was always met with *let's just get home* from most people in the car. Sharon remained silent throughout the entire journey. Sophie eventually forced a toilet pit-stop at a supermarket, which was in fact only about ten miles from home.

Charles pulled onto his driveway; the same frosty atmosphere hanging in the air as when they had set off home from their caravan several hours earlier. The car was quickly vacated as its occupants raced inside the house, leaving Charles alone in the driver's seat to savour the *coming home* feeling for himself. He opened the car boot and gazed down at his three perfectly loyal dogs. They stared longingly back at him.

"At least you still love me," Charles said, giving each one a pat and stroke for being so good on the journey home.

"You all right, mate?" came a voice from over the boundary garden fence. "Did you have a good holiday?"

"Some are better than others, buddy," Charles muttered as he ushered his dogs out of the car and into the safety of his garden.

"Come on round, I've got something to show you," added Simon, the neighbour, not really giving Charles any choice in the matter. Charles hesitated; he had just driven for nearly two hours (which had seemed more like six) and desperately needed the toilet, as well as a cold beer, but the neighbour had already disappeared back inside his house.

Well, at least it delays the verbal assault I am almost certainly about to receive from my wife, he thought. He turned round, feeling sorry for himself he let out a big sigh, but proceeded to go and see what it was his neighbour wanted.

Charles walked around the end of his driveway to the main road and then up his neighbour's drive. He couldn't remember when he last went inside his neighbour's house, but he now noticed that things were starting to look a little tired and unkempt. Since his neighbour's divorce, things had gone downhill compared to how they used to keep their house. It was always kept lovely, with clean windows and a permanently pristine tidy front garden. Charles neared an open front door and he peeked inside a dark gloomy house. There came a shout from inside.

"Come in. Come in." It was the smell Charles noticed first; not a really bad smell, just an untidy dirty odour from a house that wasn't getting cleaned or aired as often as it should, reminiscent of a divorced man, a man living alone. Charles ambled inside and on into the lounge. The fixture and fittings were just how he remembered from only a few years ago. Nothing had changed. Simon was tall and lean and a very likeable man. He looked a little older than his years, and his clothes needed updating but Charles thought it was time he met someone else. Someone who could pull him out of this rut he was in. He has a full head of hair, his own teeth, and this house. Surely there is someone for him. A couple of years ago, Simon's wife had gone away for a long weekend with her girlfriends to someplace in Spain. Whilst waiting at airport arrivals, his wife's travelling companions came giggling through the arrivals gate and handed him a letter. Simon subsequently found out that she had met a man some ten years her junior on a beach and she had moved in with him. He was hopeful that she would only be gone a few weeks, come to her senses, and come home, but here he was years later and no sign of her. Charles entered the lounge and looked at his neighbour sat on the sofa.

"Watch this." Simon pointed a remote control at an exceptionally large flat-screen television in the corner of the room, and up came a view of the main road and most of Charles' driveway. Charles knew his neighbour had CCTV cameras, he could see them hanging up, but he never imagined for one minute that the cameras were also pointing at his house and recording every move he made in his front garden.

Charles, still standing, opened his mouth to offer an objection to this invasion of his privacy, when on the screen appeared a large expensive-looking blue saloon car. It had pulled up at the end of Charles' driveway, blocking his entrance.

"Sit down, sit down, man," insisted Simon, pointing at the sofa and then gesturing back towards the television. "This afternoon, this car arrived – wait for it." Charles didn't get a chance to say what he was thinking as Simon continued.

"One woman first, the pretty young one." Charles watched the screen in silence. He witnessed a woman get out of the blue car and walk up Charles' driveway. She disappeared for a minute, out of view, and presumably stood at his front door. The television screen remained focussed on the stationary blue car. Nothing happened for a minute.

"I shouted over the fence that you were out," Simon added his commentary without looking away from the television.

"The cheeky cow only then comes and knocks on my front door." Without looking, Simon pressed a button on his remote control and a different CCTV camera view came up on the television screen. Charles was now looking at the camera view that covered his neighbour's front door. The face on the screen was now clear and bright.

"What did she want?" Charles asked with some hesitation, unsure how to cope with a sudden bout of anxiety. Charles had gone red and he felt cold then hot. He couldn't explain these emotions.

"I didn't answer the door. God knows what she wanted but the car looked expensive. The other one was just as pretty."

Simon clicked back to the first camera view as the young woman walked back to the waiting car. Charles watched as she was now standing next to the passenger door of the blue car. It was then the passenger door opened, and another woman got out.

"Beatrice," Charles blurted out loud.

"Ah Hah. You know her, then!" Simon asked, searching for more information with a barrage of questions. He was interested now, and clearly proud of his CCTV equipment and technical operator skills. Charles looked back at the TV and remained silent. Blocking out the noise he attempted to process what he had just seen in his own head.

"Can you get me a copy of this?" Charles asked. Not really knowing what or how he could get a copy of it.

Simon grinned smugly. "I'll message you the clip. Who is it then?" After a pause, "… if you tell me who it is, come on, mate … what you been up to? Spill the beans."

Charles' mind was racing. He looked across at his relentless neighbour.

"Beatrice was my first wife," replied a shocked and bewildered Charles.

Simon grinned, and very quickly offered, "I knew you'd been married before but thought she was called Megan or something. Didn't know there was another one before that, you dirty dog. And that's your kid, isn't it? She looks just like you." Simon was excited at his observations. Not much had been happening recently in his life and he relished a little bit of gossip. Charles took a moment to gather himself. He had told his family about Beatrice out of the blue, and at the same time she was at his front door. Charles was taken aback, more by the timing rather than seeing his first wife on the screen. Simon was right. The younger woman certainly did look like him. She looked exactly like him. Charles needed air right now and he needed to leave. He needed to take back control of his life. He stood up and was out the front door in just a few long strides. It was a few moments before he turned and called back to his neighbour. "Cheers, mate, you're a good neighbour. I need to tell Sharon."

*

"David. David." Without looking at him, Owen shouted as he ran around the side of the bar into the lounge and hurriedly headed for the clubhouse exit.

"Watch the bar, mate, you're in charge. The police are on the beach." David was unable to offer a reply as Owen ran out the door and was gone. He looked around at a silent, empty lounge. It was slightly eerie when empty. He picked up his coffee cup and walked over to bar. *Thank goodness there is nobody here,* he thought. He went round the back of the bar and smiled to himself. It brought back all those cruise ship bartending memories. He liked the feeling and leant with one hand on a bar pump, remembering when he would talk for hours with the passengers in this exact same position. It was always easier to tell the American passengers that he was from London, no one ever knew where Doncaster was.

Familiarising himself with all the spirit bottles, David strutted around looking at beer bottles and glasses with not a care in the world.

"I'm going to have another free coffee," David told himself, glancing over at the coffee machine. He justified it as wages for tending bar. Selecting a crisp white saucer, he reached for a cup. As he was looking at the wide variety of trendy coffee pods on offer, his peace was soon interrupted by a barrage of noise and voices shouting outside the club house. Almost immediately the doors burst open with a thud and a stream of half-naked people filed in. Some were wearing swimming trunks, some with towels around their shoulders and carrying all manner of chairs and umbrellas. One person even had an inflatable pink flamingo round their waist, which at first didn't fit through the door. The relentless hordes of people pushing from behind forced the flamingo through and the noise got lounder and louder as they all talked over each other.

The crowds seemed to automatically divide themselves. One half started to fill up the lounge, moving chairs and forming circles around tables. The other half headed straight for the bar. They all stared at David at the same time.

A tall middle-aged man, wearing aged skimpy blue swimming trunks (who should really be covered up for a family bar) was the first to catch his attention. David's eyes moved up to his face as he neared the bar. It never occurred to him that they might all want a drink … he was the only bartender on duty!

"Two pints of Best, a pink gin and slim line and three diet cokes please, mate. No ice," said the well-endowed, blue-trunk-wearing chap. At the bar counter he appeared naked from the waist up and David liked that he was very muscular indeed. For several seconds, David was lost in his sky-blue eyes and intrigued with the fact that almost the man's entire upper body was covered in an array of tattoos. David found his eyes exploring the gentleman's smooth, firm, hair-free chest but that moment was soon shattered with numerous other loud requests for drinks.

"Eer yes of course," replied David, who hadn't really prepared himself for actually serving anybody. Where had Owen gone? Turning, David reached down for two-pint glasses and repeated the word 'Best' with a puzzled look on his face and a shrug of his shoulders.

"Best. Best. Best bitter, man," came a prompt stern reply from the tattooed man and a heavy tap with his index finger on the relevant brass beer pump. David started to pour the pint of beer. It was probably down to stress, but David believed that the beer on that pump came out the slowest he had ever seen in his life. He made an attempt at small talk to try and appease the long line of customers who were now all staring at him in silence.

"The place was empty only a minute ago," David attempted to speak to the crowd, his antics were lost on the angry thirsty revellers. He broke eye contact and looked down at the beer glass which by now was half full as he tilted it to one side. He didn't need to be taught this; he had done this many times in his life as a younger man.

"Unexploded bomb found on the beach apparently. Everyone has been evacuated off the beach, 500 metre cordon the police chap was shouting."

David acknowledged the information from the man, nodding in thanks for the update as he placed down the first pint of Best and reached for his second glass.

"From World War Two someone said on the way up. Bomb squad are on their way apparently. That bloody lanky idiot of a metal detector bloke found it someone said." This thirsty customer had both his elbows on the counter and was staring at the beer as it filled the glass.

"My goodness. A bomb," David replied in general to the line of faces in front of him. Things were all happening very quickly now, and there were at least twenty customers at the bar all waiting for his attention, fanning their cash as if it would get them served sooner. David couldn't concentrate and all he could think about was his beloved family.

"I'm sorry," David said, putting down the half-poured beer glass and getting his mobile phone from out of his pocket. David attempted to obtain a moment of privacy and turned his back to the bar and found comfort squashing up next to the coffee machine. Thankfully, Debbie answered her phone immediately and agreed to come straight away to the clubhouse to help him out.

"I'm back. Sorry," David said, offering open palms as an apology and he finished the second beer which by now had big frothy white heads. The customer felt he had been waiting so long he was past caring about his beer froth, and anticipated David's next question.

"Pink gin and slim line tonic. That one there. No next one yes, make it a double," he said, guiding David around the bar for his wife's preferred gin choice. David was getting into his stride now, the old memories of bartending flooding back. He was onto his third customer as Debbie appeared and ducked under the bar counter. All of a sudden, the mood at the bar seemed to calm.

Debbie had made an effort in her appearance. She was wearing one of her lowest cut tight tops and a bra that exaggerated her ample cleavage even more. All the men at the bar waiting to be served seemed to not be in as much of a rush anymore. Debbie took up the mantle and flirting with the first customer that caught her eye she began serving drinks. Drink after drink Debbie was offered tips as she plucked the customers' cash from their hands with a smile and a hair flick. David had not been offered a single drink by any customer, but Debbie seemed to be offered a drink from almost every person she served, including the women. David decided he was going to have one of his wife's paid-for drinks and pulled himself a pint of the expensive premium beer, finding one of the new logo beer glasses at the back of the shelf. He took a huge gulp and placed it down next to the coffee machine. Refreshed, he turned around with an open gesture and a smile.

"Now who's next?" David said and gently clapped his hands. The initial crazy rush of customers slowed as the lounge was now full of all the beach goers and south-side caravan residents who also had been evacuated. They had been ordered to go as far away from the beach as possible whilst the bomb squad defused the unexploded bomb. Everyone was told to go as far as the clubhouse and take this as the safe zone distance and the outer cordon limit. This had been interpreted as everyone must evacuate to the clubhouse. David and Debbie were receiving regular updates on the events down at the beach from customers. It turned out that Tony, the onsite artist come metal detector enthusiast, had really found an unexploded bomb. It was under the excavated sand dune and more down towards the Sunny Sands caravan site, but the police had been moving everyone back a good distance for their own safety.

Chatting with his wife in between customers, David had managed to update her on what happened with Owen and that they had been here on their own, but that he had ran out in a hurry. Debbie informed David in return that she had seen Owen walking towards the beach with Crawford and two men in army uniforms, and there were flashing blue lights everywhere.

With no customers left to serve, both David and Debbie leaned back up against the fridges and looked out over the full clubhouse bar. It was noisy and unusual to see as most people were still parading around in their beach bikinis and swimming trunks. They looked out of place in a formal bar setting with pints of beer in their hands. They had quite enjoyed this experience together and congratulated themselves on their excellent teamwork.

"Quick. Go around the other side of the bar and take some pictures of me serving drinks!" Debbie directed her husband, at the same time she handed him her mobile phone which was already in camera mode. David was used to these requests by now and knew how to get the best side of his wife. He had been skilled in the art of glamour photography and knew it was all about the amount of skin on show. He started clicking away as Debbie started pouring pints for imaginary customers from the beer pumps. She reached up with one hand for a glass, at the same time forcing her chest to practically fall out of her top and onto the bar counter. Debbie smiled and giggled and with only the word 'Boomerang' uttered by her, David knew exactly what to do and where to find the app on her phone. David gave a nod of his head and Debbie jumped in the air and spun around, all with outstretched arms laughing and flicking her long hair. David clicked away on the phone's camera, Debbie continued pouting and pushing her shoulders back, laughing and generally just being silly and sexy, all for her online direct debit customers.

They both served a couple more customers as the two evening bar staff members arrived, and David and Debbie were released from their duties. They helped themselves to several drinks, informing the staff members who didn't really care anyhow, that they had been paid for already. They went back around the other side of the bar and moved over to a nearby empty table. It took them at least two trips to the bar to clear the table of the numerous empty glasses and ripped crisp packets. They settled down together, several drinks in front of each of them, all paid for as tips offered to Debbie.

"I surprisingly enjoyed that," David said to his wife with a reassuring and loving hand on her arm.

"I did as well. These are great pictures," Debbie replied, smiling as she browsed through her camera roll and examined her husband's photography work. David leaned forwards and took a sip of his pint of beer, tasting even better as it was free. He looked around the lounge bar, smiling contentedly to himself that he had somehow helped people during this time of crisis. Debbie scrolled and worked her social media pages, uploading picture after picture of her chest, at the same time sipping on a large glass of sparkling pink wine.

*

Charles busied himself around his house. There were always a few jobs to do after visiting their caravan. Any uneaten food that could be saved was unpacked from their respective ice boxes and put back in the fridge. He emptied his car of any rubbish. He piled up all the dirty clothes by the front of the washing machine. Milling around the house, he was aware he hadn't seen or heard his wife for a few hours. He did wonder if she had taken the dogs for a walk, but he could see them in the garden. Had she gone out, he thought, but then he heard the toilet flush in their en-suite bathroom, and he knew she must be upstairs, sulking in their bedroom. He also knew she had the right to sulk, and he owed it to his wife to go and talk to her and apologise but he wasn't in any rush. He was also processing his own thoughts, but perhaps everyone had forgotten about this. He decided he would start to prepare the family evening meal first before checking on her. Tonight, he was making a family sized spaghetti Bolognese with locally sourced pork meatballs and homemade garlic bread. Silently, Sophie came and sat down at the kitchen table. Charles had his back to her as he peeled and chopped the endless amounts of garlic he required and, on turning his head, noticed that she had joined him with her notepad and pens.

"Hi," Charles said, smiling at his daughter with his half-turned head. "Are you OK?" and even though he didn't get an immediate reply, Charles carried on with his task in hand. He knew she would reply and talk to him when she was ready. There was several minutes of silence before a soft reply arrived.

"I'm OK." Sophie casually shrugged her shoulders but she did not deviate from the colouring book task at hand. Several more minutes of silence passed before Sophie spoke again.

"Can I meet Beatrice?" This time looking up from her colouring book as Charles, wearing his blue striped chef's apron, one hand holding a knife, the other a full clove of garlic, turned to face her with the biggest grin on his face.

Before Charles could reply, and at the exact same moment the word *Beatrice* was said out loud, Sharon walked into the kitchen. With a face like thunder on hearing her daughter say the word *Beatrice,* and presuming this was the current topic of conversation, Sharon spun on her heels and turned a complete exaggerated 180 degrees. She stormed out of the kitchen and with the sound of heavy footsteps echoing around the house, she retreated promptly back up the stairs to her hiding place.

"Sophie, darling," Charles said in his serious tone, "in exactly five minutes would you just turn off this pasta? Don't move anything, just turn the knob to the left. Is that OK?"

"I'm not a baby, Daddy. I can turn off pasta!" Sophie said, raising her eyebrows and smiling back at her father. Charles left Sophie alone in the kitchen and with four good lengthy strides he reached the top of the stairs. His bedroom door was closed, and he gently put pressure on the door handle and opened the door. Sharon was face down on the bed, her bum in tight jeans was facing Charles and was looking very attractive. Charles' immediate thought was to remove those jeans and for a moment he forgot why he had come upstairs. He closed the bedroom door and slid the lock behind him gently. He knew that Sharon would hear the lock of the bedroom door click. Historically this had always been the signal for sex between them, but he knew that wasn't the case now. Or was it? Charles sat down on the bed next to his wife. He reached across for reassuring physical contact but with the angle Sharon was laying, all he could do was put his hand on her bum. Sharon could feel his hand on her bum and with her eyes open she waited for what was going to happen next. She hadn't done anything wrong, so she wasn't going to talk first she decided.

"I owe you an apology. I'm sorry I didn't tell you first. In my defence I have tried to tell you several times over the years but it just didn't seem the right time. Before I knew it, years had gone past and everything was going so well between us and ..." Charles hesitated in what he was saying. He didn't move his hand whilst he was speaking but with no response he squeezed as hard as he could and then forcibly slid his hand down and in between his wife's legs, moving his hand up and down as he caressed her inner thigh and bum over her tight jeans. Charles knew he had to continue, and he had to make a real effort to not just switch the moment to sex. He was out of practice, if Charles had placed his hand in this position before, Sharon would have been up and sprung straight into action and not wasted a moment. Charles continued in his best sincere voice that he could muster.

"The last thing I want to do is hurt you. It all happened so long ago, and then this bloody hospital scare." At that Sharon spun round and sat upright so she was face to face with Charles.

"I can forgive you for *what's-her-face,* that was years ago, before you even met me, but we are supposed to be a team. You have to tell me about anything medical," Sharon said almost tearfully, she knew she was right.

"I mean it when I say I am sorry," and Charles leaned in and kissed his wife full on the lips. His right hand instinctively reaching up and cupping her face to bring her closer. Sharon placed her hand on his chest and without waiting any longer, she had unbuttoned several of his shirt buttons, and had her hand inside his shirt caressing his massive solid chest. She weaved her hands through his deep chest hair, and with desire building inside him, he continued to kiss his wife more passionately. He had an overwhelming urge to reach for her breasts, but deciding to let her take the lead, he continued to slowly caress her lips with his kisses. He knew now she wanted him and moving his lips gently down her neck and onto her soft-skinned shoulders, he began to undo the buttons of his wife's blouse. He freed her breasts from the fabric and reached for her bra strap.

"Everyone's gone out and Sophie is colouring in the kitchen. We will have to be quiet," Charles whispered into his wife's ear as she unbuttoned his jeans and was frantically reaching inside for his now expanding hard manhood with both her hands.

It was enough to satisfy her for now, Charles thought, knowing that they had lots more to discuss in the coming days and weeks. He got up from the bed, he still had a substantial erection and Sharon watched as he pulled up his jeans and attempted to force his girth back inside his clothing. He looked across at his naked wife who was still still laying on the bed. She returned his smile as Charles, also satisfied, quickly unlocked the door, gently closing it behind him. Charles switched his mind instantly, as men can easily do. It was time to check his pasta, he thought.

*

Tony started to dig. He had only moved four spadefuls of sand before he picked up his metal detector again. He waved it over the hole to check for a tone, and to make sure he was still digging in the correct spot. It came again, even louder this time in his headphones and indicating it was only about a foot deep. This strange, deep, long tone excited him, and Tony was hoping this time it was gold, and he had found a fortune in buried treasure. His imagination was running wild now. There had been a large sand dune about four metres tall over this exact spot only a few weeks previous. Anything buried here must have been lost long before the sand dune had built up over it. This item he was digging for could be from the Victorians or even the Romans when they came ashore all those years ago. With all his strength, Tony continued to dig with more and more enthusiasm for what he might find.

Tap. Tap. His shovel had hit something hard, and it sounded as if it was big and made of metal. Spade discarded, Tony dropped to his knees and with his bare hands he began removing the remaining loose sand from around his *pot of gold*. As the shape was beginning to show, it seemed to have the appearance of a pipe. A sewage pipe was Tony's first thought, his dreams of Saxon gold disappearing with every handful of sand that he scraped away! More of the item came into view, and he uncovered a cone shape at one end which had previously been painted red and was now a combination of red, rust, dirt, and sand. Tony's attention turned to finding the other end so he could lift it out. He was digging frantically now, and he was so close to the object, yet he couldn't make out what it was. A small brown terrier dog came sniffing over the edge of the hole, and as its owner came to retrieve his pet, he shouted a word out loud that no-one expected, least of all Tony.

"Bomb. Bomb. Bomb," repeatedly and without hesitation was shouted by the dog walker. "That's a bloody unexploded bomb, man. Run, man. Run." The dog walker scooped up his prized poodle and was away on his toes at a gentle half-wobble half-run through loose sand down the beach.

Tony stood up and wiped his brow with a sandy forearm. With his hands on his hips, he looked down into his hole. He was still hoping for gold. He took a step back and sighed, only then did he recognise it, he didn't believe it but there was no mistaking it, he was looking at a bomb. It looked just like what he had seen in the movies. His first reaction was not to run, he wanted to appraise his find. It was most probably from World War Two, and it was about four feet long, but it might be bigger. This was a big bomb.

"Bugger me," Tony said out loud, the reality dawning on him, and he began to stride towards a group of people who were walking directly towards him. He was still bare chested and covered in sand and he began waving frantically and directing them to turn around and to carry out his instructions immediately.

"Get back. Get back. There's an unexploded bomb. Get everyone back this side back towards Sunshine's. I will do the other side." From the anxious tone and seriousness of Tony's voice, they knew he was serious. Tony turned and ran shouting back over his shoulder with more frantic instructions to his recruited helpers. He ran back past the bomb, he could have given it a wide birth, but curiosity made him get close, just one more time. It was his find; he was an accomplished metal detector, and at the top of his game. He looked down into the hole in despair. He began waving his arms as he ran back towards his own caravan site. The situation was serious, and he was scared. The people on the beach were under no illusion how critical the situation was. Surprisingly they did exactly what Tony asked, and he saw people turning around and moving back, guiding and directing others. The word 'bomb' captivated everyone's attention. With wet, sandy hands, Tony telephoned reception. He told them to call the police immediately as he had found an unexploded bomb with his metal detector, and to get Owen down to the beach straight away. Ten minutes of Tony's mind racing passed, before he could hear the two tones from the police sirens coming from the town along the main road towards Pebbles.

*

On this particular visit to her caravan by the sea, Alison had gone without her husband. He had wanted to come on the trip but, at the last minute, his work had taken him overseas, but Alison decided she was still going to go. After a hectic few weeks, she wanted a few days on the beach and decided it would do her and the children some good. It was a dry, sunny autumn day and the children were busy doing their own thing. She could hear several other children she recognised from the site laughing, as they all played together around their pitch. Alison, however, was starting to get a little bored and frustrated on her own. It was late afternoon, and she was nearing the end of her first bottle of wine. Slightly intoxicated and by now as horny as ever, her thoughts turned to men and how she would welcome any naked man at that very moment. She stood and looked across at her neighbour's caravan. There were no cars or sign of anybody home, and Alison sat back down on her sofa, and flicked through the TV channels. Her thoughts again drifting to sexy bald men and specifically her caravan neighbour, Charles. It had been the same thought she had had that very morning. Over the last couple of weeks all the girls had confessed on the chat group that after the night out, they had each purchased a sex toy. Alison hadn't wanted to be left out. Not being short of money she had purchased the most expensive one on offer. It had been delivered in its discreet box and had features printed on the box to include that it was waterproof and specially designed for use in the shower. That morning she had given her toy its first outing with Charles in mind.

*

"I'm calling a family meeting," Charles shouted upstairs to his children. The hallway and stairs were empty, but he knew they would hear the words *family meeting*. Charles had already spoken with his wife Sharon about the content of this meeting and he had promised her that there would be no new surprises ever again. One at a time, his children finally filed into the kitchen. The last being Jackson who said as he walked in with a smile on his face, "Another family meeting, Dad! What is it this time? You have twins someplace you haven't told us about?"

Emily, who was already sat at the table messaging her online friends about her families' antics, laughed at her brother but didn't find it funny enough to look up from her screen. She kept her close friends updated that she was indeed about to be subjected to yet another family meeting and included her annoying brother's humour. The replies ranged from laughing emoji's to comments about how fit her brother was, which of course she ignored.

"No. I don't have twins," Charles replied, glancing over at his son. Charles continued.

"I just wanted to tell you all that I am going to go to London to speak with Beatrice." With no pre-rehearsed speech, Charles paused and looked around the table. He had everyone's attention and he continued.

"I have discussed this at length with your mother." Everyone appeared to relax as Sharon reached for her husband's hand in a display of support.

"Your mum is not going to come with me, but I was wondering if anybody else wanted to come to London?" he looked at each sibling in turn around the table. There were immediate replies from both Jackson and Emily displaying no interest in searching for their father's first wife. They added further that they in fact had lives of their own and were busy meeting friends and attending parties, and even fidgeted on their chairs in a pretence to immediately leave. Sophie took a little longer to reply, but added that although she wanted to meet Beatrice, London was a long way to go, and she would rather stay at home with her mum.

So, it was decided. Charles was going to London, on his own, to find his first wife and meet his eldest daughter for the first time. Charles had contemplated not telling Sharon about the house visit on the CCTV cameras by Beatrice and a young girl the other day (who was presumably Charles' daughter), but from her response to the previous escapade he thought better of it. He had told her everything. He had even shown her the CCTV clip on his phone and Sharon's reaction had been surprisingly understanding, and she had remained calm and constructive for several days.

"When are you going, Dad?" Jackson asked as he stood up from the kitchen table, presuming and wanting to confirm the family meeting was over.

"Tomorrow, son. I'm only going for a few days to sort everything out. You will be the man of the house whilst I'm gone," Charles said, smiling with pride at his son who was getting tall and turning into a man right in front of his eyes. Emily felt the meeting was uneventful and questioned the need for even calling a family meeting, and took the opportunity to negotiate her corner, and see if she was indeed still banned from calling them. Sharon went to the task of preparing the family's evening meal, and the house fell silent as everyone became lost in their own activities and thoughts.

Charles kept one eye on Sophie who had remained sat at the kitchen table. She had not said much and had continued, as she always seemed to lately, drawing in her books. He sat down next to her and didn't speak. He leaned one arm on the table and just watched his daughter at work. He gazed at her with complete and unconditional love as she scribbled away, and she smiled occasionally with a tilt of her head in his direction, acknowledging and appreciating that her dad was spending some time with her.

*

"It's been a busy one," Owen said as he leaned back on his big leather chair and looked across at the colourful yearly calendar on the office wall. Pam knew Owen was referring to the caravan season that they had just all gone through. The site was still open for another couple of weeks, but technically it was all over for another year. Soon everything would officially close to mark the end of the caravanning season. Caravan owners were allowed to visit their caravans during the closed season for repairs and maintenance only, but they were not allowed to stay overnight. These were the local authority's rules on caravan site residency.

Pam now also took a moment to reflect on what the site had gone through during this past year. She smiled inwardly with pride at her contribution to the business, and in the knowledge of her plans to play an even more important role next season. Secretly, she knew that Owen had been pleased with her ideas and suggestions. The biggest hit being the ballroom dancing classes. The unexploded bomb drama tested the resolve of the staff on site, and Owen had discussed this several times after the event with his wife. Owen had plans to conduct regular fire and emergency drills in the future for his staff and guests. He wanted to be prepared if anything like that were to ever happen again. The big hole left on the beach after the bomb squad had carried out their controlled explosion, after several high tides, had now been covered in by the sea. Mother Nature was remarkable and there was no trace of anything ever happening. Owen had plans for even more site modernisation and landscaping during the closed season, and he had booked in the builders for the pool renovation. He had ordered the parts for the sites eagerly awaited facial recognition keyless entry to access the pool area. Of course, this would be for the south side customers only. Pam had other plans for the closed season which included a holiday in the sun, wearing a bikini and more sex, preferably with her husband, but as she got a little older, she felt she could easily be persuaded otherwise.

CHAPTER 19

First Class

After only a couple of days at her caravan, Gabriella had managed to clean the entire place from top to bottom. With her cleaning done, she was now starting to get a little bored. The site was very quiet, as the end of the caravan season was in sight, with little or nothing happening. Her beloved son, Fabian, was out most days with his new girlfriend. Her husband, Andy, had stayed at home working. Her secret lover Crawford had gone off to France, working as a seasonal ski instructor. Gabriella craved male attention, but she had resigned herself to the fact that it wasn't going to happen.

She was messing about in front of her mirror, and in the process had removed her bra. She stood admiring herself in her white vest top and her short denim shorts. She secretly felt quite sexy for a middle-aged mum, and decided to go for a walk, perhaps to the on-site shop for a can of something, or maybe an ice-cream. She didn't really need anything, but she thought the exercise would be a good distraction as well as something to do. As she sauntered along in the sunshine, she didn't see a single person. Curtains were closed, BBQs covered, and outdoor furniture strapped down alongside mini sheds, almost as if everything and everybody had gone into hibernation ready for winter. When she arrived, she half expected the shop to be closed, but was pleased to see the lights on inside and the flashing red *open* sign illuminated next to the front door.

Inside the shop there wasn't much to choose from. The shelves were mostly empty and any items they did have left had been pulled to the front of the shelves to make them look more well-stocked and plentiful than they were. The newspaper stand, however, was still full of today's newspapers and several local editors were still running the headline of 'Unexploded BOMB found on local beach'. Gabriella was greeted with apologies from the young, pierced man behind the counter, as he explained that stock was being run down as the shop was closing next week. He sported a gold stud lip piercing and black earlobe rings, he was pleasant enough she thought. But he wasn't her type. As he made small talk, he asked her if she was looking for anything specific and added an unexpected wink. Gabriella continued browsing, mostly to pass the time, whilst contemplating the wink she had just witnessed. Eventually she selected two big bars of plain chocolate and a bottle of slim line tonic water. She considered asking the young man behind the counter for his telephone number, on the proviso that she may need to buy some weed from him later. She interpreted the wink as either an offer of casual sex, or that he was dealing, but it had been a long time since she had dabbled, and she knew she would be unable to hide the smell from her son. She paid for her goods using her contactless phone. It was a new iPhone, and she needed to operate the contactless payment in a slightly different way. Her attention was 100% focussed on her phone and making sure the transaction had completed correctly. She didn't hear the footsteps of someone approaching behind her.

"Hi sexy," Crawford said seductively with a smile as he grabbed her bottom and held it in a tight squeeze. Leaning in close over her shoulder, his eyes were drawn to Gabriella's hard nipples that were erect under her vest top. Gabriella smiled and turned with a slight startle as she looked up at him, almost melting as she stared into his blue eyes.

Crawford quickly anticipated her next question and said, "No snow, so I have come home for a couple of days. Do you fancy getting a drink?" Gabriella beamed back, leaning her head to one side slightly and letting her shoulders drop, knowing her day would now be filled with excitement and shameful pleasure.

*

David was busy watching the outside caravan tap as the water started to slow to a trickle and eventually stop. He was also making plans to leave and had drained down his caravan's water system for the end of the caravan season. The site was still open for a few more days, but Debbie had plans for a long weekend trip with her girlfriends, and David also had plans to spend a little time with his new partner, Conrad.

He wasn't a big believer in draining down the caravan's plumbing and boiler system at the end of the season, but it meant they would be still insured if he did, and it wasn't a big job to do anyhow. He had been made aware previously from other site guests that the end of season preparations were a mammoth task. Some would wrap all their cutlery and plates in newspaper, take down all their curtains, leave bowls of salt by the windows, and other pointless exercises. For David, end of caravan season was as simple as turning the drain down tap. He would ensure all the interior doors of the caravan were left open to allow the air to circulate, prop open the fridge and freezer doors, and turn the electricity off. Job done.

He started his engine and drove slowly out of the site, waving only to Owen, who was stood by reception. He was alone for once, and he knew he had a couple of hours' journey ahead of him. He also knew he wasn't going to get any phone calls, as the mobile reception wasn't great on his journey through the Welsh valleys and mountains. He soon found himself smiling as he reflected on the previous year. Who'd have thought things would turn out like this? Life was good. His wife was quickly becoming a famous social media influencer. He was certain she was making more money than him now through her Instagram and various online social media accounts. He still didn't understand how she got paid, not that it really mattered. David had a new companion in Conrad, and he was really enjoying his company. His daughters were growing up and turning into women right in front of his eyes. The roads were empty, and as was very rare in Wales, the sun was shining. Life was OK, he thought as he drove through the town, he spotted a parking space directly outside the bakers. *Perfect,* he thought, *bacon roll and a coffee for the journey home,* and he clicked his indicator to pull over.

*

"I'll ring you tonight," Charles said as he placed a kiss on his wife's lips.

"You promise?" Sharon questioned with a small tear forming in the corner of her eye. He stared at her with a smile and the tear burst and rolled down the side of her cheek.

"Oh, come on. It's all OK. We have discussed this over and over. You know I have to go and speak to her, she has been to *our* house," Charles said with raised eyebrows as he held his wife's cheeks in his hands. Looking directly into her eyes, he added, "I love you with all my heart."

He waved out of the window for the last time as his London-bound train pulled leisurely out of the station. Sharon had booked his seat in first class, with a return date in two days' time. Charles had with him his small black North Face holdall containing just a few clothes and toiletries. Sharon had selected his outfits and pressed and folded them nicely. He assumed they would be all boring and unflattering clothes, seeing as he was going to pay a visit his first wife. He smiled to himself, lay back in his seat, and contemplated the enormity of his journey. He was travelling on his own to find his ex-wife in London, and more importantly, and only known to him, he knew he still adored her. Oh, and he was going to meet his teenage daughter, whom he had never met before. What could possibly go wrong?

Over the next few hours seated in his plush seat, he was awash with a variety of emotions. They ranged from guilt for not being there for his daughter whilst she had been growing up, to being scared in case she had come to his house to tell him he was a bad father and she wanted nothing to do with him. Charles declined any drinks from the persistent on-board waitress service and stared out of the window, surprised at the number of green fields this country still had left. It seemed that where he lived every patch of grass was having houses built on them. In the end Charles must have briefly fallen asleep, as in no time at all he was woken by an on-board announcement telling him the next stop would be Kings Cross station. *Well, I'm here now, no turning back, it's now the adventure really starts,* he thought as he stepped off the train and onto a busy noisy platform.

All those years ago, Beatrice had left Charles to go back and live with her parents. Charles knew where her parents lived, or at least where they used to live. One tube ride later and then a walk up what felt like a thousand steps to exit the tube station, Charles walked out into the busy London sunshine. He waved down a black cab, but then changed his mind and told the cab driver he was sorry, but he was going to walk instead. The memories flooded back, and he recalled walking hand in hand on this very path with Beatrice along the side of the river Thames. Charles saw a pub which was now a coffee bar that he had frequented many times with Beatrice, and he felt very comfortable in the area. He knew he was close now and he made the last familiar left turn. Things had changed slightly. The street now had a grand gated entrance and he had to sign in with a security guard and show ID just to be able to walk up the tree-lined street. The area was all very grand looking, and each house looked expensive and very well maintained. He didn't see anybody else and, as he walked, he could see the overpowering white Georgian mansion house of Beatrice's parents directly ahead of him at the end of the street. It was now probably worth many millions of pounds in this up-market, gated community. The last time Charles had knocked that front door he was a desperate, lost young man and he recalled being sent packing by a smartly dressed butler in a black three-piece suit. Back then, there had been no barrier or security guards and he had spent many hours just walking around the area, not wanting to leave London without at least talking with Beatrice.

That was nearly twenty years ago, but apart from the added security, the area had pretty much remained the same and Charles knew his way around the streets. Beatrice's parents' house looked enormous. It had a freshly painted white facade with beautiful and intricate iron railings, all guarding the perfectly manicured lawns. There were several, skilfully placed enormous grey slate planters, full of an array of brightly coloured tropical flowers. The entrance was protected by tall imposing electric black gates. Looking through them, Charles could see the driveway which led down to an underground carpark area. He stood for a moment, getting his bearings and gathering his thoughts. He wanted to be sure he had the right house. It was noticeably quiet, no one was around. He thought he saw a curtain move from a house to his right, but it could have been the sun on the window.

Unexpectedly, and startling Charles a little, there was a *click* as the metal gates directly in front of him started to move. He couldn't see anybody, and he thought at first he had activated the gates as he leaned on them to look through. The gate moved graciously to one side as it slid on rollers to the right and out of view into a white rendered wall. Thinking he had been spotted from the house, Charles stepped to one side. He wasn't ready. He needed a few more minutes to think. The gate now fully open, stopped with a knock and then nothing happened for a second before it started to close again. It moved a few inches before it again jerked open as a large blue car appeared from out of the ground. It travelled up the ramp from under the house before speeding out the gate. The car passed Charles who had stood perfectly still, unnoticed by anyone as the gate began its slow retreat to close. The lone female driver drove past Charles at speed, and his heart missed a beat as he glanced in through the car window. Behind the wheel, it looked to him like the same young lady he had seen on his neighbour's CCTV camera. The car carried on a short distance and then Charles, without looking behind him, heard the car's brakes screech as it came to an abrupt stop. He didn't turn around, for the first time in his life, Charles, all confident, larger-than-life man of the world, didn't know what to do. He was petrified and frozen to the spot. He then heard the words that can melt the heart of any man and bring him to his knees.

"Daddy?" Charles turned around slowly in nervous anticipation and staring right back at him was the most beautiful young woman he had ever seen. He knew instinctively this was his daughter and the only words that came from his mouth were, "I'm sorry," and his eyes started to tear up as he repeated this several times. His daughter was walking towards him, she ran the last few meters and with no words uttered, she greeted him with wide open arms. It was the most poignant and affectionate hug Charles had ever received. They both stood there on the pavement hugging, the car had its engine still running with the driver's door open. For Charles, the world had stopped turning for a second. Charles recognised that feeling he had at that very moment, it was an indefinable and overwhelming feeling of warmth and adoration that a father has for his daughter.

*

Alison picked up a leaflet from the site reception which had instructions and guidance on closing down a static holiday home for the winter. The other option was to book a slot for the site to do it for you. All she would need to do is make sure they had a door key and message them to let them know when she was leaving and wouldn't be back until the spring. The site would then add £65 to her site fees bill and Crawford, or another staff member, would go and drain down her van, put some antifreeze in all the sinks and toilets, and make sure it was all locked up for winter. Alison took up the offer from the site and sent a text message saying she was going home in the morning and wouldn't be back until the following spring. Just after sending the text message, her phone rang with its unmistakeable ringtone.

"Hello, my love," Alison said, greeting her former husband, Adam. "You haven't rung for a while, have you been busy? What's wrong?" Adam proceeded to inform Alison all about some bodyguarding work he had managed to secure for a few famous actors on a TV show. Recently the work had dried up, and he wanted to know if he could spend some time with his daughter.

"She's here with me at the caravan, and no, Clifford isn't here," Alison added as she sneaked a sip of her gin and tonic whilst waiting for his reply. The conversation continued and a slightly inebriated and sexually frustrated Alison hinted to Adam that he could drive down and see his daughter right now if he really wanted to. This way, Alison would have some male company after all, although she wasn't so sure her husband would be keen on her choice of visitor. Alison poured herself another large pink gin and tonic and waited for his response. Two minutes later it was all agreed; Adam would be coming to visit his daughter and he would be here within the hour. Also agreed, and reiterated several times by Alison, was that he would be sleeping on the sofa. As soon as the call ended, Alison wandered straight to her bathroom, placing her G&T down next to the sink. She had been alone and off her game the last few days and had gotten behind on her personal grooming. She started the shower and with two new lady razors at the ready, she proceeded to get herself ready, even though nothing was going to happen.

It was a good hour before Alison heard a car stop just behind her caravan and, in that time, she had consumed at least two more gins, possibly three, she had started to lose count. Alison was wearing a black bikini top, and she had applied an all-over fake sun-tan cream. She was bare footed and wore a small tartan red skirt, no underwear, and was a little drunk. In Alison's eyes, Adam looked as muscular as ever and now he was sporting a suntan after weeks of working outside on a film set. He had shaved and wore fashionable jeans with brown, expensive-looking leather shoes. There was no military insignia in sight. His shirt was new, tight crisp white around his six-pack stomach and open at the neck. He smiled at Alison as he entered the caravan, recognising the signals that Alison wasn't hiding; he knew he was going to take her tonight. Adam immediately spent some time with his daughter. He was patient and listened to all her stories and nodded at all the interesting things she had been up to. Alison knew this was important to them both, but with copious amounts of gin running through her veins, she started to become a little impatient. Sitting at the end of the couch, she wriggled a little to remind Adam she was still there. He briefly looked up at her from the book he was reading to his daughter. She grabbed him another beer from the fridge and walked towards Adam, maintaining eye contact, as she crossed the lounge seductively. Certain her daughter's attention was on the book at hand, she handed Adam the beer, spun round, and, as she walked away, she flipped up the back of her skirt. Adam stared at a firm, round naked white bottom and something stirred in his groin. His thoughts turned to their married years together and the endless hours of pleasurable intercourse they had shared. Alison's thirst for Adam hadn't really diminished over the years. She returned to her empty seat on the sofa, knowing she would need to stay in the queue and wait patiently for Adam's attention. Sitting back down, she slowly crossed her long slim legs and played things cool, pretending to search her phone. Adam's full attention stayed with his daughter until it was time for her to go to bed. Adam and Alison both knew what was going to happen next and the anticipation was growing between them both.

With the two children finally asleep in bed, Adam sat back down on the sofa, this time next to Alison. Without being asked, he placed his hand between her naked thighs, forcing her closed knees slightly apart. Without saying anything Alison swivelled on the sofa and faced him. She was now half sitting on top of Adam and tightened her grip on his hand which was now wedged tightly between her thighs. She stared him straight in the eye as she used both hands to slowly unbutton his shirt. She separated his shirt, revealing his solid bulk of muscular chest, and with one swift move she forcibly pushed the shirt over his shoulders, trapping his arms. He had a thick coating of soft chest hair running across his ripped suntanned torso. At the same moment, like a caged animal Alison lurched for Adam's neck and began to kiss him passionately.

"Hope you've brought some condoms," she said directly into his ear and then bit down on his ear lobe with some force. "Clifford has had the snip and I am *not* getting pregnant," Alison continued into Adam's other ear as she flicked her hair around passionately. Her loose breasts hung down and her hard nipples ached as they swung back and forth across Adam's chest and face. Adam had not brought any condoms and he ignored the comment. His desire now to ejaculate was overpowering his common sense. He managed to free one of his trapped hands and knowing what was coming she assisted him instinctively by slightly raising her bottom in the air.

*

David enjoyed his drive home through the countryside. On route he had received several text messages but had decided he would leave his phone alone until he reached his front door. Unable to contain himself, he reached for his handset which had slid across the passenger seat, as soon he pulled onto his driveway. He saw he had a message from Debbie and three messages from Conrad. A generic message from Debbie was just wishes of love and to drive safely. David hadn't finished reading it all before moving swiftly onto the messages from Conrad. David's relationship with Conrad was getting serious now and he knew Conrad was ready to take things to the next level. David had told him he was nervous about this next step as he had only ever been in a sexual relationship with a woman before; adding that the vast majority of his experience was with his current wife and the mother of his children. Conrad was very understanding and had suggested they go away together for a few days just as friends. David had told Debbie all about this, as he told her everything about his new relationship. She had encouraged him to go on the trip, and she had even offered to check hotels and look around and sort out the arrangements if he wanted. David had declined the offer and stated he would talk to Conrad about it first and organise it himself.

Well, that was several days ago now and very soon it would be turning into a week and David hadn't done anything about it. Conrad, however, as is expected from a famous actor, had a personal assistant, and all the arrangements for their trip had been made. All the details had been explained in three long messages. David read the messages twice and was left in no doubt as to what was going to happen, when he had to be ready, and what country and environment he had to pack for. Sat on his driveway for over ten minutes now, his imagination was racing. What was different this time was that David felt as excited as a teenager on his first date. More importantly, he said to himself, he only had twenty-four hours to get himself organised and packed. A car was coming to collect him at five p.m. tomorrow night, to take him to the airport.

"Ooh is he sending a car for you?" Danielle asked jokingly of her father. "Conrad loves Dad. Conrad loves Dad," she sang whist walking upstairs and at the same not removing her eyes from her mobile phone. David was pleased that his oldest daughter was cool with Conrad, but he was acutely aware that his two twin daughters, however grown up they appeared, were in fact only eleven years old and didn't really understand what their big sister Danielle was singing about.

"I'm going away with my friend Conrad. Just for a few days holiday! Is that OK, girls?" David enquired of his two twin daughters as he sat down on the sofa next to them. Both were watching TV and, using the remote control, David lowered the volume slightly. It was important that his daughters understood that Daddy was only going away on a short holiday and that he would be back very soon. He didn't want them to think that their mum and dad were splitting up. He finished the conversation by promising that he would of course bring them both back a present from his trip. This went down very well indeed. Even Danielle from upstairs in her bedroom heard the mention of the word 'present', and proceeded to shout the names of two or three different perfumes and bottle sizes she wanted from the airport Duty Free.

*

Across town at Melissa and Patrick's caravan site, the end of season site rules were very different. They never actually closed for the end of season and stayed open all year round for their guests. There was, however, a practice of draining down your caravan and emptying the water pipes in preparation for the unexpected freezing cold winter weather. But mostly, on this particular site, people lived in their caravans all year round. A caravan was really a home from home and, like a normal house in the winter months the risk of frozen or burst pipes was a common problem.

Due to Melissa's injury, they had not visited their holiday home for nearly two months. She was, however, feeling a lot better and well on the way to making a full recovery. Whilst on police duty she had been involved in a road traffic accident. Most of this time Melissa had spent in hospital with one operation after another. But she had been discharged home now and Patrick had been allowed a little time off work to look after her. Melissa had been double crewed on a uniformed night shift routine patrol. A report had come in of a robbery in progress at a local supermarket. She and her partner had been close by in their patrol car and were the first to arrive on the scene. They arrived just as the offenders were making off in their car with several thousand pounds worth of stolen cigarettes spilling out of their open boot. In order to prevent their escape, Melissa's police car had attempted to block their path, and in doing so the offenders had rammed it violently, causing it to flip over, smashing the blue lights mounted on top. Her partner had managed to escape uninjured by crawling out of the driver's broken window, but Melissa unfortunately had been badly injured and had got trapped inside, breaking both her legs. Her partner had managed to extinguish the flames, but Melissa had been trapped with both her legs crushed for over an hour. The fire brigade eventually managing to cut her free from the police car by taking the roof off. The suspects' getaway car had been damaged in the crash, so they hadn't gone far. After a foot chase all three suspects had been caught and arrested. Melissa had heard that one of the suspects had refused to obey the commands from a police dog handler after repeated requests to comply. The dog handler had released his dog and the man had been bitten badly. He also attended the same hospital as Melissa for his bites, but after his treatment he was remanded straight to prison. Melissa's leg injuries had been complicated, with numerous pins and casts resulting in a prolonged stay in hospital. She had stayed positive throughout; she was slim and healthy and had healed quickly. More importantly she was out of hospital now and recovering well. She had started to get used to her wheelchair as her main option for getting around.

They both arrived at their caravan in Wales on a cloudy and overcast day. There had been some intermittent rain, but as Patrick always said, if you don't go to Wales when it's raining, you would never go to Wales at all. He had pre booked a supermarket delivery, scheduled to arrive within the hour. His order included food, wine, and plenty of beer, enough for both of them for the next few days. He had also booked a table at the onsite restaurant for later that evening.

"I can manage," Melissa blurted out, something she was saying more and more often as she pushed herself along in her wheelchair down the path at the side of their caravan. When Patrick had built the decking all those years ago, both his two sons had been well out of their pushchairs and Patrick had just built three steps up to the front door. At that time, he had given no thought to any wheelchair ramp access and as Melissa stopped just short of the decking steps it made Patrick think again about his design.

"If you just get me up the steps *then* I can push myself," Melissa said, raising her left arm in what was now a well-practised signal to be picked up out of her wheelchair. Patrick, bending down, picked up his wife easily and lifted her out of her chair. He carried her up the three steps and lowering her down slowly he kissed her on the cheek at the same moment as her feet touched down. She gently put all her weight onto her stronger left leg, and she steadied herself using the handrail. Patrick rushed to carry the wheelchair up the steps, Melissa scathingly told him not to hurry as she was OK to stand. In fact, it was nice to be standing for a few minutes. She was high up and was able to see the fields and hills surrounding the site and the view out to sea, a view she had missed. The wheelchair moved easily around the decking, but the door into the caravan was not a normal size door. The wheelchair didn't fit through. She couldn't help but feel annoyed and also slightly upset at the small door. The slightest thing seemed to upset her now. She was surprised that even in these modern advanced times, things were not really geared up for wheelchair access.

Melissa knew she was only likely to be in a wheelchair for a few months, but even this short period of time had really brought things into perspective as to how difficult it can be for wheelchair users. Patrick opened the caravan door and after collapsing the wheelchair he took it inside. Melissa insisted on using her crutches to enter the caravan. He stayed directly behind her and guided her slowly to the sofa; he wasn't comfortable until she was seated.

After much discussion, it was agreed that the wheelchair would stay outside. There wasn't much point in bringing it inside the caravan; it didn't fit past the kitchen table, and it didn't fit through the bathroom or bedroom doors. They both agreed that if Melissa's disability had been more permanent, then they would have had to change caravan models to something specifically designed to accommodate a wheelchair. Melissa had plenty of time to think whilst she healed. She had decided that she was going to campaign and make sure that there were more wheelchair-friendly caravans available in the future.

Twenty minutes later, Patrick had managed to unload the car and bring everything into their caravan ready for their short break. Starting to feel relaxed and wanting to lighten the mood he suggested, "I've an idea, darling – why don't we bring that wheelchair inside and see what positions we can discover?" He pretended to dance towards his wife whilst slowing unbuttoning his shirt to reveal his toned stomach muscles. Melissa was not sure what he was suggesting, but feeling his question was not worthy of a reply, she looked down at the remote and proceeded to change channels. Patrick wasn't getting it, he was becoming restless and as nearly all married men do when the sex dried up, he was starting to look.

*

"It's here. It's here," Danielle shouted frantically from upstairs. A startled David tilted his head to the left and looked out of his kitchen window which had a long view down his driveway. Sticking out from behind the hedge he saw the end of a dark, highly polished vehicle. Danielle's heavy footsteps could be heard as she frantically ran downstairs, and almost out of breath she darted into the kitchen. She was just as excited as the rest of her family who had all gathered in the kitchen. Danielle was aware that she was the only one that had seen the car arrive and she went onto explain how she had seen the car take a long slow turn in front of the house out of her bedroom window. Hurriedly, and with a massive smile on her face, Danielle added, "It's a blacked-out limousine, Dad. It's gorgeous. OMG Dad, just like on TV. I'm well jell."

David smiled, sharing a *moment* with his eldest daughter. Debbie was also excited, and a little jealous, and she considered for a moment asking if she could pose for a social media picture whilst stood in front of the car, her mind racing as to what sexy outfit she could wear. Wearing something skimpy was always the favoured articles of clothing for her glamour social pages. She did, however, remind herself that she was also a mother and wife, and decided to take charge of the situation in hand.

"Right, my darling. Have got your passport? Your wallet? Have a lovely time and ring us when you can, won't you? And put some pictures on the family group chat!" Debbie lovingly smiled at her best friend and kissed him full on the mouth. How things had changed in such a short space of time, she pondered. David spoke to each of his children in turn. He reassured them again he was only going on holiday for a few days, and he would be home very soon. Debbie ordered everyone to wait inside the house and play it cool for David who was now walking down his driveway. The waiting chauffeur, who had an air of authority, stood perfectly still with his hands behind his back.

David walked towards him carrying his new fashionable overnight bag that Debbie had recently sourced for him. He was also wearing his new wardrobe, again a gift from his now financially better-off wife. He wore expensive designer shoes, slim fitting light tan jeans with an open neck white shirt and a blue casual jacket. He had had his teeth whitened and she had also taken him into the city recently and had paid over a £100 for his haircut, something David struggled to justify, but he wasn't paying. With his shoulders back, David approached the smart-looking chauffeur who was wearing a dark blue suit with matching tie. He held open the rear door with an air of authority and a smile. The chauffeur held out his hand with a request to take David's bag from him. David handed over his bag and with both hands now free he turned and waved to his family. He expected to wave to them all as they looked through the kitchen window, but instead they had all come running outside onto the driveway, including Debbie who was jumping up and down and waving frantically.

David offered a casual single wave and settled himself onto the back seat. Whilst he felt the soft cream leather seat beneath his fingers, the door closed firmly behind him with a satisfying clunk. David turned to see the car boot closing automatically behind him after his luggage had been carefully placed inside. The chauffeur then disappeared out of view towards the front of the vehicle. He sat looking out the window at his family, who were all still waving and giggling. He felt an overwhelming sense of love and pride wash over him, mixed with excitement and apprehension for his forthcoming trip.

"Good afternoon, sir. My name is Marcus. I am Conrad's personal chauffeur, and your flight is on time, sir," the good-looking chauffeur said. The vehicle was now pulling away gently. Marcus checked his rear-view mirror to see David frantically fiddling with all the buttons on the door but had only succeeded in lowering the tinted window after Marcus had driven some distance. Conrad had briefed his lifelong friend and employee Marcus on the circumstances surrounding his new partner. Marcus was understanding and knew David's current family situation.

"Would you like me to go around again, sir? So you can wave goodbye?" Marcus said, smiling into his rear-view mirror.

"Thank you," David replied with a nod of gratitude, and he relaxed back into his seat.

"It's turning around. Come back. Come back everyone," Daisy screamed, jumping up and down on the driveway. As they hadn't been able to see David waving back at them through the one-way glass, everyone, apart from Daisy, had been slightly disappointed and underwhelmed that their dad had just driven off. But Daisy had stayed on the driveway. She knew her dad would never leave without waving goodbye. Debbie ran out of the house first, followed by her daughters. They all huddled together, hugging each other and smiling. They could see the black limousine make a sweeping turn and it passed slowly in front of the house again. David was half hanging out of the rear car window, and he was waving uncontrollably with the biggest smile on his face.

"I love you all," David repeatedly shouted unashamedly at the top of his voice. Everyone, including Debbie, waved and jumped up and down hysterically. Debbie found that her eyes had watered slightly as she had waved off her husband. Her lifelong partner was going away without her. This was the first time this had ever happened since they had got married, all those years ago. She thought she was prepared for this but clearly, she wasn't.

"It's approximately an hour's drive, sir." Marcus allowed David to settle, and after a few minutes he calmly offered, "There are refreshments in the fridge, sir, behind the seat in front of you and a selection of movies for you to watch on the monitor if you so desire."

"Thank you, Marcus," David immediately replied then, after moments of silence, said, "Thank you for going back, meant a lot to me that, I appreciate it." David offered a nod to the person looking back at him in the rear-view mirror and in that moment, he cemented a lifelong friendship with a man he had only just met. A friendship bond, unbeknown to David, that would last for many years to come. David's shoulders relaxed and he settled into being driven around by somebody else. He was happy looking out of the window at the passing fields and houses. He certainly wasn't used to being chauffeur-driven, but certainly liked how smooth and quiet this vehicle was, and how comfortable the seats were compared to his little white painter's van.

*

"I'm Evangeline. Are you, my father?" the emotional young lady said inquisitively. She was unable to stop staring at the face of the man standing directly in front of her. Charles was still lost for words, and he stood trembling, just staring back. She looked so much like him, he was taken back, and his eyes filled with tears. He knew he was looking at his daughter. She was so strikingly beautiful with her long straight brown hair, her beautiful golden skin, and a smile of perfect white teeth. She was tall and slim, composed and with a kind and confident manner.

"Mummy has told me everything. But she only told me recently, or I would have come and found you sooner. It's OK. It's OK, you know. Grandma and Grandad can be very bossy. They still are, but they are older now and keep themselves to themselves." Evangeline just continued talking and Charles didn't hear all of what was being said. He was well out of his comfort zone now and still utterly lost for words. He broke eye contact for the first time and bent down to pick up his bag. Evangeline took hold of his hand and she guided him in the direction of her car. Her car had its driver's door still open and engine running. It looked like it had been abandoned the way it had suddenly just stopped in the middle of the road.

"Let's go for a coffee first before we go inside. Just us two, is that OK? I want to know everything," Evangeline said as she continued to direct Charles towards her car. Charles remained silent and did as directed. As he got closer, the car boot opened automatically and she signalled for Charles to put his bag inside. He sat in the front passenger seat and as he pulled his seat belt across his lap, he could see Evangeline's eyes had also watered, but she couldn't stop smiling and Charles couldn't help looking at her. Evangeline chatted away about a little coffee shop that her best friend owned just down the road. More importantly, they could park at the rear in the staff carpark, a little perk she had made use of a few times.

*

Lucy was into double figures now on her bookings. Things had settled down a little as she was becoming more comfortable and more familiar with her new business venture. At first it had just been an off-the-cuff comment by one of the old timers down at her local pub. One night the drunken pub regular had said aloud that he had read someplace that down south *naked cleaning* was all the rage. He suggested that there was big money to be made if Lucy got her kit off whilst cleaning. They would pay her money to watch her clean their house, whilst completely in the buff. Lucy had a fit, toned body, something she was immensely proud of, but under no circumstances was she getting naked and being leered at by groups of strangers. She had several girls on her books through her massage business who were interested in the extra money, but she wanted to try and separate the two businesses if she could. Lucy wanted her massage business to continue as it was. The girls she knew performed *extras* for their caravan clients if they asked, and they kept the extra money. Lucy wanted this new business venture to be professional and tasteful. Above all she wanted it to be very expensive, she would charge big money for an hour of naked cleaning.

With each customer, a list of rules would be agreed in advance, which included no touching, no stag parties, and no large groups. It would be a maximum of three persons per cleaner and with a minimum of two hours cleaning. All paid for in advance. Specific cleaning requests would be catered for but, only if the cleaner felt comfortable performing the requested role. They would be expected to tip if the clean had gone well and was warranted. Lucy had already secured a repeat customer who had booked a single clean for the first Friday morning of every month and had paid in full for the next six months. He ticked his preferences as wanting a more mature, busty type of female cleaner, preferably with dark hair who would just clean his kitchen. In the *any other comments* section at the bottom of the registration form, a form that every respective customer had to complete, he had also requested that the cleaner should wear red high heel shoes at *all* times whilst cleaning. For Lucy this was easy money, and she liked this particular customer, having met him in person on the first clean. This was one of Lucy's company policies, that she would accompany the cleaner into the premises on their first clean and supervise for the first ten minutes. The partner or driver of the cleaner was authorised to wait in a car down the street and not directly outside the premises, in case there were any issues and the cleaner had to end the clean prematurely.

From the start, Lucy had been very comfortable with this new client. He was a wealthy stockbroker from the city who worked from home a few days a month and enjoyed women's company, other than his wife. This customer was accustomed to the rules of brothels and other forms of sexual stimulation, but on these occasions, he preferred to only observe. It was of course an added bonus that his kitchen was also spotlessly clean at the end of the session, in readiness for his wife's return home from her monthly trips abroad. Lucy had agreed a gold member's rate for this customer, and she charged him £265 per hour, of which Lucy kept £150 for herself, the cleaner being very pleased with the remaining wages.

In Lucy's inbox today she had received her first request for a man and woman team to clean a house together. This was Lucy's first request of this nature and she had lined up Crawford and Adrianna for the clean. Adrianna, however, had got herself mixed up in a dispute with her neighbour over some criminal damage to her car and, with her fiery Italian temper she had gone and got herself arrested overnight.

"But I could really do with the money," Crawford said to Lucy.

"If Adrianna's not available I'm going to have to cancel the clean," Lucy replied, phone resting in her left ear she turned the pages of her contact's book.

"What if I get another cleaner? I know somebody. I think she'd be up for it," Crawford uttered, already regretting saying it as the words came out of his mouth. Crawford was thinking about Gabriella. He was certain that he could persuade her if he offered his body in payment. He was secretly hoping she didn't want paying as well and would perhaps regard it as more of a favour to help him out.

"Details please. The client is specific," Lucy replied in her stern business tone. She didn't want to risk losing this contract so early, this was going to be an easy £300 for her if she could find another cleaner at short notice.

"Tall, blonde, and looks like a model," Crawford replied. He was ready to add more complimentary adjectives to describe Gabriella, but he was interrupted by Lucy.

"OK. Perfect. This afternoon, 4 p.m. start, don't be late. I will text you the address and I will meet you there. Come to my car first, I will be parked up nearby. This is a new customer. It's a big client, Crawford, don't blow this," Lucy said in military precision and then hung up without saying goodbye.

In his head, Crawford was already spending his share of the cleaning money, he had a few debts to sort out. He was still hoping Gabriella wouldn't want any money, but he was going to offer her £50 if she wanted paying. Oh, and sex of course – that was a given. Crawford made the telephone call to Gabriella.

"Hi. Are you OK? It's me. I need to speak to you; I need a favour!" Crawford continued, not giving Gabriella a chance to say anything. "It's a big favour but you will be really helping me out and it's only for two hours. Starts at 4 o'clock today, are you free?" Crawford said in his calm, soft, sexy voice and with his fingers crossed. He was unsure if Gabriella would be up for this, but she was game for most things. He explained everything in detail, including how he desperately needed the money. When she had paused, he had added that he hadn't asked her for anything before.

That afternoon, Gabriella found herself sat in the front seat of a stationary old land rover.

"Being honest, I'm really not sure about this. I'm actually a bit scared," Gabriella said softly.

"I promise it's going to be fine. We say hello and then just start cleaning. We just take our clothes off, that's all. Just look at me all the time, don't look at them. Whoever is watching we can talk to them if you want, or just ignore them. I promise it will all be OK. You're doing it for me, remember." Crawford offered a reassuring smile and placed his hand on Gabriella's knee. "You look amazing. It's a husband-and-wife team so just the two of them in the house. The man will probably watch you and the lady will watch me. That's it, easy money. No touching and you are doing me a big favour," Crawford said. Holding his breath, he tentatively added, "You can get paid if you want?"

"It's not about the money," Gabriella replied immediately. Crawford squeezed Gabriella's leg and moved his hand up the inside of her bare thigh to the base of her denim shorts. She smiled and instinctively parted her knees slightly. He began to lean in to kiss her on the lips. Crawford jumped and before his lips touched Gabriella he blurted out:

"Lucy's here. Let's go," Crawford said and darted out of the car. He didn't wait for Gabriella to catch up and walked directly towards Lucy's car. Lucy was pulling over into a parking space a little further down the street. Lucy started offering her hand from a distance as she walked towards them both.

"Pleased to meet you, Gabriella," Lucy said, looking her up and down and cementing their new friendship with a firm handshake. Gabriella reciprocated and they shook hands. Gabriella was unable to offer any verbal interaction due to her nerves. Lucy carried on walking, and then turned right up a cobbled driveway, the entrance to a large grand mansion town house. Crawford followed closely on her heels, trying to not look at Gabriella so as not to invite any last-minute nerves or giving her an opportunity to back out. They didn't have to knock as the imposing front door opened immediately as they approached. A slightly plump, middle-aged gentleman who was wearing a sky-blue V-neck jumper with an open neck shirt underneath greeted them.

"Come in. Please do come in," he said and then left them alone at the door to enter and settle in their own time. He disappeared out of view down the long corridor. The house was amazing thought Gabriella as she looked around her. She followed Crawford down a long, well-lit hallway, eventually opening up into a bright, airy, modern, open-plan kitchen and lounge area that Gabriella thought looked out of this world. She checked out her surroundings, and with her professional cleaning eye she thought this place is immaculate and certainly doesn't need cleaning. Lucy was speaking with the homeowners who were sat on separate brightly coloured sofas, positioned so they faced each other off to the left. Gabriella, who had stayed at Crawford's side, saw them both sign a document that Lucy presented to them on a grand polished chrome coffee table, positioned between the two sofas.

Lucy retrieved her signed contract and she turned and looked at Crawford, saying aloud:

"The two hours starts now. If you can clean the kitchen first, please."

The gentleman of the house only spoke to offer calm instructions that the cleaning materials were located in the cupboard just to the left of the dishwasher. Crawford smiled at Gabriella and immediately pulled his tight white T-shirt over his head. He remained smiling as all three ladies in the room looked straight at Crawford's suntanned, solid, muscular body. He had a chiselled six pack torso and muscular big arms and he flashed them each an individual smile of his perfect white teeth. He leaned over, exaggerating his stance to deliberately show off his bum in his tight jeans, and opened the designated cleaning cupboard. Lifting out numerous cleaning chemicals, bottles, and cloths, he placed them slowly and carefully on the kitchen counter. Lucy stood up, as if preparing to leave the house. She was already comfortable with the new client and was indeed preparing to leave, she just needed to see Gabriella participate. She needed her to get naked, so she knew that the contract would be fulfilled.

With a smile, Crawford whispered to Gabriella., "Take your clothes off." Gabriella looked back at him with wide eyes and then looked across at the couple still sat on the sofas. She looked over at Lucy who had now moved again and was standing by the entrance to the hallway.

"Lucy won't go until you're naked," Crawford added again in a whisper and a reassuring smile. Gabriella started to unbutton her long sleeved blouse and, after removing it, she looked around for somewhere to set it down. She laid it slowly over the back of one of the many red leather stools which sat perfectly spaced around an oval centre island. Gabriella had specifically selected what she regarded as her sexiest black bra, and as she stood there in a stranger's house wearing only her bra and a pair of skimpy denim shorts, she felt empowered. She was tingling with excitement and the overpowering feeling of being alive and free to make her own choices left her almost breathless. In that moment, she knew she was going to enjoy this just as much as the paying customers were. Gabriella picked up a can of furniture polish and a yellow duster as Crawford unbuttoned his jeans. He lifted out one suntanned muscular leg at a time and again the three ladies' eyes were all drawn in Crawford's direction. He was not wearing any underwear and his ample weighty manhood flopped about as he folded his jeans. Naked, he deliberately walked towards the female paying customer. Smiling and maintaining eye contact with her, he placed his folded jeans on the arm of the sofa where she sat. He came within only a few feet of the woman and, since she was sitting down, she was in the direct line of sight of Crawford's biggest asset. Gabriella couldn't take her eyes off Crawford's body as he then walked around and started to clean the kitchen counters. He was at least making an effort to clean, or at least pretend to clean the counters. With skilful practice he did, at all times, make sure that the female customer was able to see him easily both from the front and rear. He knew if he didn't look at Gabriella, he wouldn't get an erection, and he tried to blank out his surroundings and just clean. Gabriella smiled at Crawford and lifting her eyes from his naked body, she looked him in the eye and put her right hand around her back and popped her bra clasp open. Lucy turned and said she was leaving. Crawford leaned into Gabriella and whispered, "Thank you, my darling. Swimming pool later?" and wiggled his now semi-erect penis in her direction. He smiled and watched as Gabriella unbuttoned her denim shorts and they fell to the ground under their own weight. She left them where they lay on to the kitchen floor. Gabriella was now completely naked apart from the black high heel shoes she was wearing. She was proud of her body and with her shoulders back she walked around the kitchen, revealing her perfect slim and completely naked suntanned body. Crawford was as aroused as Gabriella, and he was in the stage between floppy and fully erect where his penis projected straight out. Every time he turned it waved from side to side as it gained in girth and size from its unconstrained movement. The female homeowner followed its every move and bounce around *her* kitchen.

*

Over a single cup of coffee, Charles and his daughter spent the next few hours chatting endlessly as if they had known each other their entire lives. He disclosed to her all about his second wife Megan and that they had a son together, Jackson, her half-brother. He told her all about his current wife Sharon and her two half-sisters.

Evangeline in turn told Charles all about her boyfriend that she hoped to soon marry. She had already decided that she wanted Charles to walk her down the aisle and not her current stepdad. She told Charles about her mum and that she didn't marry for many years, but that she has now met a good man and all three of them live together in Grandma and Grandad's enormous house.

They both knew the circumstances of how Charles and Beatrice had separated all those years ago. Charles recalled his version of events and almost immediately Evangeline began to weep. She interrupted Charles many times, explaining how she was finding it hard to get over the fact that her mother had lied to her for all these years. She was struggling with the anger she felt inside towards her mother, and she regarded this time as wasted years. Time she could have spent with her biological father. Charles stretched his arms across the table and reached for his daughter's hands. It felt comfortable to do this. He told her about their time together at university and the crazy student things they had done. He told her about how much he loved her mother and the details about their small, quick wedding. He confessed that, in a way, he still loved her as he had never fallen out of love with her. She left him; he didn't leave her. He didn't have to tell Evangeline, but Charles wanted to say it, and he reminded her that he was young and back then he did what he was told and that it was a different era to nowadays.

They both told each other everything. He told her the details of when he came to London to find Beatrice and he had banged on her grandparents' front door. He explained how he had been refused access to his wife and how he then just sat on the doorstep for hours without moving. He knew Beatrice was inside the house and just the other side of the door. Memories came flooding back to Charles as he recalled the events, and he told his daughter that he had slept that night on a park bench around the corner. He had been a student and was unable to afford London hotel prices. He had walked for hours along the river and that the next day he had come back to the house and explained how he had stood just staring at the house. He described how there wasn't a gate at the end of the road then and he sat on the kerb for hours, but nobody came out and he eventually gave up and caught the train home. He told her all about his adventures around Europe and the particular night when he was working in a French restaurant when he found out that Beatrice was still pregnant. He skirted over how he had punched another chef on the nose and the fact he had to immediately leave France.

Evangeline looked down at her phone again and said, "Mummy has messaged five times. She wants me to come home. I've already told her you are coming with me!" Evangeline looked at Charles and he knew he was going to meet his first love again and of course her new husband. Charles picked up his mug as if to finish his coffee, a cold cup that was long ago empty. Evangeline's best friend who ran the coffee shop had been hovering and knew all about Charles, and as they both started to gather their things at their table, she pounced. Evangeline introduced Charles to her friend and they both shook hands with reassuring smiles, and he attempted to answer her endless questions that proceeded the handshake and the walk through the kitchen to the staff carpark.

The short drive back to the house was in silence, both overwhelmed by the enormity of what was happening. As they neared the house the gate swung immediately open and Evangeline, with raised eyebrows, said aloud, "Security. They are always watching." Charles at first didn't know what she actually meant but later in the evening he became aware of the 24-hour security guards that patrolled the house and gardens. The security guards monitored the numerous CCTV cameras located everywhere from a monitoring room in the adjoining property which Grandma and Grandad also owned. The former military security team lived in the house next door, and they provided security for the several houses in the street and manned the gated entrance. One of many companies owned by the affluent grandparents.

Charles, with nervous anticipation, watched as Evangeline parked in an underground carpark. It contained at least a dozen other cars and Charles thought he was in some sort of office block car park, not underneath someone's home. Several of the cars caught Charles's eye. There were sports cars and vintage models he could only ever dream of owning. He was directed to retrieve his overnight bag from the boot and was told that he must of course stay the night at the house. Charles explained that he had made a hotel reservation and insisted that he couldn't possibly stay. Evangeline skilfully deflected his decision by adding that she wanted to spend as much time as she could with him, and that the house was like a hotel anyway. They had staff who would prepare a room.

Impatiently, Evangeline led Charles to a staircase in the corner of the car park. The black electric doors opened automatically as they approached, and Charles said aloud the word "Security" and Evangeline casually nodded her head without looking back. They walked up a beautifully wide, marbled, partially carpeted staircase to the next floor as Gabriella attempted to describe the layout of the house. Charles struggled to take everything in, he thought he was in a film set of a grand hotel as, whilst looking at her phone, he heard his daughter end her sentence with the words, "Everyone's in the kitchen."

Evangeline in front and Charles following very close behind, they approached a large open-plan, very striking kitchen area. Charles could hear several voices up ahead and he had visions that there was going to be a houseful judging by all the cars downstairs in the garage. As they neared the high ceiling entrance, Evangeline took Charles' hand in a show of support, and they walked into the kitchen side by side. Charles saw five people in front him, who all fell silent and stared straight at him as he entered. Evangeline stopped, squeezing Charles' hand as an indication for him to do the same.

"Everybody, this is my biological father, Charles," Evangeline said in a firm business tone and then added, "Please come and meet my dad," with the biggest grin on her face you could imagine, all whilst holding firmly onto Charles' hand as she looked at everyone in turn. Charles scanned the room and his eyes stopped firmly on Beatrice. She looked amazing, he thought, and she hadn't changed in the slightest. He immediately thought that he had aged and that she must be thinking, I've aged and got fat. For what seemed like an age, no one said anything, until …

"Hello Charles," Beatrice said gently with a smile and a slight tilt of her head. The mood broken suddenly by the words "Ding Dong" being said aloud from a slightly overweight middle-aged brunette lady. Without removing her eyes from Charles, she lifted a glass of white wine to her mouth and took a gulp. She then continued to stare over the top of the glass at Charles, offering him a wink as he turned to look in her direction.

Charles later found out this was Angelica, who was the single, divorced many times over, extremely wealthy and amorous best friend of Beatrice.

Charles greeted Beatrice's husband with a nod and a firm, respectful handshake. He said hello from a distance to both grandparents who acknowledged Charles with just a nod of their heads, and then after briefly speaking with Beatrice in hushed tones, they both made a discreet exit from the room. Angelica had insisted several times that Charles should sit down next to her on one of the numerous leather sofas that surrounded the kitchen cooking area. Evangeline, however, made sure she always stayed at Charles' side and quickly reminded all persons present that her father was currently married. She guided Charles to an empty sofa and sitting down on the other side of Charles she took his hand in hers in a daughter-father show of affection.

CHAPTER 20

You Have To Go Right Now

After an hour, Evangeline, not wanting to share her father any longer, dragged him away from everyone and gave him the obligatory tour of the house. As Charles expected, it was all very grand and very big. As they toured, they stayed away from the west wing and the grandparents' side of the house. Charles was genuinely impressed; he had no idea that this is where his first wife had grown up and called home. In a way, it helped him understand a little as to why her parents had decided they wanted more for their only daughter than to marry an unemployed, over-weight university student who drank too much and had only just scraped through his degree.

Evangeline was keeping up a relentless pace on their grand tour, so Charles attempted to slow things down a little, not really wanting to get back to the kitchen for fear of more interrogation and awkwardness.

"This is a wonderful house. I can see why your grandma and grandad wanted more for your mum," the doting father exclaimed, wanting to savour every moment he was sharing with his daughter. Evangeline stopped suddenly and turned. Staring at her father she dropped into an immediate rant about how she had been lied to, and that her mother was lucky to have him. Charles closed the gap between them in a show of both affection and support. He was quite accustomed to daughters who vocally expressed their emotions and opinions.

"I understand a bit more now, that's all," Charles added with raised palms as he followed on behind his daughter, the house tour continuing erratically. Evangeline wasn't having any talk that discredited her father, it was all *nonsense*. In her eyes, her biological father had done nothing wrong. He was a victim, just as she was, of a Victorian parental dictatorship. Evangeline's biggest gripe, which she repeatedly vented, were the lies she had been told, and as they walked and talked Charles just let her get it out of her system. They continued down the long endless carpeted corridors, occasionally opening doors to empty, grand, well-illuminated rooms. It was easy for Charles to get his daughter back on track by relaying stories of their student life. His stories included when her mother had got very drunk on vodka jelly shots at the student bar and between them both they had ended up losing their campus front door key. Being locked out of their rooms, Charles had convinced Beatrice to climb up the drainpipe to reach a partially open window on the second floor! They laughed together at the stories, and the physical contact of holding hands cemented their newly found love for one another, their special father-daughter bond. Evangeline barely recognised the adventurous and fun-loving crazy party woman he described as being her mother.

Bored of showing off the house, Evangeline decided to end the tour early. She directed Charles back to the grand kitchen and the beating heart of the house. It was an even bigger space when empty, everyone had gone to bed. All that was left to remind them of their presence were numerous empty wine bottles and glasses, along with several half-eaten terracotta bowls of Tapas dotted around the gleaming white marble worktops.

"Mum messaged me. She's left us some food in the top left oven." Evangeline indicated for Charles to select a seat. There was a long line of elegant black leather bar stools lining the edge of the counters. As he sat, his daughter left his side for the first time since he had arrived in London. She opened one of the many oven doors that were at waist height and integrated around the kitchen island. Charles felt very comfortable, and he watched with pride as his daughter began fussing over him.

"He has his faults, old Rupert," Evangeline said, adding "My *step*" with eye contact towards Charles. Looking away, as she continued to prepare the meal for them both, Evangeline carried on talking and Charles just listened. They were both very comfortable in each other's presence. "But he always buys nice wine," Evangeline added out loud, and at the same time pulled out a long single cork from what looked like an expensive bottle of French Bordeaux wine. She left the cork still twisted on its corkscrew and dropped it down on the counter, the red wine from the wet cork briefly staining the surface. She plonked the open bottle down in front of Charles. Looking around the kitchen and without leaving his bar stool, Charles reached over and managed to grab two nearby empty wine glasses. One had probably been used earlier in the evening, but it was getting late, they looked clean enough to him and he was past caring. Without being asked, Charles poured himself and his daughter a glass of wine, only filling each glass a third full. Charles couldn't resist offering the wine to his nose and the bouquet was indeed reminiscent of his time spent travelling around France in his youth. Evangeline began placing more ceramic terracotta bowls down in front of him, warm from the oven and containing an array of colourful spiced meats and vegetables. With efficiency, she added two square multi coloured plates, several white crisp folded linen napkins and a fistful of various silver cutlery which she grabbed from a drawer with one hand without even looking.

"Will you stay the night, Dad?" Evangeline asked, and then immediately laughed and babbled on about using the word 'dad'. A word she had never used before today. Charles never had time to answer, and Evangeline continued to chatter whilst he filled his plate with heaps of food, and with a single gulp he emptied his wine glass and poured himself another. He hadn't eaten since leaving home and he was famished. After several minutes of eating, drinking, and more talking, Charles was feeling pretty full and replied to his daughter's earlier question.

"Of course I'll stay the night. Do you have a spare room?" Charles enquired with a grin, at the same time picking up the wine bottle again.

"Just one or two. I think there's twenty or so in total. I lose count, pick one!" Evangeline laughed, flicking her long hair back. She moved along the marble counter to open another oven door and began lifting out even more bowls of food.

"I need to ring Sharon," Charles said between mouthfuls, phone aloft in one hand and wine glass in the other.

Excitedly Evangeline had a new interest: "Can I say hello?" Charles was unsure on how to reply to that question, so he just propped up his mobile phone against the now almost empty wine bottle and pressed the video call button. On loudspeaker Evangeline could hear her father's mobile phone ringing, shortly followed by a woman's voice.

On answering, the voice was initially firm and frosty, but as a woman can easily do, on realising her husband was not alone, Sharon skilfully changed her tone to one of calmness and friendliness, and utter pleasantness. Evangeline made a purposeful sweep of the kitchen, approaching her father from behind as she slowly appeared in the screen. She carried over more food and placed it down next to Charles, as she perched herself on the bar stool next to him. Leaning forward, she placed her arm around her father's shoulders in a show of physical contact for the woman who was looking back at her. Offering her biggest smile, she said excitedly, "Hi. I'm Evangeline!"

Sharon did her best to attempt a posh accent and was as polite and affable as possible. Unfortunately, her face appeared larger than normal as she was holding her handset very close to her face, in an attempt to shield it from her children. They should have been in bed of course, but Sharon had let them stay awake to speak to their Dad, and in the hope that they may get a glimpse of their new half-sister. From Sharon's perspective, she was pleased and relieved at last to see her loving husband looking back at her, although she was unsure as to why he was sitting on a bar stool in a very luxurious hotel restaurant, it wasn't the hotel she had booked for him that was for certain. Beside him was a pretty, slim young girl, sitting very close to her husband. She was a strikingly beautiful young woman, thought Sharon, and she continued to scan the rest of their surroundings; the grand open plan modern kitchen with its high ceilings, the numerous empty wine bottles and the copious bowls of overflowing food that surrounded them both. Sharon had flashes of nervous anticipation mixed with twinges of jealousy in the pit of her stomach; she had experienced these feelings many times before, being married to hunky good-looking Charles.

*

"Time to leave, kids," Alison shouted, and at the same time adding a few hard knocks on each of her children's bedroom doors. No one stirred. She decided she would leave them just five more minutes before trying again.

"And *you* have to go right now," Alison said, almost shouting at the half-naked man asleep on her caravan sofa. With a crushing hangover and overpowering guilt, she now regretted what had happened last night, but she had been a willing participant in wild drunken sex with her soldier. Adam, now half sitting but still laying on the sofa, cupped a cup of coffee in both hands and he had a big grin on his face. He watched Alison in silence as she busied herself around the caravan.

"And don't look at me like that, cover yourself up," Alison glared at him seriously, her eyes drawn to his morning erection as she snatched up a pair of her crumpled knickers from the lounge floor and noisily dropped copious empty beer and wine bottles into the kitchen bin.

"Up. Up. Come on, get dressed!" Alison shouted again with a swiftly aimed kick directed at Adam's bare thigh. In silence Adam just smiled at his ex-wife, admiring her voluptuous body as she moved with haste and purpose. Adam decided it was time to try and win her over. He had enjoyed last night. Now wearing only a towel around his waist, he stood up and offered an open arm as he approached, adding;

"You were amazing last night. You know it was. I know it was, but it was a one off. We both know that. You get off with the kids. I will tidy up the place and lock up." Alison looked him up and down. She too had enjoyed last night; it had been a long time since a man of his stature had taken her with such passion. She was unable to resist him, his manhood still not relaxed and unmistakeable under the towel. Dragging her eyes away and annoyed at herself that she had even briefly contemplated a morning quickie, she opened the fridge door.

"There's bacon and eggs left, you can have them for breakfast and then make the place spotless. Someone from the site is coming to drain down, so when you go, lock up and leave this key in reception," Alison instructed, waving a single gold-coloured key in the air, before slamming it down on the kitchen counter in front of him.

"Kids, my god, let's go!" Alison screamed as she began pulling two huge bags of dirty laundry out to the car. Almost instantly, she heard movement from the bedrooms beyond. The kids had heard that scream before, and knew their mum meant business.

Just over ten minutes later, no thanks to the kids, the car was packed. As they drove away from the caravan at an unnecessary speed, Adam stood on the decking waving off his ex-wife and daughter, like the doting ex-husband he was. Adam went back inside to a warm, empty plush holiday home. He liked being here, he felt comfortable, and, as he sat himself down on the sofa, he reached for his mobile phone with one hand and the television remote control with the other. Finding a football match on the television, he lowered the volume and telephoned the caravan site reception. Like a light switch being clicked, he quickly turned into the more formal and professional Adam.

"Hello, this is Adam. I'm a family friend staying with Alison and Clifford up on the north side. When's the end of the season, sorry what I mean is when do I have to be off the site? Oh, four days yet, OK that's great. Alison said she has booked a caravan drain down or something like that and she has left me a key to hand in. Yes. OK. I will drop the key in reception in four days when I go. Oh thank you so much. Cheers have a lovely day, goodbye!" Sorted.

Adam lay back even further on the sofa with a big grin on his face. Four days of free holiday, Adam thought. Jackpot. Great sex last night, with what has to be one of the sexiest women around, and a free holiday. Bacon and eggs, and free beer in the fridge. Things are certainly looking up he thought to himself as he began to search the kitchen cupboards for a frying pan.

Several weeks passed and Alison had not heard anything from her ex-husband. In a way she was pleased. She had not trusted Adam to remember to hand in her caravan key, so she had telephoned the site to check. Everything was OK and their caravan had been drained down and locked up for the winter. Her key was in an envelope in the site safe marked with her name and plot number. With that knowledge, Alison relaxed for another week or so, and was able to start the process of trying to forget about her one night of straying. She did this by (a) trying to convince herself it never happened and (b) believe it was not her fault as she had been very drunk.

What she couldn't get out of her mind, however, was that her period was now three days overdue. She was never late. Ever. In the chemist she found herself looking at the pregnancy tests. They were cheaper if you bought a pack of three. *What am I going to say to Clifford?*

"Sorry, darling, I know you've had a vasectomy, but sorry I slipped and fell pregnant. Oh and by the way, my ex-husband is the father. Oh you do forgive me, thank you, darling!" What a complete and utter mess, she thought. The words 'I am never *ever* drinking again' came to mind, as she tearfully selected a three-pack of pregnancy tests from the shelf and placed them into her shopping basket, hiding them under a family multi-pack of crisps.

*

"That beep is my watch, it's been two hours. I hope the place is all nice and clean enough for you?" Crawford politely said out loud, whilst standing naked in front of the paying customers. His penis was not fully erect, but he was large from being aroused whilst watching a naked Gabriella moving around the house. The customers had moved onto one sofa together, and by now were not paying any attention to what Crawford was saying. They couldn't keep their hands off each other, and the female party was in a state of undress. Crawford turned to Gabriella with a big grin and signalled for her to get dressed, it was time to leave. They both smiled at each other as they repeatedly glanced across at the now affectionate couple on the sofa. Gabriella wasn't wearing many clothes when she arrived, so she dressed quickly and had a few seconds to cast her professional cleaning eye over the kitchen. The place was spotless. She had realised it wasn't really about the cleaning, it was about injecting some sexual excitement back into the paying couple's marriage, but Gabriella always took her house cleaning seriously. She watched as Crawford got dressed. He was still completely naked, and she was enthralled to watch as he carefully pulled his jeans over his enlarged manhood and, taking his time, he carefully applied his zip. He was such a big man and she smiled and laughed as she moved closer to him. With one hand she caressed Crawford's firm bare muscular chest, scrunching his chest hair and with the other she squeezed his stiff penis as hard as she could, whilst they both laughed together.

Crawford collected the padded envelope containing the payment from the arm of the sofa and, with a beckoning gesture, he nodded for Gabriella to follow him out. He smiled as he offered an unnoticed polite gesture to the couple who were still on the sofa, lost in each other's companionship, and who were now in the process of undressing each other.

"We'll see ourselves out. All the best," Crawford shouted and with a giggle he pulled the front door shut behind him quietly. Crawford took hold of Gabriella's hand as they walked down the driveway.

"You looked amazing. You are a complete natural. Thank you so much," and he squeezed her hand lovingly and held it tight as they both walked hand in hand towards their parked land rover.

When they reached the side of their vehicle, Gabriella said, "I really enjoyed myself," with her sexy smile, at the same time she lowered her hand and massaged his groin area again, she couldn't keep her hands off him. She could feel he was still hard, and his penis was still easy to locate through his jeans. She was about to speak again and tell him what she wanted, when suddenly a car pulled up next to them. It was Lucy, her driver's window was coming down as she came to a sudden stop.

"Well?" Lucy asked, looking at Crawford through her open driver's window.

"Went good. Really well, they loved it. Gabriella was *amazing* and we have left them tearing each other's clothes off," Crawford replied confidently and instinctively he handed Lucy the padded envelope. Lucy went into businesswoman mode, and she flicked through the contents of the envelope. She moved the envelope ever so slightly, a move that went unnoticed by Gabriella but who was now unable to see what Lucy was doing with the envelope. In one swift movement,

Lucy removed some of the money and discreetly folded the notes and tucked them away in her bra. Lucy handed the envelope back to Crawford. Instinctively she turned all sincere and gentle and with a friendly smile she thanked Gabriella and uttered that she hoped to see her again soon. Handing Gabriella her business card, almost instantaneously Lucy then drove away. They were alone again; work was over and they climbed aboard the land rover like a couple of naughty newlyweds on honeymoon. In the privacy of their vehicle, Crawford said;

"Right, young lady. Time to show you some attention," and he turned to face Gabriella and placing a gentle hand either side of her face he passionately kissed her full on the lips. This was too much for an already aroused Gabriella and she went weak at the knees. She pushed Crawford back into his seat and leaned over him, forcibly pulling down his jean zip. She could feel Crawford still had his firmness and knew she was going to enjoy this just as much as him. She began to jostle and wobble his now even larger manhood in her grip, and without saying anything she looked him directly in the eyes. She smiled and then, looking back down, instinctively her eyes closed and her mouth opened as she took in as much as she was able.

That evening, Crawford and Gabriella made love many times. The onsite swimming pool. This fantasy of Gabriella's had now been fulfilled, arranged by Crawford with the consent of his good friend, Owen. The following day, Crawford left early on the first morning train for the airport. He messaged Gabriella that the snow had arrived, and he had to get back to his skiing instructor's work.

Later that morning, Gabriella emptied her caravan fridge, and turned off the gas and water. She jumped in the car to pick up Fabian who was waiting by the clubhouse. He had wanted to say goodbye to somebody and had been out all morning.

"You OK?" Gabriella said to her son as he climbed into the front seat of her car and pulled across his seat belt. Fabian just nodded, offering no verbal reply, and sat staring out the car window as they drove out of the site. As they turned right up the lane, Gabriella shouted out loud, "See you next year caravan," and they continued in silence. This marked the end of their first caravan season for them both. Gabriella's thoughts turned to the one man who could satisfy her, and she suddenly had an empty feeling in the pit of her stomach. It would be months before she would see Crawford again. Fabian's thoughts turned to the girl he had just left behind, and seeing his mother going into the closed swimming pool the previous evening with a man that wasn't his dad, but more importantly to the video game he was going to play on the journey home.

Back home life was the same for Gabriella. Weeks turned into months and Gabriella continually checked to see if the tick on her message had turned blue to confirm that Crawford had read it. The message had been delivered but Crawford had not read any of the numerous messages she had sent. Gabriella didn't know what to think. She couldn't get this man out of her head. The new spring caravan season was only days away, and Gabriella began to resign herself to the fact that Crawford had most likely moved on, changed his number and not told her, and she should try and forget about him.

But she couldn't forget him and had turned into a desperate schoolgirl looking for answers. Under the pretence that she had agreed some landscaping work on her caravan plot, Gabriella rang the caravan site reception asking to specifically speak to Crawford. She was placed on hold and passed around several people before she was eventually informed that Owen, the site manager, would ring her personally later that evening, she couldn't provide a time. Gabriella didn't know what to think or feel. All Gabriella could think about was herself. What was the manager going to say? Was he aware about the two of them? Did he know they had been having sex in the swimming pool? She began to make herself sick with worry that she had been found out and how it was going to affect her current comfortable married position.

Owen rang just before midnight. Her husband had gone to bed and Gabriella was sat alone in the dark of her living room staring at her empty handset, constantly checking she had a signal. An empty wine bottle sat on the coffee table. Owen first apologised for the lateness of the call, and Gabriella listened as Owen told her everything. He informed her he wasn't at the caravan site, but he was in Paris. He said he had been there for over a week, and he had been visiting the British embassy every day. Owen knew they had been close. Crawford was in trouble. He proceeded to explain that Crawford was a very dear friend, but also that his friend was a deep and complex man with issues and fingers in lots of different pies. Gabriella listened without interrupting but after Owen began talking about the caravan site again, she spoke and brought the conversation back to Crawford.

Owen, now back on track, cut to the chase and informed her he had just left La-Santé Prison in the centre of Paris. That it had taken all week for him to be able to get a thirty-minute prison visit with Crawford along with a British Embassy representative. In the thirty minutes Crawford had said that an amount of white powder had been found at the airport, inside his ski bag. It had been wrapped in pink plastic bags and hidden in between his skis. It had been discovered on his flight stop over on his way home and during tears he had strongly denied he knew anything about the drugs. Gabriella was silent for a few moments and Owen thought the telephone connection had been lost.

"Do you believe him? Do you believe he is innocent?" Gabriella asked after a few moments. Owen didn't immediately reply.

"He looks well, he says he has to share a cell with only three other people and one of them speaks English so he can talk to someone."

"How do I get a prison visit?" Gabriella asked. She recognised how she felt inside and she knew things were going to change. Her life was going to be different from now on, but she was in love.

*

David had never experienced an airport VIP lounge before. He didn't even know such a thing existed. With a smile, he thanked Marcus for being an excellent chauffeur and then exchanged a firm handshake. Marcus returned the smile and at the same time commanded a business-like nod to a young man who was hovering nearby.

"This is Stefan. He will show you to your plane, sir. Have a safe flight and I hope to see you again soon." Marcus smiled again.

Stefan leaned in and with efficiency and grace, picked up David's bag from the open boot. With similar grace, Marcus disappeared into the driver's seat and almost instantly the car began to slowly pull away, the boot lid still closing itself as the car glided away effortlessly. David was sad to see Marcus go. Even in their brief encounter, David knew he liked him.

"Sir. Please follow me if you would. If we hurry, we have the chance of an earlier take off slot," a perspiring Stefan said hastily as he led the way at pace. They passed through some smoked glass doors which were covered in security warning stickers and proceeded down two flights of illuminated, clinical-looking stairs. David followed on in silence, with Stefan respectfully holding open the many doors behind him. Suddenly stopping near a locked steel door, Stefan spoke into a small chrome intercom box on the wall. Offering his name, he then read the long number from the front of his laminated pass that hung on a bright orange lanyard around his neck. The flashing red lights on the intercom box turned a solid green colour and the door opened with a purposeful click. Without being asked, David followed at pace down a long corridor. The corridor opened out into the sunshine and onto the airplane runway. David's bag was dropped into the back of what looked like an electric golf buggy and Stefan gestured for David to take the rear seat. Instantly the fluorescent-wearing bald driver flicked a switch which started a bright orange light flashing on top of the buggy. As they moved their way around the concourse, they passed near and under numerous sizeable commercial planes. David recognised the well-known company logos embossed on their tails and wings, and it fascinated him to see these aircraft from this angle, and so close up. The buggy sped at a fast but comfortable pace and soon David spotted a small, expensive-looking white jet plane sitting alone in the distance. It was situated on the edge of the runway with a bright red carpet running along the ground and leading up to the plane steps. David smiled, assuming the plane with the red carpet was for a famous person or even royalty and he looked around to try and spot them. He was mistaken.

With a sudden stop, Stefan grabbed David's bag, fled up the carpeted steps and disappeared inside the jet plane. David spent a few seconds looking around, taking in his surroundings, and savouring every minute of this fabulous adventure. He slowly alighted from the buggy. He felt like he was on some sort of movie set, it was all so surreal.

The mood was soon broken by Stefan calling out from the landing at the top of the stairwell, making various gesturing arm movements.

"Sir. If you could take your seat, please. I am terribly sorry to rush you, but this take off slot is disappearing fast. Sir. Please."

With this, a startled David dashed up the plane steps and ducked slightly as he entered the cabin. He was guided to one of the eight large, leather spacious empty seats as he heard the engines roaring. Stefan placed a seat belt around his bag on the adjoining seat.

*

Debbie's wealthy parents had taken the children away for a week on a special child-friendly cruise around the Mediterranean. Danielle wasn't sure about a cruise with her grandparents; she was far too cool, but she was now getting interested in improving her own online social media profile, all influenced by her now-famous glamorous mother. She was impressed with the amount of money her mother was making online, all from advertising. She didn't really agree with how her *mother* displayed every part of her anatomy, curves and all, regularly for the whole world to see, but when it was explained to her how much her mother made from just wearing one particular brand of bikini or lingerie, Danielle was suddenly very interested indeed in this choice of career. She thought a cruise holiday was a very mature thing to do, and she had plans to post daily about her on-board adventures including descriptions of the three different outfits she had planned for each day. It had been two weeks since she had last seen Fabian, and his snapchat messages were drying up. She always knew he would be a difficult boyfriend to keep, but she was glad to say that he had been her first.

Debbie's work schedule was now constant. She loved the attention this brought her, and with over two million online followers, she had now employed two members of staff to manage all her accounts. Debbie would check in digitally with her team on the day's business schedule, sending them notes of what she had been up to that day and forward pictures she had taken of herself. Her team would ensure that all the current top-paying products Debbie had to endorse were shipped promptly to her, with any specific instructions from the vendor. Sometimes Debbie needed to just hold the item or wear the item. Sometimes it was enough the item was seen in the background of a selfie picture Debbie had taken of herself.

Along the way to stardom, Debbie had received lots of advice from her fellow social media influencers. One reoccurring suggestion was not put all her eggs in one basket. Listening to this advice, Debbie had started a new Instagram page called *Mums Bums*. To help advertise her new page, in her other accounts her bio read 'Creator and founder of Mums Bums'. Debbie relished the challenges of starting a new business venture. The page was certainly starting to explode. It was not just about Debbie; anybody could submit pictures of their *bum* for approval before being posted. Her goal also with this new account was to venture into YouTube and OnlyFans when the moment presented itself. She was now well-practiced in holding her phone as she walked along the pavement so she would talk about what she was up-to on that particular day. Debbie would always be mindful to hold her phone aloft, making sure she captured her best bouncing assets on the screen.

With this invaluable child-free time, Debbie was going on a bikini shoot. An all-expenses paid trip to Barcelona for four nights and more importantly, she could bring a plus-one. She wouldn't be allowed to share pictures from the photo shoot on her private social media accounts, but after it was over, she would spend most of the day lounging around the pool snapping suggestive pictures of herself for her online admirers. Life was good, and she would smile and laugh with her family on video calls most nights. They would all share their adventures from the day, always remarking on how things had dramatically changed for them all. Debbie didn't mention the plus-one and she would make sure she was alone on the video call when she spoke with her family. She didn't need to, everything was cool, but she was still married, and she didn't want to rub David's face in the fact she was now sleeping with other men. More importantly she didn't want her husband to know who she had selected as her plus-one, as it was slightly delicate, since he was married. Debbie had secured a hotel suite with vast panoramic sea views, and an enormous four-poster bed that got tested daily. Just being around this man when he was naked made her become uncontrollably aroused, and every time he touched her, he would set her feet on fire. They made love to each other every morning and evening with a desire of complete passion and lust. They experimented and explored areas of each other's body in ways they had never dreamt of with their current partners. Debbie was introduced to bondage on this trip, and she liked it and rose to the challenge of being tied down across the bed with silk scarfs and leather belts.

*

Lucy missed Crawford being around, and her business suffered because of it. She didn't show any surprise when she heard that he had been arrested. Over the years she never wanted anything to do with his dodgy business ventures, he had asked her many times over for investment. International drug smuggling was not something Lucy thought had a long-term future, and she was right.

Her naked cleaning bookings were down as a result of not having Crawford's body to put on display, but the business was ticking over, and she had several new male cleaners ready in the wings. Her repeat customer for the first Friday of every month had booked and paid for another six months in advance again. Lucy had just received a telephone call from the cleaner who had let her down at the last minute, offering up a feeble fanciful excuse. Not wanting to lose this customer, she decided to offer her apologies in person, and drove in her own car to his house. She was surprised that she had made the journey. Parking a little way from the address, she walked purposefully up the road. Lucy was freshly showered and changed. After all, it was important that she projected a professional image to all her clients. By offering a personal touch, Lucy was hoping to reassure her good customer that she would be able to sort a suitable cleaner very soon. The last thing she wanted was to refund his fee; she couldn't afford to, and besides, she had already re-invested the money.

Lucy knocked the grand front door and within seconds it was answered by the tall good-looking homeowner. Paying more attention this time, Lucy noted he had whispers of grey in his beard with a full head of unruly dark hair. He greeted Lucy and smiled, remembering her as the big boss lady from his first ever clean. Lucy immediately dropped into her rehearsed speech about being let down by his pre-booked cleaner. Lucy had always liked what she saw, it may subconsciously have been why she had made this personal visit. She tried to convince herself that she didn't remember him being such a masculine, well-dressed man and more importantly she didn't remember how good looking he was with his chiselled jaw line. He invited her inside but with a fluttering in her stomach, she initially declined. The gentleman was insistent, adamant that she needed to come inside and chat over a drink regarding how they were going to move forwards in their business relationship. Lucy soon found herself admiring his beautiful home and surprised herself at how comfortable she felt in his presence and she was unable to resist his hospitality and smile.

"Coffee or tea?" asked the customer, adding further, "I'm going to have a G&T," and at the same time, without waiting for a reply, he reached up with giant hands and took two tall slim glasses from a cupboard and placed them down in front of her.

"Make yourself comfortable," and he gestured to an area just off the kitchen, which was airy and modern, with a smart leather sofa. Lucy wandered over slowly and dropped her coat over the arm, placing her handbag down next to where she sat. She lifted her bum and attempted to pull her short black leather skirt over her bare legs as far as it would go. The sofa was a quality leather and very comfortable and Lucy sank into it, her skirt riding even higher up her thighs. She surveyed her surroundings. His house was impressive; modern, bright with unique items on display which oozed quality and style. She admired his sense of style as he prepared her drink. He wore a smart, fitted navy suit with a crisp white open-neck shirt, his tie hanging loosely around his neck. Wandering over he smiled, and his eyes dropped to Lucy's toned legs. He handed her a glass, and placing his down on the table, he proceeded to pull off his tie and unbutton another shirt button. The tie was thrown over the arm of the sofa along with his suit jacket and he sat down. He had an overpowering presence, and he was unable to not make physical contact with Lucy on the sofa.

Now comfortable without jacket and tie, he leaned forwards and picked up his glass. "Cheers," he said, turning to face Lucy. Lucy replied likewise as they clinked their glasses and she smiled over the top of her glass.

"So," the customer said with a grin.

Lucy was already under this man's sexy charm and said gently, "I'm breaking my number one business rule by being here," as she sipped from her drink and suggestively smiled at her host over the top of her glass. Lucy knew what she was doing, and she wanted it to happen. Oh, she wanted this man. She liked him and she liked being in this house.

"This is a very grand house. Is anyone else here?" Lucy asked.

"We are all alone. I find you very attractive," the customer said and, as he broke eye contact, his eyes wandered over Lucy's body and suntanned thighs. Lucy wanted to rip his clothes off there and then but restrained herself and lifted her glass, emptying its contents in one go. Standing, she walked slowly and seductively towards the kitchen counter, and with her back to him, and in silence, she poured herself a second drink. Turning, she began a very slow walk back towards her host, holding her glass in one hand, and using her free hand she began to unbutton her blouse.

The customer remained on the sofa staring and slowly he parted his legs to make himself more comfortable. Lucy was now standing directly in front of him and with an open blouse she reached around and pulled down the rear zip on her skirt. Knees together, her skirt fell to the floor, revealing Lucy's toned, tanned legs. He reached forward, running his hands on her outer thighs, he reached round and cupped each of her buttocks. He had large firm hands and Lucy was surprised at how aroused she became at his touch. Lucy wasn't going to clean his kitchen, that was for certain.

It was dark as Lucy walked down the street back to her car. The smile remained on her face as she walked, realising she had been completely and utterly seduced by this gorgeous handsome man. It had been a long time since she had had a man make love to her, and she enjoyed the feeling of being in control of the situation. She knew he was married, and it was only going to be once a month. But that was enough for Lucy for now. She wouldn't want any more from him, she wasn't the relationship type. Or at least she thought she wasn't.

*

Evangeline eventually said goodnight to her father, it was very late. She repeatedly made sure Charles had everything he needed before she left him alone and disappeared upstairs to her room. Charles had been allocated the bedroom just off the kitchen area. It had a double bed, a single desk, and wardrobe. It was very light and modern, and the only items left in the room were several handbags and a lot of expensive looking ladies' shoes. Evangeline had explained that the room had been designed and built for her mother's best friend, Angelica. When Angelica drank too much wine, which was most nights, she would stay over and crash out for the night. Its location was ideal as it meant that any guest staying over would have easy access to the carpark and could sneak out in the morning without waking up the household. Charles didn't lock the room door; it had gone three a.m. He laid down on the bed, fully clothed, and found himself smiling at the ceiling. He was still in complete shock and bewilderment at what had taken place that day. It was surreal that he was in his first wife's house. He was tired and decided he would climb between the crisp white sheets, but first needed to go in search of a clean glass as he needed a drink of water.

Now topless and barefoot, wearing only his partially open jeans, he wandered back into the kitchen. Not wanting to go searching the vast array of cupboards, he selected his used wine glass, rinsed it out and filled it with ice-cold water from the water dispenser on the fridge door. He had originally planned on returning directly back to his room, but he sat down on the barstool where he had spent most of the evening and sipped his water. He had been furnished with expensive wine all evening by his daughter; wine was something Charles was not used to drinking. He sat in silence for a few minutes, savouring every mouthful of the crisp, fresh, ice-cold water, still not quite believing where he was. Relaxed now that he was finally alone, Charles leaned forward on the counter to assist himself to stand up, as he heard footsteps behind him. He immediately assumed it would be his daughter returning to check if he were OK. He was wrong.

"Hello, handsome," Beatrice said as she brushed his naked upper arm and leant over to pour herself a glass of wine from one of the many open wine bottles on the counter. Beatrice was just as beautiful as Charles remembered, and his heart thumped as she sat down next to him.

She wore long flowing pyjamas bottoms and a tight, white vest top. Charles could clearly see she wore no underwear and her nipples projected through her top and were enticingly hard as they brushed Charles' naked arm purposefully as she sat down next to him. Her skin was silky smooth, and her eyes glistened in the dim lighting. Using the counter for support, she leaned towards Charles and turned his stool so they faced each other. Charles sat in silence, he suddenly felt vulnerable, being partially naked, and under this woman's spell.

Beatrice closed her eyes as she kissed Charles full on the lips. He couldn't help himself and he kissed her back just as passionately. Instinctively he reached up with his hands and placed both hands onto her bare shoulders, the way he remembered she liked from all those years ago. They kissed like they both had never been kissed before. The mood was intense; they both felt it. Beatrice pushed Charles away with both hands and jumped to her feet. She grabbed his hand with determination and without speaking she dragged him along in the direction of the adjoining kitchen bedroom. He had no choice but to follow her, by now nearly full aroused. Beatrice was in charge, and immediately upon entering she again pushed Charles backwards with her kisses and he just managed to close the bedroom door as he was forced backwards. Beatrice reached for the remaining button on Charles' jeans as they fell to the floor under their own weight, only Charles' erection supporting them for a brief moment before they fell. Beatrice reached down and firmly gripped Charles. She started stroking him vigorously back and forth. She did this only briefly before she let go and stepped back, she liked what she saw. She lifted her vest over her head and threw it into the corner and, reaching down, she unfastened the button and her remaining clothes fell silently to the floor. Charles could see that Beatrice was in great shape. Her nipples were erect with desire, their large dark areola enticed Charles to step forward and he reached for her breast. In his grip he held her tight and remembered her smell and the softness of her porcelain skin. He cupped her buttocks firmly to bring her even closer, noticing the shape of her breasts, still as firm and responsive as he remembered. He lowered Beatrice down onto the bed, he couldn't wait even a second. His erect penis sought the gap between her thighs on its own and his mouth again closed over hers. Charles was completely and utterly aroused and still overwhelmingly in love with the woman who stole his heart all those years ago. Charles didn't know he was capable of his next move, but with an overpowering loyalty of love towards Sharon that he didn't want to gamble with, in one swift violent roll he broke free from Beatrice.

"I have never stopped loving you," he said through gasps of breath. Beatrice, still laying on the bed, was also breathing heavily. Charles stood naked and proud in front of her. "I am so sorry it ended like it did—"

Charles was interrupted as Beatrice opened her legs wider as she whispered, "Charles, I want you now," glancing down, infatuated with the size of Charles' glistening erection. "I love you, Charles," she said and offered her hands up between her raised knees, gesturing for Charles to lower himself down on top of her.

"I never stopped loving you," Charles repeated, but with surprised hesitation he stood looking down at Beatrice. Flashes of brief moments filled his head as his thoughts turned to his wife, but this was all lost in years of supressed anger and desire to recall the moments of true love from his carefree university years. Charles reached forwards and took hold of the outstretched hands belonging to his first and only true love. He never broke eye contact as he gently lowered himself down on top of Beatrice. They made passionate but gentle love into the early morning hours and Charles knew things were going to change in his life forever. Beatrice finally left him alone and bare footed, she quietly sneaked out of the room. Charles slept heavily in what was left of the morning. When he woke, he lay on his back looking at the ceiling. He looked across at the closed bedroom door as he heard noises from the kitchen beyond. Charles liked being in this house.

*

"Good morning, sexy," Patrick whispered into his wife's ear as she slept. He wasn't sure if she was still asleep, but he was awake and he had woken up like most men do with a partial erection and the desire for procreation. He was going to ask and try and get his wife to get into the same mood as himself.

"Can we have sex in your wheelchair?" Patrick whispered again into the same ear and this time he got a response.

Smiling, Melissa rolled over and facing him she said, "I didn't think you found me sexy anymore," opening both her eyes and staring at her husband with a smile.

"WHAT. Come here," and Patrick tickled and pulled his wife towards him under the duvet. Passionately he began to kiss her, and his hands explored her breasts before he pulled down her knickers with one forceful action. He disappeared under the duvet to get them off and over her feet, at the same time being gentle with his wife's injured legs. Patrick was a skilled love maker and he reminded himself to slow down in an attempt to entice his wife to arousal with his tongue. The desire to powerfully enter his wife had already started to consume him.

Afterwards, he let Melissa lay with the promise of bringing her breakfast in bed. From the kitchen Melissa could hear her husband moving around and the sound of the kettle boiling, and drawers opening and closing. Patrick picked his moment and he shouted from the kitchen;

"Do you know Terry? From C shift?"

"Who?" Melissa shouted back whilst she searched around the bedroom floor for her phone. It had been knocked off the bedside table during their enthusiastic love making.

"Tall guy, marrying a nurse I think she is, anyway he is having a stag-do next week. Just a couple of days I think it is, in Portugal someplace. His brother is best man, and he is organising everything. All expenses paid as he is loaded, so won't cost us much, I just need to book a flight." Patrick carried on cooking breakfast as if what he had said was un-remarkable. He was hoping no inquisitive questions would follow. He knew his wife had orgasmed during their love making and he knew her well enough that she would be relaxed and receptive for the rest of the morning.

Several minutes passed before Melissa shouted, "Have you heard anything from Frank lately? Sylvia is not responding to any of my messages! Been over a week now!"

Patrick smiled inwardly, pleased he had dodged any detailed questions regarding his forthcoming trip, and he entertained this new line of conversation with gusto.

"You will never believe it, I should have said. Frank told me the other week they have sold the motorhome!"

"NO," Melissa shouted in astonishment and then she instigated more details about their mutual friends. Patrick was happy to talk all day about Frank and Sylvia as this would avoid any questions about what he was up to next week.

"Honestly I thought you would know everything," Patrick said in reply, facing in the direction of the open bedroom door so his voice would be heard. He continued to make his wife breakfast and as he was romantically preparing the breakfast tray he continued, "You know they had that guy, what's-his-name came on a Sunday, the weekend and he would tidy their garden, clear the leaves," Patrick paused as he removed his dressing gown and threw it over the back of a chair at the kitchen table. "Well, Frank came home early from the pub and only caught them at it in the utility room."

"Sylvia and the gardener?" Melissa said, adding further, "I don't believe you." But then she flashed back to how horny Sylvia was on their night out by the sea. She recalled in her head how her friend had told everyone, including strangers, that she had needs and she wasn't getting it from her husband.

"I can show you Frank's messages. Anyway, he said they have sold the motorhome and Frank has bought a boat. He has set off sailing towards the Caribbean or in that direction. To find himself apparently." Patrick finished heaping scrambled egg onto his wife's breakfast plate. He was ready to take the breakfast tray into the bedroom and present it and himself to his wife who was still lying in bed.

He removed his boxer shorts and glanced at himself in the full-length mirror. He was good looking and in a good muscular toned shape, and he knew it. He was still brandishing a semi erection and his penis was large and protruding straight out in front at nearly a 90-degree angle. He picked up the tray and wandered into the bedroom completely naked. She screamed slightly and laughed as he placed down the tray down onto the bed. With one hand she picked up a slice of toast, with her other hand she flicked Patrick's penis from side to side which was becoming even harder as he was about to suggest that they go again, after breakfast of course. His penis wobbled arousingly up and down and, he knew he was going to get sex for a second time that morning.

With Melissa safely carried to the car, Patrick completed the final checks of closing their caravan for the winter. Inside the caravan all the doors had been left open for air to circulate, all the taps were open and Anti-freeze had been poured into all the bowls and sink u-bends. Outside the mains water was turned off and the drain down plug was left open. The fresh water that was left in the caravan pipe drained away slowly and disappeared into the grass. The shed was locked and tied down with old fisherman's rope that Patrick had found on the beach. He had looped it over the top of the plastic shed and anchored it into the ground on long steel spikes. The winds rolling in off the sea could be strong and Patrick had hammered the spikes into the ground to stop the shed blowing away. The gas was off at the main tap, and each of the two big red gas bottles were individually turned off. Patrick double checked all the windows and then for one last time tried the front door handle again before climbing into the driver's seat of his car.

"Another great season; loved it," Patrick said as he started his engine. Caravan parks up and down the Welsh coast were all closing for the end of season.

The following week, Patrick was away on his stag trip, but he hadn't managed to ring Melissa every morning and every night like he said he would. She wasn't concerned at all and was secretly enjoying her time alone. She was still off work with her leg injury so had been unable to ask around the police station and gather any details regarding the stag-do.

What she had done though was sneak a look at her husband's online airline booking. She knew he always used the same password for things like that online. She had found the booking and discovered he was flying to Barcelona, not Portugal, and it was for four nights, not a *couple* as he had casually offered from the kitchen. For a brief moment Melissa was annoyed, but realising it was probably just a miscommunication or a last-minute change (typical men!), she flopped onto the sofa in her lounge wear and reached for the television remote control. Whilst her husband partied with groups of stupid drunken men, she had plans for catching up with *The Crown* TV series. Looking down at her phone she checked in with her now famous and glamorous best friend Debbie. Her friend's naked body was sure to be dominating the many social media pages! Starting on Instagram she began flicking up, scrolling through the endless shots of Debbie in a bikini from both the front and the rear. All the pictures were very similar 'selfies', all apart that is from one video clip which caught Melissa's eye. Debbie rarely posted video clips. In the 15 second clip, Debbie was seen running in a skimpy black bikini and being very suggestive at how her boobs bounced up and down. She ran along the side of an empty private swimming pool; it was all very posh looking, and she appeared to be on her own with numerous empty glamorous looking wooden sun loungers. Except she was being filmed by someone else, this other person was recording Debbie as she giggled and flirted, Melissa thought. As Debbie ran along the pool edge, the camera panned from left to right, the last second catching the side of the hotel building. In the patio door glass, Melissa caught sight of the reflection of the person holding up the phone camera. It was only a partial second of a shot and could easily have gone unnoticed, but Melissa's heart missed a beat, she recognised who it was in the reflection. It was a tall, muscular dark-haired man wearing only shorts, but the angle of the phone obscured his face. She didn't want to admit it to herself, and she buried her thoughts deep, but her heart was racing and she had the beginning of a headache.

Immediately she messaged her friend on the secret mobile number which was reserved exclusive for a few select friends. Debbie would normally always instantly reply to this number. Her mobile phone was her gateway to her business and her handset was never far from her hands. Twenty minutes passed and still no reply. This was unusual for Debbie. Melissa nervously laughed and immediately assumed that Debbie was in the throes of being thrown around the bedroom, those massive boobs would be wobbling now, she thought to herself. Several months ago, Debbie had told her friend that she had years of missed sex to catch up on and she wasn't going to be choosy! This at the time had made Melissa laugh. The TV hadn't been switched on yet, and Melissa looked across at her boring fish finger sandwich that was her evening meal. The only excitement for her was pouring the chilled mayonnaise on her sandwich. She began to gently cry. In the silence and alone she continued to scroll through her friends' recent social media posts. She searched all Debbie's different platforms, looking for clues. She found one. Melissa's hands began to shake. The previous day on Twitter. The posted picture in the sunshine was of a glamorous Debbie arriving at an expensive looking restaurant. Her friend looked amazing with a wonderful glow about her. She was scantily clad in designer clothes, with ample cleavage on show. The smartly dressed waiter at the restaurant entrance was very dashing and Debbie was clearly flirting with him.

Again, the photograph had been taken by someone else, who had stood back to take the photograph. Captured in the picture were Debbie, the waiter, and the surrounding beautiful restaurant building and its historical architecture. Melissa closed Twitter and researched the restaurant name. There was only one Google hit with a restaurant of that name. The restaurant was in Barcelona.

THE END

ABOUT THE AUTHOR

Former P&O Princess Cruises, cruise ship bartender who spent many happy years travelling the world's oceans, serving fine wines and cocktails to the rich and famous. Now, semi-retired from the beverage industry and working shoreside, I purchased a static caravan in a beautiful remote village in North Wales. As a family, we spent most weekends and wonderful summer holidays at the caravan, where I watched my sons grow into fine young men. Making lots of good friends and enjoying many adventures along the way.

Printed in Great Britain
by Amazon

81187407R00200